on borrowed TIME

BLOSSOM PEAK SERIES

Contents

To all of the people that are chasing your dreams, even if someone has
made you to feel that they're stupid or unrealistic.
Don't listen to someone if you wouldn't trade lives with them.
Live your life for you!
And don't forget that it's okay to change your dreams too.

That dream was planted in your heart for a reason.

CHASE IT.

-Unknown

Prologue

Henley

Age Twenty

Those Three Little Words

"I'm so proud of you!" Carol, my foster mom, runs up to my little sister, pulling her in for a hug as confetti rains down around us.

"Peace out, bitches!" Dilynne shouts as she tosses her graduation cap in the air.

My foster dad, Nick, and I share a laugh as Carol wipes a tear from her eye. "I'm so glad to be done with high school. Time to dominate the automotive industry!"

"Those men won't know what hit 'em." Nick steps forward, hugging Dilynne tightly as she closes her eyes. "You make me proud, kiddo."

"I love you both so much," she whispers back, and unease twists my stomach. When my sister releases Nick, she barrels toward me. "I did it, Henley!"

"You did, Dil. But did you really think you wouldn't?"

She leans back with her arms still around my neck. "I don't know. It was touch and go for a while."

"How so?"

"Math homework, big brother. That shit was the bane of my existence."

I laugh and rub her head affectionately. "Yeah, I have to agree with you on that one."

"Let's take some pictures," Carol says as my sister and I part, posing for the camera. Another parent offers to take a picture of the four of us, and for a moment, it almost feels like we're a family.

But we're not.

The only family I have is my sister. She's the only person I've ever cared for so deeply that I would gladly sacrifice my life for hers. In fact, I've always put her needs before mine. But now that she's graduated from high school, it's finally time for my life to start.

I'm not sure what that looks like yet, but seeing her in this moment feels like a weight has been lifted from my shoulders.

After a celebratory dinner, Dilynne goes out to celebrate with her best friend, Laney, and a few other friends. I wasn't aware she had other friends besides my buddy Rhonan's little sister, but I'm not mad about it. She's always been sort of a black cat, dancing to the beat of her own drum, reluctant to let people in, and never apologizing for who she is.

Honestly, I wish I could be like her in more ways than one.

"How are you feeling?" Nick asks me from the recliner on the other side of the living room. It's late and he has the History channel on, as usual.

"What do you mean?"

"I mean, your baby sister graduated today. You've got to be feeling something after all you've been through."

Dilynne has told Carol and Nick about our childhood, but she doesn't remember it the way I do. Sure, there were times when she'd cry because she was scared, and she always asked when our parents would return, but for the most part, I tried to shield her from the reality that we were basically on our own.

Making sure she was safe and fed was my only priority. Even after we ended up in foster care, things weren't stable until we were placed with Carol and Nick Vance.

"I'm proud of her," I say, not sure what he wants to hear.

"So am I. I swear, watching you two grow up these past few years has been the biggest blessing."

"Still not sure I've grown up yet, Nick."

He chuckles. "You'll figure it out. Most of us do eventually. But just remember, you always have a place right here. The two of you have changed Carol's and my life, and we will always care about you."

"Thank you."

He clears his throat and then says something to me that I can't remember hearing from another adult. "I love you, Henley."

Little did I know how badly those three words would haunt me for years to come.

Chapter 1

Henley

You Know There's a Baby in There, Right?

"So, if I call your references, they'll tell me the same information?" Hector nods from his seat across from my desk.

"Okay, then you'll get a call from me by the end of the week."

"Thanks for the opportunity." He stands and reaches out to shake my hand before heading toward the front door of the lodge, giving me a moment to rub my temples as the headache I've been fighting off all morning throbs with each hum of the ceiling fan above.

Finding good help these days feels damn near impossible. Most people don't have experience working at a ski lodge to begin with, and if I had a dollar for every fake or embellished reference I've checked, I would be a millionaire.

The truth is, I never planned on owning Sky's the Limit Ski Lodge & Adventure Park in Blossom Peak. Yet here I am, still in North

Carolina, and I actually love it. After high school, I had no idea what I was going to do with my life. Academics weren't my strong suit, and the only things I cared about were football and girls. If it weren't for my near-death experience and my sister's pleas for me to stop chasing the adrenaline that made me feel something for once, I wouldn't be standing here today with something to show for myself.

I honestly don't want to know where I might have ended up otherwise.

My phone vibrates in my pocket for the tenth time today. When I glance at the screen and see the same number that's been calling non-stop for the past two months, something in me snaps.

"What do you want, Meghan?" I shout as I bring the phone to my ear.

"Henley?" She sounds shocked. "So you *do* know how to answer the phone..." Her tone is clipped now, laced with the same irritation I'm feeling.

"What about one-night-only did you not understand?" My response has a bite to it I'm not proud of, but honestly, the only reason I even have her number is because she saved it in my phone herself. I never planned on calling her back, but having her number means I can dodge her calls. She was a tourist anyway, and we met outside of town. There's not much information she has about me other than my number, so I didn't feel threatened by her relentless calls. But after months of this, I've finally had enough.

I thought I clarified the type of relationship we would have before our night even began—sex, one time only, no repeats. It's how I've lived my life up until this point, and I have no intention of changing that anytime soon. I've never been interested in relationships. The house, kids, and white picket fence most people dream about? No fucking thank you.

My childhood was a far cry from that picture-perfect fantasy, so a so-called normal life of checking boxes, playing house, and pretending life is sunshine and rainbows never appealed to me. Still doesn't.

"What do *you* not understand about answering your phone when someone calls multiple times?" she fires back.

"I was hoping you'd get the hint and I wouldn't have to tell you out loud that..."

"I had a baby," she says, cutting me off.

"Good for you."

"She's yours, Henley."

And yet again, three little words flip my entire world upside down.

***

Standing in the parking lot of Hart Winery with a baby carrier in one hand and a diaper bag in the other is a situation I never thought I'd find myself in. But here I am, still trying to process what just happened.

"Fuck," I mutter to myself before spinning on my heels and heading back inside to the party for one of my best friends, Fletcher Adams. He's the wide receiver for North Carolina's NFL team, the Carolina Thunder, and their preseason games start this coming week, so tonight's the last hurrah before he disappears for the next four to six months.

As soon as I walk through the arched entrance of the main tasting room, my sister's eyes meet mine, bugging out when she sees my new accessories.

"Is—is that a baby?" Dilynne asks, but I don't bother answering her as I make my way over to my friends gathered around one of the tall, cocktail-style tables made from old oak wine barrels. "Why do you have a baby, Henley? You're aware that a *baby* is in that thing, right?" She points to the carrier in my hand.

I set the carrier on the table as I let out a heavy sigh. The baby girl dressed in pink is sleeping soundly inside, her jet-black hair combed to the side, but everyone's eyes are locked on me. "Yes, I'm aware there's a baby in here, Dil. Let's just say, I finally found out why that girl Meghan has been calling me so much."

"Who's Meghan?" Laney, my sister's best friend, asks.

"Shit," Fletcher mutters beside me. "Meghan is a woman Henley slept with last year, and she's been calling him for months." Even though I could have answered for myself, I'm grateful to my friend for explaining the circumstances with words I probably couldn't form easily right now.

"Oooookay…" Dilynne drags out, not putting two and two together yet.

"Your brother thought she just wanted a repeat with him, but looks like that wasn't the reason she was calling." Fletcher jerks his chin in the direction of the baby.

Dilynne gasps as everything clicks. "You have a daughter?"

My brain starts to catch up with the conversation happening around me, even as I come to the conclusion that condoms really aren't one hundred percent effective because I've used one every time I've had sex in my life.

Now I know how Ross felt when Rachel told him she was pregnant on *Friends*.

"I—I guess I do."

Dilynne leans in to assess the baby. "How old is she?"

Clearing my throat, I reply, "She's three months old."

"And where's Meghan?" Fletcher asks, his arm slung around Laney's shoulders. They finally admitted their feelings for one another about a month ago, much to everyone's surprise. Now they're inseparable. I'm still trying to get used to it, among other things.

I take a deep breath. "She's gone. She said she never wanted kids but thought she might feel differently once the baby was born. Clearly that didn't happen and I had been blowing her off, so it's not like she had help. It took her awhile to make a final decision and for me to pick up the phone, but once I did, she felt confident in her decision, and just left the baby with me."

My friends glance around at each other, completely shocked and clearly at a loss for words—because the reality is, I'm the last person any of them expected to have a kid.

Laney's older brother, Rhonan, comes over to the table now, followed by my other friend, Elliot. Rhonan is our town's sheriff, a single dad, and the one who had the hardest time accepting that Fletcher was in love with his sister. He seems to be warming up to the idea now, though. Either that, or he puts on a good show.

"Um, is that a baby?" he asks, his brows drawn tightly together.

Elliot snorts around the rim of his beer glass. "I love how everyone is asking that question like you all don't have eyes. Yes, we've established that it's a fucking baby."

Elliot Thorne is the last of my three best friends and a lawyer at his father's firm in town. Normally, I'd comment on his piss-poor mood and sarcastic reply, but it's only been a little over a month since his fiancée left him at the altar and ran off with her boss. So, he gets a pass for a while.

Dilynne glares at Elliot across the table. "Look, Grumpzilla. There's no need for you to speak if you're going to act like even more of an asshole than usual."

Those two can't be in the same room without biting each other's heads off. Before Elliot can spit something nasty back, Laney asks, "How do you even know she's yours, Henley?"

I push the canopy of the carrier back. "Those are Clark ears. Come on, Dil, back me up."

My sister peers into the carrier and sighs. "Shit."

"I still think you should get a paternity test," Elliot grumbles as he lifts his drink again.

Rhonan clears his throat. "He's right because then you're not legally responsible for—"

"And what if she's not mine?" I say, cutting him off. I know my friends don't want me to be taken advantage of, but the only thing I'm feeling right now is guilt. "She ends up in the system?" I turn and look at my sister because she and I both know what that life is like, and hell if I'm going to put another human being in that same situation. "Not on my fucking watch."

I should have answered the damn phone the first time she called. Maybe then, Meghan wouldn't have been so desperate to leave the baby behind. Maybe we could have co-parented or figured something else out that would be best for this little girl. Because I'm the last thing she needs—a single parent with no knowledge of how to care for a baby. But I'll be damned if I'm going to let this innocent baby end up in foster care like me.

"I can't abandon her," I continue, staring down at the little bundle of pink, sleeping peacefully and blissfully unaware that her entire life just changed. "Even if she's not mine, she's—"

"A *child*, Henley," Dilynne cuts in. "A baby. And the last I checked, you don't have any experience with that. Hell, none of us do."

Rhonan clears his throat and raises his hand. "Uh, pretty sure I have a daughter."

Dilynne smacks her forehead. "Shit, that's right."

Elliot chuckles. "Forgetting about Ellis? I didn't think you were *that* self-centered, Dilynne."

My sister begins to round the table toward him, cocking her fist back, but I intercept her before she gets within arm's reach. "Dil..."

"You're lucky I feel sorry for you." Her teeth are clenched as her gaze penetrates Elliot.

"I don't need your fucking pity," he slurs.

"Maybe you've had enough," Rhonan says, reaching over to take Elliot's glass from his hands.

Elliot pushes his arm away, draining the last of his beer. "I'm not a fucking child."

"Then stop acting like one," Dilynne snaps.

Laney clears her throat. "Look, Elliot, I think you should go cool off for a minute. Let me take you back to my dad's office."

Elliot wraps his arm around Laney's neck, stumbling slightly as she leads him away. "I wish I had a sister like you," he mumbles just loud enough for all of us to hear.

Fletcher pushes a hand through his hair. "Is he always like this now?"

"Well, while you were at training camp, he mostly drank at home. Now, he's making a sport out of it," Rhonan answers. "I don't know how long we're supposed to let this go on until we intervene."

Dilynne scoffs. "Maybe you give him some Everclear or tequila next time, and then when he's so hungover he feels like he wants to die, he'll stop."

I shake my head, glancing back at the baby just as her eyes start to flutter open.

Blue eyes as dark as the ocean meet mine and my chest twists.

"Oh my God," Dilynne whispers. "She's awake."

"What do I do?" My eyes dart over to Rhonan and my heart begins to race in my chest.

"Did Meghan leave you any formula? Diapers? Wipes? She's probably going to be hungry and need a diaper change soon." His eyes drop down to the diaper bag.

I push it toward him. "I haven't even opened this thing yet. I don't know what any of that shit is." Clutching my hair between my fingers, I pull it up until it's standing on end. "Fuck, I can't do this."

Fletcher rounds the table and puts his hand on my shoulder. "Just breathe, Henley. Rhonan, maybe you should go home with Henley and walk him through a few things. Tomorrow, you can wake up with a fresh mind and tackle this thing head-on, okay?"

"Yeah, if the baby even lets him sleep," Rhonan mutters as he digs through the bag.

"What do you mean?"

He glances up at me, and then to Dilynne and Fletcher as Laney comes back from her dad's office, minus Elliot. "She's only three months old. She probably doesn't sleep through the night yet."

"Jesus Christ." I pinch the bridge of my nose. "I can't fucking handle this right now. I have a job, a life. I have interviews tomorrow…"

Rhonan shrugs. "Welcome to parenthood. You have to juggle that and take care of another human being. That's why I hired Joanne."

Joanne is the nanny Rhonan hired to help with his daughter right after she was born. Unfortunately, Rhonan's wife, Sarah, died during childbirth, so if there's anyone who understands an ounce of the responsibility I've just been given, it's him.

"Can I take Joanne from you?" I ask, a little too desperately.

Rhonan laughs before growing serious. "Fuck no. I can't survive without that woman. Find your own nanny, Clark." Returning to the bag, he finds a canister and pulls out an empty bottle. When he pops the lid and looks inside, he winces. "There might be enough formula to last you another day or so, but I could be wrong. It's been a long time since I've had to worry about this." Ellis is almost five, so I can imagine he's rusty with the baby stuff. But he still knows a hell of a lot more than I do. "Even still, you need to get more supplies—fast."

Sighing, I stare back at my daughter, inhaling her scent, absorbing just how small she feels in my arms, and wondering for the hundredth time what the hell I just got myself into. "You're stuck with me now, Remy."

"Remy?" Dilynne asks.

"Yeah, it's short for Remington. That's what Meghan named her."

With a lift of the corner of her mouth, my sister glances up at me. "Well, at least she has a badass name. It almost cancels out the fact that her father doesn't know what he's doing."

I know my sister's trying to make light of the situation, but I can't help but think just how wrong she is.

This girl needs a dad, someone to look up to, someone who knows what they're doing. And that definitely isn't me.

***

"If you keep this pillow on the other side of her, then she won't roll off in the middle of the night." Rhonan fluffs the pillows he placed near the edge of my bed.

"What if I roll over on her and squish her?"

He pushes a hand through his hair. "I remember worrying about the same thing with Ellis, but I promise, you're more aware of her presence than you think. It's instinct."

I'm standing in my room as Rhonan walks me through a few things for my first night alone with my daughter.

Even though I'm fairly certain a paternity test is unnecessary, my friends still suggested that I get one, so I added that to the long list of things to do and items to purchase over the next few days—the first of which is a crib.

"I don't have any instincts when it comes to babies, Rhonan. I have no fucking clue what I'm doing."

My eyes sting with the threat of tears. I think I'm more nervous and unprepared than scared or sad. Four hours ago, I was conducting interviews at the lodge. Now I'm a dad.

"I get it, Henley. I do. After Sarah…"

Guilt slams into me. Here I am freaking out about doing this on my own, but that's been Rhonan's reality since the day Ellis was born—the same day he lost his wife. Ellis's mom would have been there if she could, but fate had other plans. He's the only one who remotely understands what I'm going through here.

He shakes his head. "I just don't understand how someone could abandon their child—"

"Honestly, I think Remy is better off," I cut in.

"Why?"

"Because having a parent who's around but doesn't give a shit about you is no better, Rhonan."

We share a look, silently speaking words neither of us needs to voice. While my parents were MIA, Rhonan had two of the most loving parents a kid could ask for. Sadly, his mom passed away when we were twenty, but he and Laney were always loved, cherished, and wanted.

And that's when it hits me—that's exactly how I want my daughter to feel.

Even though I have so much to learn, Remy deserves every ounce of effort I've got. The overwhelm is flooding my body right now.

"No one's ever ready to be a parent, and no parent is perfect," Rhonan says, breaking the silence. "But my mom used to say that the best parents are the ones who just never stop trying, even when they screw up."

Nodding, I glance over at Remy sleeping soundly in her carrier again. "I'm so out of my depth here."

"You'll adjust. But seriously, try to find some help."

Turning to face him again, I nod. "I'll add it to the list."

Rhonan glances down at his watch and sighs. "All right. Well, I need to get going if I'm going to make bedtime. Ellis is probably going to pick the same story we've read all week, but if I'm not there to read it, I feel like shit."

"You read to her every night?"

"On the nights I'm not working, yeah. Why?"

"I don't know." I shrug. "My parents never did that."

He tilts his head. "Will she remember the story? Probably not. But will she remember me being there? Yeah, she will. And that's what matters, Henley." He casts his eyes on my daughter. "Parenthood is going to teach you a lot about yourself, my man. Just wait and fucking see."

With that, he's out the door.

I let out a heavy sigh. "Well, I guess it's just you and me, Remy." Bending down, I lift her from the carrier and adjust her awkwardly in my arms, not yet used to holding a baby.

Will I ever get used to this?

She stirs awake, letting out a wail that could shatter glass. "Shit. Shhh. I'm sorry. Please go back to sleep, baby girl. Please..."

Spoiler alert: there was very little sleep that night.

Chapter 2

Henley

Spilled Coffee and an Interview

"Jesus Christ, you look like shit." Warren, one of my ski instructors and most dependable employees, gawks at me as I walk through the front doors of the lodge a not-so-fashionable twenty minutes late. When I finally figured out how to dress Remy in one of the tiny outfits from the diaper bag and managed to leave the house, she threw up formula all over both of us. I had to change into a new shirt, but then she projectile pooped all over my fresh shirt before I had a chance to change her outfit too.

I never knew that getting out the door in the morning could feel like an Olympic sport.

With my third shirt of the day on, I head for my office with Warren hot on my heels. "Thanks, Warren. If I fire you later, just remember this moment."

"Well, what's with the bags under your eyes, the bedhead, and the, uh...*baby* that you're carrying in that car seat?"

Setting the carrier on my desk, I look down to find Remy sleeping peacefully. Of course she fucking sleeps now.

Last night, it took me three hours to get her to calm down, and then she only slept for an hour before she screamed again for another two. By the time she finally passed out, I was nearly in tears and went through almost all of the diapers and formula Meghan left me. As soon as I'm done with my interviews this morning, I'm headed to Asheville. We don't have a store big enough here in Blossom Peak that would have everything I need for this little bundle of screams and shit—I mean, my daughter.

Transfixed by how fucking cute she is as she's sleeping, a mixture of feelings rolls through me. Last night, I seriously thought the Devil himself had possessed my child. But as she drifted off to sleep and laid her head on my chest, where she slept for the remaining hour and a half before my alarm went off, I couldn't help the overwhelming streak of protectiveness that lodged itself in the center of my chest and calmed me quicker than I could have imagined.

I don't know if I've ever seen a baby as cute as mine.

And now I'm thoroughly convinced that the reason why babies are so adorable is so that you don't scream back in their faces when they won't stop crying.

"This is my daughter," I tell Warren, waiting for his reaction.

His eyes bounce between me and my baby before he clears his throat. "I'm sorry, did you say, your *daughter*?"

"That's exactly what I said."

"Uh...how did you...when did you..."

"Yesterday. I found out yesterday." Keeping my eyes on Remy, I say, "And even though I'd love to fill you in on all of the details, I have three interviews this morning, so I need to get back out there."

I turn to leave, but Warren calls out to me the second my hand hits the doorknob. "Henley?"

"Yeah?"

"Are you forgetting something?" Warren points to the carrier still resting on my desk.

"Shit." Smacking my palm to my forehead, I retrace my footsteps, grab the carrier by the handle, and head back toward the front of the lodge where I set Remy's carrier beside the empty booths of the restaurant, where I'll be conducting the interviews.

I can't believe I almost forgot her in my office. Looks like I won't be winning Dad of the Year anytime soon. My quest to find help for the upcoming winter season is still in full force, though, so it's time for me to take off my dad hat and put my boss hat back on so my business doesn't fall apart like the rest of my life.

During the winter, this place draws skiers, snowboarders, and families with young kids to enjoy the winter activities, scenery, and Santa's Village that the resort transforms into in December. But during the summer, the adventure side of the property opens with ropes courses, ziplining, bike trails, hiking trails, rock climbing, and other activities that allow us to operate year-round.

And this year's numbers have been record-breaking. I don't want to burn out my employees or myself, so I need to hire more help fast. But finding reliable help isn't easy.

"Hey, Henley." Jessica, one of my employees, comes up to me with a cup of coffee as I exit the hallway by my office. "You look like you could use this."

Eagerly, I take it and drink like my life depends on it, not even caring that it burns my tongue in the process. "What makes you say that?"

She offers a sympathetic smile. "I heard about the baby." She nods toward Remy. "How are you holding up?"

"Well, it hasn't even been twenty-four hours, even if it feels like I've been awake that long. Check back in a few days."

Jessica nods before glancing at the waiting area. "Two of your interview candidates are here, waiting and ready. The other one—"

But she doesn't get a chance to finish because as I spin to look at the waiting area, coffee cup still in hand, a warm body runs right into me and sends scalding hot coffee flying.

"What the fuck?"

"Oh my God!"

Jessica gasps. "Holy crap! Are you two okay?"

Wincing, I wipe the coffee that splashed on my face so I can open my eyes. But when I do, I'm met with the most stunning pair of gray eyes staring back at me.

"Oh my God, I'm so sorry," the woman says, reaching out to my chest, trying to wipe away the coffee that's already soaked into my shirt. All she's really doing is running her hands up and down my pecs and abs, which isn't helping the situation at all. In fact, it's actually making my dick wake up even though he's as tired as the rest of me. But I haven't been touched by a woman in a few weeks, so my body is appreciating the attention, regardless of the timing.

I catch her wrists and gently create space between us. "It's okay. It was an accident." Remy decides to make her presence known at that moment, fussing in her carrier. "Shit, I need to get her."

Jessica clears her throat. "Let me get you two some clean shirts from the back. Elodie?" Jessica says to the woman.

"Yeah?"

"Follow me this way. I can show you where you can clean up."

Elodie.

Fuck. That's a beautiful name.

And as I watch the woman walk away from me, I determine she has a beautiful ass as well.

Shaking off my natural instinct to follow her and find out what she looks like naked—because that's exactly what I would normally do—I turn back to Remy who isn't fussing anymore, but looking up at me with wide eyes.

"This day is just off to a great start, huh, Remy?"

Warren comes up behind me, holding out a brand-new Sky's the Limit T-shirt and a warm, wet towel. "You look like you could use these."

"Thanks." I shuck my ruined shirt and wipe my chest, arms, and face off before replacing my shirt for the fourth time today. When I look up, I find Jessica and Elodie staring at me.

Elodie's cheeks flush and she looks away quickly, heading toward the waiting area and taking a seat with the other two women waiting for their interviews.

"Is she..."

"One of your potential new hires?" Jessica finishes for me. "Yup."

Jesus Christ.

Warren stifles his laughter behind his hand. "Nothing like a human resources nightmare to start off the hiring process, am I right?"

"Your commentary isn't necessary," I grumble, trying to focus on my next task while simultaneously avoiding looking at the woman with the stark gray eyes. "Now, both of you get back to work before I find replacements for you too."

Warren and Jessica share a laugh. "It's funny that you think you could replace us," Warren says as they walk away.

Remy starts to fuss again, making me sigh. "All right, little one. I've got you." Unbuckling and lifting her from her car seat, I struggle to find a position to hold her that's comfortable. Remy's head lolls around as I fumble, but before I can find the right fit, a throat clears behind me.

"Need some help?" Elodie is there, arms outstretched.

I momentarily hesitate, this protective instinct flaring in my chest, but when Elodie smiles at my daughter, Remy lunges for her, so I have no choice but to hand her over.

"There we go," Elodie coos, holding Remy in her arms like it's the most natural thing she's ever done. "Well, aren't you a beauty?"

"Thanks."

Elodie quirks a brow at me. "I was talking to the baby."

"Well, that's half of my DNA you're holding, so I figured I could take credit." I reach out to shake her hand. "I'm Henley, by the way."

Her hand meets mine, soft skin and warmth. "Elodie. Sorry again for spilling coffee on you."

"Trust me, compared to what else I've been covered in today, coffee's an upgrade."

Her brows draw together, but thankfully she doesn't press for details about the many fluids that I've already encountered today. "Don't take this the wrong way, but if she's yours, why were you holding her like she was a bomb that was about to explode?"

"If you'd seen how this little thing fills up a diaper, you'd understand."

Elodie rolls her eyes, laughing. "She's a baby."

Rubbing the back of my neck, I stare down at the ground. "Yeah, and I didn't know she existed until yesterday."

She freezes. "What?"

Sighing, I say, "It's a long story. Anyway, you ready for your interview? Might as well do you first since you're here." Her lips fold in on themselves as she fights her smile, and that's when it dawns on me what I just said. "Shit, I didn't mean it like that...I meant—"

Warren was right. Everything that's happening with this woman is an HR nightmare.

"It's okay," Elodie cuts me off, shuffling Remy in her arms as she slides into the booth. "Let's just move forward. Huh, baby bear?" Looking down at my daughter, she rubs their noses together. Remy lets out a squeal I haven't heard from her yet, followed by the most precious, gum-filled smile.

Jesus, I have a kid.

When I take my seat opposite them, something shifts in my chest, but I can't quite put a name to it. "You're good with her. Do you have kids?"

Elodie snorts. "Yikes. Sorry, that wasn't cute."

Actually, it kind of was.

Fuck. That's the last thing I should be thinking about when it comes to this woman, but I can't deny how captivating she is. Her long, dark hair glistens under the light hanging above us, spilling down her back like silk. Those sparkling, gray eyes are so unique, I can't help but stare. And her lips—plump, a deep rose, and spread into a grin as she studies my daughter—make me wonder what they would look like pressed against my chest, trailing lower as she makes her way down my abs to my...

"Henley?"

Her voice breaks through my daydream. Clearing my throat, I focus back on what she's saying. "Yeah?"

"You looked like you were lost in thought there for a second."

I was. I was thinking about your fucking mouth. "Sorry. I, uh, didn't get much sleep last night."

Elodie bounces Remy in her arms as my baby girl rests her head on Elodie's shoulder. The sight makes me want to snap a picture, like it's a moment I want to remember forever.

My mind is being taken over by thoughts and feelings that are so foreign to me, I'm truly wondering if the lack of sleep is altering my brain chemistry.

"How old is she?"

"Three months. She was born in May." Though I had no idea until Meghan told me last night, I still feel guilty for all that I've missed.

"She's such a doll." Remy wraps her hand around Elodie's finger, pumping her tiny fist up and down.

"Yeah, you wouldn't think that when she's screaming bloody murder at one o'clock in the morning."

"Aw, it's normal for babies to fuss in the middle of the night."

I extend a hand toward them. "Well, she obviously likes you."

Elodie shifts Remy on her chest where she's dozing off, her little eyes fluttering open and closed.

"It's the boobs."

Fuck, don't look at her boobs, Henley.

"To answer your earlier question, no, I don't have kids." Elodie's eyes scan my face for a few seconds before she says, "My mom owns a daycare. I've been around little kids my whole life. Before I moved out, I helped her take care of her little cubs, as she calls them."

"A daycare, huh?" The lightbulb practically blinds me when it clicks on in my mind, a solution to one of my problems becoming clear as day. Shuffling in my seat, I prepare what I'm going to say. "Look, I know you came here to interview for the restaurant job at the lodge, but I actually have another position I think you'd be perfect for."

Her mouth falls open. "Really? What is it?"

I take a deep breath and say, "My nanny."

Chapter 3

Elodie

Not the Job or Boss I Had in Mind

Stuttering, I try to string together the words spinning around in my brain. "You want me to be your...nanny?"

Henley clears his throat, as though he needs a second to gather his composure as well. "Look, you have experience with babies that I don't. Like I told you, I just found out about her last night. I have no clue what I'm doing, and I could use the help. I'll pay you way more than what you would make working here." His eyes search mine, heavy with hope. "So, what do you say? Will you be my nanny, Elodie?"

Coming back to Blossom Peak was just supposed to be a pit stop, a way for me to regroup before I either head back home with my tail tucked between my legs or I decide to go back to Los Angeles and give my dream another shot. Never in a million years did I think applying to work at the ski lodge temporarily would lead to me becoming a nanny for one of the most precious little baby girls I've ever seen.

But when I glance back at Henley, the desperation in his eyes nearly undoes me.

God, he's entirely too good-looking—a problem in itself. As soon as I saw him walk into the lodge, I was drawn to him. He's the definition of tall, dark, and handsome—thick, black hair cropped close on the sides, matching scruff lining his jaw, and a hard body encased in denim and soft cotton that hugs him in all the right places.

My eyes wouldn't move from where he stood, especially holding that car seat with a diaper bag slung over his shoulder. There's just something about the sight of a man being a father—it does things to my libido that should be considered illegal.

Maybe it's because I was raised in a home where my father never helped my mom with us kids or the children at her daycare because that was a "woman's job." Maybe it's because I rarely saw fathers come to pick up their children from the daycare or make an effort to be involved in their children's upbringing. Or maybe it's because the dream of having my own kids has always been in the back of my mind, especially with a husband who actually gave a damn about being a father—the opposite of the man I grew up with.

So, the way this man makes my body react should be reason enough why being his nanny is a horrible idea.

"I'd prefer if you lived with me as well, that way you're there when I need you." Waving his hands around, he says, "This is my home away from home, and sometimes that means being here at odd hours. I don't know how to juggle a job and a baby." Leaning forward in his seat, he clasps his hands together on the table, staring me down. The heat of his stare makes me clench my thighs together. "I'm seriously so out of my element here, Elodie, and I'm not too proud to beg."

"You...you want me to live with you?" I dip my eyes down to Remy where she's sleeping peacefully on my chest now, her eyes completely shut and her little mouth slightly open.

"My friend, Rhonan, has a live-in nanny and I've seen how much easier it's made his life. I just think it would make the most sense with my schedule. Having Remy in one place just seems less complicated, and with your experience with kids through your mom's daycare, I feel like I can trust you."

I twist my head from side to side, trying to figure out if this is a joke and I'm being filmed.

"Elodie," Henley says in a commanding tone that makes my eyes snap back to his. "Please?"

Oh my God. He *is* going to beg.

"Okay." The words leave my lips before I can think twice. When I see his shoulders sag and an exhale of relief falls from his lips, the man across from me looks like I just solved all of his problems with one word.

"Thank you. God, thank you, Elodie."

I hold my hand up to stop him. "Don't thank me just yet, Henley. I want to be clear about something."

He leans back in the booth, his brows drawn together. "All right."

"This is temporary. I only planned on being in Blossom Peak until Christmas."

One of his brows lifts as irritation begins to paint his features. "Were you planning on telling me this after I hired you for the other job?"

"I would have told you, yes. But being a nanny makes this more complicated."

"How so?"

Now isn't the time to divulge what brought me to town in the first place, how my own daddy issues may have influenced this decision, or why there's a timeline associated with my stay. "It just does. So, you have my help for the next four months, but after that, you're going to need to find someone else."

He casts his gaze off to the side of the room, his jaw flexing as he thinks for a minute. But when he turns back to me, he nods slowly. "Honestly, I don't have another option right now, so I'll take what I can get."

Swallowing down the lump in my throat, I stare down at Remy. "If you just got her last night, I assume you don't have much for her? Clothes? Toys?"

"That would be correct."

"Okay. Then we need to go shopping."

"I already planned on it after these interviews." He gestures toward the waiting area. "Now that we agree on your position, do you mind sliding out of the booth so I can finish what I came here to do?"

I maneuver my body across the booth and stand slowly so as not to stir the sleeping baby on my chest. "No need to be so testy."

Henley lets out a sigh, pinching the bridge of his nose. "I didn't mean for that to come out like that. Again, I didn't get much sleep last night and my mind is just spinning with everything I need to get done." He lifts his gaze to mine. "I promise, once I get some rest, you'll see that I'm not a complete asshole."

"Just do what you need to do. I'm going to walk around and check out the place while I wait, and then later we can go into more detail about pay and time off." I take two steps before a warm hand comes down on my forearm, barely grazing Remy, but singeing my skin and stopping me cold.

"Thank you again, Elodie."

Our eyes catch and hold for a beat, the silence stretching between us. His touch is electric, sending shockwaves up and down my arm and making my toes curl in my sneakers.

"You're welcome, Henley."

He releases me, pushes a hand through his hair, and reaches for the clipboard on the table behind him. "I'll finish up as soon as I can."

While I wait, I hold Remy in my arms and wander over to the picture windows that overlook the surrounding mountains. My stomach twists at the reminder of why I came here, why this place felt like the perfect spot to lick my wounds and regroup.

Blossom Peak was a place of peace, fond memories, and somewhere that made me feel like I belonged as a kid. When I was here, I always felt calm, solid, and inspired, which is exactly what I need right now—reassurance that what I've worked for since childhood isn't just a pipe dream that won't ever happen for me.

***

"This one has some great safety features." Henley and I are standing next to each other in the crib section of the department store in Asheville, scouring the options. "Although none of them will prevent her from ripping her diaper off and playing in her poop."

Henley looks at me, horrified. "She'll do that?"

I shrug as I walk over to the next option. "Some kids do, some don't. We had one kid at the daycare we had to duct tape into his diaper during nap time. Because that's the kind of painting nobody wants hanging on the walls."

"Is that...legal?"

Glancing over my shoulder at him, I say, "It was his mom's idea. Apparently, he'd made many masterpieces at home."

Henley pushes the cart behind me, barely able to see me over the pile of stuff he's buying for his daughter. It's been a long time since I've cared for an infant, and there are so many new gadgets in the stores now that are purely genius—like a single-serve, no-mess formula dispenser. I can't tell you how many times I've knocked over an entire can of formula just trying to get one scoop into the top of a bottle.

I told Henley he might be going overboard on some stuff, but turns out, the baby's mom didn't leave him with much.

I still can't wrap my head around how a mother can leave her child, but then again, I don't want to assume or judge. I'm sure there has to be a logical explanation, but Henley was quite the closed book on the drive here. I got one-word answers and plenty bouts of silence.

All I kept thinking about is how am I supposed to live with this man? I'm a talker. I'm an over-thinker. But those two qualities make me good at writing songs and telling stories.

Not good enough though, huh, Elodie?

Shaking off my internal self-doubt, I point between two of the cribs we've looked at. "I would go with either of these because they also convert into a toddler bed, so you'll get more use out of it as she grows. More bang for your buck."

Henley's eyes bounce back and forth between the options. "I honestly don't care. You pick."

"Well, what color is her room going to be?"

His brow furrows. "Her room? She's a baby. Last night she just slept in my bed with me..." I can practically see the wheels turning in his head. "Well, for the short amount of time that she *did* sleep. But I didn't even think about a room for her. I mean, I have a guest room, and one I can clean out and make baby-friendly, but—"

Sensing the overwhelm and irritation building in his voice, I interject. "Let's go with the dark brown wood. It's neutral enough that you can decide on a theme later and it will hide the wear and tear that comes with having kids."

Henley's shoulders fall as he nods. "Okay."

"You head to checkout. I'll grab someone to load the crib." I walk away to find a store employee and make a mental note to call Lennon, my best friend back home, as soon as possible to fill her in on my life change. Then I head to the aisle with the teething gel because the moment we'll need it will be the time we don't have it.

We.

As in, Henley and I are a team now when it comes to taking care of this baby girl.

Shaking off that thought, I focus on the task at hand.

You're just helping this man, Elodie. He's paying you, so it's a job, just like you wanted. It's just not the one that you'd thought you'd land. But the money will help you pay down your debt just like you wanted and buy you time to come up with a plan.

That's the thing about plans, though—they rarely go the way we want them to. And I've got firsthand experience with that.

***

"There you go. Keep your hand over her forehead so the water doesn't get in her eyes. The soap is supposed to be tear-free, but you still want to be kind to her about that."

Henley is focusing so hard on bathing his daughter that he looks like he might pass out from the stress, and I've been fighting back my grin the entire time.

"You're doing great." Reaching for his forearm, I give it a squeeze, but boy, was that a mistake.

His skin is warm, dark from working in the sun, and covered in a dusting of dark hair. But that's not the part that startles me—it's the way he tenses under my touch, the way the veins pop out under his skin that makes my breath hitch as I hear him do the same.

God, why do forearms have to be so sexy?

Clearing his throat, he turns away from me as I release him. "Thanks. It's not as terrifying as I thought it would be."

"That's the beauty of using this little tub over the kitchen sink. You don't break your back bending over the bathtub."

"Yeah, thanks for that tip." He cleans the little rolls under Remy's chin for the third time, being thorough since I warned him it's a common place for babies' skin to get irritated. At least he's listening. "Anything else?"

"Nope. I think she's good. You can take her out now."

He reaches for the towel I picked out at the store earlier and holds it open. "Uh... Could you hand her to me?"

"Sure." I carefully pick up the slippery little girl from her tub and place her in Henley's waiting arms.

He wraps the towel around her and holds her to his chest, far more comfortably than he did earlier. I cautiously corrected him on his baby-holding technique once we got home, and now he looks much more at ease holding his daughter. "I hate to ask you, but can you help me dress her, please? It took me almost thirty minutes to figure out the outfit she had on earlier."

A chuckle leaves my lips, but I nod and follow him down the hall to his room. For now, he's going to continue to use his room as his "Remy Headquarters", as he called it.

"Those outfits with a million snaps should be banned, if you ask me."

He places Remy on his bed, drying her off a bit more as I hand him a diaper. "Is there a petition? Because I'll definitely add my name."

I rifle through the clean clothes I took out of the dryer earlier, locating a pajama outfit that has a zipper. "If I find one, you'll be the first person I tell." Nodding, he puts a fresh diaper under Remy's butt and then quickly fastens it in place.

"Hey, you did that pretty fast!"

"Well, she shit right on my chest earlier today, so I learned that speed is a necessary skill when it comes to diaper changing. Who knew projectile shit was a thing?"

My laugh bursts out before I can stop it, clutching my stomach. "Oh my God!"

"Glad you find it amusing."

"I'm sorry," I say, wiping away the tears from under my eyes. "But you have to admit that it's pretty funny."

The corner of his mouth lifts, a quirk of his lips that is the closest thing to a smile the man has shown me all day.

God, I only met him today, but it feels like it's been a week after everything that's happened. But if there's anything I've learned about Henley in that time, it's this: the man is way in over his head here, so all I can do is try to give him the confidence he needs to know he can handle being a father to his daughter, especially after I leave.

Christmas is just a little over four months away. It was the deadline I gave myself to figure out my next moves, and the longer I stand here and stare at one of the sexiest men I've ever met, the more I have to remind myself of that fact.

"Elodie?" His voice breaks through my mental spiral.

"Yeah?"

"She's dressed."

My eyes move down to Remy happily kicking her feet and smiling up at Henley. "She is. You did it!"

His lips quirk up again. "I couldn't have done it without you."

Those words do something funny to my chest, making my heart twist in a way I haven't ever felt—like I'm needed, like I have a purpose, like I'm being seen for what I have to offer for the first time by someone other than my family.

Too bad it's not in the way I'm craving.

Remy's fussiness breaks through the silence, the happy girl suddenly irritated with the world. I glance down at my watch. "She's probably hungry."

Henley lifts her from the bed and then hands her to me. "Do you mind feeding her for me, please? I'm in desperate need of a shower and then I can order us some pizza for dinner, if that's okay with you?"

The idea of this man wet and naked in the shower enters my mind just as quickly as I push it back out. "Sounds great."

He reaches up and squeezes my shoulder. "Thanks, El. I won't be long."

El.

God, he's given me a damn nickname already.

After I prepare a bottle and find a comfortable spot on the couch, I place the feeding pillow around my waist and press the button on my phone to call my best friend, Lennon, who still lives back in Garnet Valley.

"Well, good to know you're alive," she says in greeting.

"Sorry I didn't call sooner, but after I got here yesterday, I crashed early so I wouldn't look like a total zombie for my interview this morning."

"And? How did the interview go?"

"I got a job."

"Heck yes!" she squeals. Somewhere down the hall, I hear a shower starting. "So what do they have you doing at the lodge? Waiting tables like you wanted so you can rake in the tips?"

"Uh, well... Not exactly."

Lennon clears her throat. "What do you mean?"

My eyes drift down to Remy in my arms, her big eyes blinking up at me. "I sort of became the owner's nanny instead."

Dead silence.

"Lennon? Are you still there?"

"A nanny? You're...you're a *nanny*?"

"I know it sounds crazy but—"

"I thought this was only supposed to be for a few months?"

"It is. I told Henley that—"

"Henley?"

"Yeah, he's my boss and he was desperate, Lennon. I swear, I couldn't handle watching him beg for my help." I spend the next several minutes filling my friend in on everything that has transpired today.

"So you're going to live with him and take care of his daughter, but you still plan on leaving Blossom Peak?"

"Exactly. Honestly, it's perfect. More money, I won't have to worry about rent, and it will help me pay down my debt sooner and save up for my next move. Plus, you know I love babies."

Living in L.A. isn't cheap, especially when you're trying to juggle bartending hours and writing with multiple roommates in the house, so credit cards became my best friend. Well, now they're my worst enemy, and something I want to get rid of faster than a zit that pops up out of nowhere.

"Yeah, I know. I'm just worried..."

"About what?"

"Well, what does your boss look like? You know those stories where the nanny falls for the boss are popular for a reason."

My brain filters back through every mental snapshot I've taken of Henley today, flipping through the rolodex of how I've organized every photo—his smirk, his ass encased in denim, and his forearms.

Yup. Those forearms are a problem.

"He's…uh…" I hear the water shut off, making my heart rate instantly spike. "Hey, Lennon?"

"Yeah?"

"I've gotta go."

"This conversation isn't over, Elodie. In fact, maybe I need to make a trip down to Blossom Peak to make sure you're not in over your head here. I mean, you just agreed to move in with a man you've barely met, and I know you go silly for a sinful-looking man, especially if he wears flannels…"

I'm listening to her, I am. But before I can reply, Henley comes walking down the hall with nothing but a towel wrapped around his waist, droplets of water cascading over the mountains of muscles on his chest and abs.

Screw a flannel when he looks like that underneath.

"Dear God," I pant breathlessly, but thankfully, Henley doesn't seem to notice.

"Sorry. I just realized all of my clean clothes are still in the laundry room," he explains, completely oblivious to how he's practically rendered me speechless.

"Uh huh…"

"Elodie!" Lennon shouts through the phone.

I fight like hell to divert my gaze from the walking lumbersnack before me, failing miserably until Remy decides to burp loudly against me, saving me from further humiliation.

"I'll call you later, Lennon," I say into the phone.

"This isn't over, Elodie!" she yells before I end the call and toss my phone to the couch, hoisting Remy up to my shoulder, patting her back in an attempt to get another burp from her tiny body.

Triumphantly, she lets out a rumble that stops Henley in his tracks as he heads back to his room. "Was that her?"

"Sure was," I say, smiling at Remy, her face right next to mine.

Henley chuckles. "Damn. That was actually impressive. Maybe she really is my kid."

I glance between the two of them. "I don't think there is any doubt about that. I mean, have you compared your ears and hers?"

That tilt of his lips shows itself again. "Yeah, that's what I said, but everyone's insistent that I get a paternity test."

Debating if now's the time to pry, I cautiously ask, "What happened with her mom?"

Henley lets out a sigh, running a hand through his wet hair as the other one continues to secure the towel around his waist.

Just look into his eyes, Elodie. That's right. Above the chest. Do not look down. I repeat, do not look down.

"It was a...short-term thing. I didn't even know she was pregnant, but it's partly my fault. She tried calling me months ago, but I didn't answer, thinking she was a stage five clinger." He casts his gaze to the side of the room. "Anyway, she never wanted kids but thought she might feel differently after Remy was born. Turns out, she didn't."

"I'm sorry."

"Don't be. This is for the best, especially for Remy."

"What do you mean?"

The brief glimpse of vulnerability this man just displayed vanishes right before my eyes—as if someone flipped a switch.

"It's not important." Holding up his clothes, he gestures toward his room. "I'll be right back. Pizza is already on its way. I hope you like anchovies."

My stomach turns as my lips follow suit. "Uh..."

That smirk makes an appearance again, which makes me think it's not so rare after all. "I'm just kidding. I hope you like cheese and pepperoni. I'm sort of a child when it comes to pizza toppings."

"Cheese and pepperoni are great," I say as my pulse races as fast as a hummingbird's wings.

With a nod, he retreats to his room and I let out the breath I was holding. My phone buzzes next to me on the couch.

Lennon: *You'd better send me a picture of your boss, stat. Otherwise, I'm going to assume that he's hot, which means you're in more trouble than I thought, and I might have to rescue you and drag you back home sooner rather than later.*

Sighing, I steady Remy in my arms while I text her back.

Me: *Fine. He's attractive, but I have it under control. And I need this time, Lennon. Please. I told you, I'm making the decision by Christmas, okay?*

Lennon: *Fine. But I still want a picture.*

"Come here, little one." Henley appears in front of me, reaching out to take his daughter from my arms, holding her to his chest now which is fully covered—*thank God*—smiling down at her.

I stand from the couch, holding my phone out to snap a picture of them.

"What are you doing?" Henley asks as I glance at the picture on my screen while my ovaries practically melt inside of me.

"Taking your picture."

"Why?"

"Because you're going to want these memories one day. Remy is going to grow faster than you can possibly imagine."

His eyes move to his daughter again. "I'm not so sure. Today has been a year long."

Chuckling, I say, "My mom used to always say that the days are long, but the years are short."

He nods, processing my words. "Never heard that."

"Really? Your mom never said anything like that?"

Henley's brows draw together, pain washing over his face, but the doorbell rings, snapping him out of it. Clearing his throat, he says, "That would be the pizza. My wallet is on the counter. Would you mind grabbing it for me?"

"Oh. Uh, sure."

After we eat, I stifle a yawn as I glance at my watch. "I'd better be going."

Henley reaches for Remy, who's been sitting in my lap for the past fifteen minutes. He hasn't put together any of her furniture yet, like the high chair, so we passed her back and forth while we ate. "All right. I promise, I'll have the guest room ready for you tomorrow, and at least the high chair built."

"It's okay. No rush."

Henley stands as I do. "There is a rush. The sooner I get that room situated, the sooner you can be here for Remy."

Nodding, I say, "Well, I wish you luck tonight." Remy rests her head on Henley's chest as she looks at me, and I fight the urge to take a picture of them again. "But I have a feeling she's going to sleep a bit better for you this time."

"Why?"

"She's exhausted from screaming all night last night." Shrugging, I head for the front door, grabbing my purse from the couch on the way.

"I'll text you in the morning once I get back from the clinic," he says, referring to his appointment for his paternity test.

"Sounds good."

"Thank you again, Elodie."

Turning to face him, I stare up into his dark, brown eyes. "You're welcome. Just don't get too used to me being around, remember?"

"Too late," he jokes, as evident by the tilt in his lips—that same tilt that's been taunting me on and off all day.

"Have a good night." With a wave and backwards glance, I hop in my car, noticing that Henley watched me leave until I was safely inside. And as I head back to my cabin, prepared to pass out the second I arrive, I play back the events of today and beg for something—anything—to spark inspiration.

But all I can hear in the pit of despair deep in my mind is silence.

And that fear that I'll never write another song again comes back with a vengeance.

Chapter 4

Henley

An Explosion and Donuts

"What are you doing here?"

When I open my front door and find my sister standing there, smacking her gum with her signature bandana wrapped around her head, I try to ignore the disappointment that lodges in the center of my chest because I was hoping to see someone else.

"Nice to see you too, asswipe." Dilynne scoots past me and straight toward Remy in her high chair. It was the only piece of furniture I've been able to build since I got back from the clinic three hours ago, which is frustrating considering I should have way more done by now. Turns out, taking care of an infant means it's virtually impossible to get anything done.

At least I got four hours of sleep last night. After the disaster of the night before, it felt like winning the lottery.

My sister showing up unannounced has instantly soured my mood, though.

Remy squawks from her high chair when she sees my sister.

"Well, hello to you too! Can you say Auntie? Auntie Dilynne?"

"She's three months old, Dil. Words aren't on the horizon anytime soon."

My sister glares at me over her shoulder. "And how do you know that?"

Elodie told me, I think to myself. But instead, I say, "I looked it up."

"Thank God for the internet, huh?" Dilynne plays peek-a-boo with my daughter a few times, making her giggle before she stands up tall and turns to face me. "So, how did the test go?"

"Simple. I should have the results in a few days."

"I'm glad you went through with it. I know it seems pointless, but..."

"It's all right. I know it's the smart thing to do."

"Exactly. And now you can focus on finding a nanny and getting this house put together for your daughter."

I survey my home, realizing for the first time just how pathetic it appears. I mean, for a single guy, I never gave much thought to what the inside of my house looked like. My furniture is all dark gray and nice quality, and I have the biggest television I could buy, but the walls are bare, the decorations minimal, and after talking a bit to Elodie, apparently there's a bunch of baby-proofing that needs to be done.

"Actually, I already found a nanny."

Her eyebrows lift. "That fast?"

"Yeah. It's a long story, but..."

"Is she friends with Joanne?" Dilynne asks, referring to Rhonan's nanny, who is old enough to be his mother.

Elodie is definitely *not* old enough to be my mom. In fact, I don't even know how old she is, but my gut is telling me she's too young to find so damn attractive.

Hiring her wasn't a well-thought-out plan, I'm aware. But desperation fueled many of the decisions I made yesterday, and I'm actively avoiding the reservations that I'm feeling—particularly about how enticing my new live-in nanny is.

"She's not, but she's actually on her way over to start moving in, so…"

"Wait. She's going to live with you?"

"Rhonan suggested it. Joanne lives with him, and it really helps."

"Yeah, but Rhonan's known Joanne for years. Where did you even find this woman?" Dilynne asks just as the doorbell rings, and this time, I know it has to be Elodie.

"She actually came to the lodge to interview for the waitress position, but then there was a coffee incident…" Dilynne tilts her head at me with curiosity, striding toward the front door to beat me there. "Anyway, we got to talking and she's worked with kids. She's smart, and kind, and I would have been a fool not to hire her…"

Dilynne races to the door now, and when she opens it, the smirk on her face tells me everything she's thinking. "Oh, a fool you most certainly are."

Groaning, I peek my head around my sister, but she speaks before I can.

"You must be the new nanny."

Elodie's eyes bounce back and forth between me and Dilynne before she musters a smile and reaches out to shake my sister's hand. "I'm Elodie. It's so nice to meet you. I, uh, didn't realize that Henley had a date tonight…"

Dilynne dry heaves. "Ew, gross! No hun, I'm his sister."

Elodie's cheeks turn pink with embarrassment, which is way cuter than it should be. "Oh God. I'm so sorry!"

"I'll let it slide this time, but just know that the only reason I tolerate my brother is because shared DNA obligates me to." Dilynne elbows me in the ribs as she pushes the door open wider for Elodie, who has a duffle bag slung over one shoulder and a box tucked under her arm.

"Elodie, this is my sister, Dilynne. She's annoying, nosy, and stopped by unannounced, just so you know."

"Forgive me for wanting to check up on you and my niece. After the other night, I felt guilty letting you go home alone."

"I managed," I reply as Elodie fights her smile. She knows the hell I went through the first night, and thankfully, she was correct about Remy sleeping better last night. "But now I have Elodie's help."

"My mom owns a daycare, so I have a ton of experience taking care of kids."

"Remy already loves her too," I add in an attempt to convince my sister that hiring Elodie wasn't a calculated decision like I know she assumes.

Elodie holds up the box in both hands now. "I'm gonna drop this stuff off in my room and grab a few more things from my car."

"I can help you," I say as Elodie heads for her room.

Dilynne yanks me toward where Remy is still sitting in her high chair, perfectly content watching all of the adults around her. "I can't believe you thought this was a good idea."

"What do you mean?"

She pushes my chest. "I mean, it's clear that you were thinking with your dick here, Henley."

Crossing my arms over my chest, I glare down at my younger sister. "Contrary to what you might think, the only thought going through my mind when I hired her was that I needed help and she knows more than I do."

Dilynne mimics my stance. "You know you can't sleep with her."

"Yes, Dil. I'm very aware. Besides, she's not going to be here for long."

Dilynne drops her arms to her sides. "What do you mean?"

"She's only here temporarily. She applied for the seasonal job at the lodge, and she plans to be gone by Christmas."

"And what will you do then?"

Pushing my hand through my hair, I stare down the hall. "I haven't thought that far ahead. I mean, look at my house." Turning back to her, I fan my arms around the room and the stacks of boxes, bags of clothes and toys, and half-built furniture. "Cut me some slack here, will ya? I just became a dad overnight."

Dilynne sighs. "Fine, but you and I both know that this girl is beautiful, and not being able to keep your dick in your pants is what got you into this situation in the first place."

I flash my sister a deadpan stare. "Thank you for that."

Smiling proudly, she pats me on the shoulder just as I hear the sound of Elodie coming back down the hall. "Just speaking the truth."

"Still need help?" I ask Elodie when she comes into view.

She tucks her long, dark hair behind her ear. "Yes, please. There's only a few more boxes."

Glancing at my sister, I say, "Do you mind keeping an eye on Remy while I help Elodie?"

Dilynne looks at the baby. "Uh, I guess. Not sure what to do with her, though."

"As long as she's not crying, just leave her."

Dilynne nods. "Got it."

I follow Elodie out to her car. "Sorry about my sister, by the way."

Elodie chuckles. "She seems harmless," she says as she opens up the trunk of her car, revealing a few small boxes and another duffle bag.

"Uh, Dilynne is the furthest thing from harmless. Seriously, I love her, but she's a lot to handle."

"Women don't really like to be told that," Elodie counters, lifting one eyebrow.

"Trust me, it's true when it comes to my sister."

"Have you ever considered that maybe she's just self-sufficient and aware of who she is, and *you* are the one who's a lot to handle?"

I stare down at her, transfixed by the challenge in her voice. "Look, we're getting off topic here. All I'm saying is, don't feel the need to entertain her. And if she tells you any stories about me, believe less than five percent of them."

Elodie huffs out a laugh. "That basically means she'll tell me anything I ask, won't she?"

I pinch the bridge of my nose. "Based on this conversation, I have a feeling you two will get along just fine."

"Well, she is Remy's aunt, so it would be good for me to get to know her, right?" Elodie loads the boxes into my arms and then grabs the duffle bag, slamming her trunk shut before heading back up to the house.

When we walk back inside, Remy is fussing in her high chair, and Dilynne is standing right in front of her, pinching her nose closed with two fingers.

"What's going on?" I ask.

The nasally voice that comes out of my sister almost makes me lose my composure. "That little girl exploded. Seriously, it sounded like a bomb went off in her pants and then the most horrific stench I've ever smelled filled the room."

Setting the boxes down on the kitchen counter, I rush to the high chair and lift my daughter out of it. Brown liquid drips down her legs. "She just pooped, Dil."

Dilynne dry heaves again. "That is not just poop, big brother. That is vile, disgusting soup dripping down her legs." She gags again. "I can't handle this. I—I have to go." She rushes for the front door, but not before turning back to Elodie. "It was nice to meet you. Hopefully we can talk more when I don't feel like I'm inhaling pollution that could destroy the ozone." Elodie laughs out loud. "But if you're ever interested in hanging out or have any questions about my brother here," she says with a toss of her thumb over her shoulder, "my best friend Laney and I would be happy to oblige."

And then she's gone, leaving us standing there in relative shock before we both burst out laughing.

"I take it your sister doesn't have experience with babies either?" Elodie manages to finally ask through her laughter.

"What gave that away?"

Elodie winces when she sees the back of Remy's outfit as I continue to hold her at arm's length before casting my eyes toward the wipes, debating how I'm going to clean her up.

"That outfit is probably unsalvageable."

Sighing, I accept the clothing's fate. "In the trash it is, then."

"Honestly, you're better off just stripping her down and washing her off in the sink."

"You can do that?" I ask as I hold Remy over the kitchen sink and Elodie begins to undress her.

She chuckles as she carefully removes the soiled clothing and diaper. "You bathed her over here last night, didn't you? It's better to rinse her than waste all of those wipes. She'll be much cleaner this way anyway."

Setting Remy down in the porcelain sink, I turn on the faucet, wait for it to warm up a bit, then put it on the spray mode and gently rinse her off.

"I'll go get her an outfit and new diaper," Elodie says.

Once Remy is clean and redressed and the high chair cover is in the washing machine, Elodie heads for the front door.

"Where are you going?" I ask.

"I left something in my car. I'll be right back," she says, as though she needs to reassure me that she's not about to run away. Maybe that's my own insecurity coming out, but I push the thought away.

When Elodie returns, she's carrying a guitar case.

"Please tell me you don't also have a drum set in your car."

Laughing, she props the case upright. "Nope. I'm a one-instrument band."

"So you play?"

"No, this is just for decoration." Her sarcasm is becoming oddly comforting. With an eye roll, she says, "Yes, Henley. I play." She leans the guitar case against the back of the couch, surveying the state of my house. "So, looks like you didn't get much done today."

"Honestly, I don't even know where to start. I was lucky to get the high chair finished and put Remy in that. I swear, it's impossible to get anything done with a baby in tow."

Elodie takes Remy from me, settling her on her hip with ease. "Okay, let's start with the crib. That way she can sleep in her own bed tonight, and maybe you can get a little more sleep."

I almost tell her that having Remy sleep on my chest last night was much more pleasant than I care to admit. Holding her close was a surprising comfort, especially for a guy who likes his space. But with my daughter? It's a different sort of bond, one in which it feels like she's been missing from my life this entire time.

Fuck. There's another thought I don't want to tackle right now.

"Crib it is." I drag the box into the only empty space on the floor in the living room before taking my utility knife from my pocket and slicing through the tape.

"Sorry for assuming that Dilynne was your girlfriend, by the way," Elodie says, breaking through the silence.

Lifting my head, I meet her eyes. "No need to apologize."

Her cheeks turn pink again behind the curtain of her hair. "I know you said that Remy's mom took off, but I wasn't sure if you were seeing someone." Our eyes meet and she shakes her head. "I guess I just wanted to be prepared if someone else would be around the house," she explains with a shrug.

"Nope. It's just me, and that's the way I like it. Relationships aren't my thing." The moment the words leave my lips, I glance back up at Elodie to catch her reaction, even though I shouldn't care what she thinks.

The truth is, if it were anyone else, I wouldn't.

Her eyebrows lift, but then she focuses on Remy. "I haven't had much luck with those either."

Standing tall again, I remove pieces of the crib from the box. "Uh, how old are you by the way? I probably should have asked that the other day, but...well, you know what a flustered state I was in."

She chuckles. "I'm twenty-five. You?"

"Thirty-two."

Christ, she's seven years younger than me. Maybe that will make it easier to keep my thoughts about her strictly platonic.

Elodie crosses the room and scoops up a toy, holding it out to Remy. But the bounce in her breasts and sway of her hips as she strides toward my daughter makes it difficult to keep the level head I know I need to find.

I clear my throat and continue our conversation. "So, what brought you to Blossom Peak? This isn't exactly the type of place people move to out of nowhere. Most of us who live here permanently were born here or transplanted here for work or for family. The rest are tourists."

"I used to come here as a kid," she says while showing Remy how to shake the toy to make noise. "My parents booked us a trip each summer where we'd stay in a cabin, swim in the lake, and hike. I needed a break from LA, but I wasn't ready to go back home. This was the first place I thought of."

"And where's home?" Taking a seat on the ground, I lay out the crib's pieces and screws before opening up the instruction manual.

"Garnet Valley. Have you heard of it?"

"That's in Tennessee, right?"

"Yeah, about two hours from here, tucked up in the Great Smoky Mountains."

"So, your parents would leave their mountains to come to our mountains?"

Elodie laughs. "That's what my dad used to say to my mom, but she loved the cherry blossom trees here. Coming here felt different—like a real getaway. And honestly, this place holds some of my favorite childhood memories. Like this scar," she says, holding out her leg to me and pointing to the divot in her shin. But all I can focus on is her smooth, tan skin and muscle tone in her calf. "I got this from racing my brother through the woods behind our rental cabin. One wrong step and I fell shins-first into some rocks."

"And that made you fall in love with Blossom Peak?"

"Yes, Henley. The blood overwhelmed me and I've associated pain with love ever since."

"You know, I didn't think anyone could perfect sarcasm quite like my sister, but it seems I was wrong."

Elodie flips her hair over her shoulder as she walks into the kitchen to pour herself a glass of water. "Then maybe I need to take her up on her offer to hang out."

The idea makes me uneasy, but I'm sure Elodie could use a friend or two while she's here. Even I can admit that my sister is someone you want in your corner. "That's if you can convince her to step away from her shop. My sister owns Clark Customs & Auto Repair and she's been known to sleep in the garage when she's knee-deep in a project."

"She works on cars for a living?"

"Yeah. Trust me, she's taken a lot of shit in her life because of it too, so don't bring it up unless you want an earful about stereotypes."

Smiling, she heads back into the living room and takes a seat on the couch, watching me work. "Oh, I know all about stereotypes. I carry around a guitar case and suddenly, I'm out here just trying to be the next Taylor Swift."

"Well, are you?"

Sighing, she looks down at Remy. "I'm not sure what I want anymore."

I want to press her further, to learn more about what that defeated reply really means, but Remy starts fussing. With one glance at her watch, Elodie hoists Remy on her shoulder and stands. "I think she's ready for a bottle and a nap."

I stare down at the half-built crib.

"We'll try the crib tonight. She can nap on me this time." Elodie makes a bottle for the baby with one hand like it's nothing and then heads toward the hall.

Before she gets too far, I call out for her. "Elodie?"

"Yeah?"

"Thank you again."

Her smile is soft, but I don't miss the pink hue that rushes across her skin as she looks away. "You don't have to say that every time I do what you've hired me to do."

"Yeah, I actually do."

With a shake of her head, she retreats down the hall before I focus back on my task, thinking about how normally I'd be finishing up things at the lodge and wondering which bar I would hit up to find my companion for the night.

Oh, how things have changed.

***

"Oh my gosh, I haven't been here in ages." Elodie's entire face lights up the second we walk into Bites & Bliss Bakery, a staple here in Blossom Peak. The purple and white walls are bright and inviting, providing the perfect backdrop for the bakery, and the view of the mountain peaks surrounding our town is one of the best things about this place.

"I wonder if they still have that blueberry-filled donut..." Elodie muses.

"We do, but we're almost out. If you want one, tell me now and I'll put it aside." Carolina, the owner of the bakery since I was a kid, wipes her hand on her apron as she watches Elodie survey the case of baked goods.

Elodie practically bounces on her toes. "Yes, please."

Laughing, Carolina moves toward the case and takes out the donut in question as I adjust Remy's carrier in my hand, drawing her eyes to the sight. "Henley Clark, is that..."

"What?"

She plants her hands on her hips, moving her eyes between me and Elodie. "I know it's been a long time since I was in school, but if memory serves me correctly it takes nine months to have a baby, and I didn't even know you were dating anyone."

Elodie's eyes snap to mine at the same time I look at her. "Uh, we're not…"

"This is my nanny, Carolina," I say a little too quickly.

"When the hell did you hire a nanny?" Carolina glances at the clock and then back over to me. "How did I miss this?"

"Probably when you were too busy making penis-shaped cakes," I mutter.

"I heard that," Carolina fires back.

Elodie's eyes move between us. "I feel like there's a story here that I'm not privy to."

Sighing, I ignore Elodie's comment and focus on clearing the air. "I just found out I have a daughter, Carolina. She wasn't planned and I didn't even know she was coming until her mom dropped her off with me. Elodie was interviewing for a job at the lodge, but I hired her to help me instead."

Carolina snaps her towel on the counter in front of her. "Well, heck. She must be something if you hired her on the spot like that," she says as she directs her gaze to Elodie. "If he gets to be too hard of a boss, come work for me. I could always use help, and the blueberry-filled donuts will be on the house."

Elodie twists to face me, an impressed look on her face. "I'll keep that in mind."

"Now, now… No one needs to jump the gun here. Elodie, I'll buy you all the donuts you want. And Carolina?" I say, leaning over the counter, "Stop trying to poach my nanny."

There's a sentence I never thought I'd say.

Elodie's laugh bursts from her lips. "Never thought I'd see the day when people would be fighting over me. Hell, at my last job, I was just grateful if someone remembered my name."

"Well, at least you'll be working for someone who will appreciate you now," Carolina says, winking at me. This type of repartee is normal anytime I pop into the bakery, but I don't want to make Elodie uncomfortable.

I can't lose her. Not yet, at least.

Out of the corner of my eye, I see Elodie's smile fall as she registers Carolina's implication. "Yeah, I guess you're right."

Hating to see her frown and alarmed by my own reaction, I return my focus to why we stopped here in the first place. "All right, I think we obviously know what Elodie wants, and I'll take a breakfast croissant. Do you want a coffee too, El?"

"Yes, please." She bites her bottom lip between her teeth. "Is it possible to get a coconut cream cupcake for later as well?" Shrugging, she explains, "I have a bit of a sweet tooth."

"You and me both, hun," Carolina says, smacking her ass. "Where do you think all this junk in my trunk came from?"

"Nothing you make is junk, Carolina," I quip before leaning over and whispering, "Your frosting is the best I've ever had."

It's Carolina's turn for her cheeks to turn pink. "Oh, Henley. You know just what to say to the ladies, don't you?"

Staring down at the baby sleeping in the carrier in my hand, it dawns on me that my sister was right—apparently my flirting skills *are* part of the reason I'm in this predicament in the first place.

After Carolina fills our order, we take a seat at one of the empty tables. Carolina takes Remy in her arms, parading her around like she's a proud auntie. The boys and I have frequented the bakery since we were in high school, so Carolina is an extension of our family-of-choice.

"Oh my God," Elodie moans, closing her eyes as she savors the first bite of her donut. "These taste even better than I remember."

My dick stirs in my shorts at that, but I divert my focus to what she said instead. "I honestly think Carolina has gotten better with age."

"I have," Carolina agrees as she bounces Remy in her arms, moving right past us.

Laughing, I take a bite out of my egg, bacon, and cheese croissant before asking Elodie, "So, what are your plans today?"

"I thought I'd go out and explore a bit with Remy. Is that okay?"

The idea of leaving Remy makes me nervous, but this is why I hired Elodie—so I could go to work and continue my life as normally as possible. I mean, I know nothing will be exactly the same, but suddenly leaving my kid seems difficult.

How did that fear creep up on me so fast?

"Yeah, that's fine. I should be home around four today, so I guess I'll just meet you there later?" We drove separately because I knew I'd be leaving from here to go to the lodge, but I guess it just hit me that Elodie wouldn't be coming with me.

"Sounds good." As if she could sense my apprehension, she reaches out and places her hand over mine. "She's going to be okay, Henley. I promise, I know what I'm doing."

Nervous laughter leaves my lips. "Honestly, you know more than I do, which is why I don't understand why it's so hard to leave her."

"It's actually really sweet," Elodie says. "You've barely just become a dad and you're already worried about leaving your daughter." She squeezes my hand again, her warmth actually soothing me, which makes me more nervous, but for an entirely different reason. "The fact that you're already worried lets me know you'll be just fine once I'm gone."

As soon as she says the words, that invisible clock on our time together starts ticking louder and louder.

But Carolina returns with Remy, snapping me out of it. "If you don't get going, you're gonna lose your daughter *and* your nanny to me."

"You'd better watch it, Carolina."

Laughing, she kisses Remy's cheek and hands her back to me. "Henley, I know kids weren't on your radar, but this one is a doll. Just remember, everything happens for a reason. You may have limited time with your nanny, but this little girl isn't going anywhere for the rest of your life. That's a huge responsibility, and if there's one man I know can handle it, it's you."

Emotion clogs my throat. "Thanks, Carolina."

She squeezes my shoulder. "Anytime. And Elodie? You know where to come if you need some sugar or a place to enjoy the view." Fanning her arms out toward the window, she smiles.

"Thank you. I'll definitely be back."

I place Remy back in the carrier and then walk her and Elodie out to her car. "All right. Text or call if you need anything. The lodge isn't too far, so if you need me…"

"Henley, it's going to be fine."

I lean down and kiss Remy's cheek, breathing in that faint powdery scent clinging to her skin. "Bye, baby girl."

And with one last glance at the two women who just crashed into my life, I hop into my truck, knowing that nothing will ever go back to the way it was.

Chapter 5

New Friends, Accusations, and Sleepless Nights

The buzz of power tools mixed with the rumble of engines greets me as I open the door to Clark Customs & Auto Repair, Dilynne's garage located on a corner in The Village, a neighborhood of shops and restaurants centrally located in town. I remember walking these streets and sidewalks with my parents each summer, visiting the ice cream shop and gift shops full of souvenirs and knickknacks, but many new stores have popped up since then. Suddenly my lack of plans for the day has been solved as I plan to walk around and check out everything new after this stop.

A man behind the counter pops up from the floor, startling me and making me question if being here is okay

"Hey there. How can I help you?" Tattoos snake down his arms and gray and black whiskers dust his jaw, but his smile is extremely friendly.

"Hi. I'm, uh…looking for Dilynne. Is she working today?"

The man chuckles, scratching his chin. "Oh yeah, she practically lives here." His words remind me of what Henley said about his sister. "Let me go see what she's up to. Hold tight."

I watch him walk through a door with a half-window into the garage where the sounds of metal on metal echo, making my ears ring. While I wait for him to return, I peek inside the stroller to find Remy blissfully sleeping still.

After seeing Henley off to work this morning at the bakery, I decided to stop by Dilynne's garage to smooth over our rough introduction from yesterday and also prod a bit more about my boss.

Henley's nerves this morning before he left made me soften even more for this man, which only adds to the list of inappropriate feelings I have toward him. But it was sweet, how anxious he was about leaving Remy. After assuring him that she'd be fine and that he should let me do the job he hired me to do, he reluctantly left the bakery, which gave me a moment to breathe.

The door from the garage opens, interrupting my thoughts as Dilynne, the man from earlier, and another woman I don't know all stride through.

"Elodie? What are you doing here?" The three of them stare at me as Dilynne wipes her hands on a rag.

"Hi. I hope I'm not bothering you, but uh…"

Dilynne clears her throat, gesturing to me as she twists her head between the other two people flanking her sides. "This is Elodie, you guys. She's Henley's nanny."

The woman on Dilynne's left beams as her eyes shift to me. "Oh! Nice to meet you. I'm Laney." She reaches out to shake my hand as her name rings with familiarity.

"Laney is my partner in crime," Dilynne explains.

The man scoffs. "First of all, Laney would never commit a crime. And second, I thought I was your partner?"

Dilynne rolls her eyes. "Steven, this isn't the time for you to complain about how we classify our relationship, okay?"

Finally. A name for this man.

"I'm not complaining. I'm just looking for validation."

Laney shakes her head, crossing her arms over her chest. "Careful, Steven. Dilynne is already in a mood."

Dilynne grumbles. "Well, this freaking engine is giving me trouble."

"I'll go take a look at it then while you all do your girl-talk thing. But if I figure out the problem, you have to admit that you couldn't run this place without me." Steven places his hand on the doorknob, waiting for Dilynne's reply.

With a heavy sigh, she says, "Fine. Just don't fuck it up further."

Steven laughs. "Yeah, like that's going to happen."

Once he's gone, Dilynne turns back to me. "Sorry. Steven really is my right-hand man, but he's a lot to handle some days."

Laughing, I say, "I can see that."

Dilynne and Laney lean over the stroller, greeting Remy and gushing over how adorable she looks in her yellow onesie before Dilynne stands back up to full height. "Anyway, this is Laney, my best friend. She owns..."

"The beauty salon across the street," I finish for her. "Your brother told me last night."

"So he's actually talking to you?"

"Yes." Confusion builds in my mind. "I mean, it's kind of hard to take care of Remy without communicating."

A knowing smile spreads across Dilynne's lips as she mimics Laney, crossing her arms over her chest as well. "And has he been on his best behavior?"

My brows draw together more, wondering what she's alluding to. "Why wouldn't he be?"

Dilynne's eyes move up and down my body before she drops her arms. "Look, I know we don't know each other, but I'm going to say something honest because that's the only filter I have."

"It's true," Laney interjects.

Dilynne shrugs. "And I don't apologize for it. But, my brother is a bit of a manwhore, and well...you're hot."

A manwhore? Well, that's interesting...

Unfortunately, Dilynne's comment makes my cheeks burst into flames. "Oh, uh... Thank you?"

"Don't be shy, girl. Own it," she continues, leaning up against the counter resting between us. "But just be careful. I saw the way he looked at you yesterday."

"What do you mean?"

"Let's just say that his eyes were fixated on your ass as you walked around his house."

Laney shrugs. "Sounds about right."

"Don't all men do that though?" I ask matter-of-factly while thinking back to how many inappropriate encounters I've had with men throughout my short lifetime, the most recent one scarring.

I developed pretty early, so at thirteen, I already had an ass and boobs that made me look far older than I was. It was annoying and made me want to cover every inch of my body some days. But as I got older, I just started calling out men for staring, which became way more fun and helped boost my confidence.

Dilynne taps her fingers on the counter. "Yeah, but my brother has a type, and I hate to say it, but you're it."

Uneasiness twists in my stomach. I thought my attraction to him was one-sided, but if Dilynne's right, perhaps Henley feels it too, which only makes this situation more complicated.

"I'm glad he has you right now though, because lord knows I have no idea what to do with a baby," Dilynne continues.

Stifling my laugh, I say, "Yeah, that was evident by your reaction to Remy's poopy diaper yesterday."

Laney snorts. "I'm so mad I missed that."

Dilynne's lips curl up in disgust. "It was vile, Laney. Insanely vile."

I lean forward over the handle of the stroller. "She acted like a bomb exploded." Laney's giggles intensify as Dilynne dry heaves, reliving the scene. "Let's just say I won't be asking Aunt Dilynne to change a diaper anytime soon."

Once Laney has composed herself and Dilynne gathers her wits, she narrows her eyes at me. "I like you."

My smile is instant, a warmth spreading through my chest as the people-pleaser inside of me gets a huge dose of dopamine. "Right back at you. But I think Henley and I will be fine. I mean, he's my boss. This is strictly professional." The words lack confidence even to my own ears.

"Uh-huh. That's what I told myself when I had to work a wedding with one of my brother's best friends. Didn't stop me from acting on my feelings for him," Laney says.

With a jut of her thumb over her shoulder, Dilynne nods. "Yeah, delusion was her best friend."

"No one is being delusional here though," I counter quickly. "Henley knows I'm only here for a few months, and hopefully by then he'll feel confident in his ability to take care of Remy. Besides, manwhores aren't my type."

Dilynne tilts her head. "I don't know… I just have a feeling here, and my gut usually steers me straight. I mean, hell, I called it that Elliot's fiancée was a witch in disguise."

"Who's Elliot?"

Laney and Dilynne share a look, having a silent conversation between themselves before they step out from behind the counter. Dilynne motions me toward the waiting area. I give Remy a quick check, finding her still out cold, so I brace myself for what I'm about to hear while also tickled within that I'm getting some adult interaction besides my new boss.

Back in Los Angeles, my roommates were all struggling singers, actresses, and creatives. We were all in the city for the same reasons, so while it helped having roommates to keep costs down, there was also an unspoken competitiveness, which didn't lead to close friendships. But yesterday when I met Dilynne, I just knew she was genuine and honest, and for some reason, I want to trust her and hear what she has to say.

"So, I know you're only here for a few months, but you need to understand what you're walking into," Dilynne starts once we're all settled. "My brother has three best friends that he's known since their freshman year of high school, and they're sort of the glue that holds us all together."

Laney clears her throat. "Actually, that's you and me, Dil. Let's be honest."

Dilynne huffs out a laugh. "Yeah, you're right. Men are horrible at making plans and remembering shit."

Laney nods. "Anyway, Fletcher Adams is my fiancé," she says, steering us back to the topic at hand.

I snap my fingers. "That's where I recognize you from! My family loves football. I knew you looked familiar."

She smiles. "Well, glad you're not one of the women ready to fight me in the grocery store for taking him off the market."

"Girl, you locked him down and have his ring on your finger. Be proud of that," I say, grinning as her smile widens.

"Thanks."

Dilynne clears her throat. "Yes, Laney and Fletcher are engaged, which her older brother, Rhonan, didn't exactly love the idea, seeing as he's also a member of the Blackjack Brotherhood."

Laney shakes her head, glaring at her best friend. "Why do you call them that?"

Dilynne chuckles, holding her stomach. "Because it's hilarious."

"Blackjack Brotherhood?" My eyes bounce between the two women sitting across from me, waiting for more information.

Laney nods. "The four guys started playing blackjack in high school and it's sort of a tradition they've kept going. They try to keep up a monthly game, though they weren't consistent with it until Fletcher and I got together." Sighing, she says, "Anyway, I won't bore you with the details, but let's just say the guys have all been a little rattled lately—with Henley's sudden fatherhood on top of everything else."

"I see."

Dilynne clears her throat. "Anyway, Laney's brother is one of the sheriffs in our town and also a single dad."

I nod in understanding. "Okay, that makes sense. Henley has mentioned that name before."

"My brother helped him the night that Remy's mom dropped her off, and he's the one that suggested Henley hire a nanny."

"Well, he found one," I say jokingly, holding my hand in the air, making both of the girls sitting across from me laugh.

"That he did. Which brings us to the last of the four men, Elliot," Laney says, side-eyeing Dilynne for a beat. "Elliot was supposed to be married earlier this summer, but his fiancée ended up leaving before the wedding started and ran off with her boss."

I cover my mouth. "Oh my God, that's terrible."

"Bitch," Dilynne mutters under her breath. "I knew she couldn't be trusted, but no one wanted to listen to me," she continues.

"So just know that when you meet him, his surly attitude has nothing to do with you, okay?" Laney explains.

"Got it."

"The boys truly are four of the best guys you'll ever meet, but Elliot's wedding and everything that transpired after that sort of shook up their friendship." Laney folds her hands in her lap. "Not to mention Henley finding out he was a dad out of nowhere took everyone by surprise and has made all of us worried."

"What do you mean?"

Laney turns to Dilynne, giving her a small nod.

"My brother and I didn't exactly have the best upbringing, and he never wanted kids after what we went through. So, the fact that he was suddenly thrown into parenthood has me worried about him," Dilynne says, her voice shaking slightly with emotion. "So do me a favor, and let me know if you notice him struggling, okay? I've dealt with most of my shit from our childhood because I refused to walk around with a chip on my shoulder forever, but he hasn't. And I doubt he ever will. Whether he wants to face it or not, it's only a matter of time before all that shit catches up with him."

Laney squeezes Dilynne's shoulder. "He'll be okay."

"Yeah, I hope so. At least he has Elodie now. That makes me feel a little better."

Suddenly a weight comes down on my shoulders. So, not only am I responsible for taking care of Remy, but I'm also on "new dad" watch too? And what does Dilynne mean about their upbringing? Now I have even more questions about the man I'm living with.

"Speaking of meeting everyone, did Henley mention the movie night at the winery next week?" Laney adds.

I tuck a strand of hair behind my ear. "Nope. Is it at Hart Winery though? That's the one I remember visiting when I was a kid."

Laney nods enthusiastically. "It is! That's my family's winery. My parents opened it when I was a child, and I've been helping my dad run it since my mom passed twelve years ago."

"Oh my gosh. I'm so sorry about your mom," I say, thinking about how I should probably call mine and let her know that I'm no longer in California. I've been avoiding that call because I just know I'll get the same criticism as always when the conversation moves to me thinking I could make it as a singer-songwriter.

My parents have never supported this aspiration of mine, and I know the first words out of their mouth will be "I told you so" when I tell them that I'm considering giving up.

I know I have it in me, and I know I have stories to tell through music. But I need that breakout hit, that chorus or melody that resonates with people and makes a music producer say, "We want your song. We want *you*."

It sucks to want to be wanted and feel like you're never going to hear that from someone who matters, like someone that holds the fate of my career and future in their hands.

And the scariest thought I'm refusing to face right now is, if I don't sing and write songs for a living, what else do I do?

"Thank you," Laney says, brushing a hand through her hair. "My mother was the one who started our event series, so we hold movie nights once or twice a month during the summer, and there's one next week. You should come. Convince Henley you should go. You bring a blanket, pick a spot on the grass, and relax. We have snacks, games, and of course, plenty of wine."

The idea of sitting on the grass at a winery on a crisp summer night makes me feel energized. Maybe it will help spark some creativity. If anything, it will give me the opportunity to people watch, which always gives me some kind of inspiration. "With or without Henley, I'll be there."

Dilynne rubs her hands together. "Fantastic. Let me give you my number so you can get in contact with us as well." The three of us exchange numbers, and just as we're finishing up, Steven comes back into the office.

"Hey, boss. I think I found your problem." His cheeky grin is brimming with pride.

Dilynne practically launches herself from her chair. "Show me." Without a backward glance, she follows Steven into the garage, the door slamming shut behind them.

"And we've lost her," Laney says with a sigh before turning back to me. "Anywho, I'm right across the street if you need a mani-pedi, facial, or a trim." She laughs and tilts her head. "Or, you know...a friend.

"I appreciate that. I came here on a whim to recuperate but haven't met many people yet."

"Well, now that you have mine and Dilynne's numbers, you're definitely not alone." Laney tilts her head at me. "Do you mind me asking what brought you here in the first place? Dilynne told me you applied for the seasonal job..."

Sighing, I debate how much I should divulge, but I feel comfortable with Laney, and I can't avoid discussing my career aspirations forever. "I moved here from Los Angeles. I'm originally from Garnet Valley and went to the University of Tennessee before moving to the West Coast."

"I know where Garnet Valley is. That place is beautiful—and just as small as Blossom Peak, right?"

"Exactly, but I couldn't go back home just yet."

"How come?"

Sighing, I continue. "I went to L.A. to try to make it as a singer-songwriter. I've been out there for three years without any luck, and if I go home, my parents are just going to rub it in that I'm delusional for thinking I could actually make a living doing something like that."

Laney frowns. "I'm so sorry, Elodie. That sucks that your parents don't believe in you."

"Thanks." I shrug, glancing into the stroller really quick to check on Remy. "I've made my peace with it, but I'm just not ready to face them. I don't feel like there's anything left for me back home. I got my degree in business because the agreement with my parents was that I had to go to college first and get something to fall back on in case music didn't work out, but I never wanted to do anything else in my life. Music is a universal language, you know? Everyone can relate to it. I just want to write something that means something to someone else, words and a melody that can transport you to a moment and allow you to relive a feeling over and over again. I want to leave behind a legacy, have a purpose in this world, make a difference in someone's life with a song. Does that make sense?"

Laney practically has tears in her eyes. Brushing her cheeks, she says, "I'm sorry. I didn't mean to tear up but I'm slightly hormonal at the moment. PMS is a bitch."

I laugh. "I agree."

She reaches out and grabs my hand, squeezing it slightly. "I know we just met, but if you can bring me to tears with just that little speech, I have no doubt that you have it within you to change someone's life with your music. Don't give up on yourself, okay? Speaking from experience, I put a dream of mine on the back burner because I felt it was no longer important. When Fletcher and I reconnected though, he was the one that pushed me to chase after it again because he believed in me, and didn't want me to live my life with regrets. My mom wouldn't want that for me either."

"If you don't mind me asking, what was it that you pushed aside?"

"Writing a novel."

"That's something I've always wanted to do too."

Laney smiles. "See? There are so many ideas I had, but after my mom died and I stayed in town to help my dad, it just became something I forgot about, thought I'd never end up doing because I was needed elsewhere. Fletcher helped me see that it's still important, so I decided to give it a shot."

"You're lucky to have someone like that."

"And now you do too. *Me*," she says effortlessly, like her words didn't just make my eyes tear up as well. "Take this time like you said, help Henley because lord knows that he needs it, and then chase your dreams once you're rested and inspired again. There's no timeline for aspirations, right? That's what I keep thinking. Who says you have to achieve something by a certain age? People who were too scared to keep trying, that's who."

I swallow the lump in my throat. "Thank you, Laney. I really think I needed to hear that today." Maybe that's the reason I walked in here on a whim, to hear the words that would help me feel like it's okay to breathe and rest.

"My pleasure. But, if you need some sarcasm or tough love, Dilynne and I are more than qualified to offer that as well."

We both stand as Remy stirs in the stroller. When she wakes up, she's going to want to eat and probably need a diaper change, so I need to find somewhere I can complete those tasks. I saw a sandwich shop down the street that had lunch specials, so I'll probably go there to stretch my dollar further, my daunting credit card balance reminding me of how necessary keeping this job is.

"I really do hope to see you at movie night," Laney adds as we move for the door.

"Honestly, I can't wait. It's been a long time since I've actually done something like that. For the past three years, all my life has been about is work and trying to get my big break."

"I understand that more than you know." With a wave, she heads across the street, and I make my way toward the sandwich shop.

I wasn't lying when I said that I've been working non-stop, and maybe that's the problem. I turned a creative outlet into a job.

The question that scares me though is: is it possible to have both? A job that requires creativity at all hours of the day?

Have I even had enough life experience to write a song that's worthy of being heard by the masses?

Or are my parents right, and I need to think logically for once?

But like Laney said, I have some time to figure it out. I just hope I don't get myself into a bigger mess in the process.

***

"Uh, it looks like I interrupted something."

The sound of my voice makes Henley collapse into a heap of bare skin and muscles on the living room floor, where it looked like he was doing some sort of martial arts when I walked in.

"Shit," he mutters, his arm slung over his face, sweat dripping down his torso.

And what a torso it is.

Holy mother of chest and abs, this sight will never get old.

This isn't the first time I've seen the man without his shirt. In fact, it's actually the third, but who's counting?

However, this is the first time I've seen him glistening with sweat and in a pair of athletic shorts that do very little to hide the bulge between his legs.

God, Elodie. Stop staring.

Clearing my throat, I bend down to take Remy from her car seat, pulling her to my chest as I stand tall again, only to find Henley standing up now as well.

Eyes on his face, Elodie.

"Were you just doing karate when I walked in?"

Henley huffs out a laugh, his smile effortless until his lips fall almost instantly, as if he realized he was actually smiling and had to put a stop to it. "It was supposed to be yoga, but I'm not very good yet."

My chest starts to tighten. "You were doing yoga? That's not what I expected from a man like you."

He arches an eyebrow. "A man like me?"

Heat crawls up my neck. "I just meant..." My eyes skim over his broad shoulders before I can stop myself. "You look more like a weights-and-bench-press guy. That's all."

He pushes a hand through his sweat-soaked hair as his eyes land on Remy. "Yeah, well...I blame Laney. She does yoga and wine events at her dad's winery and Fletcher dragged me to one without telling me what it was. Despite nearly dying that night, I felt more challenged by that workout than I had been in a long time, so now I've been trying to incorporate it into my routine."

He reaches for his daughter and she lunges for him as he presses a kiss to the top of her head—and I'm pretty sure my ovaries just wept. "How did she do today?" Glancing at the clock, he continues, "I thought you'd be home sooner."

"She did great," I reply, heading toward the kitchen for a glass of water, parched from the walking I did today. "We walked around The Village, and visited Dilynne and Laney, actually."

He stops dead in his tracks on his way to follow me into the kitchen. When I turn around to look at him, his eyes are focused on my ass.

Looks like Dilynne was right about his visual appreciation of my body.

You shouldn't care, Elodie, remember? He's your boss.

"You went and saw my sister?"

"Yeah. I mean, you kind of told me to and I wanted to smooth things over from yesterday. Laney happened to be there at that time too, so I got to meet her. She seems amazing and really sweet."

"Yeah, she's a lot happier now that she's not busy hating Fletcher's guts."

"Fletcher Adams," I say, followed by a whistle. "What a lucky girl."

Henley's jaw ticks. "You have a thing for Fletcher?"

I fill up my glass at the fridge, gauging his reaction before I speak. I shouldn't be enjoying the way his body looks even more tense than when I found him earlier, or how adorable he looks shirtless while holding his daughter, but I am.

"Just appreciating an objectively good-looking man, Henley. Nothing to get worked up about."

"I'm not getting worked up. I just..." His voice is tight. "I don't need my nanny swooning over my friends."

I pause mid-pour and turn to face him. "Excuse me?"

He shrugs. "Fletcher is engaged, and I don't need any more drama in my life."

Like a match has been lit, anger races through me. "You actually think I'm here to...what? Hook up with your friends instead of doing the job you hired me for? I actually met Fletcher's fiancée today. She was lovely and we made plans to hang out soon."

His face instantly relaxes and then regret takes over the lines around his eyes. "Elodie..."

I hold my hand up to stop him. "I know we don't know each other very well, a detail that is becoming glaringly obvious as each day passes, but I'm not a homewrecker, and definitely didn't come here to find a man, okay? So I'd appreciate being given the benefit of the doubt."

"Fuck, Elodie," he mutters, moving closer to me, but I shake my head.

"Your daughter and I had an amazing day, by the way. She napped, we walked around, and I took her to the park and pushed her on the swing in my lap, which she loved. I took pictures and wanted to show you, but right now? I think I just need to be alone."

"Elodie," he starts once more, but I walk around him and down the hall to my room, closing myself inside, hands shaking.

How dare he accuse me of being here under the wrong intentions.

How dare he question who I am.

Even though we don't know each other well, I need him to trust me, given that I'm caring for his daughter.

But maybe Dilynne is right. Maybe Henley has a lot of shit to work through and the best thing for me to do is keep the distance between us, especially because I won't be here for long.

We don't need to be friends for me to do my job.

And honestly, it would make everything I'm feeling easier to deal with if we weren't.

***

The sleepy haze I'm in dissipates as the sound of Remy's cries cut through the fog. When my eyes pop open, the sound is much more distinct. For one split second, I debate staying in here and letting Henley handle it, but when I hear his pleas for her to go to sleep and stop crying, I launch from my bed and tiptoe down the hall to find him pacing in the living room, trying to soothe her.

"Please baby girl," he whispers. "I don't know what else to do."

"Well, pleading with her isn't going to make her stop anytime soon."

His head twists in my direction. "Shit, I'm sorry, Elodie. She woke up and I fed her, changed her, but now she won't stop crying. I—I don't know what the hell she wants."

A tiny bit of pity builds in my chest, even though it shouldn't after what he alluded to earlier this evening. But with a glance at the clock, I realize it's actually early in the morning, which means this is a new day and everyone deserves a fresh start, even asshole men that think I'm here to hit on their friends.

Sighing, I close the space between us and reach for the baby. "Let me take her."

He turns away from me, bouncing her further. "No, you go back to sleep. I can handle this."

"I'm already awake, Henley. Will you just let me see if I can get her to at least calm down?"

Eyeing me wearily, it doesn't take him long to relent as he hands Remy over to me. "What's going on, baby bear?" I brush her hair back across her head, inhaling her sweet baby scent as I press my cheek against hers. "What's got you so upset?" Her cries become quieter, but she's still angry.

Henley groans as he pushes both of his hands through his hair, drawing the strands to stick straight up. I don't have the energy to tell him he looks like a mad scientist right now, especially when I can see the despair on his face. "I just don't know what she wants."

"Sometimes babies just need to cry, or it could be gas. Have you tried bicycle kicks with her?"

His blank stare shouldn't be funny, but it is. "You act like I should know what that is."

I take a seat on the couch, laying Remy down on the cushion in front of me. Her cries grow louder until I grab both of her legs and begin to move them up toward her stomach and back down, alternating them in the same motion as if she were riding a bike. "Moving her around like this can get the gas to move." Henley studies what I'm doing with laser focus. "Wanna try?"

Nodding, he switches places with me and repeats the same motion I was just performing. Within a few seconds, Remy lets out a fart that startles us both. He peers up at me with shock, and then we both burst into laughter.

"Holy shit!" Henley says through a laugh. "I think most grown men couldn't compete with that."

Holding my stomach, I fight to contain my giggles. "See? She's just gassy. Keep moving her legs around." Henley repeats the motion until Remy lets out a few more farts that seem to have alleviated some of her discomfort. But when he lifts her from the couch, she burps and spits up all over him.

"Shit."

"Aw, poor thing. Her stomach is clearly upset. Did you burp her after she ate?"

"I tried to," he says as he carefully stands from the couch and heads to the laundry room, removing his soiled shirt. "But she didn't let one out."

And once again, this man is standing in front of me, shirtless.

Is this God's way of testing the lines of temptation? What kind of karmic retribution am I suffering through right now?

He sniffs himself dramatically. "Shit. I need another shower. Do you mind..."

"Not at all. Go ahead, we're good."

Henley heads for his room and I take Remy into mine to change her outfit since she spit up on herself as well. Once she's in a clean pajama outfit, I head back out to the living room, but she starts crying again.

"What's wrong now?" Henley's voice startles me as I move gently around the room, trying to soothe her by bouncing her softly.

"She's just fussy, Henley. That doesn't mean something is wrong with her."

He sighs, brushing a hand through his wet hair. "I'm sorry you're up too. I wish I knew how to calm her down."

"You'll learn."

He scoffs, taking a seat on the couch. "Not sure that's true. Having kids was never on my radar, and the past few days have only proven that maybe I was right in avoiding this responsibility. It's not like I had amazing parents to look up to as an example." As soon as the words leave his lips, I can see the recognition on his face that he said more than he wanted.

"Dilynne said you two didn't have the best childhood," I say cautiously. "What happened?"

His eyes dart to mine. "Nothing," he says curtly in an attempt to shut down the conversation.

"Wow. Okay."

"Okay, what?"

Remy's cries still echo around us as I glare at him. "You know, I'm just trying to help, Henley. Dilynne wanted me to make sure you were okay..."

"My sister needs to mind her own business." He stands from the couch and heads toward the kitchen for a drink.

I shake my head, trying a different motion as I walk around with Remy. "Guess I'll be going to the movie night at the winery by myself," I mutter.

Henley walks back into the living room. "What?"

"I said, I guess I'll be going to the movie night at the winery by myself."

His brows furrow. "The girls told you about that?"

"Yeah. They invited me actually, and I said I'd be going with or without you. I think you've made it abundantly clear that you have no interest in being friendly with me and think I'm just here to hit on your friends, so..."

His feet carry him across the room in slow motion until he's standing right in front of me. And before I can breathe, he's lifting my chin up so our eyes meet, the callus of his fingers branding my skin. "I'm sorry," he says, the deep timbre of his voice coating me in a warmth that travels down all of my limbs. "I tried apologizing to you earlier, but you ran off."

"You accused me of something that I would never do."

"I know. Deep down, I know that, Elodie. I just..." He blows out a breath as his face contorts. I can practically see the wheels turning in his mind. "I'm frustrated and tired, and I'm—I'm taking it out on you."

My eyebrows lift. "Wow. That's mighty big of you to admit."

The corner of his mouth lifts. "What can I say? I have my moments. But I mean it. I'm sorry. It's not fair to you that you're getting the brunt of it." His thumb strokes my jaw and suddenly I forget how to breathe.

Our eyes remain locked, which is how I catch it when his dip down to my mouth for a split second. But as soon as he realizes what he did, he releases my chin and gives me his back, sighing out loud.

"Thank you," I whisper, barely loud enough for him to hear me over Remy's shuddered cries. All I get is a nod from him before he heads over to the couch and takes a seat, burying his head in his hands.

The only sound in the room now is Remy's fussing, and without thinking, I try one tactic I haven't yet.

I start to sing.

Henley's head snaps up, both he and Remy suddenly fixed on me. I find my voice that I haven't used in a while and close my eyes, letting the lyrics carry me as I softly sing "Breathe" by Faith Hill.

My mom is a huge country music fan, and all I remember growing up was listening to Faith Hill, Reba McEntire, and Shania Twain records while I helped her clean the house on the weekends.

When I open my eyes, I find Henley staring at me but Remy has finally laid her head on my shoulder. I begin to taper off, but she stirs again so I keep singing, moving around the room while swaying from side to side.

By the time I've finished the song, Remy is out cold on my chest. And when I glance back at Henley, I'm caught off guard by the sight of his massive frame slumped in the corner of the couch, also fast asleep.

Chapter 6

Henley

Parental Pressure and Job Duties

"That bus from the elementary school will be here in ten minutes, boss," Jessica calls out as she blows right past me, headed to the lodge restaurant with a pot of coffee in her hands. If she weren't so damn fast, I'd ask her to come back and refill my coffee mug for the third time this morning, which is better than the five cups I've been averaging for the past few days.

My body hurts all over this morning, but I can't tell if that's from the yoga or falling asleep on the couch in an awkward position last night. All I know is I got the best rest I have in the past week, and it was all because of my new nanny.

God, her voice.

I thought only angels could sing like that.

Elodie is talented, which makes me question what the hell she's doing here. With a voice like that, she should be singing on stages all across the world. But watching her walk around and soothe Remy last night with that song only made me realize how little I know about the woman.

She's right. We don't know each other, and even though every part of me is fighting the idea of broaching that issue, the rational part of me knows that I should be more familiar with the woman I entrusted with my daughter. I mean, hell...I knew her for all of twenty minutes before I hired her.

Is that the type of shit that gets CPS called on you?

"Henley Clark!" I can count on one hand how many times I've heard that voice at that volume, but all I know is when she gets that loud, that means I've done something terribly wrong.

Spinning around, I come face-to-face with Carol Vance, my foster mother and the closest thing to a real mom I've ever had, her husband Nick hot on her heels.

"Carol? Wh—what are you doing here and why are you yelling?"

She waves her finger in my face, or as close to my face as she can because the woman is barely five feet tall, yet still terrifying. "Don't act all coy with me. How come I had to find out from Carolina down at the bakery that you had a baby?"

Fuck.

"Well, uh..."

"I'm sorry, but is now a bad time, Henley?" Spinning around, I find Elodie standing to my right, Remy on her hip with her hand outstretched toward me.

Wait. Is that my wallet?

I pat the back pocket of my jeans and realize that I did, in fact, leave my house this morning without my wallet.

"Henley!" Carol forces my attention back to her.

Dragging a hand down my face, I groan. "Carol, look. I'm sorry that I didn't tell you about Remy, but..."

She turns to Elodie, and her face instantly softens as she takes in my daughter. "Is this her?"

"Yes," I reply.

"And you must be the mother," Carol says to Elodie.

Elodie's eyes widen as I reach out and place my hand on Carol's shoulder.

"No, Carol. This is Elodie, my nanny." Sighing, I guide her over to a booth. "Here, take a seat and I'll get us some coffee, okay? I'll explain everything."

Nick clears his throat and leans over to mutter in my ear before taking a seat. "I tried to tell her not to bombard you at work, but..."

"Telling her anything is impossible, I know."

He nods. "Take your time. It's not like we have anything else to do today."

Carol and Nicholas Vance were foster parents for many children over many years until they took in me and my sister.

Dilynne was nine when my parents started disappearing, leaving us home alone at all hours, two kids under the age of eleven left to fend for themselves. When the food started disappearing and the electricity and water got turned off, I knew I needed to find a way to keep us safe. Finally, after a few months of barely surviving and stealing anything I could, one of my teachers reported suspected child abandonment, and CPS picked us up and put us in foster care. We went through three families before landing in Blossom Peak with Carol and Nick, the closest thing to actual parents that we've ever had and the best thing that ever happened to us.

We were the last siblings Carol and Nick helped raise before closing that chapter on their lives. Now as retirees, they spend their days kayaking on the lake, driving around the state going to antique shows, and keeping an eye on me and my sister, even though they don't have to anymore.

They're the closest thing I have to parents, but it still doesn't occur to me to keep them in the loop about my life. My instinct to lean on others left my body long before Carol and Nick took me and Dilynne in. I respect them, but I've always kept to myself.

I would have thought to tell them eventually, but after how chaotic the past week has been, it's no wonder it slipped my mind.

I stride back over to Elodie, taking Remy from her arms and planting a kiss on my daughter's cheek. "Sorry about that."

She pushes the few strands of hair that have fallen from her ponytail away from her face. Wearing denim shorts and a plain white tank top, she looks far too tempting, like the girl-next-door a guy like me doesn't deserve.

But I push that thought away as fast as I can.

"That's all right. I feel bad for just showing up here, but I figured you'd probably need your wallet."

She holds it out to me again, and this time I take it and shove it in my back pocket. "Thank you. I appreciate it, even though that's not in your job description."

"Yeah, well since you never really provided me with one, I've taken the liberty of fulfilling any tasks that need to be done. Speaking of which, your fridge is pretty bare, so I was thinking of going grocery shopping today. Is there anything in particular you want?"

"Oh, you don't have to do that."

She laughs. "I do if we want to eat anything besides Hot Pockets and plain noodles."

Shaking my head, I pull my wallet back out and hand her my credit card. "Fine. Take my card. I'll eat pretty much anything."

"Are you sure? No allergies I should know about?"

"Nope. Strong as an ox."

Her eyes dip down my torso before glancing away, heat flaming her cheeks.

Fuck, she's adorable when she blushes.

"So, I take it those are your parents?" she asks, brushing past her embarrassment.

"Uh, well..." Now's not the time to get into my relationship with Carol and Nick, so instead, I clear my throat and then gesture toward the restaurant. "Have you eaten?"

Her eyes slide to where Carol and Nick are seated, but thankfully, she doesn't push for more information. "I—I haven't. I'm not a big breakfast person."

"Well, at least have Jessica pour you a cup of coffee to go. I'm going to take Remy over to see Carol and Nick really quick, and then I'll meet you back over here."

She nods curtly. "Okay." Reaching out to smooth Remy's hair back, she says, "I'll be right back, baby bear."

Remy and I both watch her walk away before I snap myself out of staring and brace myself for Carol's reaction when she meets my daughter. "This is Remington," I announce when I arrive back at the booth I left my foster parents in. "I've been calling her Remy for short."

Carol practically launches out of her seat. "Oh my gosh, she is just too precious," she says, reaching to take Remy from me, arranging her in her arms while she gazes down at her. "And that nanny of yours is pretty cute too." Her eyes lift with that knowing glint in them, making Nick laugh.

"Not sure Henley hooking up with his nanny would improve his situation, hun."

"Oh, hush. We don't know the whole story yet," she fires back.

So, as Carol coos and gushes over Remy, I fill them in on the past few months—the phone calls from Meghan, her dropping the baby off, and how I ended up with Elodie as my nanny.

"She's awfully beautiful, Henley. I mean, if it were me…"

Nick clears his throat. "Are you alluding to you becoming a lesbian, hun?"

She bats at him. "You know what I mean." Turning back to me, she continues, "Having a baby changes things, Henley. Nick and I can't speak from experience, but the first time we fostered, we knew our lives would never be the same, and now yours won't be either. Parenting is a full-time job, even when you sleep you'll be worrying. Having someone else to lean on makes it a bit easier though. Maybe it's time to consider settling down and finding someone to be with."

"Look, I appreciate your concern, but the last thing I need right now is a relationship. Besides, she's technically my employee, she's only here until Christmas, and she's seven years younger than me. So what you're suggesting is just batshit crazy."

"First of all, never tell a woman that she's crazy," Carol snaps, pointing a finger in my face as soon as I'm finished recalling the reasons why I need to continue to think with my head, and not the one in my pants. "And second, what are you gonna do when she leaves?"

"I haven't thought that far ahead yet."

"Well, you know you can count on us if you need extra help, but Elodie—that's her name, right?"

"Yeah…"

A throat clearing behind me makes me pause.

"Oh, hello dear," Carol says brightly.

"Hi. I was just, uh…" Elodie stammers. "I got my coffee, so if you're ready for me to take Remy again…"

Heat crawls up the back of my neck. *God, how much of that did she hear?*

Luckily, Carol speaks before I can embarrass myself further. "I hope you weren't offended by my little interrogation." She kisses Remy on the cheek before handing her back to Elodie. "I can't help but want what's best for my kids, even if they're too stubborn to see a good thing when it's right in front of their face."

"Thank you for not making this worse," I mutter under my breath through clenched teeth.

Elodie doesn't seem fazed, though. "Oh, trust me, I understand parents wanting what's best. But as Henley said, this is just temporary." Smiling, she peers up at me. "I'll see you when you get home?"

"Yeah. Thanks." Leaning forward, I kiss Remy on the cheek. "Be good, little one."

Elodie picks Remy's hand up and waves to us before leaving the lodge, my eyes trailing her the entire time.

Carol's snort breaks through my perusal. "You might think I'm off my rocker, but I'm not blind, Henley."

Nick shrugs behind her. "The way your eyes were locked on her ass as she walked away doesn't do much to support your argument."

"Look, I appreciate your concern, but I haven't even been a father for a week yet, okay? Can you please just give me time to adjust to that before trying to marry me off? Jesus, is this what it's like to have overbearing parents?"

Carol swats my arm. "Watch who you're calling overbearing."

Pinching the bridge of my nose, I say, "Seeing you always reminds me where Dilynne gets her sass from."

"Damn right. The last thing I want is for any of my kids to roll over and just take what life throws at them. You're a fighter, Henley, just like your sister."

"Yeah, well, I'm not feeling very victorious right now."

No. The past few days feel like all of my questionable decisions over the years are coming back to haunt me.

Living for today, never settling down with one person, having the freedom to come and go as I please—I never realized how much I took those things for granted until Meghan dropped a baby bomb on me.

But that doesn't mean that I need someone else in my life, a woman to complete my little family.

Families disappoint you. Parents turn out to be selfish.

Remy already got the short end of the stick with me as her father, and a mother that left her behind without a second thought. The last thing I want to do is bring in another person who might end up disappointing her too.

***

The smell of garlic and herbs hits me when I walk through my front door, finally home after a long day at work. The field trip today went well, except for the group of fifth graders who thought it would be funny to fill condoms with water and throw them at each other on the obstacle course. Not even sure where they got condoms from, but honestly, it was hilarious.

Remy sees me first, letting out a coo that pulls Elodie's attention from the stove where she's stirring something. "Hey, you made it."

"Yeah. Long day."

"Well, dinner's almost ready, so wash up."

"Yes, Mom."

Elodie rolls her eyes with a hint of a smile. "Well, they say the older you get, the more you turn into your parents, right?"

"I wouldn't know." Comments like those always sting because I didn't have stellar parents as examples and by the time Carol and Nick took us in, I was a thirteen-year-old kid, jaded by the cards life had dealt me. Even though I respected them and appreciated everything they did for me and Dilynne, I fought like hell not to let them close enough to hurt me.

Elodie keeps talking as I wash my hands at the kitchen sink. "This recipe is one that my mom makes, one-pan chicken and rice. It's just a few simple ingredients, but it packs a punch of flavor."

"It certainly smells good, but you don't have to cook, Elodie. I've managed to feed myself over the years just fine."

Shrugging, she begins dishing out the food onto two plates and sprinkling something green on the top of it, along with freshly grated cheese.

Is this woman the baby-whisperer and *the long lost child of Gordon Ramsay?*

After drying my hands, I walk over to my daughter and lift her from the high chair, pressing a kiss to her cheek. "How was your day, little one?"

Elodie places the plates down on the table that's perfectly set with placemats, silverware, and napkins—little things that make this place feel more like a home.

"She got a little fussy today at the grocery store. She kept trying to eat her toy and was drooling everywhere. I think she could already be teething."

"This soon?"

Elodie nods. "There was a baby at the daycare that cut his first tooth when he was four months old. Every kid develops at different rates." Taking her seat, she reaches for her glass of water, takes a sip, and then inhales deeply over her plate. "God, I've been thinking about this all day."

My mouth begins to water as I assess my plate. "It smells amazing, but again, you didn't need to cook."

"Well, like I said, you haven't exactly given me a list of job duties and cooking is something I don't mind doing, especially when I have a proper kitchen to do it in. My place in L.A. barely had room for a microwave."

I blow on my first bite, watching the steam waft through the air. "I didn't even know I owned placemats."

Elodie covers her mouth as she chews. "I actually bought those today at the store. Your table needed some color, and they help protect the wood."

"Ah. Good to know I'm not just that sleep deprived." When I finally taste her cooking, I have to fight the urge to moan from how good it is. "Damn, El. This is incredible."

"Thanks." Her proud smile almost makes my lips tilt up too. "I still think my mom's is better, but that just might be me being too critical."

"Your mom taught you how to cook?"

"Yep. Me and my brother. She was a big believer that homemade is always better."

I keep shoveling food in my mouth. "I'm more of a convenience guy, myself. Never really was taught the basics of a kitchen, but I manage. I can grill a mean burger."

"I honestly don't mind cooking, Henley," she says softly. "You can add it to my list of duties."

I wipe my mouth with my napkin. Remy continues to sit on my lap, kicking and waving her hands around while watching us eat. "I'm paying you to take care of Remy, not be my personal chef."

She finishes chewing, dabbing at the corner of her mouth with her napkin. "I'll tell you what. How about I make a list of the jobs I'm willing to do, and then we can agree they are included in what you're paying me, especially since you're letting me live here rent-free."

I twist my lips as I consider her proposition. "Fine."

She claps her hands once, standing from her chair and walking over to the couch, flipping pages of scribble over until she finds a blank one. "Okay. Elodie's duties," she says as she writes, her handwriting just as soft and feminine as the rest of her.

Jesus Christ, Henley. You're admiring her handwriting now?

"So, we agree that anything pertaining to Remy is my responsibility, and I agree to cook at least three nights a week. The other nights you can eat cereal for dinner if you wish. But please let me spend some time in your kitchen while I can."

I look over my shoulder to admire the kitchen with its top-of-the-line appliances that I barely use. "Fine. Three nights a week and no more."

"Deal. Now, what about laundry?"

"You can do yours and Remy's, but I'll do my own."

"That's fair." She scribbles more words on the paper. "What about cleaning?"

"Cleaning?"

"Yeah, mopping floors, dusting..."

I hold up my hand to stop her. "You're not a fucking maid, Elodie."

She's taken aback by my tone. "I know..."

"I have a cleaning company that comes every two weeks to do the deep cleaning. If you want to tidy up between those visits, you're more than welcome to. But you are not going to mop my fucking floors all the time, do you understand me?"

I can't tell if the look in her eyes is one of fear from my command, or appreciation. If this woman only knew how commanding I can be in other aspects of life. "Understood," she finally croaks out, swallowing roughly. "Okay then." Turning her attention back to the paper, she writes a few things down and then glances back up at me. "Grocery shopping is okay?"

"Yeah, I can handle you taking on that responsibility. I don't remember the last time I saw my refrigerator that full."

She chuckles. "Any other errands you need done?"

"No. Just make sure that my daughter is okay while I'm at work. Knowing you're here with her this past week has made this transition a lot easier to handle."

She reaches over and places her hand on top of mine, but almost immediately, she retracts it—as if the touch burned her. There's definitely electricity coursing through me now, and I'm wondering if she feels the same. "I'm happy to help, Henley. You've given me purpose when I really needed it."

Purpose. There's a word that's unfamiliar to me as well.

Is Remy my purpose now?

My daughter peers up at me from my lap in that moment and when our eyes meet, that feeling I've been fighting returns—panic mixed with infatuation. Panic for the tiny human I'm now responsible for, and infatuation with how incredibly perfect she is. I never knew I could be so obsessed with another human.

God, I have a daughter.

Clearing her throat, Elodie motions to my plate. "Are you finished?"

"Uh, yeah. But you cook, I clean."

"Sounds fair." She heads to the kitchen and I watch her go.

There's a woman in my house—my house that no other woman besides my sister, Laney, or Carol has ever stepped into—and part of me is surprised by how much I like it.

I've gotten used to coming home to silence and bland evenings with no one to talk to but myself. Do I miss my space? Maybe a little. But this place is different now—the smells, the sounds, the *feelings*.

Yeah, I think my nanny is part of what's making me feel panic mixed with infatuation as well.

"So, are you just gonna watch sports again tonight? Or are you up for a movie?" Elodie asks as she walks back to the dining room.

"Sorry. I'm a creature of habit. My evening routine was sort of on repeat before..." I gesture to my daughter.

"I can tell, but maybe you'll be open to something new? I just need to check out for a while."

Her comment makes me pause. "Check out?"

"Yeah. Don't you have a ritual that you do when you just need to turn your mind off for a bit?"

"Yeah. I drink."

Placing her hands on her hips, she scolds me with her gaze. "That's not a very healthy way to escape."

"Wasn't asking for your opinion."

She rolls her eyes and sits back down in her chair, reaching out to play with Remy's hands. "Sorry, but there's got to be a better outlet than that."

"It's not like I'm an alcoholic. But when I've had a long day or something is on my mind, I like a drink to take the edge off. Why? What do you do? Eat celery?"

Her mouth falls open before a laugh escapes. "What?"

"I don't know. That was the first healthy thing that popped into my head."

She shakes her head. "No. No celery. Popcorn is more my snack of choice, but besides that, I listen to music."

"What kind of music?"

"Any and everything. Just depends on my mood. But lately…" Her heavy sigh sounds like she's been carrying a weight on her chest. "It's just not helping."

"So, movies?"

"Yup. That's the next best thing."

"Do you have a favorite?"

"*Now and Then*," she says proudly. "A classic, and one that never lets me down."

"Were you even born when that movie came out?"

She swats at me playfully, but my lips curl up into a smile I can't control. Fuck, she's fun to get riled up. And as soon as I realize I'm enjoying myself, my lips fall and I drop my gaze back down to my daughter who lets out a big yawn.

"No, I wasn't born yet. But my mom let me watch it when she deemed I was old enough, and I became obsessed. To this day, I still want to go to a cemetery at night and see if I can talk to the dead."

"You're all on your own with that one."

Laughing, she says, "Are you scared of ghosts?"

"No, but I know better than to mess with shit I don't understand."

"Life after death fascinates me," she continues. "Especially those that die young. It always makes me so sad to think of people not getting to leave a mark on this world."

"Is that important to you?" I ask, even though my heart is pounding as I realize how deep this conversation is getting. But fuck if I don't want to keep talking to her, keep getting to know who this woman really is.

Her smile is soft and quick. "It is. But lately? I just don't know what that mark will be."

Remy starts to get fussy, squirming in my arms. "Looks like she's had enough of this conversation."

Elodie nods, reaching for her. "Yeah, probably a little morbid for a three-month-old." Kissing Remy's cheek, she meets my eyes. "I'll handle bath time while you do the dishes, and then maybe we can watch that movie?"

Nerves race through me, but I'm not sure why.

Maybe it's because you've never watched a movie with a woman at home before, Henley.

But the look in her eyes right now—hope mixed with sadness—has me agreeing to her request. "Sure." The smile that blooms across her face makes my chest swell with panic and infatuation again. *Fuck.*

"Sounds great. Thanks, Henley," she says and then heads down the hallway to bathe my daughter while I sit there, wondering what the hell is happening inside my body.

You're getting attached, Henley.

"Shit," I grumble, standing from my chair and heading to the kitchen sink where a pile of dirty dishes awaits me.

As I clean, I wrestle with the realization that I'm getting used to this woman being around.

Finding Elodie in the kitchen, cooking me dinner, smiling at me as I walked into my house.

Having someone to talk to in the evening about the day and having conversations with her about nothing and everything at the same time.

Her dropping off my wallet this morning when I left it at home.

I like having her in my home and in my life. And that's a real fucking problem because she's not staying.

Nope. Remy and I are better off alone.

And I've been left one too many times to hold out hope that this time could be different.

Chapter 7

Henley

Popcorn, Paternity Results, and Peer Pressure

A pack of screaming kids rushes past me as I enter the Hart Winery courtyard with Remy strapped to my chest in a carrier and my new diaper bag slung over my back.

The pink, flower-patterned bag that Meghan dropped off with my daughter has been traded in for one a bit more tactical—khaki canvas material that's stain resistant, pockets for all of the necessities like bottles and binkies, and a compartment that folds down into a changing pad for when I have to change a diaper in a pinch because the men's restroom has no changing table.

Seriously. When are public restrooms going to get with the times? And what about the single dads, like me? Why are we not being thought of?

It's been a little over a week since Remy came into my life, and I'm already forming a list of parenting issues I feel I'm developing strong stances on, with the changing table debacle at the top of the list.

But today also marks ten days of Elodie living with us, and adjusting to having a woman in my space has been its own adventure.

The woman in question is currently gliding next to me in a floor length cotton dress, printed with a tropical pattern in teal and purple. Her hair is down in soft waves, and she has on a pair of earrings that sparkle every time the sun hits them, making her eyes stand out even more.

After the run-in with Carol and Nick the other day, I was expecting Elodie to push me more about my relationship with them, but she never brought it up again. Instead, I came home to a fully stocked fridge, clean and folded clothes, and organized baby items in my daughter's room, along with the amazing meal she had prepared for me, and two more since then.

That night—sitting there and talking to her, seeing a look of sadness but also unexplainable joy in her eyes—it's had my stomach in knots the past few days. Watching her as she watched her favorite movie was an experience. I was invested in what she was feeling—her laughs, her shock at certain parts even though she knew what was going to happen, and her tears when the end came.

The entire evening has been on replay in my mind and is causing an uneasiness to grow inside me, even though I have nothing to be wound up about. Elodie is incredible, and between the two of us, we're starting to get a routine down.

Remy's crib is still in my room for the time being, but she's not sleeping in the bed with me anymore. The past few nights have been decent thanks to Elodie's suggestion that we change her formula to one more sensitive for her stomach, which has definitely helped with her gas and projectile vomit issues. I'm confident that if she wakes up, my subpar fatherhood skills are enough to get her back to sleep without my nanny's help—a thought that I have to keep reminding myself of since the night she sang my daughter and me to sleep.

"Hey, you made it!" Laney walks up to me, pressing on her tiptoes to kiss my cheek, then Remy's.

"Well, not sure how much of the movie I'll get to watch, but I don't want to let a baby prevent me from supporting the winery."

Laney runs a finger down Remy's cheek. "I'm sure she'll be fine, but if you need a break, just let me know." She turns to Elodie, tossing her thumb in my direction. "You convinced him to come?"

Elodie rubs my arm, so natural I don't even flinch.

Fuck. I like her touching me way too damn much.

"Honestly, I think he's just scared to be left alone with Remy."

I shrug. "She's not wrong, but it's a beautiful night. I don't want to waste it because before you know it, the snow will be here."

Laney huffs out a laugh. "Yeah, but that means it's snowboarding season, which you love, remember?"

My lips quirk up. "And you're not wrong about that."

Elodie turns to me. "You snowboard?"

"And ski. Wouldn't make sense that I own a ski lodge and don't have some sort of experience on the slopes, now would it?"

"Henley used to be a bit of a daredevil back in the day."

"Is that so?" Elodie studies me before Remy squawks from her carrier.

"Laney!" A voice carries over the noise of the growing crowd, drawing my attention to the right. George Hart, Laney's father, is waving her in his direction.

She turns back to me and Elodie. "I'll catch up with you guys later, okay? But don't forget about the popcorn. The new cart is working great, and we've added some new flavor options."

Elodie watches her walk away and then gestures to the grass that is filling up quickly as families mark their spots with their blankets and lawn chairs, the sun falling fast in the sky.

"Shall we find a spot?" she asks.

"Yeah, probably should."

"Good, because I'm a bit of a popcorn fanatic and if I miss out, I'm going to be pissed."

Chuckling, I lead Elodie over to a spot that has just a sliver of shade created by the tree that's been here for at least as long as I have. Hart Winery is a staple in Blossom Peak, and part of the reason is the history of this place. Laney and Rhonan's parents opened this winery when they were kids, and that type of legacy is pretty normal around here—generations of families continuing to build Blossom Peak into a town and home that draws people from all over this country.

Since her mom passed, Laney and her dad have kept this place thriving, and people visit from all over to sample their wines or host their weddings on the beautiful grounds.

The lawn stretches wide wherever the concrete paths don't, providing plenty of space for people to spread out. Trees, shrubs, and flowers are planted around the property as well as a playground off to the left for kids to enjoy while parents relax with a glass of wine. To the right are several cornhole sets, bocce ball courts, horseshoe pits, and fire pits for the colder nights, which also allow them to offer s'mores for the kids.

One day I'll be able to do that with Remy.

"You weren't kidding about popcorn being your favorite snack, huh?"

"Nope." Elodie spreads out the blanket she brought and I drop the backpack on it to keep the breeze from blowing it away. "Even when I had braces and it was forbidden, I snuck it every chance I got."

She kneels and starts taking out a few toys for Remy while I unclip the straps and extract her from the carrier without dropping her.

Ha! Parenting win for the day.

I shake my head at her admission. "Looks like I wasn't the only one that was a rebel."

She grins. "Guess not. So, what did Laney mean about your daredevil days?"

Handing her Remy, I gently lower myself to the ground, still sore from yoga the other day. "Let's just say that adrenaline is a powerful drug."

"How so?" She sits Remy in her lap, her legs tucked behind her as the breeze blows her long hair to the side. Fuck, she looks gorgeous right now—especially holding my daughter.

I brush off that thought. "Football was my outlet throughout high school, but after that, I had no plans to continue playing or go to college for that matter, so I chased new highs—snowboarding, skydiving, and anything else that made me feel invincible at eighteen and nineteen, since touching drugs wasn't an option for me." *Especially after I witnessed what happened with my parents.* "But once Dilynne graduated from high school, I took off and traveled for a few years, seeking any thrill I could find. It was the first time I felt free in my life, and then when I was twenty-two, I injured myself pretty badly in a street luge accident."

"Pretty badly? You almost died." I peer up to find my sister staring down at me, her hands planted on her hips.

I scowl up at her. "Oh, it wasn't that bad."

"You had six broken bones, and they had to cut a piece of your skull off to relieve the swelling in your brain. At this point, you should be grateful you still have some ability to think straight." Glancing over at Elodie and then back to me, my sister continues, "Well, I guess that's debatable."

"Nice to see you too, Dil," I mutter as annoyance builds in my temples. It's not that I don't love my sister, but I was actually enjoying the conversation I was having with Elodie.

Plopping down on the blanket, my sister pushes her hair from her face. "I'm just speaking the truth." Dilynne turns to Elodie. "Don't let this guy fool you into thinking he was okay. If I hadn't begged him to stop trying to kill himself and come home, who knows if he'd still be alive."

Elodie shakes her head at me, even though there's a smile pulling at her lips. "Well, then you wouldn't have this little bear cub, would you?"

If she'd made that comment a week ago, I'd probably grunt with annoyance. But honestly, seeing my daughter in front of me makes me feel as though there has been a piece missing in my life all these years. And if she hadn't appeared the way she did, I don't think I would have been as receptive to it.

"She's definitely changed things," I reply instead.

Dilynne reaches out and grabs Remy's hand as her tiny fingers curl around her thumb. "How are things going with you two?"

My head snaps to my sister. "What do you mean? Elodie is my nanny." My question comes out a tad more defensively than it should, which of course, she picks up on.

Dilynne twists her lips. "I was talking about you and your daughter, but good to know you're keeping your dick in your pants too." Rolling her eyes, she turns to Elodie. "I told you my brother has issues."

Elodie hides her smile behind her hand. "Believe me, I'm beginning to understand that. But to answer your question, I think their father-daughter bond is developing well. He's no longer afraid of bathing her, he's become a pro at changing a diaper, and she reaches for him when he gets home—all things that point in a positive direction."

My sister slaps me on the back. "Look at you, acting like a dad and shit. Carol and Nick would be proud."

"Yeah, they came by the lodge the other day. Let's just say Carol wasn't pleased that she found out about Remy from someone other than me."

Dilynne cackles. "Damn. I'm sad that I missed that." Before I can say another word, Dilynne is pushing herself up from the grass. "Well, I just wanted to come over and say hello. Laney is putting me to work tonight, so I'd better get back to it. The girl is lucky she's my best friend. I wouldn't do this for anyone but her." Looking at Elodie as she begins to walk away, she says, "Text me tomorrow. Laney and I usually have dinner one night a week and you're more than welcome to join us."

"Thank you. I will."

"Hey, I'll be right back," I tell Elodie, not bothering to wait for her reply as I launch myself from the grass and catch up to my sister. "Dil—"

"What's up?" she asks while casting a glance at me over her shoulder.

I pull her to a stop. "Hey. Stop for a minute, will ya?"

"I told you. I need to help Laney."

"Well, I don't appreciate you saying shit like that to Elodie."

"What shit?"

"About me and my—" I clear my throat before continuing. "Issues."

My sister plants her hands on her hips. "First of all, you're the one that alluded to something going on between the two of you, not me. And second, I was just warning the woman you barely know that's now living with you that you're a grenade that might explode at any given moment."

"That's not true."

She places a hand on my shoulder. "Henley, I love you, but your emotional intelligence is...under construction."

"So you think I'm immature?"

"I think you've avoided a lot of shit from our childhood," she fires back. "And now that you're a dad, I think it's going to come back and bite you in the ass."

Irritation is flooding my chest because deep down, I know my sister is right. But that doesn't mean I like hearing it from her. "Well, I don't appreciate you talking about my personal business to my employee."

"Why is it such a big fucking deal? She *lives* with you."

"Because she doesn't need all of the details, and she's leaving anyway. She's leaving just like everyone else does." The moment the words leave my lips, my sister's grin grows into a full-blown smirk.

Yeah, I'm the one with zero emotional intelligence.

"God, it's already happening."

Pushing a hand through my hair, I let out a growl. "Nothing is happening."

My sister softens her voice. "Not everyone leaves, Henley. The boys haven't left you, right? I haven't left you. Carol and Nick haven't left you." I shoot her a glare but remain silent. She takes that as permission to keep talking. "And besides, Elodie's living with you and taking care of your daughter. She deserves to know you in some capacity, and if you'd take the time to get to know her too, you just might find she's pretty amazing. I mean, she was in Los Angeles trying to make it as a singer and songwriter before she moved here. Did you know that?" *No, I didn't, but that definitely explains her vocal talent she showed me the other night.* "She's funny and kind, and I'm pretty sure I'm developing a girl crush on her, and the last time that happened was with Laney."

"You were eleven."

"Exactly, so that should tell you something."

My frustration is starting to subside, but something else is filling my chest instead—yearning, curiosity, and a need to get back to my girls.

My girls? Where the fuck did that come from?

"All I'm saying is, one, I'm not going to apologize for warning this poor girl about who she's living with and asking her to keep an eye on you. And two, maybe it's not the worst thing that you're not alone right now. Lord knows I wouldn't be any help with Remy, so count your blessings and treat the woman with some respect, okay? And that starts with getting to know her and vice versa. Just please don't sleep with her," she pleads. "I like her, and that would just make things awkward for everyone."

"Trust me. I have no intention of doing that. Which is part of why I'm pissed at what you said."

She crosses her arms over her chest, staring at me like I'm a lying sack of shit. "Then stop staring at her ass."

"I don't."

"Yes, you do. I don't blame you, it's very nice. Round and voluptuous. But there's no good that can come from you crossing that line, Henley. Keep it professional. Make a friend of the opposite sex, for once, and I think you'll find it's something you've been missing."

"So are you saying you have guy friends I don't know about?"

Her glare is alarmingly effective. "I work in the automotive industry. You already know the answer to that."

I mimic her stance, crossing my arms over my chest now. "You know, if memory serves me correctly, you once mixed business with pleasure too."

She huffs out a laugh. "Yeah, and look at how well that worked out for me." Patting me on the chest, she says, "Now go back to your daughter and nanny, and try to enjoy yourself, okay?"

A detail I've been meaning to share spills out before she can walk away. "By the way, the paternity tests came back yesterday, confirming what I already knew. Remy is definitely my daughter."

My sister flashes a soft smile up at me. "Well, we already knew the ears locked that in, but good to know it's official." A curt nod is all I can muster at the moment. "Now, unclench your shoulders, stop stressing about something you can't control, and embrace this new life of yours."

Rolling my eyes, I grumble, "Yeah. Fine."

Dilynne might think she's healed, but I know there are still demons she fights too. No one handles what life throws at them without a scar or two. And even though it's not Elodie's fault that I'm in this predicament, I still think it's best that I focus on the fact that she works for me and keep that line drawn in the sand.

I trek back across the grass to find Elodie feeding Remy a bottle as I take a seat back on the blanket, the opening credits to *Toy Story* playing through the speakers around us. "Sorry about that."

"Everything okay?"

"Yeah, just sibling stuff." Sighing, I watch Elodie adjust Remy in her arms.

Silence rests between us until she says something that only further fuels my irritated mood. "So, you had foster parents?"

"I was wondering when you were gonna bring that up," I mutter, reaching into the diaper backpack for a few bottles of water I brought for us, unscrewing the cap on mine and taking a drink.

"Honestly, I was waiting for the right time but realized there probably isn't one."

"You're right about that."

Shaking her head, she looks down at Remy. "I couldn't imagine not having my parents in my life. Even though they both had their faults, I was lucky to be raised in a home with a mom and a dad, a brother that I got along with for the most part, and I never felt unsure of what the day would bring."

"Yeah, well, some kids are better off without their biological parents." Jutting my chin toward Remy, I say, "Her mom didn't want her, and I'm going to make sure that I do everything in my power to make sure she doesn't ever feel like she's missing something because of that."

"Carol and Nick seemed pretty great."

"They are. Honestly, I'm not sure where we would have ended up if it weren't for them. I had to write a letter to the deputy district attorney, pleading for us to be able to stay with them when they moved us. Carol was the first foster mom we had that Dilynne connected with. I didn't want her to lose that, and luckily, the DA listened. We got placed back in the home and were able to stay with them until we both turned eighteen."

Our eyes meet, hers glistening with unshed tears. "Remy and Dilynne are so lucky to have you, Henley. I know your life has completely changed in the past week or so, but this little girl has a family here—her aunt, Laney, your friends." Tilting her head, she asks, "Family doesn't have to be blood, does it?"

A wave of contentment rolls through me. "The only family I have besides Dilynne isn't related to me at all, El. And frankly, I think chosen family is the best kind. There's no obligation, you know? No guilt for cutting things off. Toxic people are toxic, regardless of if they're related to you or not." I reach out and stroke Remy's tiny arm, her soft skin making my chest grow tight with a protective instinct that's only growing stronger by the day.

"I get that," she replies, but doesn't elaborate further.

And it's at this moment I decide it's time to turn the tone of the evening around. I opened up a bit, even though I didn't want to. But Elodie makes me want to fucking talk. It's like every time I talk to her, her sunshine sucks the darkness from my soul.

Too bad Dilynne wasn't around to hear it, though.

Emotionally immature, my ass.

Standing, I say, "I'm going to get us some popcorn before it's all gone. Any flavor requests?"

Looking up at me, her gray eyes shining in the orange sunlight, she flashes me the most annoying smile—annoying because it makes me want to smile right back at her. "I told you. I want them all. Don't let me down, Henley."

And as I walk across the courtyard to the popcorn cart, my stomach twists with the reminder that I could let her *and* my daughter down in more ways than one—especially if I act on this attraction to my nanny that's growing stronger with each passing day.

***

"So, she's definitely yours?" Rhonan asks as we wait for our turn at the bocce ball courts, where I just told him and Elliot about the paternity test results I received yesterday, feeling more at ease now that I got to tell my sister first. The Hart Winery courtyard is filled with people taking in all of the activities tonight. Most families are still trying to watch the movie, but there's a bustle of movement and chatter all around from those that can't sit still.

Honestly, movie nights usually end up like this. The movie is there for entertainment, but groups use it as an excuse to hang out and support the winery and community of Blossom Peak. This winery attracts a lot of tourists, so all businesses profit from their events.

I glance between two of my best friends, silently wishing the third was here as well. Fletcher is in Charlotte this week, deep into the preseason. We have plans to head down there next month to catch a game with our whole crew, which hasn't happened in a few years. But now that Laney and Fletcher are together, I'm sure it will happen more often.

"She is." I take a drink of my soda, opting not to drink wine tonight since Elodie mentioned wanting a glass earlier, and I don't want her to feel like she can't enjoy herself. "I knew it from that first day, but it feels good to have it confirmed. Now I just need Elliot to draw up the custody papers and send them to Meghan."

Elliot arches a brow at me. "You sure that's what you want?"

"Absolutely," I say without hesitation. "Meghan made it clear that she doesn't want to be a mom, and the last thing I'm going to do is let her try to go in and out of Remy's life when she feels like it. My parents did that shit to me and Dilynne—swearing to us that things would change, promising us trips that never happened, and leaving us disappointed time and time again. I'll be damned if I let someone do that to my daughter."

"And what about Elodie? You gonna introduce us to her tonight?"

"You guys could have walked over to us and said hello earlier."

Elliot chuckles. "No way. My first order of business when I arrived was getting a drink in my hand."

Rhonan and I share a look, debating between our silence if one of us should say something. Rhonan clears his throat first, so I let him take the reins. "Don't you think it's time to cut back a bit, man?"

Elliot tips his wine glass to his lips. "What do you mean?"

Rhonan sighs, pushing a hand through his thick hair before straightening his spine. "The drinking, Elliot. I know you're hurting right now..."

"Look. You guys didn't want me sulking at home, so now I'm sulking in public. Either way, the only way I choose to be around people right now is if I can do it with alcohol in my system," he fires back, cutting off Rhonan. "If you don't like it, then I'll march my ass back to my house."

"Having a few drinks is fine, man, but lately..." I start.

"Lately, what?" His jaw clenches.

"Sorry to interrupt," Elodie says from behind me, and the three of us spin to face her.

"By all means, do," Elliot says before reaching out to shake her hand, his signature grin spreading across his lips. "These two were just lecturing me."

Elodie smiles, intrigued. She shakes Elliot's hand with her free one, holding Remy on her hip with the other. "Well, I'm happy to help."

Elliot's eyes dip up and down Elodie's body, causing an inferno of irritation to ignite in my body. "I'm sure you could help me in other ways too."

I shove his shoulder. "What the fuck is wrong with you?"

He puts his hands up, playing stupid. "What?"

Elodie plants her hand on my chest in an attempt to calm me down, but I've never had as strong of a desire to punch one of my best friends as I do right now. "Henley, it's fine."

I jab a finger at Elliot. "Fucking apologize."

He snaps out of his annoying smirk, as if the reality of what he just said registered in his brain.

"I'm sorry," he says, shaking his head. "You didn't deserve that."

"Thank you. No hard feelings, I promise. Laney and Dilynne told me what happened earlier this summer and I can't imagine what you're going through."

"Of course they fucking did," he mutters before draining the rest of his wine glass, glancing around the crowd as if everyone was watching him. "Look, I'm fine." Bracing myself for more of his attitude, I'm shocked when he turns away from us and heads to the nearest bar for a refill.

I let out the breath I was holding with a heavy sigh, facing Elodie now. "Sorry again."

"You don't need to apologize for him. He's a grown man and he's hurting. I don't take it personally."

Mumbling, I say, "I wish I could say the same."

I've never felt rage like that in my life. But it wasn't just anger. There was something else there too.

Fuck. Was I jealous?

The thought of Elliot with Elodie makes me want to vomit.

I turn my attention to Remy, taking her from Elodie and pouring my attention into her as a distraction. "Is everything okay?"

"Yeah. I was just going to ask Rhonan what wine I should try." She twists to introduce herself to my other best friend. "I'm Elodie, by the way. Nice to meet you."

He reciprocates with a friendly smile that isn't flirtatious in the slightest. "Likewise. I'm glad Henley found you."

The two of them share a laugh. "Yeah, I think desperation won out over rationality, but I'd say we're doing okay."

Rhonan glances between the two of us, but my eyes are transfixed on the brunette vision standing next to me.

I'm fucking glad I found her too.

"Right?" she asks me with a nudge.

"Yeah. We're getting a routine down," I reply, clearing my throat.

Rhonan blows out a breath. "Routines are crucial. Trust me. It's part of the reason why I hired Joanne, my nanny, so my daughter Ellis could have stability."

Glancing around the property, I say, "Where is Ellis?"

"Joanne took her to the playground to play for a bit, but she's probably with my dad bossing the employees around." His eyes dart around the open space. "Everyone thinks it's hilarious, but my daughter takes it very seriously."

Elodie laughs. "I love that. Bossiness is a great personality trait to have, despite what people might tell you."

"Yeah, I've gotten a little glimpse of your bossiness already," I say as Elodie smirks back up at me.

"Well, you hired me for a reason. I'm just trying to be the best employee I can be."

I can still feel Rhonan's eyes on us, but mine remain locked on the woman standing beside me.

Rhonan clears his throat. "To answer your earlier question about the wine, do you prefer red or white?"

"White. I wish I liked red, but it's just not for me."

Rhonan nods. "I get it. It took a long time for me to adjust to the taste, but if whites are your thing, we have a white cabernet that is one of our most popular wines for a reason."

"Excellent. Thank you." She turns to me now. "You'll be okay with Remy while I'm gone?"

No, I want to say because I'm getting used to her being nearby. But instead, I fake confidence. "Of course. Go get yourself a drink."

"Thanks." Squeezing my forearm, she presses a kiss to Remy's cheek and walks away, releasing me from her grasp as I watch the distance between us grow.

I don't realize how long I've been staring until Rhonan's laugh cuts through my thoughts. "Oh, shit. You're so screwed."

I spin back to face him. "What do you mean?"

"You've got the hots for your nanny."

Dilynne barks out a laugh as she joins us. "You saw it too?" she asks, right as Laney appears at my side.

"What are we talking about?" Laney asks.

"How my brother has a boner for his nanny," my sister says without missing a beat.

"First, please don't talk about my dick. And second, no I don't. Elodie has just been a huge help and I wanted to make sure she found the bar all right."

Laney points to the giant sign above the outdoor bar. "Not sure she could miss it, Henley. But it's cute that you couldn't come up with a better excuse."

Rhonan holds his stomach as laughter pours out of him now. "Oh, fuck. This is great. I mean, how much more cliché could you get?"

I point a finger at him. "The only reason you think this is funny is because your nanny is old enough to be your mom, so no one's accusing you of the same thing."

Elliot walks up to the group with a fresh glass of wine, inserting himself back into the conversation. "Hey. Don't knock older women. Cougars need love too, and they are amazingly confident in the bedroom." He bounces his eyebrows up and down. "Trust me."

Rhonan stops laughing and glares at Elliot. "If I find out that you've hit on Joanne, I'll be the one putting a hand on you next."

"What have Dilynne and I missed already this evening?" Laney looks around at all of us.

"Nothing. Look, just keep your fucking mouths shut, all right?" I snap. "I don't want Elodie feeling awkward around our group. She's only here until Christmas anyway, but I don't want her counting down the days until she leaves."

"Why only until Christmas?" Rhonan asks.

"She moved here from LA," Laney replies. "She's a singer and wasn't having much luck, so she's trying to figure out what her next move is."

"Fuck. That's a rough industry to break into," Elliot adds. "But why not go home? I mean, where is she even from?"

"Garnet Valley," Laney answers. "Her parents weren't exactly supportive of her dream, so she's not ready to face them yet."

"How do you know all this?" I ask, dumbfounded by how Laney already knows more about my nanny than I do.

My sister leans closer to me. "It's called asking questions to get to know somebody, big brother. You know, that thing I was trying to convince you to do earlier?"

"What were you trying to convince him of?" Elodie asks as she reappears with a glass of wine in hand.

Dilynne glares at me and her lips spread into a mischievous grin. Fuck, I know that grin. That means she's about to say or do something that's going to make me want to strangle her. "Laney and I were just trying to convince my brother to let us take you out one night next week."

"Uh, Dilynne..." Laney taps my sister on the shoulder. "I'm going to be in Charlotte next week, remember?"

Dilynne shrugs. "Fine. Then we can go out just the two of us. But I think it would be fun for you to let loose a bit and enjoy this time away from mounting decisions about your life, you know? Maybe find a man to help you release any tension you've been holding onto."

Elodie looks between me and my sister while the urge to tape Dilynne's mouth shut grows stronger by the second.

"Sorry again for my comment earlier," Elliot interjects.

Elodie places her hand on his shoulder, stroking it softly. "I told you. No hard feelings."

"You hit on her?" Dilynne asks, her lip curling in disgust.

"Don't fucking worry about me and what I do," he fires back. "And while we're at it, stop sending—"

Ellis comes running over at that moment, which cuts off what Elliot was about to say. And I think I can speak for the entire group that we're thankful—because that means he and my sister won't be able to verbally spar like they normally do.

I swear, sometimes I think that putting them in boxing gloves and sticking them in a ring together might be the best way for them to take out their aggression on each other.

"Daddy!" Ellis shouts as she jumps up into Rhonan's arms, looping her arms around his neck. "Grandpa let me drive the tractor and take all of the money from people!"

"It's a Rhino, Ellis. Not a tractor, remember? And I'm sure you did a great job."

"Duh." Ellis rolls her eyes as if she's already a teenager and not a four-year-old who will turn five next month.

Jesus, is this what I have to look forward to with Remy?

Then, she turns to Elodie. "Who's that?"

"I'm Elodie." She offers her hand, and Ellis shakes it like a pro. "It's nice to meet you."

"Your name rhymes with melody," Ellis points out, making us all laugh.

"It does."

"Who is your favorite princess?" Ellis continues, asking the most important question in her mind.

"Disney princess," Laney clarifies.

"Oh, that's easy. Ariel."

"Mine is Elsa," Ellis replies. "But I like the mermaid too."

Studying my nanny, I ask, "Why Ariel?"

"Because she gave up her gift for the man she loved. I mean, the whole movie is completely unrealistic, but she was willing to sacrifice her voice to follow her heart. I think that's pretty brave."

"My daddy says that girls should never give up anything for a man," Ellis counters. "That's why we like Elsa and Anna."

Rhonan nods proudly. "That's right."

"That's a very valid argument. I think in a movie, it's romantic. But in real life, it's not a wise decision."

"Can I go play on the playground again, Daddy?" Ellis asks Rhonan, already bored with this conversation.

"Yeah. Let's go." Rhonan lowers her to the ground and takes her hand. "I'll catch up with you guys later."

Wondering if Remy will love playgrounds when she's older, I watch them walk away. But after a few seconds, I realize that Dilynne has picked up the conversation that Elliot and Ellis interrupted.

"So, about our girl's night..."

"I mean, I'd love to. I'd just have to ask my boss for the night off." Elodie looks up at me and winks.

Fucking hell. The idea of Dilynne going out to a bar with Elodie makes my skin crawl.

But you don't have a reason to be jealous right, Henley?

"I'm sure he won't have a problem with it," my sister says, winking over at me now. "I mean, the last thing he wants to be known as is a demanding boss. And besides, you're young. You need to have some fun, maybe stay out all night. Taking care of a baby has to be exhausting."

Elodie reaches for Remy as my daughter reciprocates. Once the baby is safe in her arms, Elodie kisses her on the forehead. "I'm honestly having the best time with this little baby bear."

"Aw, you call her baby bear?" Laney interjects.

"Yeah. My mom used to call all of the kids that were in her daycare her cubs, so it just felt natural."

Laney's hand covers the center of her chest. "That is just too freaking adorable."

I want to say that I thought so too, but I refrain.

My sister claps her hands together, startling our group. "Well, then it's settled. We will make plans for next week." Then she turns to me. "Your nanny is gonna need a night off, big brother. I'm gonna take her out and show her a damn good time."

"Wonderful," I mutter between clenched teeth because the calculated grin on my sister's lips makes me want to throw Elodie over my shoulder and carry her out of here. I could lock her up inside of my house like Rapunzel and never let her leave, that way no other man could hit on her.

Where the fuck did that thought come from?

Laney pouts. "Well, now I'm sad that I'll miss it."

"Don't worry," Dilynne says, wrapping her arm around Laney's shoulder. "We'll plan another night out soon."

My daughter may not have an aunt for long if my sister doesn't stop talking.

"You guys could go out when we have our blackjack night next," Elliot suggests.

"Uh, I kind of need my nanny to watch my daughter so I can go, unless you want to change dirty diapers in between hands," I explain.

"Have you ever considered letting the girls play during blackjack nights?" Elodie asks.

Elliot and I answer simultaneously. "No."

Elodie's mouth drops open. "Why not?"

"Because it's our manly bonding time," Elliot retorts. "No girls allowed."

Dilynne leans forward and stage whispers, "It's really just because they're afraid they're going to lose to a bunch of girls."

Elodie laughs. "Yeah, probably. I mean, my grandma taught me how to play poker, and I love screwing over an unsuspecting, cocky man when he thinks I'm just an innocent girl who doesn't understand the game." Batting her eyelashes, she pretends to be a damsel in distress, making Laney and Dilynne laugh.

Only the sight makes the corner of my mouth tip up.

Dilynne moves to high-five her. "Hell yes! Call these boys out!"

And in this moment, I know that Elodie fits in just perfectly with our group, which means there's one less thing for me to worry about.

Now if only I could make this fuzzy feeling I get when I'm around her go away.

Chapter 8

Elodie

A Charming Bull & An Asshole Boss

"You know, you don't have to go out with my sister. It won't hurt my feelings or anything."

My eyes land on Henley where he's watching me put my lipstick on in the mirror by his front door. It's one of the only things he has hanging on the walls in this house, and luckily, it's in a very useful spot. "*You* might not care, but *she* probably will." Turning around to face him, I put the cap back on the tube of lipstick and stick it in my purse. "And your sister scares me more than you do."

He crosses his arms over his chest while tilting his head at me. "Doesn't surprise me. She scares me too, but you don't have to go out with her out of obligation. I can handle her."

I drift my gaze over to Remy sitting in her high chair, shaking one of her toys around. "You can be honest, Henley. Do you not want me to go because you're scared of being here alone with your daughter?"

Remy lets out a garbled noise, making us both laugh.

"Actually," Henley says, stepping closer until I can feel the heat of him, "I feel a hell of a lot more comfortable now than I did two weeks ago before you came into our lives." His eyes move up and down my body appreciatively, which I shouldn't notice or enjoy, but I do. "I don't know what I would have done without you, El."

When he says things like this, it makes it even harder to resist getting lost in those hazel eyes of his. "You would have figured it out."

He shakes his head slowly. "Doubtful. I'd probably still be cleaning up projectile vomit and poop."

Laughing, I turn back around to check my appearance in the mirror one more time, fluffing my hair that I curled to give it volume, and making sure there's no black specks of eyeshadow or mascara under my eyes.

It's been a long time since I've dressed up for a night out, and honestly, seeing myself all dolled up is renewing that urge I have to perform. Part of the fun of singing in front of a crowd is slathering my face with makeup, putting on an outfit that's both sexy and fun, and talking to a crowd while singing songs and listening to them sing them back to you.

But it's been a long time since I've had that rush.

And I'm not sure if I'm willing to give it up.

I adjust my jean shorts, pull up my socks so my cowboy boots don't rub against my calves, and smooth down my white tank top. "Hey, at least you have the internet to turn to. Can you imagine what our parents did before that magical invention? I mean, it wasn't the powerhouse it was back when we were kids, but it still beats having to look stuff up in books, or worse, encyclopedias."

Henley grunts. "Even if my parents had reliable access to it, they probably wouldn't have used it for parenting tips."

Each time he makes comments about his childhood, it makes me want to push him further and ask him so many questions I'm fairly certain he won't answer. Because deep down, I know Dilynne was right—him becoming a father is forcing him to confront feelings he's never dealt with. I can practically see when his mind ventures back to a memory each time either of us brings up his parents, biological or foster. And even though I still consider my childhood pretty great compared to others, I can't imagine what he and his sister went through, and I want to be someone he can talk to about it.

"Even still. No one has all of the answers, and every child is different. You would have had to figure things out on your own, and for what would work with Remy."

Remy tosses her toy to the ground. "Apparently what works for her is watching me pick this up a hundred times."

I chuckle. "Well, you have fun with that tonight. And to your earlier claim, I'm not going out with your sister out of obligation. I genuinely like her. It's been a long time since I've felt welcomed by someone like that, and since I've felt like I could be myself around them."

"No super friendly people lining up to be your friends in Los Angeles then?"

His comment catches me off guard. "Oh. Uh…"

"Dilynne and Laney mentioned it the other night at the winery. If it makes you feel any better, it made your little performance last week make a lot more sense," he explains.

"My performance?"

His eyes bore into mine, as if he's recounting the exact memory, bit by bit. "When you sang to Remy to get her to fall asleep."

"Oh. Yeah." My heart rate climbs as we stare at each other, as I remember watching him sleep peacefully on the couch for almost an hour before I finally laid Remy down but didn't wake him up to go to bed because he looked so exhausted.

"Don't be upset with them. The guys were curious about you, and Laney explained—"

"I'm not mad," I say, clearing my throat and turning my back to him while attempting to get my pulse to return to normal. The truth is, I was kind of enjoying no one knowing why I'm here licking my wounds. I told Laney because I felt compelled to in that moment, but something about Henley knowing makes me feel inadequate. I mean, he hired me to be his nanny, but that's not even close to what I was doing before this.

Honestly, I've felt more purposeful in the past two weeks as Remy's caretaker than I have in the past three years.

The reality of that slams into me like a freight train.

"You sure?"

Spinning around, I paste on my most convincing smile. "Of course. It's fine. I mean, it's the truth."

"And is it true that your parents don't support you wanting a career in music?"

I shrug. "Pretty much."

He takes a step closer, a pinch in his brow as he places two fingers beneath my chin, tipping it up so I can meet his eyes. It steals the breath from my lungs.

Up close like this, I can make out each of his eyelashes and count every piece of dark stubble dusting that hard jaw, and as I watch his Adam's apple bob, I clench my thighs together because God, this man is rugged and handsome, and right now, his attention is purely on me.

"I'm sorry they don't support you," he says, his voice low and rough. "Because listening to you sing the other night..." His eyes close, almost as if he's transporting himself back to that moment, inhaling deeply before releasing his breath and snapping back to the present. He jerks away and turns his back to me, pushing a hand through his hair. Glancing at me over his shoulder, he says, "You're really fucking talented, El. Don't give up on what you want for your life, okay?"

Stunned and confused, I stand there and finally release the breath I was holding. "Thanks." That's all I can manage to say.

"You should get going."

"I'm—I'm waiting for Dilynne to pick me up."

As if on cue, a car horn honks from outside. Henley strides over to the front window, peeking through the blinds. "Looks like your ride is right on time."

I reach behind me and grab my purse from the entry table and sling it over my shoulder. "Okay. Well, you have my number if you need anything."

Nodding, he turns back to Remy. "We'll be fine. Have fun."

But the tone of his voice sounds like he doesn't mean those words at all, not even one little bit.

***

"So...you told your brother about my singing aspirations?" Taking the tiny straw between my teeth, I sip my whiskey and Coke as Dilynne waits for the bartender to finish making her drink.

"Well, Laney told me and I didn't realize he didn't know." Her eyes meet mine. "Is that a problem?"

Shaking my head, I stir my drink slowly. "No, it just caught me off guard when he brought it up."

She turns to face me head on now, placing her hand on my shoulder. "Hey, I'm sorry. We didn't know you weren't sharing that with any-one. Otherwise, I totally would have honored that. So would Laney."

I shrug. "It's no big deal." Meanwhile, inside I'm still replaying the look on his face when he told me how talented he thought I was.

And it wasn't that his words didn't mean anything.

It's that I've heard those words before from a man, and believing them cost me much more than just my pride.

Shaking off the melancholy that the conversation with Henley caused, I turn my back to the bar to survey the room around us.

It's been years since I've been to The Charming Bull, a two-story bar and dance spot located about forty-five minutes from Blossom Peak. And the only reason I'm familiar with it is because it's about the same drive from Garnet Valley.

Taking a drive to The Charming Bull was like a rite of passage once you reached the age of twenty-one. Big groups of us would make a weekend of the trip, booking two hotel rooms for ten people, pre-gaming in the rooms before heading to the bar, dancing until they closed, and then grabbing a greasy diner breakfast the next day before returning to our regularly scheduled lives.

That last year of college was epic, even though the only reason I have those memories was from appeasing my parents' demand that I get a college degree. But I'm sort of missing what those memories made me feel—like I belonged and had roots.

Right now, I just feel like a plant that hasn't been able to really grow because I keep being moved around, exposed to the elements, and tossed on the ground when I'm no longer needed.

And that's exactly why I ran back to a place where I did feel whole—because I never felt that way in Blossom Peak.

Dilynne smacks me on the ass, making me jump. "Then let's find us a table, a spot on the dance floor, and maybe later, a man to give us some orgasms."

Laughing, I follow her lead as she pulls me by the hand, weaving us through the throngs of people. For one split second, I wonder what Henley and Remy are doing back at his house, but I shake that thought off quickly and focus on the melody of LoCash's "I Love This Life" booming through the speakers.

Once Dilynne finds a high-top table she deems suitable, we take a seat across from each other and sip our drinks.

"So, do you think my brother is surviving right now?"

The mention of Henley instantly makes me smile, and my cheeks get warm. *Damn my easy blushing.* "Yeah, I think he's fine. Honestly, he's doing so much better since those first few days."

Dilynne shakes her head, studying her drink. "I still can't believe he's a dad. He's never wanted a family, which I don't blame him for. I mean, I don't want kids, but not because of our childhood."

"You don't want kids?"

"Nope. I just don't think I got that maternal instinct. There are plenty of women who will make fabulous moms, but I don't think I'm one of them."

"Do you think you might change your mind?"

Dilynne shakes her head. "No. It's a gut feeling. Kids just aren't something I ever envisioned in my life. I like my freedom. I like being able to go to car shows on a whim or work on a car until one in the morning. I could never do that if I had a child."

"True."

"What about you?"

My smile is instant. "Oh yeah. I've always wanted kids. Since my mom owned a daycare, I was always around children and I love the chaos, watching their minds explore the world around them, and guiding them through growing up. If life is kind to me, hopefully I'll have five."

Dilynne's eyes nearly pop out. "*Five?*"

"Yeah. I have a friend back home who's one of five siblings. I used to love going over to her house. It was always loud and chaotic, but God, her family had big celebrations full of laughs and hugs. There was always someone around if you needed anything." I look back down at my drink. "I'm tired of being let down and feeling alone, and the last thing I would want is for my child to feel that way."

Dilynne covers my hand with hers. "You're not alone when you're with our crew," she says confidently. "Look, I know my brother is your boss, but if you needed anything, he would be there. Same with Rhonan, Elliot, or Fletcher. Those boys are all like brothers to me and Laney, Fletcher excluded now, of course." We share a laugh. "All I'm saying is, we are a family. It's been that way since my brother and I got placed with Carol and Nick, who are basically our parents anyway."

"Carol seems like a hoot."

Dilynne fluffs her hair. "Where do you think I got my sass from? The woman is my idol. She's not afraid to speak her mind, be herself, and stand up for what's right."

"She thought I was Remy's mom."

Dilynne stares at me for a moment. "I mean, you could be. You both have dark hair and light eyes."

"Yeah, well, watching your brother explain that I'm just the nanny when they assumed she's mine was far more entertaining."

Dilynne holds her stomach as she cackles. "I can only imagine."

The DJ comes over the speakers, interrupting the regular music. "Open mic night is almost here! If you're interested, sign-ups are at the bar to the right of my booth. We're only taking ten acts, so get your name on the list."

Dilynne turns back to me, her eyes and smile wide. "You should totally sign up!"

"Ugh. I don't know…"

"Come on. There's no pressure here, right? Half the people in this place are already drunk, so even if you suck, they're still gonna cheer."

I give her a flat look. "Gee, thanks."

She chuckles. "You know what I mean. Look, you came here to regroup, right?"

"Yeah."

"So maybe that means remembering why you fell in love with singing and music in the first place. Take the pressure off. Just sing because you love it. Hell, that's what I do sometimes with cars. I rebuild one not because someone is paying me to or because I'm entering into a show, but because I simply love the process."

Biting my bottom lip, I contemplate her words.

Maybe she's right.

It felt so amazing to just sing the other night to Remy and Henley. I haven't sung in months without trying to make it mean something, not since the night that changed how I felt about this career aspiration.

Dilynne is still staring at me, nodding her head as if that's what's going to make me decide.

"Ugh, fine." Huffing, I stand from my chair and march over to the bar then scribble my name in the second to last spot. I traipse back to Dilynne who's clapping excitedly.

"Heck yes! I can't wait to hear you sing."

"I hope I don't end up regretting this."

"Elodie? Elodie Olsen, is that you?"

I spin around to see a familiar face that I haven't seen in ages standing just to my left. "Easton Bennett."

Jumping from the table, he intercepts me into his big, burly chest. "Holy shit! It is you." Holding me out at arm's length now, his eyes move up and down my body. "Damn girl, L.A. has been good to you. What the hell are you doing back here?"

"Oh, uh...just visiting some friends," I say, not wanting to get into all of the details of how I ended up in Blossom Peak right now. Motioning to my new friend, I say, "This is Dilynne Clark."

He reaches out to shake Dilynne's hand. "Hey... You look familiar."

"I come here pretty often. You actually hit on my engaged best friend a few months ago."

"Easton!" I smack him on the chest.

He simply shrugs as those dimples of his appear, using them to his advantage like always. "Hey. I'm a grown man. If I'd known she was taken, I wouldn't have..."

"You could have asked," I counter, crossing my arms over my chest. "Besides, I thought you and—"

He cuts me off, his tone clipped. "Nothing is going on with anyone back home, all right?"

Lifting my hands in the air, I say, "Okay. Noted. Won't bring it up again."

Dilynne's eyes move between me and Easton. "Did you two ever..."

My lips curl up in disgust as Easton groans. "Absolutely not. He's like a brother to me."

Dilynne's eyes shamelessly rake all over his body. "Well, he's not my brother, and"—she takes his cowboy hat from his head and places it on her own—"it's been a while since I've gone riding."

I cover my mouth to hide my smile, but Easton's grin is stretched a mile wide. "Then maybe I'll warm you up on the dance floor, sugar."

Dilynne's face falls flat as she returns his hat. "Nope. Changed my mind."

"What? Why?"

"Sugar?" she retorts, rolling her eyes. "How much more cliché can you be? I mean, the jeans, boots, flannel, and hat are enough...but that nickname is so not hot"

Laughing, I turn to Easton and shrug. "She's not wrong."

Easton straightens his hat on his head. "Well, another lady won't mind it. Now, if you'll excuse me, I need to make sure I don't end up going home alone tonight." Tipping his hat at me, he says, "Always good to see you, Elodie. Let me know when you're in town and we can grab a burger or something."

I lunge toward him, hugging him tightly. "I will."

He saunters off as I return to my chair and find Dilynne staring at me. "What?"

"You sure you two have never banged?"

Dry heaving dramatically, I lift my glass to my mouth. "I'm sure. Trust me. Easton is way too immature for me."

"Most men are," Dilynne replies.

"Agreed, but he uses it as crutch to avoid growing up. His family..." My words trail off as I take a deep breath before continuing. "Let's just say everyone has their own way of coping with things and his is that. I know he has feelings for one of Lennon's sisters too, but..."

"Oh, so there is someone back home he's avoiding?" Dilynne leans forward in her seat, clearly invested.

"Yeah. They fight more than anything, but it's clear as day that there are feelings there."

Dilynne's grin from before falls as she clears her throat. "Yeah, well sometimes fighting is just fighting, nothing more."

I tilt my head at her. "You seem like you're speaking from experience."

"Let's just say that people usually fight for a reason, okay?"

I take my straw between my teeth again, feeling the effects of the whiskey coating my limbs in warmth as I get to the bottom of my glass. "Care to elaborate? Is this an ex you're referring to?"

She huffs out a laugh. "Yeah. I should have known better than to mix business and pleasure," she says almost painfully, making me reach out for her hand again.

"God, have I learned that lesson too."

The music cuts off at that moment, pulling everyone's attention to the DJ booth. "All right y'all! It's time for our first act for Open Mic Night. Put your hands together for Gregory Banks singing a Garth Brooks classic, 'Friends in Low Places'!"

Dilynne and I turn our attention to the stage in the corner of the bar while Gregory belts out a slightly intoxicated version of the crowd pleaser. But inside, I'm squirming, waiting for my turn. I count the acts until I know I'm up next. Dilynne rubs my back as the DJ introduces me.

"You've got this."

Nodding, I head toward the stage.

I don't know why I'm so nervous. I've sung in front of crowds hundreds of times.

But this is the first time I've sung since the night when everything changed and I questioned if this is what I wanted for my life still.

"How are y'all doing tonight?" Holding the microphone between both of my hands, I cast my gaze out into the crowd of people, receiving hoots and hollers in response. "Sounds like we're all having fun. Now, I wouldn't be up here if it weren't for my pushy friend in the back," I say as Dilynne screams so everyone can see her. "But singing is something I've been doing since I was very young, so I hope you guys enjoy this one. I think it's fitting for tonight."

I wait for the first few notes of the song to play and then I close my eyes, take a deep breath, pop my eyes back open, and let the music overtake me. Singing "Bartender" by Lady A, I tap my toes and swing my hips as the upbeat music plays and the crowd starts singing with me.

My eyes land on Dilynne in the back of the crowd, shaking her arms around and singing along, instantly making me smile.

The energy, the music, the entire feeling of the room transports me to another place—one where instead of people watching me singing someone else's song, there might be a day when a crowd would gather to listen to me sing songs I wrote myself.

By the time the song ends, reality gently brings me back to the present where the entire crowd is on their feet and cheering for me.

I can feel my cheeks heat as I wave goodbye, thank the crowd, and make my way off the stage and back to Dilynne.

"Holy shit!" she shouts when I get close enough to hear her. "I feel really bad for the guy that has to go after you."

Chuckling, I reach for the glass of water Dilynne must have ordered for me and drink down half of it. "Thanks."

"No, seriously, Elodie. You are incredible. You have a rasp in your voice that is so unique. Your energy is amazing. I hate when you go to a concert and the person just stands there at the mic. But you were moving around and having fun! Your energy was contagious."

"Being on a stage is like getting to be someone else," I reply. "It's fun to be an alter ego of yourself. You know how Beyonce says her stage presence is Sasha Fierce?" Dilynne nods. "That's how it feels. I don't feel like Elodie Olsen. I feel like this different person, someone that matters," I whisper at the very end.

"Well, hell, girl. You need to come up with a stage name then because watching you perform was entertaining as hell. And you do matter, Elodie. I mean, you're helping my brother through one of the hardest transitions of his life, you're offering me your friendship when we barely know each other, and you just brought up the energy in a room full of people wanting to escape their lives for a bit. I'd say those are all fucking important roles for someone to fill."

Dilynne's words hit me square in the chest, making my heart ache. She has no idea how badly I needed to hear those words. Choking back my emotion, I reply, "Thank you. That means more than you know."

As if she can sense that I'm on the verge of tears, we share a look before Dilynne lifts her drink to her mouth and drains it, slamming it down on the table. "All right, enough of this depressing talk. We need some more alcohol, and it's time to dance."

Chuckling, I slide off my chair as well, sucking down the final few drops of my drink. "Agreed. Let's do this. And hey, thanks for inviting me out. I really feel like I needed this, you know?"

Dilynne wraps her arm around my shoulder as we head toward the bar, our height difference making it a tad difficult since she has to lean down to reach me. At only five-two, I'm shorter than almost everybody.

"Me too. Ever since Laney and Fletcher got together, we don't go out as much anymore. I'm not mad at her, but it's nice to have someone else who's single that wants to have fun."

I don't have the heart to tell her that a night at home with Henley and Remy has become its own version of fun, and right now, I'm kind of missing them—even though I am having a good time.

"Being single is better than being with the wrong person though, that's for sure."

She nods. "So true."

Once I get a refill and Dilynne switches to soda water with lime, we head to the dance floor and move until my feet are throbbing. I dance with a few guys, but none that make me feel anything close to what Henley makes me feel.

At one point, I spot Dilynne wrapped up with a guy, kissing him hard before slipping off the floor with him.

"Where are you going?" I call to her.

"I'll be back. Give me fifteen."

Watching her walk away, I turn back to the guy I'm dancing with. His hands tighten on my hips. "Where's your friend going?" he asks, his mouth close to my ear so I can hear him.

"Probably to the bathroom," I answer.

His grin widens. "We could go to the bathroom too."

"No thanks."

He pulls me closer. "Aw, come on. You seem interested, and I definitely am."

I attempt to push him away, but his grip on me tightens. "I said no."

"I can get you free drinks. I'm friends with the owner and know a spot that's more private than the bathroom, if that's what you want. It pays to know the people in charge."

I shove him completely off of me now, my chest heaving from the exertion. "Don't you understand that no means no?"

He holds his hands in the air as a security guard comes over to us. "Is everything okay here?"

My dance partner smirks as he begins to back away. "Yup. We're good. I was just leaving this cocktease alone."

Tears prick at the back of my eyes as I spin and make my way off the dance floor. When I find a corner to catch my breath in, I stare down at my shaking hands.

Memories flood my mind, overpowering me and making my chest grow tight. I close my eyes and try to fight off the panic attack I feel coming, but luckily, Dilynne finds me before I fully slide to the floor.

"Elodie. Hey, you okay?"

When her face registers in front of me, I shake my head. "No."

"Shit. All right, let's get you out of here."

She holds me steady as we walk through the crowd, my eyes staying focused on the floor beneath me and just the simple task of putting one foot in front of the other. Once we get outside and I feel the cool breeze waft across my skin, I take in a shuddering breath. "I'm sorry."

"No, I am. I shouldn't have left you."

"Where did you go?"

"I thought the guy I was with could help me relieve some tension, if you catch my drift, but he ended up getting into a fight because some other man was hitting on his ex." Shaking her head, she continues, "I don't need the drama."

"Yeah."

Rubbing my arm as we walk to her car, she asks, "What happened in there? You looked like you were about to have a panic attack."

"I was."

When we get settled in her car, she turns to face me. "Want to talk about it?"

"Not really." I can feel my entire body shaking, but the last thing I want to do is relive what that man's words just reminded me of—one of the biggest reasons I left LA.

"Okay." Dilynne seems unaffected by my unwillingness to open up, and in this moment, I'm relieved.

"Thanks for not pushing me."

"Girl, you're talking to someone who understands not wanting to rehash shit. Trust me. Just know I'm here to talk if you need me."

We ride in silence the entire drive back to town as I fight with my mind bringing up all of the events that have led me here. By the time we pull into Henley's driveway, I feel drained, like I just ran a marathon. Fairly certain the surge of adrenaline I just had is the culprit, I slowly exit Dilynne's car as she speaks.

"You want me to walk you in?"

"No. I'm good. Thanks, though."

"You sure?"

I glance at her over my shoulder, flashing her the best smile I can muster. "Yeah, I'm good. Thanks again for a fun night...until it wasn't."

"Get some rest." She waits until I'm inside before pulling away. It's after one in the morning, so I'm surprised to find Henley on the couch scrolling on his phone.

"Hey," I say, pulling my purse off my shoulder and setting it on the table by the door.

The icy glare he gives me makes my shoulders tense. "Glad to see you're alive."

I twist my head around the room before landing back on him. "Did I miss something?"

Grunting, he stands from the couch. "I just didn't realize you planned on being out so late."

Growing instantly defensive, I cross my arms over my chest. "I'm sorry. I didn't realize I had a curfew. You knew I was going out, so where is this coming from?"

"It's after one in the morning," he replies.

"And?"

"I didn't realize you could be so irresponsible."

My blood starts to boil. I've witnessed snarky Henley before, but in this moment, he's just being an ass. With shaky hands, I inhale deeply before giving him a piece of my mind. "You think I'm irresponsible? You trusted me with your daughter—without even knowing me. So, if we're comparing responsibility, let's start there. Not to mention, I'm old enough to drink, smoke, and stay out until any hour of the night that I want. So if this is you being worried about my ability to do my job…"

He holds up a hand, stopping me. "Look, it's late."

"Yes, I'm aware."

His glare gets more intense. "I need some sleep."

"You didn't need to wait up for me."

Our eyes remain locked for some time, almost as if he's debating if he should say anything else. Finally, he shakes his head. "I know I didn't." And then he walks down the hall and shuts his door softly behind him, making me wonder how a night of fun turned into a night of me feeling more unsettled than before.

Chapter 9

Henley

Blackjack and a Heart Tattoo

"Hell yeah! Twenty-one, baby!" Fletcher lifts his hands in the air after Rhonan deals a five, making his cards total the magic number you want to see in a game of blackjack.

Elliot grunts, draining his third beer before reaching for a fresh one. "At least someone is getting lucky tonight."

Fletcher bounces his eyebrows up and down. "Oh, I'll be getting lucky in more than just blackjack, man."

Rhonan glares at him. "Please refrain from making any innuendos about your extracurricular activities with my sister. You know the rules."

I stifle my laugh behind my hand as Fletcher tsks. "Sorry man, but it's true."

"Again, at least one of us is getting lucky," Elliot grumbles as Rhonan cleans up the cards on the table and passes the deck to Elliot for his turn to deal.

It's a Tuesday night, which is why Fletcher is back in town for a few days, and his request was a night of blackjack to catch up. The NFL season is underway, so there will be few times between now and February for him to venture to Blossom Peak for more than a day or two.

My boys and I became obsessed with the game after Rhonan's dad showed us the movie 21 with Kevin Spacey. He played a college professor that recruited genius students of his to count cards and run a ring that traveled to Vegas, winning a shitload of money. We never planned on developing our own card counting group, but we still learned how to play the game and have done so since we were in high school. Now our games are few and far between, but we still make it a point to play when we can.

Elliot, Rhonan, and I share a look because we're all still single.

"You're telling me you haven't been out trying to drown your sorrows in women instead of booze?" Fletcher asks Elliot.

Elliot's eyes drop to the table. "I can't yet..."

Rhonan rubs his shoulder. "Take your time, man. Ellis was almost three before I finally felt like I could stand the idea of sleeping with someone that wasn't my wife, and it still took me six months after that before I finally did."

"I fucking hate her," Elliot grates out. "She ripped my fucking heart out—"

"Tori was not the person you were supposed to be with," Fletcher says, cutting him off. "Because if she were, she never would have gotten involved with you while she was in a relationship with her boss."

"I just can't believe I didn't see it."

"People can be blind when feelings are involved," I say.

"Are you talking about you and the way you look at your nanny, or Elliot?" Rhonan's knowing smirk irritates me instantly.

"Fuck you."

"No thank you. I'm partial to women."

Fletcher's eyes bounce between all of us before landing on me. "What did I miss?"

Rhonan lifts his drink to his mouth as Elliot begins to deal the next hand of cards. "Henley has the hots for his new nanny but is too chicken shit to admit it."

Fletcher raises one eyebrow at me. "Clark, is that true?"

"I don't have the hots for her. I mean, is she attractive? Yes. But she's also annoyingly cheerful and way too young for me. A few nights ago, she went out with Dilynne and didn't come home until one in the morning."

Fletcher's brow creases. "Did you give her a curfew or something?"

Rhonan and Elliot chuckle beside me, but I keep my eyes on Fletcher. "No, but I couldn't sleep until she got home."

"Why?"

That's the thing I've been struggling with for the past few days—*why* did I feel the need to stay up and wait for her? And why did I pick a stupid fucking fight with her when she got home?

I swear, those were some of the longest hours of my life, and that's including the first night I had Remy in my care. I kept wondering what she and Dilynne were doing, if they were okay, if Elodie was dancing with some random guy and hitting it off with him, if they would...

"Henley?" Fletcher pulls me back from my mental spiral.

"What?"

"I asked you why you waited up for her?"

Pushing a hand through my hair, I lean back in my chair. "I guess I've gotten used to her being in the house and it felt weird without her there. I couldn't sleep."

The guys share a look before Rhonan loses his smirk from earlier. "You know, it's okay to care about her, Henley."

"I don't care about her…"

"I mean in a non-sexual way. Like, she's a part of your life now. She's been in your house for almost a month. It's natural to want to make sure she's safe. I mean, I feel that way about Joanne. She's a part of my family."

"I don't have family."

Elliot scoffs. "Uh, then what the fuck are we?"

Sighing, I say, "You know what I mean."

"No, enlighten me, because the last time I checked, Dilynne is your sister and the four of us are practically brothers," Elliot says defensively.

"I just…" Looking off to the side of the room, I debate how to explain what I'm feeling. "I guess I'm annoyed that I care about her when she's just going to leave."

Rhonan nods. "That's understandable, but that doesn't mean you can't appreciate her now. You don't need to act like her father, though."

I pinch the bridge of my nose. "Yeah, I guess it kind of sounded like that when I spoke to her."

Rhonan shrugs. "I mean, unless she has a daddy kink."

I grab a few pretzels from the bowl on the table and chuck them at him. "Shut the fuck up."

Fletcher clears his throat. "Okay, so other than that, how's it going? How's dad life treating you?"

"Honestly, I didn't realize how boring my life was until Remy came into it," I say as I feel my lips curl up in a smile. "That little girl is…" My words trail off because I can feel my throat growing tight. "Her smile makes me smile. Her giggle is one of the best sounds in the world. When she takes a shit, I've never smelt something so godawful in my life, but it also makes me proud. It's fucking weird, man."

Fletcher smacks me on the back. "I'm happy for you."

"Thanks."

"Honestly, I'm surprised by how well you're handling the whole thing."

My brows pull together. "What do you mean?"

Fletcher looks between Rhonan and Elliot. "We all know what growing up was like for you, and how you never wanted kids," he says matter-of-factly. "So, I guess I'm just surprised how easily you stepped into this new role."

My momentary happiness shifts to annoyance. "Wow. Glad to know you had such high faith in me."

Rhonan interjects. "It's a good thing, Henley."

"Remy deserves at least one parent who wants her," I say, but can't deny that when Elodie, Remy, and I go out in public, I have to remind myself that we're not a family. I'm always quick to clear that up when people assume, but lately, I'm annoyed by how good it feels to have someone to talk to, to help on those days when I'm exhausted, and someone to come home to after a long day at the lodge.

Fuck. I'm really getting used to Elodie being in my life.

And that's exactly what I can't do.

"So, have you thought about what you're gonna do when Elodie leaves?" Rhonan asks as he puts two more chips on his bet.

"Not at all."

"You probably should. It could take months for you to find some-one else. Getting Elodie to agree to help you on a whim was sheer luck, my friend."

"Yeah, don't I know it."

"I could ask Joanne if she knows anyone interested in the job," he suggests.

"Having an older nanny might prevent you from developing feel-ings for that one," Fletcher teases, and I chuck a few pretzels at him this time.

Elliot chokes on his beer. "Aw, Fletch. It's good to have you around more, buddy."

"Happy to be here, boys. And you guys are still interested in coming to Charlotte next month for a game, right? I need to let the team manager know to reserve a box."

The three of us nod. "You know I'm fucking there," Elliot says.

"Are you gonna bring Remy?" Rhonan asks me.

"I—I guess so. Otherwise, I'd have to leave her with Elodie."

"What if you brought both of them?" Fletcher suggests. "I'm sure Elodie would enjoy a game. Laney mentioned that she watched foot-ball growing up."

Yet another detail about my nanny that my friends have learned first.

Shrugging, I say, "I could." Then I turn back to Rhonan. "Are you gonna bring Ellis?"

"Depends on Joanne's schedule. I mean, I know I'll enjoy the game far more without her there. An almost five-year-old doesn't exactly sit still long enough for me to watch a football game."

"Remy can just sit on my lap."

Rhonan laughs. "Yeah, for now. But in a few months, she's going to be crawling, and then she's not going to want to be held." He pats me on the shoulder. "You think the sleep deprivation is rough? Just wait until she starts moving. That's when life really starts to change."

Jesus Christ.

Just when I start to get the hang of things, it looks like life is going to change yet again.

***

When I walk into my house a few hours later, the silence is unsettling. "Elodie?" I call out, but there's no reply. The faint sound of the shower running hits my ears, and that's when I realize she must be in the bathroom.

Walking down the hallway, I head for my room to check on Remy. I still haven't put a room together for her, but having her sleep in my bedroom makes the late night and early morning wake-ups easier. Elodie has been asking me when I plan to put together Remy's own space, but I just haven't had the time.

That's a lie, Henley. You have. You've just been too busy talking to your nanny in the evenings to focus on anything else.

When I walk into my room, I see Remy sleeping peacefully in her crib. She's almost four months old now which doesn't seem possible. The past month has felt so long and yet terrifyingly fast at the same time. Her lips purse in her sleep, making me smile. Her hands are balled up in fists by the sides of her head, and her lashes are fluttering as she dreams.

I wonder what babies dream about.

I want to lean down and kiss her head, but don't want to wake her up at the same time. Instead, I head for my closet, change out of my jeans and shirt and into some pajama pants with a plain white shirt before heading toward the kitchen for a glass of water. But as I stalk back down the hallway, I run smack into Elodie as she steps out of the bathroom.

"Ooof!"

"Shit!"

Elodie loses her balance and falls to the floor, her towel coming loose to reveal her entire backside, including her bare ass perched in the air that, unfortunately, I can't stop staring at.

"Henley?" Elodie asks, face down on the carpet, snapping me out of the transfixed state I'm in.

Fuck, she's perfect. Round globes, silky white skin, and a tattoo of a heart just above her right butt cheek.

Jesus Christ. I could lick that ink. Dainty tattoos are so fucking sexy.

"Henley!" she says louder this time.

"Yeah?"

"My towel. I'm, uh..."

"Shit." I turn away from her, facing the opposite direction. "I'm not looking. You can get up now."

Groaning, she says, "Oh my God. This is so embarrassing."

My eyes drop down to my cock getting hard in my pants, the flimsy fabric doing nothing to hide how my body is reacting to seeing her half naked.

"It's fine."

"Yeah, easy for you to say. You're not the one that just flashed your boss your bare ass."

Fuck. Stop picturing it, Henley.

"I didn't see anything," I lie.

"Yeah, sure," she scoffs as I hear the sound of her coming up from the floor. Her heavy breathing fills the silence between us until she says, "Okay. I'm decent."

Reluctantly, I twist around slowly to face her, and if I thought her ass was beautiful, it has nothing on her face fresh from the shower. "You okay?"

She brushes her wet hair from her face. "Nothing is hurt except my pride, fortunately."

Chuckling, I say, "You have nothing to be embarrassed about."

Arching a brow, she crosses her arms over her chest. "I thought you didn't see anything?"

"I didn't. I mean..."

She pinches the bridge of her nose, closing her eyes. "I'm mortified, Henley."

"Again," I say, dipping my eyes down her body and then back up, secretly loving the way her cheeks are pinker than I've ever seen them, "Nothing to be ashamed of."

"Henley..." Her voice is breathy, almost like her heart is racing just as hard as mine.

Needing to change the subject, I say, "How was tonight?"

She clears her throat, pulling her towel tighter around her body. "Uh, it was fine. Remy got a little fussy around seven, like usual, but once she pooped, she was happy and fell right asleep."

"It's crazy what a solid shit does for that kid's mood."

We share a laugh. "Yeah." Elodie bites on her bottom lip before moving past me. "Well, I should probably get dressed."

"Okay." But as she gets closer, the familiar smell of lavender hits my nostrils. "Did you—did you use Remy's body wash?"

Elodie freezes right next to me, our shoulders touching, but both of us facing away from each other, avoiding the other's eyes. "No."

"Why do you smell like it then?"

"I—I bought shampoo and conditioner with the same scent so it soothes her when I hold her."

My eyes snap to hers as her head moves slowly toward mine. "You bought shampoo for yourself to help calm my kid?"

Her brows draw together. "Yeah. Is that okay?"

Fuck, this girl is trouble with a capital T.

As if I wasn't struggling with my attraction toward her already, she goes and does something like this. I didn't even fucking know that lavender was supposed to be calming until Elodie told me when we were shopping for the thousands of baby items I needed. And I can't deny that the body wash does help Remy relax after her bath.

But for Elodie to change what she uses to help *my* daughter? The strongest urge to kiss her slams into me.

Our eyes remain locked, our chests rising and falling with each of our shallow breaths.

Elodie's eyes dip down to my lips, and mine follow suit.

I bet she tastes incredible. I bet her lips are so fucking soft, like pillows, and they get swollen from being used.

God, she'd look so fucking perfect on her knees for me too, those lips wrapped around my...

"Henley," she says breathlessly.

"I don't deserve you," I say, the admission catching me and her off guard.

"Yes, you do. You and Remy both deserve someone who puts you first. And when you look for your next nanny, make sure you find that."

As if she just poured a bucket of water on the fire raging in my body, her words remind me of the timeline we're on.

Only three months remain until she's gone, out of mine and Remy's life forever.

"Get some sleep, Elodie," I grate out, clenching my teeth and pulling my eyes from hers.

I can practically hear her eyes roll. "Good night to you too, Henley."

As I finish my trek down the hall, I hear her bedroom door softly shut, allowing me to exhale heavily.

"Fuck." Pushing my hand through my hair, I think back to the image of Elodie's ass and how my body reacted to her.

This is the longest dry spell you've had in a while, Henley. You would have reacted like that if you saw any woman's bare ass right now.

My mind is trying to convince me that my reaction is normal, but deep down, I know better.

I think my friends were right and it's time I accept it.

I've got the hots for my nanny, and it's just one more problem I can add to my list.

Chapter 10

Henley

Gorilla Man & The One-Eyed Snake

When I look up from the paperwork I'm filling out, I find my sister standing in the doorway of my office. "Dilynne? What are you doing here?"

"Am I not allowed to check in on you?"

"No."

Rolling her eyes, she uncrosses her arms and walks further into the room, taking a seat in the chair on the other side of my desk. My office isn't fancy, but when I need to get things done without any distractions, I like to feel comfortable. My desk is black wood, I have a comfortable chair that I splurged on so my ass doesn't fall asleep when I sit for long periods of time, and there's a small couch over to the left that I've been known to take a nap on a time or two, especially lately.

"Well, get used to it now. You're a dad, which means your life now revolves around taking care of another human, so someone needs to make sure that you're taking care of yourself too."

"You're acting weird."

She shrugs. "Not weird. Just checking in."

Narrowing my eyes at her, I drop my pen to the desk and lean back in my chair. "Well, everything's fine."

"Fine?"

"Yeah, fine. Is that not good enough?"

"How's Remy? How's the lodge? How's..." She pauses before lifting a brow. "Elodie?"

"Remy is perfect. The lodge is still standing. And you talk to Elodie more than I do, so shouldn't you know the answer to that question?"

"I actually haven't talked to Elodie in a few days. She didn't text me back when I invited her to have dinner with me and Laney this week."

It's been a little over a week since the night I came home and got a front row seat to my nanny's bare ass, but not a day has passed where I haven't thought about it, or jacked off to the image in the shower.

My sister clearly doesn't need to know that, though.

"She probably saw it and forgot to respond," I say in an attempt to placate her. Elodie didn't mention the dinner invitation to me, so I'm just speculating here, but she also doesn't seem like the type of person to intentionally ghost someone.

"Maybe. Or maybe I scarred her for life when we went out a couple weeks ago, and she doesn't want to hang out with me again."

My pulse instantly spikes. "What do you mean you scarred her?"

"She didn't tell you what happened at The Charming Bull?"

I lunge forward in my chair. "What the fuck happened, Dil?"

"Unclench your butt cheeks, big brother," she says with annoyance. "She's fine physically. Nothing crazy happened. She sang on stage during Open Mic Night, and fucking rocked it by the way, but then she sort of had a panic attack after. I left her for a minute and when I came back, she was hyperventilating in a corner. She wouldn't tell me what brought it on, so I was just wondering if you noticed something off with her since then."

Jesus Christ. That night she came home, I was so irritated with her being out late that I didn't think twice about asking her how the night went. No. I was pissed off that I couldn't sleep knowing she was out, that she looked sinfully sexy in her outfit, and that other men got to look at her.

"You fucking left her alone, Dil?"

Her brows tighten. "She was dancing with some guy and seemed fine. How the hell was I supposed to know she would freak out?"

I push a hand through my hair and blow out a breath. "She hasn't said anything to me, but then again, our interactions haven't been..."

"Haven't been what?" my sister asks with a bite to her tone. "Are you still being a dick to her, Henley?"

"Uh, I don't know if dick is the appropriate term..."

She tosses her hand in the air, followed by an exasperated sigh. "Jesus. What is wrong with you?"

Do I tell her? Do I confide in my sister about what I realized last week after mine and Elodie's literal run-in in the hallway? She's probably the safer person to confide in than the guys at this rate, especially given the shit-talking they've done lately.

"Let's just say that you were right," I say, low and under my breath.

She cups her ear. "I'm sorry. What was that?"

"I said, you were right."

"About?"

"Elodie and my..." I cast my gaze off to the side of the room before finishing, "attraction to her."

Dilynne's mouth falls open slightly. "Are you joking?"

Shaking my head, I glare back at her. "No. I'm attracted to my fucking nanny, Dil. And I shouldn't be—"

"She's an amazing person," my sister interrupts. "And sweet, and talented as fuck, but she sure as hell doesn't deserve to be treated poorly by you because she makes your dick hard."

"I know."

"How grumpy have you been with her?"

Sighing, I lean back in my chair again and hang my arms over the headrest, staring at the ceiling. "Well, the night you guys went out, I sort of went off on her for being out too late."

Dilynne purses her lips. "Nice, dickwad. You're not her freaking dad."

"I know, she told me so."

"Good. What else?"

"Well, last week when the guys and I got together for blackjack, after I came home, I ran into her in the hallway and she had just gotten out of the shower. Her towel sort of fell off and I..."

My sister's eyes widen. "Oh. My. God. You saw her naked?"

"Just her backside, but yeah." *And the image is permanently branded into my brain.*

"And let me guess, you went all Henley on her and walked off."

"What the fuck does that mean?"

She stands from her chair and hangs her arms by her sides like a gorilla, scowling and grunting. "You know, all Henley—grumpy gorilla man." She lowers her voice. "I'm always in a bad mood and can't ever let a woman in because I'm too afraid to feel shit."

I blink at her slowly until she stops. "That was...fascinating."

She plops back down into her seat, sighing. "Well, it's extremely accurate."

"What the fuck do I do, Dil? I have no idea how to handle this. I mean, she's leaving, for crying out loud. I just became a dad too. The last thing I should be thinking about is my nanny naked."

"Well, is it more than physical? Do you want a relationship with her?"

I toss my hands in the air. "I don't know! All I know is that I can't stop thinking about her and wanting to kiss her."

My sister folds her lips in to hide her smile. "Oh my God. I never thought I'd see the day."

"I can tell you're enjoying every minute of this."

"Hell yeah, I am! I mean, there are worse girls out there you could fall for. But like you said, Elodie is leaving, and trust me—when I saw that girl sing the other night, she belongs on a stage, Henley. It's gonna happen for her." Pausing, she taps the center of her chest. "I can fucking feel it."

I echo her sentiment. "Her voice is incredible."

"Agreed. But if all you want her for is sex, you need to keep your distance. That girl doesn't need to be used by you and find herself sacrificing her dreams for an emotionally immature man."

My heart is pounding so hard that my entire body is vibrating.

Is Elodie someone I can see myself with, or is my attraction to her just physical? Is a relationship even an option for a guy like me?

I'm thirty-two and haven't dated anyone seriously in my entire life. That's not exactly a detail I would want to include on a boyfriend resume.

But I can't deny that I'm drawn to this girl. I want to know more about her, who she is, and I certainly can't forget the way she makes my dick react.

And that's a first for me.

There's a knock at the door.

"Come in."

Warren pops his head inside. "Hey, boss. The mechanic for the snow machine is here." When his eyes land on my sister, his smile builds. "Hey, Dilynne."

My sister salutes him. "Warren."

"Staying out of trouble these days?" he asks her.

"Never. Trouble is too much fun."

Warren laughs. "Sounds about right." Turning back to me, he says, "Should I tell the guy to give you a few minutes?"

"Yeah, I'll be out in five."

Warren nods and then shuts the door behind him.

"So, what are you gonna do?" Dilynne asks, bringing me back to my predicament.

"I don't know, Dil. But please, for the love of God, don't tell her anything."

She mimics zipping her lips. "My lips are sealed."

"I fucking hope so. I am not in the position to promise a girl anything, and besides, I don't even know if that's what I want."

"Well, at least stop acting like a dick to her, Henley. Gorilla man needs to stay locked up in his cage."

"When the fuck did you start calling me gorilla man?"

She stares up at the ceiling in thought. "Honestly, I think it just came to me today."

"Then can we erase it from your memory, please?"

She cackles before growing serious. "Absolutely not."

I pinch the bridge of my nose. "I don't even know why I asked."

***

"Are you eating popcorn with a spoon?"

The moment I enter the living room to find Elodie sitting crisscross on the floor next to Remy lying on her playmat, the first thing I notice is what and how my nanny is eating her favorite snack.

Elodie finishes chewing before answering me. "Um, yes. Did I not mention that that's how I normally eat it?"

My mind is still trying to process what I'm seeing. "Uh, no. You did not."

Shrugging, she empties another spoonful into her mouth. "Well, I do."

Sighing, I leave my wallet and my keys on the end table by the door and head toward the living room, taking a seat on the couch before greeting my daughter on the floor. "Hey, little bear cub. How was your day?"

Remy's response is a toothless smile and coos that I'm sure means something, but no one can decipher. I lift my eyes to Elodie. "You know that's serial killer behavior, right?"

Elodie laughs as she finishes chewing. "I think it's actually quite genius."

"Really? How?"

"Well, when I eat it with my hands—which I'm not opposed to, just don't prefer—the grease and flavoring gets all over my fingers. Napkins are essential. But with a spoon, no messy fingers." She wiggles her fingers in the air on her free hand. "If you think about it, it's kind of like eating cereal."

I can't deny that the woman has a point—a bizarre point—but a point nonetheless. "I see. Well, it's still strange in my book."

"That's just because you haven't tried it."

I lift Remy from her playmat and lay her on my chest as I lean back on the couch. She reaches for the scruff on my jaw as I kiss her cheek. "And I probably never will."

Shrugging, she takes one last bite and sets her empty bowl and spoon on the coffee table. "You're missing out."

Remy is making all sorts of noises while I study her gorgeous blue eyes. "How was she today?"

"Good. Eating a bit more than usual and she took a longer nap too. I think she's about to go through a growth spurt."

"How often will that happen?"

Elodie smirks at me. "Well, think about how small she is and how big she'll be by the time she's a year or two old, Henley. So, I'd say a lot."

"The sarcasm wasn't necessary."

"That's funny coming from you." Smiling, Elodie takes her phone from her pocket and snaps a picture of me holding my daughter, something I've grown accustomed to her doing now, so I don't bother fighting her on it.

I feel the corner of my mouth lift. "How was your day?"

She slides her phone back in her shorts before answering. "It was all right. I tried to sit down and start making a list of different jobs I could do if singing doesn't pan out."

"And what did you decide?"

She stands from the ground, taking her bowl to the sink and grabbing a bottle of water and a notepad from the counter before returning to sit next to me on the couch. "Well, a flight attendant is in the top spot right now."

"Really? Why's that?"

"I love the idea of getting paid to travel, and since I'm unattached and don't have a family, I have the freedom to do that right now."

My chest grows tight at the thought of her leaving again. "Yeah, I guess that's true."

"But I want a dog, and having a pet doesn't really work with that career. Plus, I know I want a family and a home someday, so even though the job sounds great now, it would only be temporary, and that's definitely not the sort of thing I'm looking for right now. If I'm going to make this type of decision, I want a job I can see myself doing for a long time."

A family. A home.

The exact opposite of what you've ever wanted for your life, Henley.

Yeah, but can one person change how you feel about stuff like that?

"Okay, so any other options?"

She sighs. "Nothing that doesn't require me to get another degree."

"You went to college?"

"Yeah, my parents made me get a degree before I went to L.A. so that I had something to fall back on in case music didn't pan out, which they hoped wouldn't work out anyway. I knew they were just trying to help me, but those four years were the longest of my life so far. I just can't stand the idea of sitting still for another four."

"What's your degree in?"

"Business. Something generic enough that I could use in pretty much any arena."

I nod. "I never went to college. School wasn't my thing either. But working at the lodge for seven years before the owner sold it to me was far more valuable to me in the end."

She turns to face me, propping her head up on the back of the couch, her lips curling into a soft smile that makes her look so fucking beautiful and relaxed right now, the urge to lean over and pull her lips to mine slams into me like a train. "You know, I was thinking about something when you brought this up before, and after Dilynne told me a little bit about your daredevil history."

"Okay…"

"What do you do now for that adrenaline chase? I mean, that's not something you give up overnight."

Fuck. Do I answer her honestly? Or do I spare her and me the awkward truth?

"Well, I'll still hit the slopes from time to time, but I found another hobby that gave me a thrill to chase that was far less risky, at least in my opinion."

"Which is?"

I look directly into her eyes. "You don't want to know."

"I asked, didn't I?"

I move my gaze to my daughter, bouncing her a bit as she still lays on my chest. "Let's just say, my daughter is here because of what I used to do for fun."

Elodie's smile falls. "Oh."

"See? Told you you didn't want to know."

She blows out a breath. "No, it's fine. I'm not judging. I just didn't think that chasing women would give you the same high."

"It didn't," I say honestly, pulling her attention back to me. "In fact, it didn't even compare, but the orgasm at the end of the night was close enough."

"I see." She stands from the couch now.

"Elodie?"

"Yeah?" Her voice is almost an octave higher than before.

"I'm sorry if that made you uncomfortable."

"It didn't." Her smile is quick and borderline fake. She's definitely not being honest, which doesn't sit well with me.

Does this mean that my previous extracurricular activities have made her think differently of me now?

I mean, I'm not ashamed of my past. Every woman I've ever been with has been a consensual partner. But for some reason, right now, I really wish I hadn't said anything to Elodie about it.

Before I can say anything else, my phone rings in my pocket. I fish it out and see Warren's name across the screen. "What's up?"

"You busy tonight?"

I glance up at the clock and note the time. It's just after six on a Friday, but it's the end of the week and I'm beat. "Nothing but a date with my bed until my daughter wakes up for her midnight feeding."

"I need you to come out with me tonight."

Groaning, I shake my head. "No way, man."

"Come on. My buddy that was supposed to come out with me canceled. He caught a cold or some shit. I need a wingman."

"Call Elliot." Warren knows my boys and has gone out with me and Elliot plenty of times.

"I did. He's already too intoxicated to go out. Someone needs to check on him again, by the way."

I mentally make a note to send Fletcher or Rhonan over to his house this week. It may be time for an intervention. "Well, I'm busy."

"No, you're not. You have a nanny. Come on...when's the last time we went out together? And dude, I need to get laid. This is the longest dry spell I've had in a while." *You're preaching to the fucking choir, Warren.* "Please?"

"You're begging?"

"I wouldn't if I didn't think my balls were about to explode."

"Then jack off in the shower like a normal person." I lift my eyes to find Elodie staring down at me, her brows lifted. Mouthing 'sorry' to her, I point to the phone next to my ear. "My friend."

"What?" Warren asks.

"Nothing."

"Dude, my hand is turning into the claw with how much I've been yanking the one-eyed snake lately."

"Please don't ever fucking say that again."

"You know, you might want to start watching your swearing. You don't want Remy's first word to be fuck," Elodie whispers while reaching for my daughter and picking her up from my chest.

I roll my eyes and turn my attention back to Warren. "Where are you even going?"

"Riley's."

"The sandwich shop? Dude, you must be desperate if you're looking to score at The Happy Belly Deli."

"No, fucker. Riley's Office. It's a new bar in Asheville. Just opened a few weeks ago, so there's new clientele."

I groan again, but as I look up, I see Elodie putting Remy in her high chair to feed her dinner.

I know the routine for the rest of the evening—dinner, bath, play time, bedtime story, sleep. Midnight feeding. Three in the morning feeding if she's still hungry. Waking up by six.

And Warren is right. I do have a nanny.

But I also don't want to leave my girls.

Then Elodie bends over to pick up something off the floor, and the crease of her butt cheek peeks out of the bottom of her denim shorts—that delectable, smooth skin that I've been dreaming about all week.

Fuck. Maybe I need to get laid too.

I know the talk I had earlier today with my sister is in the back of my mind, but maybe I just think I have feelings for my nanny because I haven't been with anyone in a few months. This is the longest dry spell I've had, and I literally have temptation living in my house with me.

If I can take out my frustration in another way, maybe all of my problems will disappear.

Fuck, it's worth a shot, right?

"Fine," I finally say.

"You'll go?"

"Yeah, give me a couple hours and then swing by and pick me up."

"Hell yeah! Awesome, see you in a bit."

I end the call and look up to find Elodie studying me. "Where are you going?"

Bracing my hands on my knees, I stand from the couch and stare down at her. "Warren wants me to go out with him tonight."

"Oh. Okay."

"I honestly didn't want to, but he needs a friend right now." Elodie doesn't need to know that "friend" really means wingman.

"He's not commissioning you to jack him off, is he?"

"What?"

Fighting her laughter, she says, "Your comment from before. You told him to jack off like a normal person."

"Oh, uh...no. He's just...going through a dry spell and needs some emotional support."

She nods slowly. "I see. And hey, maybe you can chase some of that adrenaline you've been missing lately too? I'm speculating, of course." Giving me her back, she picks up the jar of baby food from the counter and takes a seat in front of Remy. We've just started a few pureed foods with her this week, and so far carrots and sweet potatoes have been the biggest hits.

"Does that bother you?"

"Why would it bother me, Henley? You're a grown man, and I'm your nanny. This is what you pay me to do, right?" Her eyes lift to mine, followed by one of her eyebrows.

I can sense the irritation in her voice, but I don't want to engage with it right now.

"Why don't you let me feed her?" I say, reaching for her hand before she takes the lid off of the glass jar.

Elodie freezes but doesn't look up at me. "I can do it."

"I know you can, but I want to. I'll take the next hour or so, and then you can take over when I need to shower before I leave."

She doesn't even put up a fight. "Okay." Handing me the jar and spoon, she avoids my gaze and heads straight for her bedroom, closing the door behind her.

Sighing, I sit down in the chair Elodie just vacated and make eye contact with my daughter. "Your daddy is really good at pissing off women." Remy lets out a bunch of garbled noises I pretend to understand. "Yeah, I know." But as I sit there and feed my daughter, this dull ache builds in my chest.

I really don't want to go out with Warren tonight, but part of me thinks I need to, if for no other reason than to prove to myself that Elodie hasn't gotten under my skin as badly as I think she has. And maybe getting under another woman will help me confirm that.

After feeding and bathing Remy, I cautiously knock on Elodie's door. When she answers, I can't tell if she's irritated with me. "I need to shower before I head out."

She reaches for Remy before I can hand her off, sliding her onto her hip. "Okay, no problem. Thanks for the break, by the way."

"You don't have to thank me, Elodie. You deserve a break too."

"I know. You let me have one last week, remember?" I instantly connect that she's referring to the night she went out with my sister and the conversation that I had with Dilynne about it earlier.

"I do. Speaking of which, my sister said you never texted her back."

Elodie grows confused, her brows drawing together. She reaches for her phone in her back pocket and swipes to open it up. "Yes, I did."

"Then why would she say that you didn't?"

After a few seconds of clicking around, she groans. "I never hit send. Oh God, she's probably thinking she did something wrong."

"She was more worried about you after your...panic attack."

Elodie's eyes widen. "She told you about that?"

Taking a step closer to her, I tip her chin up so our eyes meet. "Yeah, and you didn't. If I'd have known, Elodie, I could have been there for you."

"Would you? You didn't even ask how my night went. You just jumped down my throat for being out late."

That hits me square in the chest, but I hold her gaze. "I'm sorry, Elodie. I should have put my pride aside and checked in with you."

She visibly swallows before replying, "I'm fine."

"You don't have to lie to me."

"I could say the same thing to you."

"What do you mean?"

"You tell me."

We stay there in a standoff—chests rising and falling with rapid breaths, her pulse under my fingers that have slipped down her neck, her lips slightly parted and wet from her tongue.

My dick is half-mast, quickly on its way to full, and my pulse is firing so rapidly that I can hear it in my ears.

Lucky for us both, before I can do something stupid, Remy smacks Elodie on the chest. Elodie blinks, breaking the trance and prompting me to release her chin. "Sorry, baby bear. We weren't paying attention to you, were we?"

Clearing my throat, I take a step back. "I'll be in the shower."

"Okay." That's the last thing she says to me before I walk away, strip my clothes off, and fist my cock under the water as soon as it's warm enough. Like clockwork, I think about Elodie ass up in my hallway, but instead of just standing there, I drop to my knees and bury my face in her pussy from behind, teasing her puckered hole as well.

Fuck, this woman is going to be the death of me.

I'm so fucking horny just from barely touching her and only seeing part of her naked, but it's those eyes—stark, gray eyes—that I can't look away from, especially when there's a hint of a challenge in them.

She's right. I have lied to her. I've both omitted and covered up the truth of what I'm feeling. And if I'm not careful, the truth may come back to haunt us both.

Chapter 11

Henley

Drunken Confessions & Big Mistakes

Fresh from the shower and a body-numbing orgasm, I put on a clean pair of jeans, a simple gray T-shirt, and a flannel before styling my hair and slipping on my boots. My work attire isn't much different from my normal attire, but when you live in a mountain town, that's pretty par for the course.

Part of me is nervous to look Elodie in the eye after jacking off to the thought of her. Although, I've been doing that for the past two weeks, so I'm not sure what makes tonight any different. Maybe it's because she knows that I'm about to go out and potentially chase the adrenaline I've been missing over the past month.

But the sight and sound that hits me when I walk back down the hallway leaves me stunned and completely aware that what I'm feeling for her isn't just physical.

Elodie is sitting on the couch, Remy is propped up in the feeding pillow, watching her, and my nanny is playing the guitar while singing softly to my daughter.

I have to rub the center of my chest to help ease the ache this image is causing. But before I let this yearning overtake me, I take my phone from my pocket and snap a picture of the two of them—because I have a feeling this is one I won't want to ever forget, even if it's making me want to run in the opposite direction.

"You've resorted to playing music for a four-month-old?" I ask as I step further into the living room, causing Elodie to spin around and meet my gaze.

She shrugs. "I do this every day but didn't get a chance to earlier."

Her comment makes me freeze. "You—you play for my baby girl every day?"

"Yeah. She loves it." Her brow furrows. "Is that a problem?"

Yes. Yes, it's a big fucking problem. It's the kind of problem that makes me want to run the fuck out of my house right now.

So that's what I do.

Spinning around, I reach for my keys and wallet. "I've got to go."

"Henley?"

"I said I've got to go, Elodie," I spit out, glaring at her over my shoulder before opening and slamming the front door behind me, stomping out to my truck and peeling out of the driveway.

I call Warren as I race away from my house. "You're not canceling on me, are you?" he asks when he answers.

"No, but I'll just meet you there."

"Okay then."

"See you in a few." I end the call before he can say anything else, gripping my steering wheel tightly as I head for the highway to get out of town.

And as I drive to Asheville, I keep fixating on how necessary it is that I get laid tonight. I need someone to suck this yearning from my body. I need to know that there's a cure for what I'm feeling—because no good can come from wanting Elodie, and I refuse to admit that she's breaking my carefully curated rules.

***

"I'll take another," I say to the bartender as I slam the empty glass down on the wooden surface.

Warren winces. "Dude, slow the fuck down. That's already three drinks in less than an hour."

"Yeah, well, you're the one who asked me to come out tonight, and this is what I need." Side-eyeing him, I continue, "Is that a problem?"

Warren shakes his head. "Do what you need to do, I guess. But give me your keys."

"Why?"

He leans in closer. "You're off your fucking rocker if you think I'm going to let you drive after three glasses of whiskey, with a fourth on its way."

Rolling my eyes, I dig my keys from the pocket of my jeans and slam them on the bar in front of him. "There. Happy?"

He takes the keys and slides them into his back pocket. "Almost. How about you tell me what's got you throwing back whiskey?"

"This isn't a goddamn therapy session, Warren. You wanted a wingman, so you got one. In fact, I just might try to get laid tonight too." The words leave my lips, but my body is rejecting the idea completely. In fact, nausea starts to swirl in my gut. I don't want another woman, but I have to keep fighting this need for the woman currently living in my home.

"Well, that isn't going to work out well for you, my friend, if you have whiskey dick."

"My dick is just fine." In fact, my favorite appendage is immediately half-mast as I envision Elodie bent over in front of me earlier.

Warren shakes his head, taking a drink from his glass of bourbon before surveying the bar. Riley's Office is more modern than most bars in the area. The booths are a dark burgundy, the lighting softer to highlight the sleek, black décor, and the clientele are mostly in suits, probably here to drown their sorrows from working their corporate jobs all week.

Honestly, I feel like Warren and I are sticking out like two sore thumbs, but it doesn't matter. In my experience, a woman in a suit likes a man who isn't afraid to get dirty for a living. Something about a worn pair of Levi's and work boots just does something for them.

And I need to find one to take this edge off, stat.

"There's two women directly behind us, a blonde and a redhead. White silk blouses, pencil skirts, and heels. Interested?"

The bartender slides my fresh glass of whiskey across the bar to me. "Let's do it."

Warren slaps me on the back, grinning from ear to ear. "Perfect. My dick is already excited."

***

An hour and another glass of whiskey later, the blonde sitting next to me—whose name I can't fucking remember right now—is giving me all the right signs.

She's leaning in to me, licking her lips before sipping on her white wine, and rubbing my thigh under the table. With a glance, I see that the redhead is doing the same thing to Warren, and he's eating up every second of it.

"So, you want to get out of here?" The blonde purrs in my ear. I'm waiting for my dick to have a reaction to the sound, but not even a twitch happens between my legs.

Nonetheless, I push forward with my mission. "I'm not from here and my buddy has the keys to my truck."

Warren slides them across the table to the blonde. "He's got a large backseat, but no driving, you two." Winking at me, he nods slowly.

The blonde giggles. "Fine by me."

I drain the last of my glass and stand, finding myself shaky on my feet but steady enough that I can make my way out of the bar and to the parking lot. I pull the blonde behind me, fighting to focus on putting one foot in front of the other before she spins me around and pushes me up against the side of my truck.

"I knew as soon as I saw you walking toward our table that I wanted you tonight," she says, licking her lips before reaching for the button on my jeans. Any other time a woman would say something like that to me, my dick would be racing to stand at attention.

But I feel nothing. In fact, I'm pretty sure he just shriveled up a bit and my balls just tried to climb back up inside of my body.

Focus, Henley. This is what you need, remember?

The sound of my zipper being pulled down brings me back to reality as the blonde starts to push my jeans and underwear down and drop to her knees.

Nope. I can't fucking do this.

"Stop," I slur, bracing myself against my truck.

Her hands freeze on my waist as she rises to standing again. "What?"

"I—I can't do this."

Anger paints her features, her lips pursed with annoyance. "Seriously? You were all about it earlier."

I remove her hands from my body and pull my jeans and boxer briefs back up, lifting the zipper and buttoning them closed. "And I changed my mind."

"Ha. That's rich. A man changing his mind about getting laid." She crosses her arms over her chest.

"Why does it matter if I'm a man? No means no."

Rolling her eyes, she spins on her feet and walks back toward the bar. "Whatever."

For a moment, I wonder if there's two of her and I've been oblivious to it the entire night, but that's when I realize that I'm drunk, far too drunk to drive and not stupid enough to try.

Warren is still inside talking to the redhead as far as I know, and the last thing I want to do is cockblock him after just doing it to myself. But I don't want to be here anymore. I need to lie down and get the world to stop spinning.

I want to go home to my girls.

As soon as I close my eyes, all I see and hear is Elodie—her smile, those eyes, her voice. All my body and mind want is her.

And I think my heart is making his decision known at this moment as well.

"Fuck," I grumble while attempting to pull my phone from my pocket and hit the number for someone I know won't judge me for the state I'm in.

"Henley?" Fletcher's groggy voice comes through the line.

"Hey, man."

"Everything okay?"

"No." I shake my head. "I mean, I'm fine, but I'm not okay."

"All right..." he trails off.

"I was wondering if you and Laney could come pick me up. I—I've been drinking and I can't drive my truck."

The sound of movement filters through the phone. "Where are you? We'll be right there."

"Riley's Office. It's a bar in Asheville."

"Got it. Be there soon."

"Thanks, man."

"No. Thank you, Henley. Thank you for calling and not driving."

I decide to wait in my truck for them to arrive, locking myself inside. As I doze off, I hear Elodie's voice singing, which only helps me drift off to sleep faster.

***

Bright light pierces through the window, dragging me out of my slumber. My back aches as I slowly lift my eyelids and realize I'm not asleep in my bed, but rather on a couch—Fletcher and Laney's couch.

"Jesus Christ," I mumble.

"Aw, he's alive." Laney's soft voice pulls my gaze to her, standing over me with a cup of coffee in her hands and an amused smile on her lips.

"I'm not so sure yet."

Fletcher chuckles behind me. "I'm gonna grab you some water."

"Thanks."

Laney tilts her head at me. "Do you remember how you got here?"

Slowly blinking, I open my eyes further and survey the room. I vaguely remember talking to Fletcher on the phone, but after that, the rest of the night is missing. "Not really."

Fletcher comes into the living room now, holding a glass of water and a cup of coffee. He passes the glass to me as I slowly sit up, the spinning motion from last night returning with a vengeance. "Well, that's not surprising considering you had five glasses of straight whiskey last night, or at least that's what you kept telling me while I drove you back here in your truck."

Groaning, I pinch the bridge of my nose. "That would explain the headache I have."

Laney visibly shudders. "I don't understand how anyone can drink that stuff. Wine or tequila for me. That's it."

My stomach twists at the mention of more alcohol. "Please don't talk about booze right now."

Fletcher and Laney share a laugh at my expense. I take a sip of the water, making sure it's going to stay down, before drinking about half of the glass. "God, my mouth tastes like ass."

"Should I ask how you know what that tastes like?" Laney teases.

I shake my head and lean back against the couch cushions, sighing. "Please don't make me process any sarcasm right now."

Laney leans over and kisses Fletcher on the lips. "I'll leave you two to talk. Glad you called us, Henley...but maybe you should figure out what made you get so shitfaced last night in the first place, yeah?"

With one open eye, I glare at her as she leaves the room and Fletcher takes a seat on the couch opposite me.

"So, do you remember anything else from last night?"

"Is this a hypothetical question, or are you genuinely asking me?"

"I just want to know if you remember everything you told me."

I close my eyes and groan. "Fuck. Do I even want to know?"

Fletcher grins. "I thought it was quite interesting."

"Jesus."

Leaning back in his corner of the couch, he studies me. "Let's just say, Rhonan was right to be concerned about how you feel about Elodie."

My shoulders slump with defeat as I close my eyes and sigh. I had every intention of taking a woman out to my truck and slipping back into my normal routine last night, and the blonde that almost blew me in the parking lot appears in my memory at that moment. But feeling her touch me, hearing her voice tell me how much she wanted me—it was all wrong.

Longing for one woman has never happened to me before, and I sure as fuck am not handling it well.

"She was singing to Remy last night," I say, my voice low in case Laney is trying to over hear us. "When I came out of my room, prepared to sit around and wait for Warren to pick me up, she was sitting there with her guitar in her lap and singing to my daughter." I lift my eyes to meet Fletcher's. "And I wanted to take a picture of them."

"Okay..."

"Fuck, don't you get it?" I point a finger at my chest. "I don't do that shit. I don't want to take pictures *of* women, *with* women, or care enough about the *same* woman to want to remember her."

Fletcher twists his lips. "So what did you do?"

"I left as soon as I could. I had to get the fuck out of my own house."

"Seems like you're running again, just like you did in your past," Fletcher says, making my blood pressure rise.

"Don't tell me about my past, all right? I just needed some space."

"Yeah. Space from anything that makes you feel shit."

My blood feels like it's boiling now. "You're one to fucking talk."

"Look, I'm not saying I don't understand, but I do know that facing it is much more productive than avoiding it. Have you ever finished that conversation with Nick?" My response to him is a glare, so he continues. "Maybe if you face that, you might start to feel a little lighter, and more capable of handling other feelings, like the ones you have for your nanny."

"I feel like this conversation is making my hangover worse."

Fletcher laughs. "You know, I once lived my life pretty much the same way, Henley—avoiding my dad, avoiding anything that pertained to a future without football, and avoiding how I always felt about Laney, although I wasn't out chasing women. But you know what I realized when Laney and I finally admitted our feelings to one another?"

"What?"

"The reason I didn't want any other woman is because they weren't her. The reason I couldn't think about a life beyond the game is because I didn't have someone to build a life outside of football with. And the reason I avoided my dad is because I didn't feel strong enough to do it on my own." My heart is pounding from his admission, because deep down in my gut, I know that's the fact that scares me the most. "All of that changed when Laney gave me a chance."

"Elodie's leaving in less than three months, Fletcher."

"I know. But if you don't give yourself the chance to explore how she makes you feel, then you're the one left with regrets, Henley. That's kind of what I realized during Elliot's wedding preparation when I was spending all that time with Laney. It was my chance to figure out if these feelings I'd been harboring for her for years were substantial enough to make life-changing decisions about. And I realized very quickly that they were."

"I remember. You jeopardized your friendship with Rhonan for her."

He shrugs. "And I'd do it again in a heartbeat. Do you think Elodie's developing feelings for you too?"

Staring out across the living room, I consider his question. "I honestly don't know. Although, last night when we talked about what I resorted to as a way to chase adrenaline after my accident, she seemed bothered by it."

"Then why not see if there's something there, and just take it one day at a time? No one says you have to marry the girl. But if you're feeling something for her, you owe it to yourself to see if it's more than just a crush, or the sight of her singing to your daughter making you feel emotional."

I heave out a heavy breath. "I really fucking hate you right now."

Fletcher slaps me on the shoulder. "No, you don't. Although you might hate yourself a little when you see your phone." Wincing, he hands me my cell phone, which now has a cracked screen.

"Shit."

"Yeah. You threw it against the dashboard of my truck after you got angry looking at pictures of Elodie."

Twisting the phone around, I notice there's just one crack, but it's completely across the bottom of the screen. Then my eyes land on the notifications—sixteen missed calls and nine text messages—all from Elodie.

Adrenaline races through me as I fight to swipe across the screen and click on the texts.

Elodie: *Hey, I forgot to ask you if you're coming home tonight. Let me know, please.*

Elodie: *Judging by your lack of response, I guess it's safe to say you're not. Be safe.*

Elodie: *If you could just let me know that you're alive, I would appreciate it.*

Elodie: *Henley, it's not that hard to send a text message. Let me know you're okay, please.*

Elodie: *Remy has a fever. I'm doing everything I can to keep it down, but it's making me nervous. Please call me.*

Elodie: *Glad to know that even your sick daughter doesn't matter to you right now.*

"Fuck!" Launching myself from the couch, I search the room for my keys. "I need to go."

Fletcher's energy begins to match my own. "What's going on? Is everything okay?"

"Remy had a fever last night. Elodie was trying to get a hold of me, but I didn't fucking reply."

Laney comes out from the hallway with my wallet and keys. "Here. We kept them in our room in case you woke up and tried to leave last night."

"Thanks."

I head for the front door as Fletcher's voice stops me. "Hey, just breathe. Text me later to let me know that everything's okay."

"I will. Thanks again for last night."

Laney wraps her arms around Fletcher's waist as he kisses the top of her head. "Anytime."

Without another word, I race down their driveway to my truck and hop inside, driving across town as fast as I can to get to my house. When I swing the front door open, I startle Elodie and Remy, making my daughter cry.

"Dear God, Henley. Where's the fire?" Elodie's hand is placed over the center of her chest, probably trying to calm her racing heart.

"Is she okay? Is Remy all right?"

"Her temp is still slightly above one hundred, but she's doing okay."

I head straight for my daughter, lifting her from the high chair, holding her head against my cheek. "I'm so sorry, little one. Daddy is sorry he wasn't here." Elodie walks around me, avoiding me gaze.

"Elodie…"

"I take it you had a good night." Irritation laces her words, but I don't blame her.

"Actually, it was rather shitty, but I'm sorry for not texting you back."

"It would have taken you two seconds, Henley." Crossing her arms over her body, she arches a brow at me. "I was worried that something happened to you."

"I had too much to drink…"

"Are you feeling like shit today?"

"You have no idea."

She huffs out a laugh. "No, I do because I felt like shit all night wondering if you were going to come back." Her admission catches me off guard. "I honestly wondered if you'd have come back at all if Remy hadn't gotten sick." She narrows her eyes at me. "She's doing better now, but there are going to be other illnesses and incidents over the years, and she's going to need a father who shows up."

Those words slice right through my gut. Taking a step closer to me, she tilts her head before she continues. "She's your kid, and she may be too young to remember how you're acting right now, but I won't forget it. I won't forget how fast you ran out of the house last night, how quickly you needed to get away from your new responsibility, but it's time to act like a father and stop avoiding that this is your life now."

"I'm not avoiding it," I counter, feeling myself grow more irritated by the second because even though Elodie has a lot of nerve saying those things to me, I know that she's right.

"Really? Then why haven't you decorated her room?"

Yeah, Henley. Why haven't you?

Avoiding diving into that bucket of worms, I turn the argument back on her. "Look, I'm not paying you for your opinions. I'm paying you to take care of my kid. That's it."

"Well, maybe I need a night off from this job then before the urge to quit becomes too much for me." Twisting away from me, she heads down the hall to her room, making both nerves and fury swirl around in my chest.

I peer down at Remy to find her looking in the direction that Elodie just went. A few minutes later, she comes out of her room with a duffle bag full of stuff, her guitar case, and her purse slung over her shoulder.

"Where are you going?"

"Out. I need…" She doesn't finish her thought, shaking her head and closing her eyes instead. When she pops them open, she stares directly at me and says, "I need a break."

"When—when will you be back?"

"I—I don't know."

"Elodie…" I reach out for her, but she avoids my touch.

"No, Henley." When she peers up at me again, there are tears in her eyes. "You have no idea what was going through my mind last night. And until I can look at you without wanting to scream, I need some distance."

That's the last thing she says to me before leaving my house and driving away.

Great job, Henley. Looks like your communication skills are severely lacking, and if there's any hope of fixing this, you'd better think of something fast.

Chapter 12

Elodie

A Massage and A Girlfriend

My hands are still shaking as I pull into a parking space right outside of Blossom Beauty, shut off my engine, and lean my head against the headrest. "Breathe, Elodie. Just breathe."

The words I said to Henley before storming out of his house have been on an endless loop in my head as I drove across town to Laney's salon, the only place I could think of where I could gather my nerves. I'm supposed to have dinner with her and Dilynne tonight anyway, but seeing Henley this morning just made me even more furious with him.

It wasn't just fury you were feeling though, was it, Elodie?

Luckily, the voice of reason I need right now answers on the first ring. "Elodie?"

"Hey, Lennon," I croak out, fighting off my tears that are mostly from anger. But a part of me is sad because the worst possible thing has happened to me—I've developed feelings for my boss.

"What's wrong? Are you okay?"

"I just went off on Henley."

Lennon snorts. "Okay, why don't you start from the beginning..."

"God, Lennon. He's so closed off and grumpy, but sometimes he lets his guard down, and I see what a strong man he is. He grew up in foster care, so I can't imagine what he's been through and seen, but he doesn't let people in, Lennon. Except for his friends. He has this friend group that's basically his family, and last night he went out with one of his co-workers, which shouldn't bother me, but then he wouldn't answer my texts and all I could think about was him either dead in a ditch or sleeping with some random woman..."

"Whoa, Elodie. Breathe, honey," Lennon's voice cuts through my spiral, giving me a chance to catch my breath. "That was a lot of information you unloaded."

"Well, that's how I feel this morning. Henley finally showed up at home after his daughter had a fever last night and he never responded to me. But by that time, I was so flipping angry, I went off on him and stormed out."

"Did he tell you why he didn't answer you?"

"Apparently, he had too much to drink, which is what he turns to when he wants to escape. I swear, before he left, he took one look at me and Remy, then bolted—like he couldn't handle the sight of us and had to get away."

Lennon hums. "Has he done that before?"

"I mean, he's been short with me, but never run away."

"Well, where are you now?"

"I'm sitting in my car outside of Laney's salon."

"Who's Laney?"

I spend the next few minutes bringing her up to speed on my friendship with Laney and Dilynne. "Maybe ask them if his behavior is normal."

"His sister warned me that he has issues. I just didn't realize that they'd make me want to strangle him. And knowing that he was probably out chasing women last night doesn't help."

Lennon clears her throat. "Why does it matter if he was out with other women?"

"It doesn't."

"You sure about that?"

My jaw clenches tighter. "What are you implying, Lennon?"

"That what I was afraid of happening is happening." Tears prick behind my eyes. I already know that what I feel for Henley is inappropriate, but hearing one of my best friends call me out on it isn't making my blood pressure come down any faster. "It sounds to me that maybe there's some jealousy blended with that anger you're feeling."

Sighing, I close my eyes. "I'm in a clusterfuck right now, Lennon."

"Only if you act on what you're feeling," she counters.

"I'm so mad at him right now that the only thing I'll be acting on is strangling him."

"Anger can lead to some pretty amazing sex."

I pop my eyes open and stare at myself in the rearview mirror. "You're not helping. Nothing can happen between me and Henley for a multitude of reasons. One, he's my boss. Two, I'm caring for his daughter, so that's supposed to be my focus, not the blatant display of arm and ab porn that taunts me while I'm living with him. And three, I'm leaving and he's clearly dedicated to his business and life here in Blossom Peak, so there's no chance a relationship would work between us."

"The fact that you're even using the word relationship is shocking, especially considering the last man you opened up to."

Staring out the front window, I whisper, "I had a panic attack last week when I was dancing with some guy at a bar. He kept pressuring me to leave with him…"

"Shit, Elodie. I'm sorry."

Shaking my head, I close my eyes and feel the first tear slide down my cheek. "I hate that I let a man have that power over me, Lennon."

"He only has that power if you let him."

"Well, running away sort of let him win, huh?"

"Liam was an asshole that used your dream of singing to manipulate you, and when you didn't bend to his will, he got his revenge by tarnishing your reputation. I doubt Henley has any scope of power in that regard."

"Henley will be my last reference on any job application I fill out next. I doubt anyone is going to want to hire a woman who slept with her boss because his forearms were taunting her too much. I can't be weakened by forearms, Lennon. That's not a skill employers want."

"Why would you even write that on a job application? Besides, I thought the plan was to go back to L.A. eventually? Or have you decided that's not what you want?"

"I haven't landed on any decision yet. The only thing I knew with certainty this morning was that I had to get away from Henley before I did something really stupid, and the last thing I should be doing is mixing in feelings for the man whose child I'm taking care of."

"Then keep it professional."

"He's so hot, Lennon. I mean, I never knew that blue jeans and work boots were such a turn on."

Lennon hums in approval. "Don't get me wrong, I love a man in a suit. But there's something about a blue-collar man that will win out every time."

We share a laugh. "And for some reason, I feel safe with him."

"Even though he pisses you off and won't open up to you?"

"Yeah."

"Look. You have a little less than three months left there. Just take it one day at a time, Elodie. I can't help but think that this transitional period you're in is going to lead you to exactly where you're supposed to be. Call it intuition or whatever, but when things don't work out the way we thought they would, there's usually a reason."

I groan. "I don't think I'd be this frustrated if I could write a damn song."

"Still no luck?"

"My notebook is full of bits and pieces of ideas, but nothing is speaking to me."

"Maybe you need to write something about your boss."

Just the suggestion has my pulse picking up speed. The truth is, I've been wondering the same thing because the forbidden feelings I've been harboring are speaking to me, but I've been too scared to put them down on paper.

I rest my hands on the steering wheel in front of me. "I'll consider it."

"It's going to be okay, Elodie. But in the meantime, you should probably apologize to Henley since you technically still need the job."

"Believe me. My credit card balance reminds me of that every day."

"Keep me posted, my friend."

"I will."

After ending the call, I check my appearance in the visor mirror and then head inside the salon, instantly transfixed by the beauty of the space. I'm so disappointed that I can't afford any services right now because I would love nothing more than to relax and pamper myself for a bit.

Unfortunately, I'm choosing to be a responsible adult at the moment.

"Elodie?" Laney walks over to where I stand in the waiting area. Olive green chairs line a few walls along with shelves of products, the small room slightly closed off from the rest of the salon. The walls are white, which make the space look open and fresh, each stylist station has black framed mirrors hung in front of each chair, and the gray floors provide the perfect soft background to bring the whole look together. Past the hair stylist stations on both sides of the room are three separate spaces—one for the nail technicians, one for the massage services, and one for facials and skin care.

"Hey." My throat is still tight from the emotion of this morning, but I fight to keep my composure. "Sorry to just drop by like this."

"Nonsense. You're always welcome here. Everything okay?"

"Well..." I can feel myself about to break, and luckily, Laney senses that.

"Yvonne?" she calls out to an older woman with a long, dark braid with streaks of gray in it.

"Yeah?"

"You still have a while before your next client?" Laney asks her.

"About an hour. Why? What's up?"

Laney wraps her arms around my shoulders and leads me past the receptionist counter and over to Yvonne. "This is Elodie. She's Henley's new nanny, and she looks like she needs to relax."

Yvonne drops her eyes up and down my body. "Yeah, she does seem tense. Let me work my magic on you, sweetheart." She wiggles her fingers in the air.

"Oh, that's nice of you, but I can't really afford a massage right now," I say with a hint of embarrassment in my voice, but there's no sense in trying to make up an excuse.

Laney and Yvonne share a look before Laney looks back at me. "It's on the house."

"What? No, Laney. It's okay. Really..."

"Nope." Shaking her head, she leads me forward as we follow Yvonne to the massage rooms. "You're my friend and you look like you need a moment, so I'm taking care of you. And then, you can take my keys to my house and wait there until this afternoon for Dilynne and me."

"You really don't have to do this."

Her smile is comforting. "I know I don't. But I have a lot of experience with being mad at a man, and judging by the look on your face and how early you're here in the day, I'm guessing Henley did something Dilynne's going to want to kick his ass for."

I laugh as my eyes well up. "How did you know?"

"Again, I spent years being mad at Fletcher."

Yvonne tsks. "She used to call him Lucifer if that gives you any indication of how she felt."

I chuckle through my tears. "Okay. Thank you."

"My pleasure." She rubs my back and then leaves me alone with Yvonne. "Uh, I've never had a massage before."

Yvonne rubs her hands together. "Oh, honey. You're in for quite the treat then. Let's get you ready and then leave the rest to me."

Even though this is the last thing I expected coming into the salon this morning, I'm really grateful that Laney could read me so well. The only other person that's ever been able to do that is Lennon.

And in that moment, I remember her words from earlier. This is all happening for a reason—including my argument with Henley—which means I need to embrace what I'm supposed to learn from it, even if that means what I'm learning is that a man disappointing you is inevitable, but it doesn't have to mean that you can't stand up for yourself in the process.

***

The sound of a key turning in a lock startles me from my slumber. When I open my eyes and see Laney and Dilynne walk through the front door of Laney's house, I push myself up from the couch and clear the sleepiness from my eyes.

"Good morning, sunshine," Dilynne says as she holds up two bottles of wine in her hands. "Well, technically it's the evening, which means drinking is acceptable, and Laney's dad owns a winery, so you know this shit is good."

Laughing, I clear the dryness from my throat. "I can't believe I fell asleep."

Laney walks over the couch and takes a seat next to me. "That's the post massage drug running through you. It's normal."

"Yvonne is a magician. Now I understand why people get massages regularly."

"Yup."

"Thank you again for that gift. I didn't realize how much I needed it."

Laney studies me for a beat. "Women are good at ignoring our basic needs to take care of others. You're taking care of a grown man and his baby right now. I'd say you earned it."

The sound of a cork popping turns my attention to the kitchen. Dilynne is shaking her hips to imaginary music as she tosses the cork in the trash, retrieves three wine glasses from a cupboard, and gives each of us a very generous pour. "So, Laney told me you needed to vent about my brother, and I'm the perfect person to help you plot revenge, so let's hear it. What tool do I need to threaten him with?"

I chuckle as she carries two of the glasses over to Laney and me just as my stomach rumbles. "Guess I'm hungry."

"Pizza's on the way," Dilynne says. "Now spill."

I catch them up to speed on last night's events, focusing on how quickly Henley bolted from his own house and how he couldn't even be bothered to answer my texts to let me know he was alive. When I get to this morning and what I said to him, Laney and Dilynne are both clapping in appreciation.

"First of all, I'm glad you weren't afraid to stand up to him and tell him how wrong he was," Laney says. "But second of all, I think there's one key factor that you're missing in all of this."

"What?"

"With men, it's more about actions and less about what they say. Henley's lack of words tells me everything I need to know."

My eyes move between them. "Am I missing something?"

Laney and Dilynne share a look before Dilynne speaks this time. "Nothing that isn't right in front of your face. Remember, I told you that my brother has issues."

I snort before taking a sip of my wine. "Yes, we've established that."

"Henley is a man of few words anyway, but in my professional opinion, I think he's scared," Laney elaborates.

"Scared of what?"

"You," Dilynne replies as if the answer is so simple.

"Me?"

"Yup." Dilynne pops the p before taking a drink from her glass. "And let's just say that I know this firsthand because my brother and I had a conversation about it."

"Well, your brother scares me too," I mumble in response.

Dilynne's brows draw together. "You don't have to answer this if you don't want to, but do you mind me asking why?"

Debating how much I should go into detail about everything that brought me to Blossom Peak, my gut tells me that Laney and Dilynne won't judge me. "The last time jealousy got the best of me, I ended up in a situation with a man that sort of scarred me."

"What do you mean?" Laney asks.

I stare down into the crisp, white wine as it moves in my glass, preparing myself to share the truth of why I needed to leave music behind for a while. "The music industry is cutthroat. Social media has changed the game, but I never got much traction. Honestly, writing songs is where my true passion lies. I can sing as well, but the idea of having my life plastered to the world for others to judge and invade doesn't appeal to me."

"Your voice is incredible though, Elodie. When you sang at The Charming Bull, I was blown away," Dilynne replies.

"Thank you. Performing is fun, but I'm not sure that's what I want anymore. I used to think it was."

"You're allowed to change your mind," Laney interjects. "Hell, I'm the queen of changing my mind."

Dilynne lifts her glass to her. "That you are."

They share a laugh before I continue. "Well, this girl I was friends with who was also trying to start her career got discovered by this manager. His name was Liam, and as soon as I saw the attention she was getting, something in me snapped."

Dilynne leans forward in her chair. "Did you kill her and make it look like an accident? Are we harboring a fugitive?"

"Dilynne!" Laney chastises her.

"No, nothing like that," I quickly reply, trying to defend myself. "And if I were, I never would have agreed to care for your niece, that's for damn sure."

Dilynne visibly relaxes and she leans back into the couch. "Okay, good. Just wanted to make sure."

Laney glares at her best friend. "You seriously scare me sometimes."

"Trust me. I scare myself." Motioning with her wine glass, Dilynne says to me, "Continue, please."

"Anyway, I saw what she had and wanted it. It wasn't fair to me that I'd been working longer than her to get a record label to give me a chance, so I made a point to approach Liam at one of her shows, and we hit it off. It started with a few 'business dinners,' as he liked to call them. He offered to listen to my demo tape and I was vibrating with excitement. Finally, it felt like someone was willing to take a chance on me. That's all I wanted anyway, someone to give me the opportunity to leave a mark with my songs like I wanted."

Laney winces. "I'm pretty sure I'm not going to like what happens next."

"I already have a torture plan in place. Pliers are great for extracting teeth," Dilynne adds.

"And you thought Elodie would be the one that could attempt murder," Laney mumbles before looking back at me. "Continue, please."

Sighing, I say, "He invited me to the production studio so we could talk and told me that he wanted to record one of my songs. But when I got in there, he tried to..."

"Son of a bitch," Dilynne says as she launches from the couch.

"Did he..." Laney begins to ask the question I rush to answer.

"No, thank God. I pushed him off, kicked him in the balls, and then ran out of his office. Turns out, he didn't care about my talent, he just wanted to sleep with me."

"So you left L.A.?" Laney asks.

"Not at first. I kept trying to submit more songs and demos, but then at one studio, I overheard the office staff talking about how I would sleep around to get ahead, and that's when I put two and two together."

"Liam told everyone that you did," Dilynne finishes for me.

I nod, feeling the tears build for the third time in the past twenty-four hours. "When I heard that, I had to leave. I couldn't believe that all of my talent would mean nothing going forward because of one man..."

"Oh, I fucking believe it," Dilynne grates out, drinking from her wine glass.

Laney meets my gaze. "Dilynne knows a thing or two about men and what they're willing to do when their egos are bruised."

The sound of the doorbell interrupts our conversation. Laney rushes to answer it, intercepting the pizza and moving toward the kitchen, placing a few slices on plates for all of us. Dilynne refills our wine glasses, and then we reconvene in the living room.

"Elodie, I'm so sorry that you had to go through that," Laney says after taking a bite of her pizza.

"Thank you."

"So back to the jealousy thing," Dilynne says, a look of determination on her face. "How does that apply to my brother? Just so you know, my brother would never force himself on a woman, and if he did, I would castrate him for the greater good of womankind."

"If you're wondering, yes she is always this murdery," Laney says, leaning forward in her chair while flashing me a wink.

"But I feel like we're still missing something," Dilynne continues.

Bracing myself to admit the truth, I inhale deeply and blow out my breath. "Last night, when he told me how he likes to chase adrenaline now by chasing women, and then he announced he was going out with Warren..." I swallow roughly. "Well, I instantly became jealous. I hated the idea of him being with someone else, and that's when I realized, I have a serious problem."

Laney and Dilynne glance at each other, but their faces don't move besides the motion of their eyes. No twitch in their lips, no indication of what they're thinking whatsoever.

And before they can respond, my phone rings on the couch beside me. Henley's name flashes across the screen, but I know I'm not ready to talk to him, so I ignore it.

"Sorry," I say when I look back up and see Dilynne clearly thinking heavily, her brows pinched and her lips twisted in thought.

"No problem, but I get where you're coming from. And is that interaction with Liam why you freaked out at the bar the other night?"

I nod. "Yeah." My phone rings again and when I see that it's Henley once more, my pulse spikes. "It's your brother again."

"He's probably freaking out having to take care of Remy on his own," Dilynne says with a roll of her eyes. "Just keep ignoring him."

"I really think you two need to talk though," Laney interjects. "Speaking from personal experience, if Fletcher and I had just talked about everything we were feeling a long time ago, we wouldn't have wasted all of that time not being together."

"You think I should tell him that I was jealous?"

Laney glances at Dilynne before looking back at me. "Yeah, I do. And I think you might be surprised by his response."

My phone rings for the third time, and now I'm starting to worry that something might be wrong. "Maybe I should answer him."

Dilynne scoffs. "I mean, you're only giving him a taste of his own medicine, but it's up to you."

I only hesitate for a second before I swipe across the screen. "Hello?"

"Elodie?" Henley's voice comes out panicked.

"Yeah, Henley. What do you need?"

"It's Remy," he says, and my spine instantly straightens.

"What's wrong?"

"She's hot, El. Like really hot to the touch."

"Well, she had a fever last night. Give her some Tylenol."

"I did, and it's not helping. She's almost at 104."

Standing from the couch, I take my wine glass and plate to the kitchen while balancing the phone between my head and shoulder. "That's really high."

"I know. What do I do?"

Dilynne and Laney can sense the alarm in my voice as they follow me into the kitchen. "I think you should take her to the emergency room."

"Fuck. Really?"

"Yeah, she could have a bladder infection, ear infection, or something else going on that we can't see."

"I'm scared," he whispers and in that second, my anger toward him dissipates.

"It will be okay. I'll meet you there."

"Okay. Thank you."

"Of course." When I end the call, I look up and find Dilynne and Laney biting their bottom lips. "I need to go."

"What's going on? Is everything okay?" Dilynne asks.

"Remy has a really high fever. She had one last night, but not as high as what it is now. I'm going to meet your brother at the hospital."

"Are you okay to drive?" Laney asks.

"Yeah, I'm fine." Reaching for my purse and keys from the floor by the couch, I slip my phone in my purse as I slide my shoes back on. "I'll text you guys and keep you updated."

"Please keep us updated. I don't want to crowd you two, and I know my brother will stress out more if we show up. But Elodie?" Dilynne says as I reach for the front door knob.

"Yeah?"

"Talk to my brother. Stand your ground, but tell him how you're feeling. I think he needs to hear it."

My brow furrows from her suggestion, but I simply nod and then head out to my car, driving as fast as legally possible to the hospital, hoping that the little girl I've grown to care for—and her father—are going to be all right.

***

I twist my head in every direction as I run through the automatic doors of the ER. The sun has set on this horrendous day, leaving nothing but fluorescent lights blinding me as the darkness outside is visible through the windows.

"Elodie!" Henley calls out from my left, standing from the cushioned chair he was sitting in, Remy in his arms, her cheeks bright red from her temperature.

"I'm here."

"Remington Clark!" A nurse calls out from the double doors that lead back to the triage stations.

"Perfect timing," I say as I follow Henley and the nurse through the heavy metal doors and over to a bed where the nurse pulls the curtain closed around us, providing a sliver of privacy. Henley sits on the bed with Remy in his lap, her soft cry echoing around us, breaking my heart even more than it already is. "Poor baby bear. Don't worry, we're gonna figure out what's going on with you, okay?" I run my finger down her cheek.

The nurse swipes his badge in front of a scanner connected to the computer in the space. "What brings you in today?"

"Her temperature is really high and I can't get it to go down," Henley answers on a shaky breath, bouncing Remy in his arms trying to soothe her in between cries.

"How long has it been like this?"

"About five hours," he says while I mentally take note of when her fever must have spiked again. At least she wasn't too hot when I left this morning.

"Have you given her any medication?"

"Tylenol."

"Dosage?"

"Whatever it said on the bottle," he barks out. But the nurse shoots him a glare that could slice right through him. "Sorry. I'm a new dad, and I don't know what I'm doing."

"And who's this?" the nurse tosses his thumb in my direction.

"I'm his wife," I answer for Henley, kicking myself for even saying it, but I know it was necessary so I could stay back here. If I'm not family or involved with him, they would ask me to leave.

The nurse moves his eyes between us, but doesn't fight me on it. "Let me get her vitals." He does the necessary workup and tells us that the doctor on shift will be by when she can.

As soon as he leaves, I let out a shaky breath and glance at Henley, expecting him to snap at me for what I said, but he is too consumed by his daughter. "Sorry about the wife thing, but if I didn't say that, they would have made me wait in the waiting room."

He doesn't even look up from Remy. "It's fine."

"Has she been fussy today?"

"Yeah." He continues to bounce her in his arms, even as he stands to move around the small space between the curtains.

An uncomfortable silence rests between us, a lapse in conversation that makes me spit out the first thing that comes to mind. "I'm sorry."

Henley shakes his head. "You don't have anything to be sorry for."

"I shouldn't have left you this morning."

"No, you were right to."

"Henley..."

His eyes finally meet mine. "No, El. Don't. You were right." He shakes his head again, the look of disgust resting in the lines of his face as he speaks. "You were right about so much. I just..." His words trail off. "I'm just really good at avoiding shit."

"You don't say."

The corner of his mouth lifts and I take that as a win. "And I'm the one that should be sorry."

"Let's just agree that we both reacted out of anger and frustration and move on, okay?" I reach out my hand to shake his.

It takes him a minute, but he finally reciprocates. "Fine."

At that moment, the doctor comes in and pulls the curtain closed behind her. "Hi there, I'm Dr. Miller. I spoke to the nurse, and it sounds like Remy has been running a pretty persistent high fever?"

Henley presses a kiss to Remy's head. "Yes. I've given her Tylenol, but it barely touched it. I'm worried about my daughter."

"I understand. Let's take a look." She warms the stethoscope in her hand before pressing it gently to Remy's chest, listening for a moment. Then she examines her ears, humming softly. "Oh yes. Definitely an ear infection."

Henley frowns. "Where could that have come from?"

"Pretty common at her age," Dr. Miller says, straightening. "If she's been congested, fluid can build up behind the eardrum and cause an infection."

"Her nose did start running the other day, but she's also teething, so I didn't think too much of it," I admit.

"Could be allergies or a cold, but she has fluid built up in there, so we're going to prescribe her an antibiotic. Then I want you to alternate Tylenol and ibuprofen to help get that fever down. A cool bath could also help."

"I tried a cold washcloth on her neck, but she didn't like that," Henley replies.

"Her body is fighting off an infection and the texture isn't something babies tend to like, so I'm not surprised. Don't worry, though. You did the right thing bringing her in. Give us a few minutes and we'll get you on your way."

The doctor walks back through the curtain, pulling it shut behind her.

Henley releases the biggest breath I've ever heard from that man, kissing Remy on the head again before he peers up at me. "Thank you."

"I didn't do anything."

"You're here," he says, reaching out for my hand and squeezing it. And before I can cry for the fourth time today, I simply nod and look away until the nurse comes back with a prescription and tells us we can go home.

By the time we get Remy's medicine, return to Henley's house, give her a bath, and change her, the adrenaline from today is starting to wear off. Henley's in his room, attempting to get Remy down, and I'm sitting on the couch, staring off into nothing with my notebook open in my lap, the words to a song coming together for the first time in forever.

I haven't been able to write in months, and after one of the most mentally draining days of my life, words started pouring out of me the second we got home.

Today has been a rollercoaster of emotions, but the thing that scares me the most is the jealousy I felt last night when Henley left his house. And then when he didn't answer my texts, all I could envision was him in bed with someone until the woman's face turned into mine—imagining the way his hips would roll as he thrusted into me, the way his lips would move over mine then trail down the sensitive skin on my neck, the way his eyes would darken as he held my gaze and watched me fall apart beneath him.

It's that combination of jealousy and fantasy that made a song about wanting someone you shouldn't flow so freely. I was scared to stop writing for fear that the words would disappear.

The sound of Henley's footsteps coming down the hall breaks through my fantasy, which is probably for the best.

"Is she asleep?" I ask as I stand from the couch, closing my notebook and tossing it on the cushion, watching him stalk toward me.

But Henley doesn't say a word as his feet carry him across the room, his eyes heavy from the worry of the day, his face contorted with confusion, and his hair in disarray. His broad shoulders frame his massive body, his presence becoming stronger and stronger, like all of the air is being sucked out of the room while our eyes remain locked on each other. For a moment, I forget to breathe as I watch him walk toward me with purpose, until he's standing right before me, framing my face in his hands, and smashing his lips to mine.

I freeze, completely taken aback until his tongue passes over my lips and an embarrassing moan travels up my throat. My arms wrap around his neck and I'm kissing him back.

Holy mother of God.

Henley's hands move from my face to my hips, pulling me toward him with a possessiveness that makes my entire body ignite, the peak of the warmth radiating between my legs. I move my fingers into his hair, the thick strands weaving through my nails as our tongues pass over each other. A groan from Henley vibrates against my lips as a wave of lust travels down each of my limbs.

No man has ever kissed me like this—with this much need, this much desire, this much passion. If our mouths weren't connected, I'm sure I'd be hyperventilating right now.

Our hands keep moving, lips keep seeking, and tongues keep searching until I feel Henley begin to slow the kiss. But we're still connected, his touch just softer, more reverent, less hurried than before.

With one last soft press of his lips to mine, he slowly pulls back and I barely lift my eyes before finding him staring down at me, passing his thumb over my bottom lip.

The words that leave his mouth next leave me even more dazed and confused. "Goodnight, Elodie."

And then he's gone, walking back to his room, leaving me standing there, wondering why the hell my boss just kissed me—and knowing that it was the best kiss of my life.

Chapter 13

Henley

French Toast & Pink Paint

Fuck, I shouldn't have kissed her.

"Henley? Are you listening to me?" Carol's voice cuts through my thoughts. I look up from the dining room table to find her staring at me, Remy nestled against her chest while Nick and Dilynne work their way through plates of French toast.

"Sorry. I blanked for a second," I lie, knowing full well where my mind was just now.

It's Sunday morning and Carol and Nick invited me and Dilynne over for breakfast. They'll do this every once in a while since my sister is obsessed with Carol's French toast. The other reason they invited us was to see Remy, especially after her ER visit last night, which we've already dissected in great detail. I've only been able to bring her by once since she's entered my life, but since Carol and Nick are the closest thing to grandparents she'll have, I want to make sure they have a relationship with her.

"I said, how's the lodge?"

"Good. Waiting for that first snow so we can get the slopes open, but my snow machine is on standby just in case."

"It's nearly October. Give it a few weeks and I bet we have some snow on the ground," Nick says as he cuts into his French toast. His eyes drift over to my sister who's been abnormally quiet, but that's probably because she's stuffing her face. "When's your next car show, Dilynne?"

My sister looks up from her plate, syrup dripping down her chin. "What?"

Carol laughs. "Nick, you know better than to ask Dilynne anything while she's eating my French toast." With a wink, she turns her attention back to Remy, holding her hand. "Just wait until you can try it, little girl. You're gonna be begging your daddy to bring you over here as well."

Dilynne wipes her face with her napkin. "It is obsession worthy, Remy," she says to my daughter and then turns back to Nick. "My next show is in a few weeks. I'm taking the '56 Bel Air to the Springfield Car Show in Ohio."

"Does this one have a prize?"

"No, it's more for networking. I want to get my name out there more before Motorlux next August."

"You got into that show?" I ask my sister.

Her smile is instant. "Hell yeah I did, and I'm going to auction off the Porsche 356."

Nick's mouth drops open. "Seriously?"

The look of determination on Dilynne's face shouldn't surprise any of us. "Yup. And when I get top dollar for it, Vinnie won't be able to say another word about how everything I know is because of him."

Vinnie Delatorre is my sister's one and only ex. They dated for four years when my sister first started going to car shows, but their relationship ended disastrously. Let's just say Dilynne made sure one of Vinnie's beloved cars paid the price when she found out he betrayed her. She's been on a mission to prove herself and that she belongs in the restoration industry ever since, even though no one who knows her has ever questioned that.

"Do you need any help?" Nick asks. "You know I'd love to get my hands on the car."

Dilynne covers his hand with her own. Nick's a huge reason my sister fell in love with cars. When we moved in with him and Carol, he introduced her to Barrett-Jackson Auctions on the History channel, and the rest was history, pun intended.

"I appreciate the offer, but I really want to complete this one on my own. I'm not even letting Steven touch it. I've already made some progress on the body. The engine is next and will take the bulk of my time leading up to the event."

"Then can I at least come watch you work?" Nick prods.

Dilynne laughs. "Of course you can, old man."

Nick turns to me, the smile on his face reminiscent of a kid in a candy store. "I can't believe my girl is going to Motorlux. I'm so proud."

As soon as he says the words, a realization dawns on me. Nick isn't even our biological dad, but the pride he has for Dilynne would make you think she's his own. We sure as shit never heard those words from our real dad growing up.

I glance at my daughter and wonder what she'll be interested in as she grows, and how proud the simplest things she does will make me. Will she take dance classes or play t-ball? Will she want to play football with the boys? Or will she be an artist, maybe teacher?

When I look back at Nick, he leans over and pats my shoulder. "Proud of you too, Henley. You're running a successful business and now you're a father. I'm not gonna lie, I was a little nervous about how fatherhood would impact your life. But you seem to be doing really well."

Yeah, except for kissing my nanny and acting like an ass sometimes because I hate that I want her.

"Thanks, Nick."

"Love you both," he says, and like an arrow just pierced through my heart, I stand from the chair to get some space.

How can such simple words wreak havoc on my brain and body so easily? And for years?

"How's Elodie?" Carol asks, changing the subject to the woman I couldn't get out of the house fast enough to avoid this morning.

I honestly don't know what came over me last night, but as soon as Remy was sleeping peacefully in her bassinet, I felt like I could breathe. And then when I came out of my room and saw Elodie sitting on my couch, staring off into space but looking so fucking gorgeous, completely unaware of how much her presence calmed me yesterday at the hospital, something in me snapped.

Unfortunately, the only thing I could think to do after that mind-blowing kiss was to go to my room and lock the door, because if I didn't, I sure as fuck wasn't going to stop there.

"Yes, Henley. How is Elodie?" Dilynne echoes, peering over at me with anticipation as she shoves another bite of French toast in her mouth.

"She's...good."

Unbelievably talented. Strong-willed. Patient. A remarkable kisser. The only reason why I'm not rocking myself in a corner right now as a new dad.

"Good? So you two...talked?" my sister prods further.

Snapping my eyes to her, I say, "Were we supposed to?"

"I mean, she was with me and Laney when you called her last night. She left us to meet you at the ER."

"If you need someone, you know you can always call me too," Carol interjects. "I kind of know a thing or two about taking care of kids."

"I know, Carol. And I appreciate that. In that moment though, the first person I thought to call was Elodie. Sorry."

"No apology necessary. She's a part of your and Remy's life now."

Yeah, but not for long, or at all if she quits after I kissed her last night.

Focusing back on Dilynne, I say, "What was she supposed to talk to me about?"

Dilynne shrugs, pretending like she doesn't know exactly what Elodie wanted to speak to me about, but my gut tells me she does, and partly that's because I know my sister is a horrible liar. "Again, you should talk to her."

"Why didn't she come with you today?" Carol asks. "You know she's always welcome here and there's plenty of food."

Dilynne pushes her chair back from the table, taking her plate into the kitchen and slapping two more pieces of French toast on it. "Not for long."

Nick shakes his head, amused by my sister. I look back at Carol. "Uh, Elodie was still sleeping when I left."

"It's eleven in the morning," Dilynne's brows draw together in confusion.

"I left at eight."

Her mouth falls open. "What the hell did you do for three hours?"

Go anywhere to avoid being at home and alone with her. "I drove to Asheville to the store for more diapers and stuff for Remy. Then we stopped by the bakery and visited with Carolina, and then we went to the park."

Carol, Nick, and Dilynne share a look just as my phone buzzes in my pocket. I pull it out and see a text from Elodie.

Elodie: *Hey. Not sure when you'll be home, but I'm going to go out for a while and run a couple of errands. See you later?*

Me: *Yeah, see you back at the house.*

When I look up from my phone, Nick, Carol, and Dilynne are all watching me.

"Sorry, it was Elodie."

Dilynne flicks her head in the direction of the front door. "Hey, wanna come outside with me really quick?"

"Uh, why?"

She rolls her eyes. "Just get your ass out front, gorilla man." She stabs a piece of her French toast and shoves it in her mouth before moving toward the front door.

Carol shakes her head with an amused smile on her face. "Go ahead, Henley. I've got Remy. And just so you know, once Elodie leaves, I'm more than willing to help you with her."

A tiny sliver of relief radiates through my chest. "Thanks, Carol."

"Anything for you, hun. We love you two."

That word makes my pulse spike again, but I choose to ignore it and follow my sister outside, finding her continuing to eat on the porch swing. I take a seat in the Adirondack chair next to her. "What did you need to say to me that you couldn't say in front of Carol and Nick?"

Dilynne finishes chewing before she replies. "I'm sorry. Did you want them to know that you wanna bang your nanny? Because if that's the case, we can go back in there and have this conversation in front of them."

I flash her a flat stare. "That's not necessary. Now say what you need to say, please."

"I really think you need to have a talk with Elodie. You should have seen the way that girl ran out of Laney's house last night, Henley. It was like she couldn't get to you fast enough."

My heart rate spikes with this information. "She was just worried about Remy."

"No, big brother." Shaking her head, she continues, "She was worried about *you*. It's the same reason she went off on you yesterday morning."

"Why are you telling me this, Dil?"

"Because you're a man and I know it's natural for you to be a little slow to realize things."

"And what should I be realizing?"

Sighing, she leans closer to me. "That girl cares about you, Henley. Not just Remy. She cares about *you*. That's why she was so upset with you when you didn't answer her texts. That's why she went off on you. But it seems to me like you're both too stubborn to admit what's happening between the two of you."

My blood is pumping so hard that I can hear it in my ears. My eyes are locked on my sister, and for a moment, I debate telling her about the kiss, about how I can't stop thinking about it.

But I decide not to—because until I know what I want to do about it, it needs to stay between me and Elodie. Hell, I don't even know how she feels about it. I know she kissed me back, I know that she was clawing at me just as desperately as I was at her, and I know that her eyes told me she wanted more when we were done.

But what happens next?

The physical attraction toward her has been fueling my decisions thus far. Now I need to decide if the emotional attraction is worth exploring too.

The truth is, I care about Elodie, and that's a foreign feeling for me. The small circle of people I let in is small for a reason: it means there's a reduced chance of being hurt. But can I make room for one more person in that group? And does Elodie even want that? Is it worth letting her in if she just plans on leaving anyway?

"Are you bringing Elodie to Fletcher's game in a few weeks?"

"I—I haven't decided yet. I asked him to secure a ticket for her but haven't asked her."

"I think you should. And I think you should show her that you care about her too." She lifts her eyebrow again, flashing me that knowing look. "Also, see if Carol and Nick want to watch Remy that weekend so you can get a little break."

"I don't need a break from her."

Dilynne puts her hand on top of mine. "Yes, you do. You might not think so, but Steven told me you need to make sure you get time away. I guess he and his wife make a point to do one outing a month just the two of them, no kids. Chelsea struggles with the guilt, but after they get that break, they always feel like better parents."

She releases my hand and stands from the swing. "Remember, I'm just trying to make sure you're taking care of yourself as well. Now, I'm going to practice holding my niece so one day you'll let me babysit her too."

I watch my sister move back inside the house, but I can't force myself to get up out of my chair yet.

Fuck. Maybe Dilynne is right. Maybe I do need a break. Maybe taking Elodie to the game without the baby will give us both a break.

And maybe Elodie's anger is her reaction to fighting her feelings as well.

That's when inspiration strikes, and I instantly know what I need to do.

Words may not be my forte, but actions are. And it's time to do something about these feelings and show her that I care, even if I'm risking a lot of pain in the process.

***

"Shit." Another splatter of pink paint hits my arm as I push the roller against the wall. Apparently, I forgot that less paint on the roller is better because this is the fourth time I've painted myself pink.

Twisting around, I peer down at Remy lying on her playmat, kicking and making noises, oblivious to what I'm going through. "I sure hope you like this room when it's done, baby bear, because I'm never painting it again."

It's just after five in the evening, and I've been in this spare bedroom since we got home from Carol and Nick's. As soon as Remy threw up on Dilynne and she freaked out, I knew that was my cue to leave and try to make a statement to my nanny.

The sound of the front door opening and closing alerts me that Elodie must be home.

Shit.

I was hoping to have this done, but painting a room while taking care of a four-month-old is no small feat.

"Henley?" Elodie calls out from the front of the house.

"I'm in Remy's room!"

Her footsteps travel down the hallway and when she finally peeks her head through the doorway, my heart lunges at the sight of her.

God, she's so fucking gorgeous—that long, dark hair, those gray eyes, and those lips that I can still taste. But she's so much more than her looks.

Her heart is so big that I'm afraid it might swallow me whole. Her sarcasm makes me want to know the next thing she's going to say, and she's so fucking smart that she makes me feel inadequate.

Yeah, this is so much more than physical attraction. I'm so fucking screwed.

I've never really looked at a woman beyond the physical need we could both satisfy for one another, but Elodie makes me question just how surface level my life has been until she and Remy entered it.

And now that she's back in my house, I can honestly say that I'm really fucking glad she's home.

"Henley? You do realize that half of you is covered in pink paint, right?"

"Yes, El. I'm aware."

She crosses her arms over her chest, smirking at me. "Okay, just making sure." Moving her eyes around the room, she asks, "What inspired this?"

I set the paint roller down in the tray and grab the rag off of the ladder, wiping paint from my skin while making my way over to her. Remy is still babbling, but Elodie and I are focused on each other.

"My daughter needs a room, like you said. So, I thought pink would be a good color, but I don't know what else to do." Shrugging, I reach out and gently tuck my fingers under Elodie's chin to keep her eyes on mine. "I—I need your help, Elodie, yet again."

There's such a loaded meaning to that statement, and when Elodie smiles up at me, I feel like I made the right decision today by finally doing something.

"Yes, I can help you, Henley," she says softly.

"Good." My eyes drop down to her lips, the strongest urge to kiss her again coming over me.

Remy starts to grow fussy on her playmat, which checks out. I usually get about ten to fifteen minutes before she's grown bored and needs something else to entertain her.

Elodie turns her attention to my daughter, bending over to pick her up from the floor. "Hey, baby bear. I missed you today," she says while placing a kiss on her chubby cheek. "Glad you seem to be doing better."

"She is. The medicine has done wonders for her mood, and Carol got her to nap for almost two hours earlier, thank God."

"Is that where you were? Carol and Nick's?"

"Yeah. We went over for breakfast. They wanted to see Remy for a bit and Dilynne is obsessed with Carol's cooking."

"Oh. Okay." Her shoulders fall slightly.

"Sorry I forgot to tell you about that yesterday, but with the ER visit and..." I don't want her to think I was avoiding her because she did anything wrong. I'm the one who did and I fucking hate if I've made her question that.

The smile she offers me is quick and small, but it's there. "It's fine, Henley. You're allowed to visit your family."

Our conversation comes to a halt, almost as if neither one of us knows what to say next. I hate this awkwardness, but the words aren't there. All I can focus on is the pounding in my chest while watching her hold my daughter and simultaneously wishing Remy was asleep so I could put my mouth on her on places other than her lips.

But I can't focus on the physical need anymore because this is so much more than that. And until I can put a name to it, I need to keep my hands and mouth to myself.

"Well, uh…I'm gonna try to get this room done before I pass out later," I say, tossing my thumb over my shoulder.

"Yeah. Good idea. Remy and I are just gonna hang out then, won't we, baby bear?" Elodie peers down at my daughter again before moving toward the door.

But before I can think twice, I blurt out, "Stay."

Elodie freezes. "What?"

"Stay, El. Please." I swallow roughly, the lump in my throat swelling as I read the confusion on her face. "Help me decide what else the room needs."

She licks her lips while she contemplates her decision. But when she moves toward the rocking chair and takes a seat, a wave of relief rolls through me. "I mean, I guess I could watch you attempt to get the paint on the wall instead of you. It's like free entertainment."

Elodie's comment makes me smirk as she holds and talks to my daughter. I turn back to my task and pick up our conversation like normal, hoping the control I found again today will last longer than it did last time.

Chapter 14

Elodie

Song Lyrics & An Orgasm

Your eyes say more than your mouth
Your touch says more than your eyes
And each time you look at me
All I can think about is goodbye

My hand is moving as fast as it can, trying to keep up with the words that came to me while I was cooking. As I scribble down the last line, the smell of something burning hits my nostrils.

"Shit!" Leaping from my chair at the dining room table, I rush to stir the soup on the stove and lower the heat, hoping the entire pot of my mom's chicken and rice soup isn't ruined. I take a spoon from the silverware drawer and taste it, relieved to find it still tastes the way it should.

I turn around and look over at Remy, who's banging her toy on her high chair tray. "I almost ruined dinner, baby bear." Her garbled response makes me laugh as I turn the heat on the burner to the lowest setting then return to my notebook, waiting for more inspiration to strike while simultaneously waiting for Henley to get home from the lodge.

The past few days have left me feeling both relieved and anxious. Walking into the house the other night and seeing Henley painting Remy's room made the butterflies living in my stomach multiply. They were already abuzz with excitement after that kiss, but knowing that my words the other morning must have gotten through to him made my feelings for this man sprout new roots. My anxiety is still lurking under the surface, though. Even though Henley and I seem to be on better terms, and his grumpiness has subsided a bit, he hasn't mentioned one word about our kiss.

The kiss.

The one I can't stop thinking about and may have touched myself to the thoughts of last night.

My hormones are out of control, reminding me of how long it's been since I've been with a man, and that's saying something because there haven't been many men to remember. But it's official: I'm lusting after my boss. And after that kiss, all I can think about is what other talents he possesses.

And there's that night we went to the ER. In his moment of need, when he was worried about his daughter and feeling powerless, he reached for *me*. He wanted *me* there to help him through it—and that's the part that's making these feelings build at lightning speed.

I'm just so terrified of what happens next because between his avoidance and my trust issues, I have no idea where we go from here. And apparently neither does he because we're both acting like nothing happened, and so far, it's working.

The sound of the front door unlocking pulls me from my thoughts, making me slam my notebook shut as fast as I can and going to the stove to check the soup.

"Fuck. What a day." Henley's voice carries to the kitchen, and I fight the goosebumps that travel down my arms from the sound of it while also wondering what happened to make him say that. Henley appears in the kitchen a few seconds later, leaning down to greet Remy. "Hey, baby bear. How's it going?"

My heart melts every time he uses the nickname I gave his daughter. Part of me wonders if he even realizes he's saying it.

"She's been so much happier today. I think the antibiotics have done their job and our happy little girl is back," I tell him.

"Glad to hear it." He comes up behind me, pressing his chest into my back as he opens the cabinet above me and takes out a cup. My breath stalls as he does, but he's gone as quickly as he came. "What did you make for dinner tonight?"

"Um...my mom's chicken and wild rice soup."

"It smells incredible. I've only had a sandwich today, so I'm starving."

"Busy day?"

He pushes a hand through his hair and that's when I take a moment to finally assess his appearance. His shirt has streaks of dirt on it, his boots are covered in mud, and the lines around his eyes look deeper, like he's severely lacking energy. The sudden urge to sit down and have him lay his head in my lap as he tells me all about it comes over me.

"Well, one of the pipes burst that leads to our main restrooms, so Warren and I had to find the leak, go to the hardware store, and replace it. This meant that customers had to use the employee restrooms all day. Then a kid broke his arm on the obstacle course, which made his parents threaten to sue me..."

"Can they do that?"

"No, because all parents and adults sign a release form before they get on the course or slopes." He lets out a heavy sigh. "And then there was just a bunch of little shit that piled on top of that. Let's just say I'm happy to be home with my girls."

My girls.

God, hearing him say that shouldn't make my heart flutter like it does.

"Well, would you like a beer with dinner to help wind down?"

He shakes his head, holding up his water glass. "I decided to stop drinking for a while."

"Oh." I wonder what led to that decision, but this is Henley we're talking about, so it doesn't surprise me that he offers no further explanation. And I've certainly learned not to ask. "Well, wash up and let's eat. I'm hungry, too."

After I dish out two large bowls and fill the bread basket with fresh biscuits, we sit at the table to eat. Henley's quiet for a beat before he speaks again. "So... I wanted to ask you something," he starts.

"Okay..."

"The boys and I are going to Charlotte next weekend to watch Fletcher play. Laney and Dilynne will be there too," he explains, squirming in his chair a bit before clearing his throat. "And, uh...I was wondering if..."

I can't tell if he's nervous or anxious about what he needs to ask me. "You okay over there?" I tease him, to which his response is a glare followed by a quirk of his lips.

"Yeah, I just... Well, Dilynne said I should get a break from Remy and..." He moves his spoon around his bowl, but doesn't take a bite.

"You need me to watch her?" I finish for him. "I'd be more than happy to. That is what you pay me for, remember?"

"Fuck," he grumbles, dropping his spoon from his hand and adjusting himself in his chair. "No, I don't want you to watch her, El." His eyes finally meet mine. "I was wondering if you'd like to come with us."

"So I can watch Remy? Sure."

He licks his lips, diverting his gaze for a moment before returning his eyes to me. "Carol and Nick are going to watch her."

It takes me a moment to figure out what he's implying. "You—you want me to go with you to the game *without* Remy?"

"If you want to," he says, but there's something about the look in his eyes that has me spiraling.

"Do *you* want me to?"

His eyes become darker somehow, laser-focused on me when he finally says, "Yeah. I do."

The tone of his voice almost sounds like he's commanding me to go, and I can't deny that it makes my body heat up even more than it was already when he walked through the door. But the idea of us spending time together without Remy there makes the line of our relationship grow even more blurred.

Uh, didn't the kiss already do that, Elodie?

"Okay. I'd love to." I'm smiling on the outside as I pick my spoon back up, but my heart is racing. "Thanks for the invite. That should be fun. It's been years since I've been to a game."

He scoffs, but there's a hint of a smile on his lips. "Yeah, but then you're also going to be subjected to my friend group in all its glory, and I'm not sure if that's a good thing."

"I already met Elliot and Rhonan at the winery, remember?"

"Yeah, but they weren't on their worst behavior. When Rhonan doesn't have Ellis and there's a suite with endless booze involved, things can take a turn."

"I'm sure I'll be fine, but I've been meaning to ask you something too. The next yoga night at the winery is coming up. Are you planning on going?"

He taps his phone on the table. "It's been on my calendar since the last one."

"That's adorable. I'd like to go with you because it's been a while since I've done it and would love to get back in the routine. Could we find someone to watch Remy that night? Maybe Carol?"

His smile falls as he stares at me, and I wish I could tell what he's thinking right now. Fortunately, he blinks, returns back to his soup and we sit there, finishing our dinner while Remy watches us.

"Yeah, I can ask her. And Laney runs a good class so I'm sure you'll enjoy it." Henley pushes his bowl to the side, rubbing his stomach through his shirt. "That was fucking delicious, El. Thank you."

"You're welcome. Now, would you like to see the ideas I came up with for Remy's room?"

He wipes his mouth with his napkin and tosses it into the empty bowl. "Yeah. Let's see what you've got."

Henley wasn't able to finish painting Remy's room Sunday night, but that gave me time to scour the internet to put together a few options for décor and a theme. Honestly, it took me longer than it should have because I kept getting inspired to write song lyrics, so I was wavering between the two tasks for the past two days.

"Okay, let me show you what I found online," I say, pulling out my phone and scooting my chair closer to him, which only makes his scent hit me harder.

God, he smells like cedar and laundry detergent. Why is that combination so comforting and tempting at the same time?

Ignoring the effect this man's scent is having on me, I start swiping through my phone and show the first option to him, a room with elephants. Next is a Victorian-style option, very princess-like. And the last one, which is my personal favorite for obvious reasons, has a forest theme with bears.

"What do you think?"

Henley casts his glance over to Remy as she lets out a yawn from her high chair. "I'm pretty sure it's obvious." His eyes find mine again. "The bears."

We smile at each other, and seeing a genuine smile from this man makes me feel ten feet tall. "I thought so too but just wanted to give you options."

Henley stands from his chair and grabs Remy. "I'm gonna get my daddy-daughter time in, put her to bed, and then I'll be back out in a little bit."

"Sounds great. Goodnight, Remy." I watch him walk down the hall, admiring the way his jeans hug his ass, then snap myself out of my stare and clean up the kitchen, even though I know Henley will get mad at me for it.

As I scrub the pot I cooked the soup in, the disappointment I've been shoving down for the past few days makes itself known again.

Tonight felt like we were slipping right back into our routine, boss and employee, father and nanny, friends for lack of a better term. So I guess he's just going to pretend like the kiss didn't happen, which is fine. It's probably better this way. Less messy, right?

When I'm finished, I grab my notebook and take a seat back on the couch, tucking my legs up underneath me and opening it back up to the page with the lyrics I was working on earlier.

Your eyes say more than your mouth
Your touch says more than your eyes
And each time you look at me
All I can think about is our inevitable goodbye.

A few more words come to me, so I add them to the page.

But what if this didn't have an end?
What if you decided to let me in?
I know you can be that man
This could be where we begin.

Setting my notebook to the side, I race to my room and grab my guitar so I can try to find a melody to go with the words. The last thing I should be doing is writing a song about my feelings for my boss, but I strum a few chords until I find one that I like and attempt to sing the words softly so as not to disturb Remy's bedtime routine.

I know that you're scared
Because I'm scared too.
You have the power to destroy me
And I can do the same to you.
But we can be scared together
Just put your hand in mine.
Or are these feelings fleeting
Because we're on borrowed time?

I'm so lost in the melody and words that I don't realize how much time has passed until Henley is standing right next to me, fresh from the shower, his eyebrows pinched together. "You're working on a song," he observes.

I have to crane my neck back to look up at him. "I am."

"I don't think I've seen you do that since you moved in."

I set my guitar to the side and close my notebook, resting it on my lap as he takes a seat on the opposite end of the couch. "That's because I haven't. I've been playing music for Remy, but I haven't been able to write since I left LA."

"Why did you?" he asks, resting his head in his hand propped up on the back of the couch.

"Why did I what?"

"Leave Los Angeles," he clarifies.

Avoiding his gaze, I say, "I told you. I'm trying to figure out if a career in music is what I really want."

"No, I think there's more to it than that."

My head snaps to him again. "What makes you say that?"

"Maybe that's why you haven't been able to write."

"Well, struggling with this decision is probably part of it."

"But I think there's another reason too, the one that's tied to your panic attack." My throat grows tight and tension builds in my shoulders. "Dilynne mentioned it when she was worried that you hadn't texted her back. And it wasn't before you performed, it was after, correct?" I don't say anything because my pulse is fluttering rapidly in my neck, so he takes it as permission to keep pushing. "So it wasn't performance anxiety. Something else triggered it."

Diverting my gaze, I grate out, "I really don't want to talk about it, Henley."

"Yeah, well there's a lot of shit that I don't like talking about either, but I'm realizing how much it's affecting me."

I turn back to face him, shaking my head. "Wow. That's great. I'm happy for you. But I don't think this conversation is appropriate between a boss and his employee." Standing from the couch, I attempt to walk away, but Henley reaches out and gently grasps my arm, stopping me. His touch singes my skin and my breathing picks up.

"There are a lot of things that are happening between us that aren't appropriate, El." The gravel of his voice travels down my spine as he slowly stands, putting his chest against my back and still holding my arm in his hand as his thumb passes back and forth over my skin. "Like me kissing you the other night. That was highly *inappropriate*, don't you think?" His breath skates across my neck, making a shiver run across my skin and hope surges through me.

Oh my God, he's bringing up our kiss.

The only thing I can focus on is taking in oxygen because the rest of my body feels paralyzed. But he's pissed me off now, which means sassy Elodie is ready to showcase her skills.

"So, we're gonna talk about that finally?" I quip.

"You didn't bring it up either," he fires back.

"Well, you're not the easiest man to talk to. The king of avoidance, some might say."

His hand moves up my arm and onto my shoulder as he toys with the hem of my tank top. "You're right. And that's exactly why I ran away from you that night, Elodie." He drags his nose up my neck. My eyes close instantly, savoring every second of his touch. God, it feels so good to be touched by someone that I *want* to touch me—not a man who thinks I owe him my body.

"The night I went out with Warren," he starts, his lips ghosting the shell of my ear. "I saw you singing to Remy and that's why I left so suddenly. I couldn't handle how it made me feel, so I ran."

"Henley," I say on a gasp. "I thought..."

"I know what you thought." His teeth nip my earlobe and my bottom lip trembles. "You told me so when you yelled at me the next morning. But here's the thing, Elodie. My actions have never been about my reluctance to accept my daughter in my life. Truth be told, becoming Remy's father was something I barely fought. *You* are what's made me want to run, sweetheart."

His words.

I'm finally getting words from this man and they're making so many puzzle pieces start to snap into place. So I give him mine in return.

"I was jealous," I say, looping my arm around his neck, holding him to me as he continues to toy with my ear and moves his lips back to my neck. "I hated the idea of you going out and kissing or touching another woman, especially after you told me that's how you chase adrenaline now."

"Jesus, El. Why didn't you say so?"

"It's not easy to be open with you, Henley. And then you kissed me breathless, and just...never said another word."

"Then let me be clear when I say this." He inhales deeply and then his voice vibrates across my skin as he continues. "You don't need to be jealous of anyone else...because the only woman I'm interested in—*is you*."

"Finally, some honesty from you," I whisper while digging my nails into his hair and feeling my pulse rise yet again.

I'm standing here in this man's arms and every nerve on my body is awake. Part of me wonders if I'm dreaming, but then I feel him press his erection into my back and I know without a doubt that this is real.

Dear lord, I want to feel all of him.

His voice is a mix between a groan and a growl. "God it makes me fucking hard when you call me on my shit."

I turn to face him. "See? It's a good thing I know how to use *my* words."

He presses his cock into my stomach, smirking as he says, "Oh, you certainly have a way with words, Elodie Olsen, and I'm beginning to think I don't just *want* your voice in my life, I *need* it." I'm temporarily awestruck because I think that's one of the most beautiful things a man has ever said to me in one of the most erotic moments of my life.

"You drive me fucking mad, El. You make me feel shit I've never had to put a name to. I told you that you wouldn't want to know what's going through my head because all I can think about is kissing you again, tasting you in other places than your mouth, and what those pretty little lips would look like wrapped around my cock before you gagged on it. Is that what you wanted to hear?"

"Who knew that dirty talk was how I would get the truth out of you?"

His laughter vibrates against my skin. "Fuck." His lips press against my temple. "But you deserve better than a fast and hard fuck. You deserve to be worshipped, and for the first time in my life, I want to take my time."

Those words douse the lust rushing through me, replacing it with admiration. I wrap my arms around his neck. "I'm not sure what to say to that."

His forehead touches mine, our noses brushing. I almost make a joke about how far he has to bend down to do that, but I refrain when I can hear the emotional pain lacing his words. "Just tell me that I'm not the only one who wanted that kiss."

"You're not," I whisper immediately.

"Thank fuck." When he lowers his head again, his lips brush mine in a kiss that is much sweeter than our first one, and Henley stays true to his word—he takes his time.

As he teases me with his mouth, I try to remember the last time I was ever kissed like this, and the answer comes to me quickly—never. I've never been kissed the way Henley kisses me, and that makes me terrified that I might never experience it again. "So, what happens now?" I ask breathlessly when we part.

"Now, you tell me the truth about LA."

I lean back as my eyebrows pull together, Henley standing to his full height. "Was all of that physical manipulation just now?"

"No. It's me asking you to talk first so that it might be easier for me to talk next."

Ugh, this frustratingly beautiful, scarred man.

I roll my eyes, but inside I think this man has officially made me melt. "Okay."

He leads me to the couch, pulling me close to him so I'm practically sitting in his lap. "What on earth happened that made you have a panic attack when you were with my sister?"

My eyes find my hands in my lap, twiddling my fingers as I prepare to tell Henley the same story I told the girls. "I guess I just realized how young and naïve I was about what it takes to make your dreams come true."

"Uh, uh." Henley tips my chin up so our eyes connect. "Don't talk about yourself like that. You're not naïve, Elodie. You have natural instincts that most grown adults don't, and trust me, I've seen the worst of the worst doing what I do for a living. You're witty and joyful, not too young. Hell, you make me smile and that's a feat in itself. Only someone who really has a way with words can do that."

I try to fight my smile, but it's no use. "A compliment from Henley Clark? I think I should document this moment so I never forget."

He tickles my ribs, making me squeal. "Watch it. Gorilla man can still appear at any time."

"Who?"

He shakes his head. "Never mind. Continue."

As I rehash the events that led to me leaving Los Angeles, I find it difficult to gauge Henley's reaction. His face is stoic and his jaw is hard, which isn't much different from how he normally looks. But when I get to the night at The Charming Bull and brace for his response, he asks a question I wasn't expecting.

"What's Liam's last name?"

"Uh...why does that matter?"

"Just tell me."

Narrowing my eyes at him, I say, "Henley, you are not going to get all murdery like your sister."

He arches a brow at me. "The two of us *are* related, sweetheart, which means we share a lot of the same tendencies."

I place one hand on his shoulder and frame his face with the other. "I'm okay."

"You had a panic attack because of what some stranger said to you, and it was triggered by a man forcing himself on you. None of that is okay, Elodie."

"I know, but I'm working through it."

He frames my face with his hands now, his hazel eyes boring into mine. "You know I would never do that, right?"

"Yes, Henley. I know that."

He brushes his nose against mine again. "I want you to feel safe with me."

"I do. Safer than I've felt in a long time."

"Good."

"Okay. Now it's your turn, Henley."

Leaning back, he creates distance between us and lays his head on the back of the couch, staring up at the ceiling. "I don't know if I can yet, El."

"I think you can, but I'll give you time if that's what you need. Just know that when you're ready, I'm here to listen."

"My story? What's made me so closed off from feelings?" He blows out a breath. "It's long and makes me so fucking mad that the idea of sharing it gives me the urge to hit something."

I rest my head on his shoulder. "Then don't tell me the whole thing. Tell me one part, one piece that will help me get to know you better. That's all I'm asking."

Henley is quiet for so long that I wonder if he truly isn't ready for this. But when his words come out, my heart breaks. "I didn't eat for almost an entire week when I was ten."

I lift my head to see the pain etched in the lines of his face, but his eyes remain locked above him. "Henley…"

"My parents left for six days. They left a ten- and eight-year-old alone for six days with no food in the house. It was summer, so I couldn't depend on school food to get us by. I stole a loaf of bread and a jar of peanut butter from a gas station and fed Dilynne peanut butter sandwiches for an entire week. And she didn't complain once."

My eyes well with tears.

"Survival was all I could focus on. When my parents finally came home, they yelled at me because there wasn't any bread left. And when they went to the store, they bought me a box of cereal and told me and Dilynne to make it last." I rest my head back on his shoulder as my tears fall, landing on his shirt and making the fabric wet. "That was the moment I realized how much I hated them." He goes silent again, so I let him. We sit there on the couch until I feel the tension leave his shoulders as he exhales.

"Thank you for sharing that with me," I whisper.

"Why? So now you know how fucked up I really am?"

I straighten and turn his face toward mine. "No. Because it proves you're so much stronger than I already knew you were."

Our eyes bounce back and forth between each other, and then suddenly, Henley is sliding me onto his lap, my legs draped around his hips. He buries his hands in my hair and studies my face, toying with my bottom lip with his thumb before pulling my mouth to his.

And we drown in each other.

I feel weightless, yet heavy at the same time, this physical need pushing down on me, building pressure between my legs. I know that

Henley said he wanted to take things slow with me, but my body is protesting the idea, and my hips start moving over him in a leisurely rhythm, testing the waters.

"Elodie..."

"I'm so horny, Henley," I moan, pushing down on him harder. "I've been pent up for weeks and God..." Closing my eyes, I pick up my pace, gyrating my hips over him faster. "I just need a release."

He leans back but tightens his hold in my hair. "Then use me. Let me watch you get off."

"What about you?"

Shaking his head, he says, "This isn't about me. Not tonight."

"Henley..."

He drops one of his hands to my hips, prompting me to keep moving. I can feel how hard he is beneath me, the flimsy fabric of his athletic shorts and my soft denim the only barriers between us. "Fuck, take your shorts off," he rasps, guiding me to stand and reaching for the button on my jean shorts, releasing it and helping me push them down.

My eyes fall to his erection tenting his shorts. Licking my lips, I shimmy out of my shorts, standing there in a plain white tank top and yellow lace thong.

Henley's gaze drags over me, his voice rough. "God, you're perfect."

I return to his lap, straddling him again and positioning myself so that his length lines up perfectly with my slit, the wetness on my underwear seeping right into his shorts.

"I can feel how fucking wet you are, El, how needy you are."

"I told you." Bracing my hands on his shoulders, I find my pace again and moan out loud from the difference in sensation of not having as thick of a barrier between us.

He closes his eyes, tips his head back, and groans. "Fuck, Elodie. Keep using me, sweetheart."

Our heavy breathing fills the room as I work my clit against him, wishing he was inside of me instead, wondering if him stretching me open with his cock would teeter on that line of pleasure and pain, given his size.

"Jesus, give me that mouth." He pops his head up and pulls my lips back to his as I rub my clit along his length, fighting for the friction I need to find my release and moving faster as I search for it. Those first familiar tingles appear and then I break free from his mouth, fighting for air as I feel myself get closer to the edge, pressing my cheek against his.

I whisper in his ear, "Yes...yes, Henley. I'm—I'm gonna come."

"Fuck, fuck!" he grates out as my dull cries muffle his groans, my hands burying in his hair as I clench around him, riding out the waves of my release and wishing it would never end.

When my body finally starts to relax, Henley's head is resting on the center of my chest, my hands holding him there. "Holy shit..."

A tremor races through him. "Fuck, El."

When I lean back and he follows suit, I peer down at him, smiling softly. "Well, that just happened."

His chuckle is reassuring before he points down to his shorts. "Yeah, that just happened too."

The wet spot in the fabric has me puzzled until realization clicks. "Did you..."

"Pretty sure I was a teenager the last time this happened, so be proud."

I'm not gonna lie, I kind of am. "You sure that's not just from me?"

"No, sweetheart. You made me come just from feeling you, watching you, and hearing you get off." He drags his nose up my neck. "And I've never experienced anything so...fucking...sexy."

My body is still wired from the physical release, but my mind is humming too.

"What is happening between us, Henley? What does this mean?" I whisper, afraid of what his response will be. But I need to know.

I'm not going to let this be something we brush under the rug like our kiss.

He sweeps my hair from my face, tucks a strand behind my ear, and surveys my entire face before answering. But the wait is worth the response. "It means that for the first time in my life, I'm letting myself feel something instead of running from it, and all I'm asking is that you let me while I figure out the rest."

Chapter 15

Elodie

Mud Tunnels & NFL Suites

"Thanks for offering to bring me lunch today." Laney unwraps her sandwich from The Happy Belly Deli, smiling at me from the seat to my right.

We're at a table in the break room of her salon, having lunch together since I needed someone to talk to and she has a fully booked schedule all week. I didn't just want to call or text her for advice because I feel like what's happened between me and Henley over the past five days requires a face-to-face conversation.

Remy drains the rest of her bottle, so I move her to my shoulder to burp her. "No problem at all. I appreciate you making time for a lunch."

"Well, you said you needed some advice and I'm not sure I can be of any help, but I can try."

"If this advice you need is about men, you should be talking to me, honey." Glenn, one of Laney's employees, interrupts our conversation from the doorway of the break room. He nods in Laney's direction. "This one over here used to call Fletcher 'Lucifer' until she realized that his dick could tempt her to sell her soul, so I wouldn't be so sure she's the expert when it comes to men."

Remy lets out a remarkably loud burp. Laney points to the baby. "I echo Remy's response. No one asked you, Glenn."

He leans against the doorway with a smirk. "I know, but I felt compelled to offer my two cents."

"But your expertise is in gay men, Glenn. Otherwise, I might just take you up on that."

He shrugs. "Honey, gay and straight men aren't really all that different. Put a finger in a man's mud tunnel and they'll be coming in seconds. I find that solves most problems."

Laney starts choking as my jaw drops, watching Glenn walk right back out of the room.

I turn to my friend, patting her on the back. "Are you okay?"

"I should have known better than to take a bite of my sandwich while he was talking," Laney manages to croak out, reaching for her bottle of water and draining half of it, trying to clear her throat. "Jesus Christ."

"I'm so glad that Remy doesn't understand words or repeat them yet because trying to explain that to Henley would be a nightmare."

Laney loses her composure, laughing while still coughing. "Oh God. I can't handle this right now."

Once the two of us get all of our giggles out, I place Remy back in the stroller and reach for my sandwich, finally. "I think I've forgotten why I even came here at this point."

Laney mumbles around a mouthful of food. "Well, before I forget, there was something I wanted to talk to you about too."

"All right. Shoot."

Laney swallows and then takes a drink of her water. "The winery hosts a Concert in the Courtyard each month and the act I booked in November had to cancel, unfortunately." My heart starts to race when I realize where this conversation is going. "Is there any way you'd be interested in performing?"

"I think it's my turn to choke," I say, clearing my throat so I don't start coughing. "You—you want me to do an entire set? Like...by myself?"

Laney nods, sitting up taller in her chair. "Yes, if you're interested. Dilynne mentioned that you are one hell of a performer, and she might have shown me a video she took of you at The Charming Bull."

"Oh, joy."

Laney laughs. "Look, I have another band I could call, but I figured I'd offer it to you first. Given your situation, I thought it might be a good way to dip your toes back into music with very little pressure. Plus, the locals love supporting our own, and everyone knows you're Henley's nanny now, so I'm sure the whole town will show up."

"I thought you said no pressure." I drag my palms down my thighs, trying to wipe away the sudden clamminess.

Laney's smile softens, her eyes warm with understanding. "Seriously, just think about it, but could you let me know by next week maybe? That way, I can still contact a replacement if you decide against it."

Blowing out a breath, I reply, "Yes. I can do that."

"Great. Now, you said that you needed some advice..."

"Oh, yeah." Wiping my mouth with my napkin, I adjust myself in my seat. "Not that I don't appreciate Dilynne's perspective on things, but since this pertains to her brother, I wanted a more neutral opinion."

"So this is about Henley?"

"Yeah." I bite my bottom lip before whispering, "He sort of kissed me this past weekend."

Laney's eyes widen in shock. "Oh my God."

"Yeah, and there's been a bit of…touching since then," I say, feeling my cheeks flame from the admission. I quickly add, "Nothing crazy! In fact, most of our clothes have stayed on."

Laney waggles her eyebrows. "Oh! Scandalous."

I roll my eyes. "Very high school, I know. But he was insistent about it."

That makes Laney's jaw drop. "Really?"

"Yeah." I take some time to explain what's happened from the kiss to where we are now, and just a little over a week away from traveling to Charlotte together for Fletcher's game without Remy as a buffer.

"Part of me so desperately wants to push him for more, but I also know that he has to do this on his own time. I'm just terrified of getting hurt. You heard Dilynne. She said I'm his type. The man hasn't had sex in months probably, and he's used to consistent action, so I'm sure that the physical aspect is a driving force here."

Laney tilts her head to the side, reaching for my hand. "Elodie, I want you to really hear me when I say this." I brace myself for what she's about to say. "Henley has never looked at a woman the way he looks at you."

My stomach flips, then dread rushes back in. "But I'm leaving…"

"Well, is there a scenario where you don't?"

"Music is still such a big part of my life, Laney. It's all I've ever wanted." Closing my eyes, I say, "I can still remember the first time I picked up a guitar and what that felt like." When I open my eyes again, Laney is watching me. "But being with Henley for the past two months, living with him and taking care of Remy, has shown me this entirely different side of life that I want too."

"Well, if the man is opening up to you, I think you owe it to yourself to see what's there. You don't have to be back in Los Angeles by Christmas, do you?"

"No. My lease was up with my roommates. The deadline was self-imposed so I wouldn't stall on making a decision."

"Then maybe the timeline you gave Henley doesn't really matter if you're still figuring things out. Don't tell him that, though." She taps her chin in thought. "No, I'd see how things pan out. Sometimes all we need is time to push us into taking action. That certainly was the case with me and Fletcher."

I pop a chip in my mouth. "You know, I haven't heard the full story of how the two of you got together yet. I've gotten bits and pieces, but I'd love to hear it from you. I mean, you're living out many women's fantasy."

Laney laughs. "Which is?"

"Marrying a professional athlete. There's a reason why that trope works so well in romance novels, girl."

"Yeah, well, I fell for Fletcher Adams long before he was one of the top wide receivers in the league, long before he was the man he is today." She lets out a wistful sigh. "But I think being able to know that version of him and the man he is now makes it even more fulfilling because I know how hard he's fought to become who he is today."

Her words hit me hard. Is that what Henley is embarking on right now? That same journey? And do I want to be around to watch it?

Or should I focus on my own path and the journey I've been working toward for myself?

***

"God, it smells amazing in here." Henley's voice is by my ear before I realize he's home, causing me to nearly jump out of my skin.

"Jesus Christ!" Swatting at him over my shoulder, I twist to find him smirking down at me before he leans down to place a kiss on my lips.

"Sorry. I thought you heard me."

"Normally I do," I say truthfully, but I know why I wasn't paying attention—because between the sound of the water running in the sink and my mental recollection of the words to another song that I wrote this afternoon, I certainly wasn't aware of my surroundings.

Luckily, Remy has been content in her high chair while I checked out.

I reach for the kitchen towel on the counter, wiping my hands dry. "I made lasagna. It's my—"

"Mother's recipe," he finishes for me. "Seems to me that your mom had a lot of recipes."

"I told you. Her philosophy was that homemade was always better."

He kisses me softly again, cupping my jaw. "She obviously knew something since nothing you've cooked for me so far has tasted like garbage."

"I think that was supposed to be a compliment, but I'm not sure."

Henley chuckles. "It was." Releasing me from his hold, he walks over to his daughter and extracts her from the high chair. "And how is my baby bear tonight? Did you have a good day with Elodie?" He tosses her up in the air once, making her squeal.

My cheeks are burning from how hard I'm smiling, but I can't help it. When Henley smiles, so do I.

After my lunch the other day with Laney, I decided to take things one day at a time. Her point about my timeline has also been at the forefront of my mind, that I do have the choice to stick to it or not. And while I decide on that, I want to support Henley. He seems so different since that night when we admitted the feelings developing between us. He's smiling more, cracking more jokes, and I won't lie and say that I haven't enjoyed the kisses and orgasm.

Yes, only the one. Even though I've pressed him for more, he's insisted that we take things slowly, which my libido continues to protest.

Instead of dry humping each other every night, we've spent a few hours each evening putting the finishing touches on Remy's room. The bear decals finally arrived in the mail, so the entire theme is complete. The bears have pink bows on their heads too, which totally brings the color of the walls out. Henley has finished putting all of the furniture together, and I've been organizing clothes by size, preparing for the upcoming winter season, and organizing toys and other items in her closet. Her room is almost complete and the admiration I feel for Henley for finally getting it done has been hard to contain.

Luckily, I've had a mental distraction of whether or not I'm going to agree to perform at Laney's family's winery in a few weeks, even though my heart is leaning toward saying yes. In fact, as I was writing my song today, I realized just how much I've missed that aspect, and it would be the perfect opportunity to debut some new lyrics.

"She's been a little cranky today. I think that tooth on the bottom gums is really affecting her."

Henley frowns at his daughter. "Well, that's just unacceptable, huh, baby bear?" His eyes find mine. "Did you give her anything?"

"A little bit of Tylenol earlier, which seemed to help because about twenty minutes later she passed out for two hours."

"Well, at least she got a nap."

"I'm convinced that's the only reason why she's in a decent mood right now."

Henley carries her over to the living room, setting her down on the floor in her Bumbo chair that allows her to sit up on her own. He lowers himself to the ground and then reads a book to her, making my heart melt even more for this man.

After we eat, clean up the kitchen, bathe Remy, and shower ourselves, Henley insists on putting Remy to bed on his own. We moved her crib into her room tonight, so he's nervous about not having her sleeping with him, even though he hasn't outwardly admitted it. But I think it's adorable.

I'm sitting on the couch, flipping through Netflix, trying to find a movie for us to watch when my phone vibrates next to me. My mom's name flashes on the screen and I momentarily debate not answering it. I haven't spoken on the phone with her since I moved to Blossom Peak. In fact, the last time we texted a few weeks ago, she asked me how L.A. was, and I told her things were great.

Obviously, I lied.

"Hello?" I answer, trying to keep my voice low.

"Elodie? Why are you whispering?"

"Um, I—" Struggling to come up with an excuse, I sigh and decide it's time to tell the truth. "I don't want to wake up my boss's kid."

Her silence is eerie. "I'm sorry, did you just say your boss's *kid*?"

"Yeah..."

"Elodie Anne Olsen, you'd better fill me in on what you mean by that right now."

Sighing, I lean back further into the couch cushions. "I'm not in L.A., Mom. I'm in Blossom Peak. I'm nannying for this guy and..."

"Does this mean you're done trying to make it as a singer?" The tone of her voice is more optimistic than concerned. A supportive parent would wonder why I'm giving up—even though that's not what I'm doing—but still. Sometimes I wish my parents would just support me because that's what they're supposed to do, regardless of whether they understand what I want for my life or not.

"No, I'm just taking a break."

It's her turn to sigh. "Elodie, let's call this what it is—you are finally realizing that music is not a stable career and…"

"I didn't realize that. My lease was up on the house I was renting, and I wanted a break."

"So why not come home?"

"Jeez, Mom. Why do you think? So you can stand right in front of me and look me in the eyes while you tell me that my dreams are stupid?"

Henley walks down the hall, his brows drawn together as he takes in only my side of this conversation.

"Does this mean you'll be home for Thanksgiving and Christmas?" my mom asks, ignoring what I just said.

"I—I don't know yet." Henley takes a seat on the couch next to me. "Look, this has been a great talk, but I've got to go."

"Elodie, I just want you to have a secure future, honey. You could open a daycare like I did. The money is nice and you love kids. You said you're a nanny now? I could totally see you being happy doing that."

The truth is, I am happy taking care of Remy, but that's the last thing I want to say to her right now.

I close my eyes and pinch the bridge of my nose. "I know, Mom. I just—I haven't made any concrete decisions yet, okay? And I'm sorry that I didn't tell you sooner, but…"

"I understand, honey, even though I don't." *Wow, way to make sense, Mom.* "But Blossom Peak, huh?"

"Yeah, our trips here as a kid were always my favorite, so I was hoping that being back here would help me get clarity."

"Well, I hope you find what you're looking for there, Elodie. But you know that home is just a short drive from there if you need to regroup."

"Thanks, Mom."

"Let me know about the holidays, okay?"

"I will." When I end the call, I look up to find Henley watching me. "My mom..."

"I gathered that." The crease in his brow is still there. "What did she say?"

"Well, since I hadn't told her I've been in Blossom Peak for the past two months..."

"Your mom didn't know you were here?"

"No, Henley. What part of my parents aren't supportive of my music career did you not understand?"

He holds a hand up. "Hey, I'm just trying to understand what's going on..."

I pinch the bridge of my nose. "I'm sorry. You don't deserve me snapping at you, I just—" A heavy sigh escapes me. "Every time I talk to her, there's always this voice in the back of my mind that wonders if she and my dad are right—that I need to just throw in the towel and get a regular job."

He pulls me into his arms and situates me so I'm straddling him, a position that I haven't been in since the night I dry humped him. And all this position is doing is making me think about that night, not the conversation with my mom.

"I want to say that I understand, but I don't. I didn't have parents that cared at all, El. In fact, at one point, I stopped caring too."

Remembering the lack of concern he got from his parents makes me feel guilty for being irritated by mine. "Do—do you know what happened to them?"

He shakes his head. "No. Dilynne and I made a promise to each other to never go looking for the answer."

"I don't know if I could do that, if I could live my life without knowing if they were dead or alive."

He stares up at me, pushing my hair behind my ear. "That's because you have parents who love you, who were there every day while you were growing up. When you have to raise yourself, you begin to realize there are other things that matter more. Dilynne was the only person I was concerned about. In fact, I still am from time to time because the girl does like to push boundaries."

I laugh. "I can only imagine."

"But that's not to say that you should feel any sort of obligation to them for how you live your life just because they were there. If Nick and Carol had told me not to buy the ski lodge, I wouldn't have listened to them."

"Really? I thought..."

"Did they take in me and my sister when we needed them? Yes. But I don't owe them anything for that." His statement has me confused, because he almost sounds like there's a double meaning to his words. "The only opinion that matters is mine, and therefore, yours. You're the one that has to look yourself in the mirror every day and like the person looking back at you."

"Do *you* like the person you see in the mirror, Henley?" For a second, I wonder if the question crossed a line, but he surprises me with his answer.

"No," he says, his eyes locked on mine before they move across my face and down my neck. "The man I see in the mirror has a lot of growing up to do. He's got to own the mess he's made with his emotions, take responsibility for the shit he's been running from." His grip tightens on my waist, pulling me flush against him, and I feel him growing hard beneath me. "He's also a man that wants to defile his nanny, even though he promised to be on his best behavior."

"I think his nanny would very much like to be defiled."

He licks a trail up my neck, nibbling at my earlobe and sending tremors through me. "The first time I fuck you, I want to know that you're ready for it."

"I promise, I'm ready," I pant, grateful for the change in topic because the ache between my legs has been intensifying for days and getting harder to ignore. "Please, Henley..."

He hums as he closes his eyes. "Fuck, don't start begging, sweetheart. I'm not going to be able to control myself."

I grind my pussy against his cock. "Is that what you've been doing since you kissed me? Controlling yourself?"

"You have no idea how much," he grates out.

Leaning back with his hands still on my hips, I say words I've wanted to since the night of our admissions. "Well, how about you show me what it looks like when you lose control?"

The clench in his jaw is so sexy that I have to force myself not to strip him down myself and ride him until we're both screaming. My sex drive has been non-existent for months, but Henley has made me want to be vulnerable again, to seek out pleasure with someone who makes me feel comfortable.

And even though I feel like we've been walking on eggshells around each other for weeks, I now know it's because Henley's been fighting this just as hard as I have.

But I don't care about the consequences anymore.

I see the moment his decision flashes through his eyes. Then he's lifting me in his arms and setting me on my feet before loosening the drawstring of my sweats. "This is about you, not me. Got it?"

I nod, breathless, watching him pull my pants from my legs and throw them across the room before guiding me back down onto the couch and pushing my legs open, dropping to his knees in front of me. "I'm gonna lick this pussy clean, and then you're going to bed before I take things too far."

"Why?"

"Because I don't trust myself not to, and you deserve better than that." He peers up at me from the floor. "We both do. This is different with you, Elodie."

Even though I want to argue with him, I know he's right. With the way I'm feeling right now, I'd probably let this man do anything he wants to me, but that's not the smart way to approach this shift in our dynamic. And he's right that this is different—everything about my connection with him is surreal.

"Okay," I answer him as he drops his nose to my underwear and presses his face against me.

"Fuck, El. I can't wait to taste you."

"Yes, please. God, Henley. Touch me."

He looks up at me, his head still between my legs and the sight alone of him in this position is almost enough to make me come. My body is shaking, my underwear drenched from my arousal, and I know without a doubt that this orgasm is going to come on fast.

At least I hope. Sometimes I've had trouble arriving, especially during oral and I don't want to disappoint him. My knees start to close as my mind spirals, but Henley presses them open wider.

"Get out of your head, Elodie. Trust me, okay? I know how to make you feel good. Put that other shit out of your mind. Stay in the moment with me, sweetheart."

My chest loosens from his words. "Okay."

He reaches for the strings at my hips and slowly slides my underwear down my legs, baring me to him. "Fuck, you're dripping. You're eager for this, aren't you?"

"Yes. I—I've been waiting for you to touch me again."

"Then let me take care of you. Let me stroke every inch of you with my tongue and make you fall apart." With his eyes locked on mine, he makes one long swipe through my slit and I moan embarrassingly loud. "Fuck, you taste incredible."

"God, don't stop, Henley."

He wraps his lips around my clit and sucks it inside his mouth, flicking it with his tongue as he continues to watch me. Our eyes are focused on nothing but each other, making this one of the most intimate sexual experiences of my life. There's something about watching him feast on my pussy that has me wondering if this is even happening, yet again.

But then I feel him release my clit and lick me slowly, exploring my flesh with his tongue while sliding two fingers inside of me and my back arches off of the couch, forcing me to break eye contact for the first time since his mouth descended upon me.

"That's it, sweetheart. Let me hear you. Ride my fingers and face so I can smell you long after we're done."

It's his words that make me realize that my hips are grinding against him and my moans are loud, so loud that I'm afraid I'll wake the baby.

"Fuck," I whisper as I bury my hand in his hair and watch him again, his eyes closed now.

"Don't get quiet on me, El."

"I don't want to wake Remy."

Henley freezes for a minute. "Good point, but still, I'd better hear you fall apart for me."

"Keep doing that then," I reply as he slides his fingers in and out of me, his tongue moving slowly against my clit, his pace so perfect that my orgasm is arriving surprisingly quickly.

"Tell me what you need. Does this feel good?" he asks as his tongue circles my clit again in a torturous pace, and he curls his fingers inside of me, rubbing me softly in the perfect spot.

"So good."

"So sexy," he mumbles against me. "So fucking drenched." He leans back and pushes one hand into his shorts, fisting his rock-hard erection, stroking himself before putting his mouth back on me. "That's it, sweetheart. Your pussy is gripping my fingers so tight."

An embarrassing moan leaves my lips again, but Henley keeps his pace, flicking my clit while fingering me and stroking himself, the wet sounds of our bodies making my orgasm arrive at record speed.

"I—I'm—I'm gonna come," I cry out, clapping a hand over my mouth to stifle the sounds tearing out of me.

"Fuck. Fuck!" Henley groans against me as he thrusts into the couch, pushing himself into me further and continuing to lap at me as my orgasm rips through my body. When I finally feel it start to subside, Henley's head is resting on my inner thigh, his chest heaving as he struggles to breathe. "Jesus, Elodie."

"Henley..." My eyes are closed, my legs wide open, and my body limp and spent.

He peers up at me as I look back down at him, and that smile of his is back. "I fucking came in my pants again, woman."

"What?" The word bursts out on a laugh, even as heat rushes to my cheeks, but I'm not sure if he's joking or not.

When he stands, he confirms he was telling the truth with the wet spot on the front of his athletic shorts. "Twice in a week…"

Licking my lips, I drop my eyes to his crotch and then back up. "Well, the only way to prevent that is to finish on me or in me next time. Your choice."

Henley growls as he closes his eyes and looks away from me. "God, I knew you were trouble."

And in this moment, I couldn't agree more—except *I'm* not trouble, I'm *in* trouble—because with each passing day, I'm falling harder and harder for Henley Clark.

***

"How are you feeling right now?" I ask Henley as he cruises on the highway toward Charlotte. We just finished dropping off Remy to Carol and Nick, and the clench of his jaw hasn't left since we did.

"I feel like I'm missing a body part."

Trying not to laugh at his turmoil, I reach out and stroke his arm. "It definitely feels weird without her here."

"I know I'll relax more once we get to the stadium, but leaving her was a lot harder than I thought it would be."

"You leave her with me to go to work all the time," I counter, trying to help him through his struggle.

"Yeah, but I know I'll see her at the end of the day. I won't see her tonight after the game. I won't get to read to her." Suddenly, he starts laughing. "Fucking Rhonan."

"Okay…That was a weird time to bring him up."

He leans back against his seat more, his hand still draped over the top of the steering wheel as his lips curl up into a lopsided grin. "The first night I had Remy, he told me how he tries to never miss an opportunity to read to Ellis. I thought he was crazy because she's five. It's not like she's going to remember if he missed reading to her for a night." Shaking his head, he continues, "And now here I am, feeling guilty because I'm going to miss one night of reading to Remy, and she's four and a half months old."

I rub his shoulder. "That guilt doesn't mean you aren't a good father, Henley. Trust me, you are. That little girl is so lucky to have you, but you're right. She won't remember this night, so don't beat yourself up too much."

He casts his gaze over to me for a split second, reaching for my hand on his shoulder and then bringing it to his lips, kissing the top of it. "I wouldn't be half of the father I am now if it weren't for you, El."

Cue the heart-eyed emoji.

"Yes, you would be. I'm beginning to think that your role as a father is something you avoided, but you were actually meant for."

His smile falls, but he nods. "I honestly can barely remember my life before you and Remy came into it, and part of me is glad." He blows out a breath. "Fuck, it feels good to admit that."

"Anything else you want to admit to me while you're on a roll?"

He huffs out a laugh. "Is that your way of telling me that it's time to use my words again?"

I shrug, twisting in my seat to face him a bit more. "Maybe."

Henley grows quiet for a beat. "What do you want to know?"

I decide to ask him something that's been weighing on my mind. "You said you've never been in a relationship before, but does that mean that you've never had feelings for a woman before either?"

I can see the tick in his jaw as he contemplates his reply. "I mean, nothing that made me question things like you do." My pulse spikes, but I don't say anything—because at least he's being honest about where he's at with me, which only makes my impending decisions about my life mount themselves on my chest more. "There were a few girls in high school that I thought I was falling for. Cara was the first. We were juniors and she was a cheerleader. I actually lost my virginity to her," he says, chuckling at the memory. "But we never labeled our relationship. One day at lunch, she mentioned wanting to go to college in California, ironically enough, and that's when I decided that she was leaving, so there was no reason to grow attached to her."

"Leave before you get left." *God, sounds like our situation.*

"Exactly. Then after high school, I was hooking up with another girl. She got really into smoking pot, like it became her entire personality. And look—who am I to judge a grown adult for how they choose to live their life or take off the edge? But after what I witnessed with my parents and drugs and how quickly that all spiraled, that was the last thing I wanted in my life, so I dumped her."

"No one after her then?"

He shakes his head. "Nope. No one worth mentioning, anyway."

"And then after you got injured and recuperated, you..."

"Focused on doing something with my life. That's when I started working at the lodge, and I told myself that I didn't have time for a relationship."

"Do you still feel that way?" I ask wearily.

He glances at me again, putting his eyes back on the road after only a few seconds. "No."

And that one word was all I needed to hear from him.

***

"I can't believe they're not gonna call pass interference on that!" Rhonan tosses his hands in the air as he stares down at the field from our box suite. "Even Fletcher is asking the refs for the call!"

Laney stands next to him, her hands planted on her hips. "I'm gonna hear about that call later, especially if they lose."

"It's bullshit." Rhonan turns around, grabs his drink from the table beside him, and drains half of it.

Elliot has one hand shoved in the pocket of his jeans, while the other is holding his beer. "It's only the first quarter. I don't think the game is decided from one call this early."

"Not according to Fletcher. Trust me, I know my fiancé," Laney fires back as the three of them continue to stare down at the field below them. Henley is standing there as well, remaining stoic and relatively unbothered by the call, sipping on his water.

Dilynne and I are standing off to the side in the back of the room, drinking from our glasses of champagne. "My brother is drinking water," she says, almost in a disbelieving tone.

"Is that a problem?"

"Only if he's not aware of it."

I stifle my laugh. "He hasn't been drinking since the night he went out with Warren."

She looks at me from over her shoulder. "Really?"

"Yeah. He also finally finished Remy's room and when we dropped her off at Carol and Nick's earlier, I thought he might change his mind about coming here. He looked so distraught about leaving her."

Dilynne grins around the rim of her glass. "Is that so?"

"Why are you smiling?"

"No reason. What about his alter ego?"

"Which is?"

"Gorilla man," she answers, which clicks when I remember how Henley referred to himself a week ago.

"Oh. I think the gorilla has been tamed for the time being."

"More like tranquilized," she mutters. "So you two are good?"

Is this the moment I tell her about the kiss? And about how he's been opening up to me?

Luckily, Henley takes the reins on that decision, walking over to us and kissing my temple before asking, "Do you want a refill?"

Dilynne's mouth falls open.

"No, I'm okay. Thank you."

He nods and then turns to his sister. "What about you?"

"Um, I'm good for now. Thanks."

"All right." Nodding again, he heads to the back of the suite and starts filling a plate with food that is set up for us, buffet style.

Dilynne looks back at me. "He fucked you, didn't he?"

"What? No..."

Her eyes narrow as she lowers her voice. "Well, something has definitely changed because the man that just came up to us..." She points a finger at her brother across the space. "That is not my brother."

Sighing, I pull her off to the side a bit more. "We've been...talking. He kissed me, admitted that he's feeling things, but asked me to just be patient while he works through stuff, so I have been."

Dilynne's entire face softens. "Really?"

"Yeah."

She clears her throat. "Wow."

"What are you two whispering about?" Henley asks as he comes back over to us, handing me a bowl of popcorn and a spoon.

Dilynne grows confused. "Uh, why is there a spoon in that bowl of popcorn?"

"Because that's how Elodie eats it."

Dilynne's eyes nearly fall out of her head. "Okay, who are you and what have you done with my brother?"

Henley's face transforms into the annoyed look that he normally has. "Jesus, Dil. Calm down."

She stabs a finger into the center of his chest. "No, you are acting really weird, okay?"

Laney is giggling behind her hand. "Dilynne, isn't it obvious?" she says.

"Is what obvious?"

"He likes his nanny," Laney announces, drawing the attention of the entire room to us now. My cheeks instantly grow hot.

"Thank you for that," Henley mutters before turning to me. "I'm sorry in advance for what is about to happen."

Rhonan and Elliot race over to us like teenage girls that just heard the juiciest secret ever. "Holy shit. Did I just hear what I think I heard?"

Henley groans, pinching the bridge of his nose. "Please just leave us alone."

Rhonan slaps him on the back. "No can do, my friend." Then he turns to me, brushing a hand through his thick, dirty blonde hair. "I just want to point out that I caught his crush on you before everyone else."

"Uh, no you did not," Dilynne counters. "I warned her first."

Elliot grumbles. "Dear lord, Dilynne. It's not a fucking contest."

"No one asked you, Grumpzilla."

"Okay, that's enough," Laney interjects, pointing to the windows where the game is still happening. "Need I remind you that we're here to watch Fletcher play, not interfere in Henley and Elodie's...situation," she finishes, unsure of how to classify what we are. And that makes two of us. "So, kindly return to the window and watch the game because if Fletcher asks you about a play and you don't know what he's talking about, you know how irritated he's going to get."

Rhonan and Elliot begrudgingly leave the group. Dilynne looks at Laney. "Me too?"

"Yes. I just want to speak to Elodie and Henley alone for a minute, and then we'll be right there."

She rolls her eyes. "You act like I shouldn't be privy to this conversation."

"The way you just reacted proved that you shouldn't."

Stomping off in annoyance, Dilynne finds a seat right at the glass, propping her feet up while sipping on her drink.

By the time Laney turns back to Henley and me, my pulse is firing so fast, I can feel my entire body shaking. "Sorry about outing you, but it was sort of obvious. You two all right?"

Henley pulls me into his chest, kissing the top of my head, calming me almost instantly. "I knew this was going to happen."

"Welcome to the club," Laney mutters. "I love our group, I do. But when something shifts, you'd think the damn world was ending. Just know that if there's anyone who understands the scrutiny you feel, it's me and Fletcher."

Henley nods. "Thank you for that, Laney." He peers down at me before asking, "Are you okay? I told you this game would be a lot to handle."

"I'm fine. Just trying to balance everything."

He tips my chin up and kisses my lips. "There's nothing for you to balance. I don't give a shit what any of them think, okay? I'm just trying to focus on you, so if you can do the same for me, we'll be fine."

The sincerity in his voice is such a difference from the irritation I picked up when I first met him over two months ago. "Okay."

"Good girl." With a chaste kiss, he releases me and then heads back to his seat, ignoring the questions that Elliot and Rhonan are tossing at him.

"Oh my," Laney says, pulling my attention back to her.

"Yeah."

"I take it things are going well."

The sigh that leaves my lips takes some of my nerves with it. "Yes. He's opening up to me, Laney, like he said he would. There's been more...touching," I say through nervous laughter. "But now that we're here for the night, I'm unsure of what tonight will bring."

"You two haven't..."

I shake my head. "Not all the way, no. But I don't even know if he booked one room or two."

Laney rolls her eyes. "God, I remember when Fletcher and I were taking things slow. I swear, using that word only made me want to sleep with him even more."

"That's exactly how I feel," I mumble around the rim of my glass. "It's been hard to restrain myself."

"Then my advice is to go with what feels right. Speaking from experience, by the time Fletcher and I aired everything we needed to, there was no hesitation from either of us." My heart and body are so primed that I'm sure there won't be any from me as well. "Speaking of hesitation though, have you made a decision about performing at the winery?"

"I'm not gonna lie, I haven't thought about it much this past week. I've been a little...distracted."

Laney bounces her eyebrows up and down. "What a horrible problem to have." Laughing, she continues, "But I do need a decision from you."

Part of me doesn't want to perform because I'm afraid of how it's going to make me feel, but the other part is dying to sing for a crowd. "Okay. Fine. I'm in."

Laney starts clapping. "Hell yes! Oh my God, I'm so excited. You're going to be amazing."

"I hope so. I've never performed an entire set, but I know a lot of songs and I might sing a few originals too."

"That's perfect. We can talk more about it later…"

Dilynne's boisterous laugh interrupts our conversation. "Yes, girl! Take it off!" The boys follow suit, cackling as they press their faces to the glass, peering below us.

Laney and I share a look before rushing to the window to see what's got everyone cheering.

An older woman in her sixties is twirling her shirt around in the air, standing in her stadium seat in nothing but her bra and jeans as "I Want It That Way" by the Backstreet Boys is playing through the stadium speakers. Clearly, she's enjoying herself and doesn't care what the people around her think.

Good for her.

Elliot mumbles around the rim of his glass. "And here I was thinking the saying was, 'Tequila makes her clothes fall off.' Turns out, it's songs by the Backstreet Boys."

All of us break out in laughter.

"God, if I had the chance to see them back in their prime, I probably would have behaved that way too," Laney interjects as the woman starts twerking now, her dance moves such a contrast to the beat of the song. Perhaps she has had some tequila as well.

"If I had a house, I would take out a second mortgage to see NSYNC do a reunion tour," I add.

The boys turn to look at us like we're a puzzle they can't solve.

Dilynne clears her throat. "You're on your own with this one, you two. Boy bands weren't my thing. But if I had the chance to be with Frank Sinatra or Jon Bon Jovi back in his prime, then add me to the list of fangirls gone wild."

The boys start talking shit, us girls continue to reminisce about our celebrity music crushes, and the game gets more intense by the minute. But in the back of my mind, I'm still wondering if this champagne is going to make me lose my clothes later, or if it will be my lumberjack of a single dad boss that does that instead?

Chapter 16

Henley

Only One Room with One Bed & Rocking Chair Realizations

"Can I ask you about Elodie now, or will you still get pissy?" Rhonan leans toward me, whispering in my ear as we stand in front of the windows of the suite, watching the game below.

"You can ask, but that doesn't mean I'm going to answer."

Elliot clears his throat while widening his stance, his eyes remaining on the field. "I don't think you need to ask him anything, Rho. Him kissing her head was pretty telling."

It's the beginning of the third quarter, and the Carolina Thunder are only up by a field goal. I can see the frustration on Fletcher's face every time the camera pans to him. The New York Liberty's defense is all over him, making it almost impossible for him to complete a catch. He's still managed to put up six points, but he should have had at least three touchdowns by this time in the game. New York is a dogshit team compared to the Thunder.

"I think he's ignoring you on purpose," Elliot says, bringing me back to the conversation that I'm literally standing in the middle of, pretending like it's not happening.

"I am."

Rhonan shrugs. "If Fletcher were here too, he'd make you talk. Remember, we agreed not to hold shit in anymore."

Rhonan's mention of our new pact makes me relent.

When we were teenagers, the four of us made a pact to always have each other's backs, not let girls between us, and never date any sisters. Well, given that Fletcher is now engaged to Laney, it was necessary to revamp our naïve agreement this past summer. So now, the first two points still apply, but we added not to hold shit in anymore, and to ask for help when we need it.

Rhonan's father, George, revealed to us during an intervention that his group of friends is the reason he was able to move forward after losing Rhonan and Laney's mom. His friends even convinced him to go to therapy, which none of us—including Rhonan—ever knew about. So now, over the past few months with Fletcher's pressure, of course, we've all decided that it's time to face shit that we've been avoiding.

And Elodie was the catalyst that made me finally agree.

Sighing, I turn to face Rhonan. "Look, all I decided was that I was tired of ignoring the way she makes me feel. She admitted that there's something there for her too, so we're taking things day by day. That's all I can really tell you right now."

Rhonan's eyebrows are practically at his hairline. "Wow. And you're not freaking out?"

"Oh, I'm plenty nervous about a lot of shit. Like the fact that we're sharing a room tonight, for starters."

Elliot grumbles around the rim of his beer. "Yet again, at least someone is getting lucky."

I turn to face him now. "No luck trying to move on from Tori then, huh?"

He shakes his head. "Nope. I tried going out with someone else last week and I just...couldn't."

I clasp my hand on his shoulder. "I thought trying to find another woman would make me admit that what I felt for Elodie was just because I hadn't gotten laid in a while, but it didn't work either."

"Give it time," Rhonan interjects. "I still feel guilty sometimes for moving on after Sarah." He takes a sip of his beer as the three of us grow silent. "Well, besides being alone with Elodie later, how are you feeling about not having Remy with you? This is your first time leaving her overnight, right?"

"Yes, and now that we're here, I feel a little bit better. But driving away from Carol and Nick's house earlier was tough. Dilynne was the one that suggested we take the night away, though."

"Really?" Rhonan asks.

"Yeah, she said Steven told her it was important that Elodie and I get breaks. My sister has never wanted kids, but she's been surprisingly supportive of me having Remy. She even told Elodie to keep an eye on me and make sure I wasn't spiraling." I laugh at the reminder. "Like I need a babysitter, but the concern was appreciated."

"That's just because she doesn't know how to mind her own business," Elliot mutters.

"Look, I agree she can be pushy sometimes, but she always means well. Why? Has she been checking on you too?"

"No comment," he says, bringing his glass to his lips again.

Rhonan and I share a look, and for a moment, I debate pushing Elliot further on the matter, but then Fletcher makes a catch and runs the ball in for a touchdown, and the entire stadium goes wild.

"Hell yeah!" Rhonan shouts, high-fiving Laney as Dilynne does a victory dance beside her.

I find Elodie next, our eyes meeting at almost the exact same time, and a surge of need rushes through me. Like I told Rhonan earlier, I only booked one room for the night. Even though I have no intention of pushing anything with Elodie, the thought of being away from her made my stomach lurch.

In two and a half months, she's become someone in my life that I actually crave, that I appreciate being there, and not just because she's letting me kiss her lips and other places now.

No.

She's become the person I want to talk to at the end of the day, the person I can be more honest with than I have with anyone else, even my closest friends. The story of me stealing the bread and peanut butter for Dilynne? Not even my boys know about that.

And I hate to admit it, but telling her those things, even my dating history on the drive here, is making me feel lighter, like with each memory that I vocalize, a little bit of the pain associated with it leaves my body as well.

She's the sunshine pulling the darkness from my soul.

But tonight, all I want is to get lost in her, even though I know I shouldn't. I'm terrified that if I do, I won't want to come back up for air, and for the first time in my life, I feel like I'm finally able to breathe.

***

"You—you only got us one room?" Elodie asks as I grab the keycard from the receptionist at the hotel and lead her to the elevators, pulling our suitcases behind me.

"Yes. Is that a problem?" I push the button to call for the elevator, turning to look at Elodie who's nervously biting on her bottom lip next to me.

"No. I just wasn't sure if that was the plan or not."

Leaning over, I line my lips up to her ear and whisper, "You're a fool if you think I'm going to let you sleep in a different room than me, or that we're going to be doing any sleeping at all."

Her head snaps to mine so our eyes meet, a smirk on her lips. "Is that so? I thought we were moving slow?"

"There are plenty of things we can do that don't involve penetration, sweetheart."

Her tongue darts out to lick her lips as her eyes drop down to mine. "But penetration feels so good, Henley," she whispers seductively, making my dick grow hard behind the zipper of my jeans.

"Fuck, Elodie," I groan as the elevator dings, signaling the arrival of our car. I urge Elodie to go ahead of me, pulling the suitcases behind me and then swiping the room key in front of the sensor so the elevator will take us to the correct floor.

As soon as the doors shut, I pin her up against the wall and cover her mouth with my own. Each pass of our tongues makes the sexual tension build between us. By the time we arrive at the room, I'm hard as a rock. I move the suitcases inside, shut the door behind me, and watch Elodie walk toward the window, her ass swaying in her jeans right in front of me until she's still and enjoying the view of the city around us.

But my view of her is far more breathtaking.

"Henley?" she says, her back still to me.

"Yeah, sweetheart?"

"I'm tired of slow." She looks at me over her shoulder. "I want fast, hard, and deep. Can you give me that?"

My cock rises to the challenge, making the confines of my denim even more painful. "Elodie..."

She starts walking toward me, her strides slow and deliberate until the space between us is gone and she's planting a hand on the center of my chest.

"I want to taste you, Henley," she says as she reaches for the button on my jeans and drops to her knees. "Honestly, it's all I can think about."

"Jesus Christ," I grate out as Elodie pulls at my zipper and pushes my jeans down. She's quick to shove my boxer briefs down too, and then my cock springs free. She licks her lips. "You don't have to..."

Dragging her tongue from the base of me to the tip, swirling it around the head a few times, she repeats the process and smirks up at me. "I know I don't have to. I want to. It's my turn to take care of you."

I can't be bothered to argue with her anymore because she takes me as far back in her mouth as she can, gagging on my length, covering me in her saliva as she starts to bob up and down on my cock. My hand fists her hair, holding her in place as she works me over with her mouth.

"Fuck, Elodie. God, this mouth." I tip my head back and groan before looking down at her again, not wanting to miss the sight of her taking my cock down her throat.

She hums around me, swirling her tongue, lapping at the precum dripping from my tip and licking my entire length, over and over before releasing me from her mouth long enough to say, "You sure you still want to take things slow?"

"Elodie..."

She lifts her purple sweater up and over her head, revealing her breasts encased in a black lace bra, the look of challenge flashing across her eyes. "It's your turn to use me, Henley."

Pulling her to her feet in a split second, I frame her face with my hands and her eyes widen. "I could never use you. You—" I struggle to find the right words.

Her mischievous grin morphs to concern. "I just meant…"

"I know what you meant, but I want to be clear. Nothing between you and me is transactional. Do you understand me?" She nods while biting down on her bottom lip, taunting me. "Good girl. Now, are you sure you're ready for more, Elodie? Because once I start, there's no going back. I'm fine with the pace we're at. I could lick your pussy all night, baby. But if you want my cock—if you want me buried so deep inside you that you can't tell where you end and I begin—then I'll give you that too."

Her desperate plea makes my dick harder. "Yes, Henley. God, fuck me, please."

Smashing my mouth to hers, I reach behind her and pop the clasp on her bra, releasing her breasts and tossing the flimsy fabric to the side. When I pull her into me, I can feel how hard her nipples are through my shirt. She rushes to push up the fabric, and I yank the shirt over my head, chucking it to the side and allowing our bare chests to touch. We claw at each other, swirling our tongues and murmuring words of encouragement as we kiss and pull our bodies closer.

When we part, I drop my eyes down her body, taking in her curves, her perfect breasts, and that mouth I want more of. "Strip for me, El." Our eyes remain locked as she begins to remove her jeans and I push mine completely off, reaching down to stroke my cock as I see her beautiful, bare body for the first time. "God, sweetheart. You're fucking exquisite."

Her eyes drop down to my hand pulling on my length. "So are you, Henley. I'm just—"

"What's wrong?"

"I'm not sure I can take all of..." Her eyes drop down to my cock again. "That."

The corner of my mouth lifts. "Oh, you can take it, sweetheart. You took me down your throat so well. Don't worry, I'll make sure your pussy is good and ready for all of me." I step closer to her, slowly closing the distance between us until I can pull her into my body again. Cupping the side of her face, I take a moment to memorize how she looks and how I feel—because this experience is unlike any other, all because of the woman in my arms.

"Lie down on the bed for me, baby." I watch Elodie crawl backward onto the bed, holding herself up on her elbows to watch as I crawl toward her, situating myself between her legs before leaning down and kissing the inside of her thigh. "Now watch me as I lick this perfect pussy."

She lets out a sigh as I swipe my tongue through her once, press a kiss to her pink flesh, and then lick her again, focusing on her clit this time. Elodie watches my every move, burying her hand in my hair. "Yes, Henley."

"You're dripping. So fucking drenched." I have to reach out and wipe the precum from my dick because knowing she's wet for me makes my dick more than eager to feel her wetness.

"I want you. Please, Henley."

I circle her clit a few times with my tongue before wetting two fingers and slowly sliding them inside of her cunt. "Not until you come for me like this." Slowly, I stroke her G-spot, feeling her tighten around me.

"Keep doing that and it won't take long."

My tongue finds her clit and I flick it softly while stroking her, soaking up every moan that she gives me, loving how they're coming on faster and louder until she's screaming and I can feel her soak my face with her release. As I watch her come undone, I can feel myself thrusting into the bed, knowing that my dick is ready for his turn.

She tosses her arm over her face as her body sinks deeper into the bed. "Holy shit."

"We're not even close to being done, El." Standing from the bed, I walk over to my suitcase and find the condoms I packed just in case, tearing one open and sliding it on my cock before making my way back to the bed. When I hover over Elodie, she pulls my mouth to hers, tasting herself on my tongue as I slide my cock through her slit, rubbing her sensitive clit. "Fuck, baby."

"Please, Henley..." she begs.

I reach down and tease her with the tip, pushing in slightly just to pull right back out again. "The number of times I've thought of this."

"Me too," she says, dragging my eyes back to hers.

With our gazes still locked, I push deeper inside her, watching her lips part and eyes widen as she adjusts to me. I know I'm thick, and I can see the doubt on her face as I work my way inside of her.

"You're doing so fucking good. This pussy is stretching around me, sucking me in, El, like you can't get enough. Fuck," I grate out, dipping my eyes back down to the sight of us, watching with fascination as if I'm experiencing sex for the first time. But in a way, I am. This is the first time it's actually meant something to me.

Elodie lets out a moan that makes me impossibly harder as I drive all the way to her end. "Oh." *Thrust.* "My." *Thrust.* "God." *Thrust.*

"That's it, baby. Now let me fuck this pussy until you're drenching the sheets again." As I pull back, feeling every inch of her heat, I push back in with a bit more force and watch her tits bounce beneath me as I find a rhythm she seems to like.

"Yes, Henley. Yes..." She claws at my back, marking me as I feel the sting of her nails dig into my skin.

Leaning down, I capture her lips with mine. "Goddamn, Elodie. This pussy is so fucking tight." My hips keep snapping forward as the sound of our bodies connecting fills the hotel room. I reach down and pull her legs higher, guiding them around my waist as I pump into her deeper and harder. "Jesus."

"Henley," she moans as I rest my forehead on hers, keeping this pace. "You're—you're gonna make me come."

I reach down between us and rub her clit. "Break for me, baby." And after a few minutes, she does, screaming again as I fuck her through her orgasm. And watching her fall apart makes me come almost instantly. "Fuck...fuck!"

She pushes up and kisses me as I groan, filling the condom with my cum as every drop leaves my body, shuddering through the last few tremors. When I collapse on top of her, she strokes my back softly. "Henley, that was incredible."

Incredible isn't a strong enough word for what I just experienced—sex with feelings. It was more intense, more hot, more—*everything*.

Once we clean up and get settled back in bed, I lean against the headboard as Elodie rests her head on my lap.

"Hey." I reach forward to cup the side of her face, stroking her cheek with my thumb. "That was the best sex of my life. But I just need you to know that you never have to prove anything with me. The last thing I want you to feel is that you're being pressured to do anything."

Elodie smiles softly. "I don't feel that way at all. In fact, I'm surprised by how much I wanted this. I thought it would take a long time for me to feel that way again. But it's different with you. So much is different..."

I capture her lips with mine, soaking in how every time we kiss, it feels deeper, more connected. Everything with this girl is tilting my world on its axis, and even though I feel completely off balance, I feel like I'm learning a new way to stay upright too—the one that involves being able to lean on someone and trust them completely.

But in the back of my mind, I still know that she's going to leave soon, and I don't know how to address that yet.

***

"So, do you want to tell everyone what happened last night?" Elliot asks as he holds a bite of food in front of his face. "Or can we just assume based on the pep in your step that you got laid?"

I freeze with my cup of coffee halfway to my lips. "You're really fucking lucky that Elodie isn't here to hear you or I'd punch you in the dick."

"At least then my dick would be getting some action," he quips before shoving his food into his mouth.

It's the morning after the game and the life-changing night with Elodie, and our group is having breakfast at the hotel before heading back to Blossom Peak. Laney is staying with Fletcher for a few more days, but the rest of us have to return to our lives.

Returning to real life has been on my mind all morning as I think about how things have changed in the past few weeks and what they'll look like after last night. All I know is I can't wait to get her naked again, to make her fall apart from my touch, to hold her while she drifts off to sleep, and to wake up next to her. It's insane that I even feel this way, but part of me is still holding back from accepting these feelings completely. We haven't talked any more about her next move, and until we do, I don't want to get my hopes up that she'll consider staying.

Rhonan picks up his glass of orange juice. "You don't have to answer the question."

"I know I don't. It's none of your goddamn business."

Elliot chuckles as he finishes chewing. "The fact that you won't talk about it tells me everything I need to know." He turns to Rhonan. "Another one bites the dust," he says. "Fucking idiot."

"Look, just because your fiancée fucked you over doesn't mean you get to judge everyone else's relationships, all right?"

His smirk falls. "You barely know her, Henley."

Rhonan pushes his shoulder. "That's rich considering we used to say the same thing to you about Tori."

"Yeah, and if I would have listened to you guys, I wouldn't be in this situation right now. Forgive me for trying to save my friend from the same fucking shit I'm going through." He shoves another bite of his food in his mouth.

"Relationships are hard no matter who you are," Fletcher chimes in. "But if Henley is happy, we should be encouraging, not patronizing."

Elliot scoffs. "Did your therapist help you with those big words?"

Fletcher narrows his eyes at Elliot. "He did, actually. Did yours help you with your fucking attitude?"

Elliot shakes his head. "No, 'cause I don't have one."

"Thank you for proving my point."

"Uh oh. I sense some turmoil in the Blackjack Brotherhood," Dilynne says as the girls return from the bathroom and Elodie takes her seat beside me again. I pull her chair closer, resting my hand on her thigh under the table. She leans over and kisses my cheek, making the urge to take her back upstairs grow at lightning speed.

"Everything is fine," Elliot grumbles around a mouthful of food.

"Says the guy who's the least *fine* of all," Dilynne snaps back.

"You really need to learn how to mind your own business."

"Funny, because I'm sure the guys feel the same way about you right now." My sister flashes a placating smile at Elliot from across the table.

Elliot wads up his napkin, tosses it onto his plate, and stands, pulling his wallet from his back pocket before tossing a few bills onto the table. "I'm out."

Fletcher turns to my sister. "Did you really need to say something?"

"I'm sorry, but he needs to stop using his broken heart as an excuse to be rude as fuck," she fires back. "I'm tired of it. And if he acts like that at yoga next week, I'm gonna pants him in front of everyone to teach him a lesson."

Rhonan clutches his stomach as he laughs. "Oh, fuck. Please do it anyway."

"Does that mean that you're going to participate this time?" I ask him, knowing his aversion to yoga.

"Fuck no. I told you, I'm not bending over in front of people for fun."

"It's because you're afraid to fart, isn't it?" Elodie interjects, making Laney snort.

Rhonan glares at his sister before looking over at Elodie. "No, that's not it."

"It's okay to fart, Rhonan. You don't have to be ashamed if you're an abnormally gassy person," Elodie continues, making Fletcher break this time.

I'm also fighting to keep my composure.

"I'm not afraid to fart," Rhonan counters a bit too defensively. "I just think yoga is dumb. It's not challenging, and…"

"Oh, you're afraid to be shown up by a bunch of girls and your friends." She nods. "Got it."

"It's not that. I just don't need to prove anything to anyone. Yoga isn't impressive, and I can do other things that don't involve showing my ass to a bunch of strangers."

"So, it is the fear of farting then." Elodie reaches across the table and covers his hand with hers. "It's okay. This is a safe space, right everyone? We accept you even if you can't contain your flatulence."

And now, we all lose it, laughing uncontrollably while Rhonan's face grows red. "It's not about farting," he says, standing and tossing his napkin on the table, stomping off in the same direction that Elliot went.

I lean over and kiss Elodie as everyone else is still laughing. "God, you're something, Elodie Olsen," I whisper to her as her eyes shine with amusement.

"Yeah, Henley Clark. You sure are something too."

***

"Hey, baby bear." Elodie lifts Remy in her arms before kissing her cheek and squeezing her to her chest. "Gosh, I missed you."

I lean down and kiss her cheek too. "Yeah, little one. It was really weird without you."

Carol clears her throat, reminding us that she's still there. "She was great. Slept well, enjoyed our walks in the stroller, and I can see a little tooth getting ready to cut through her gums on the bottom." She pulls down Remy's bottom lip to show us.

"Jesus, already?"

Carol rubs my shoulder. "They grow up fast, Henley. Ask me how I feel seeing you as a father?"

When my eyes meet hers, a sadness overwhelms me. Maybe it's the look in her eyes or the tone of her voice, but it's one I've never picked up on before. She sounds like a mother—*my mother*—or what I always imagined hearing something like that from my mother would sound like—that reverence of watching your child grow older and become their own person, a combination of pride and sadness.

My eyes move back to my daughter as I watch her smile at Elodie.

My daughter will never have that with her own mother either. Elodie's love is the closest thing she'll get.

God, I wonder if she thinks Elodie is her mom?

Clearing my throat, I focus back on Carol while my heart beats roughly behind my sternum. "Well again, I appreciate you and Nick watching her for us."

"Anytime. How was the trip? The game sure was a nail biter."

"Yeah, Fletcher's last catch secured the win for them, but he was irritated they didn't win by more."

"We had such a good time, though," Elodie interjects, glancing my way as her cheeks burn bright pink. She has to be thinking of last night if she's blushing like that.

Carol catches it though, smirking up at me with an arch in her brow. "Is that so? Glad you enjoyed yourselves."

Remy makes a bunch of noises, telling us that she's ready to leave—at least that's how I interpret it. "I need to get my girls home, Carol. We'll catch up more later, all right?"

Pushing up on her toes, she reaches up to hug me. "Sounds good. Let me know if you need any more breaks. I'm more than happy to take my granddaughter."

"Thank you."

"Love you, Henley." Her words slice through my chest like they do every time, but I kiss her temple and lead Elodie out to my truck without saying anything in return.

By the time we get home and unpack, Remy is ready for her afternoon nap. She's down to two naps a day now, but her afternoon one is longer. Needing to make up for lost time, I rock her to sleep in her nursery, admiring the walls that I spent hours painting and the room that Elodie decorated. Before I know it, she'll be walking around in here, potentially drawing on the walls, or asking to hang up posters of her celebrity crush.

Time moves so fast, reminding me of how just two days away from this little girl makes me think that she grew while I was gone. I reach down and stroke her soft skin on her cheek as her eyes flutter closed, and that's when it hits me—*I'm her dad*.

The truth isn't one I hadn't already known, but in this moment in time, it feels like I'm accepting it—that from now until I'm no longer on this earth, I'm the person she will run to when she needs help, the person that will always make her feel safe, the only man she will measure every other man against—if I take this responsibility seriously, that is.

I would never want my daughter to end up with a man like I was before she entered my life. I wouldn't want her with someone who is so terrified of being left that he leaves her first and breaks her heart.

And I would never want her to be with a man who second-guesses how he feels about her.

But that's exactly what I'm doing with Elodie.

As soon as Remy drifts off to sleep and I move her to her crib, I close the door to her room and search the house for Elodie, finding her in her room with her guitar next to her on the bed and a pen in her hand moving furiously across the paper. When she feels my presence, she looks up, our eyes locking as I make my way into the room and pull her up from the bed, smashing my lips to hers.

"Henley..."

"I need you," I whisper against her lips, pulling her with me and down the hall to my room, away from the nursery.

"Are you okay?" she asks once I've shut us inside and given her an inch of space.

I reach behind me and take my shirt off, tossing it behind me. "No."

"What's going on?" I'm taking off my pants when she reaches down and stops me. "Henley, talk to me."

"I need to feel you, El. Please..." The desperation in my voice surprises me, but I don't know how else to say what I'm feeling—that if I don't have her right now, I feel like she might vanish or realize that trusting me could be a colossal mistake.

Her eyes move between mine for a beat, and then she's stripping as well, throwing her clothes haphazardly around the room until we're both naked. "Okay, but we're talking afterward." I nod as she stands before me, waiting for me to make the first move before I walk toward her and frame her face with my hands, kissing her softly as I feel her hands move from my waist up my back, pulling me to her.

"Get on the bed on all fours, Elodie." I grab a condom from my nightstand as she follows my directions. "Fuck, you look perfect right now, ready to let me own you, trusting me." When I return to her, I lean down and press a kiss to the heart tattoo I memorized the location of the night I saw it for the first time. "And this. Fuck, I really like this," I say, rubbing my thumb over the ink.

"I got it when I was eighteen. Rachel from *Friends* got one, and I thought it was something I wouldn't regret."

Licking my lips, I grab both of her ass cheeks and lower my mouth to the spot again, licking the heart and then biting it gently. "It's fucking sexy."

Her entire body shivers as she lets out a moan, tossing her hair over her shoulder while peering back at me. Rubbing her ass cheek, I savor how her silky skin feels beneath my calloused hands and then move my fingers between her legs as I stand upright again, feeling how wet she already is.

"Fuck, you're ready for my cock, aren't you, baby?"

"Yes, Henley. Please..."

I waste no time pushing myself into her, filling her with every inch of me and loving how her moan drags out as I give her my cock. My need for her has spiked into a full-blown obsession.

"Fuuuuuck..." I groan, freezing to give myself time to find my control so I don't blow my load too fast.

She drops her head to the bed as I slowly piston my hips. "Oh...God..."

"Jesus, Elodie. This pussy is so fucking addicting." I go a little deeper and harder. "I can't get enough of you..."

Her eyes meet mine over her shoulder. "Show me. Tell me."

Wrapping my arm around her waist, I pull her up so her back is to my chest. I'm still standing at the edge of the bed with Elodie perched in front of me, fucking her deep and slow because I don't want this to end.

I don't want us to end either.

My head drops to her shoulder as that truth travels through my chest. "Elodie..."

Fuck, I want this woman. I need her. But what if she won't stay for me? And do I even have the right to ask her to do that?

More importantly, can I find the courage to ask her that? Because no one has ever stayed for me.

"Henley, touch me, please," she begs, pulling me back to the moment and I'm grateful because I could feel myself spiraling with indecision and fear. "Make me come."

I move my hand around her waist as her arms reach behind her, wrapping around my neck. I cup one of her breasts with my left hand, and move my right hand between her legs, feeling myself slide in and out of her before rubbing her clit softly with my fingers. "Fuck, you are dripping."

"It's so good."

My mouth travels up her neck, licking and biting her gently, teasing her skin as I attempt to draw this out, but my efforts are futile as my orgasm builds with urgency.

"You have no idea what you do to me, Elodie." I circle her clit harder and faster, and a few moments later, she's detonating, taking me with her and parting the clouds, making it clear that I'm in way deeper with this woman than I thought.

***

"You ready to talk?" Elodie asks as we're lying in my bed, soaking up the afterglow.

"No."

She pinches my nipple. "Ow! Fuck, what was that for?"

"You're supposed to be using your words. Now, what's going through your mind?"

"Nothing."

Sighing, she says, "Just so you know, you're a terrible liar, Henley Clark."

"I'm fine, Elodie." The truth is, I feel better now that we've had sex, but she's right—there's a million things going through my head right now and I'm having trouble separating them into compartments that make sense. If I can't sort through them, how the hell am I supposed to vocalize them to someone else?

She twists in my arms, resting her chin on my chest while staring up at me. "Why are you so afraid for people to see you? The real you?"

It takes me a minute to find the words. "I don't share my feelings and shit, Elodie. I don't put them out there for people to judge and ridicule like you do in your songs." Shrugging, I say, "I know it's harsh, but it's the truth."

"Sure, there are people who do judge, but most relate. You're forgetting the one common denominator that we all share—the human experience—loss, abandonment, shame, guilt, strife, but most of all, love." The second she uses that word—*love*—my heart rate picks up. "And if you won't open up to anyone, how do you think that's going to affect your daughter one day? Do you want to set the same example for her growing up that you had? Or do you want to show her there's a better way to live?"

Sighing, I place one hand behind my head, still staring up at the ceiling as she rests her head on my chest. "It's that thought that hit me earlier. I was rocking Remy to sleep and something dawned on me."

"Okay, so tell me."

"I—I realized that I would never want my daughter to end up with someone like me."

Elodie lifts her head, her brows furrowed as I peer over at her. "Why on earth would you think something like that?"

"Because it's true. I'm fucked up, El. My childhood has scarred me, and I don't know if I'll ever be able to move past it."

"What are you so afraid of, Henley?"

My mind is racing. "Let's just say that my sister was right. I have issues, and I don't want to hurt you."

She runs her fingernails through my chest hair. "Henley, you don't get it. Maybe all you can see are your shortcomings, but I see every strength that you have—your responsibility, how much you care about those in your close circle, and now your willingness to change. Plenty of people use their past as a reason to stay where they are, blaming others instead of owning the fact that they are the only person who can change their circumstances."

"My daughter has made me see the world so differently."

"Children will do that. She's made me see things differently too."

I glance down at her while rubbing her back. "How so?"

"Her innocence. Like, she doesn't have any knowledge of the evil in this world yet, you know? She doesn't know disappointment and fear. She doesn't know insecurity and anxiety. She just has this small bubble and nothing to worry about except getting her diaper changed and her next meal. I envy her, but I adore that I get to be a part of that bubble at the same time. I've never felt purpose like I do when I'm taking care of her, Henley. She's brought me so much joy, and I've loved every minute of it."

"Too bad your time with us is almost over," I say, bringing up my biggest fear, the one that made me spiral and take this woman without hesitation.

"For the past few weeks, all I've thought about is how I know she'll never remember me if I leave. But for the time that I am here, you and she have all of me, Henley." Her arms squeeze around my chest. "I promise you that."

Yeah, Elodie. I think you have all of me too, and that's exactly what I'm afraid of.

Chapter 17

Henley

Yoga & Concerts

"If you're not going to participate, why even bother showing up?" Elliot asks Rhonan as we wait for yoga to start. Fletcher is talking to Laney and her dad, helping with something before the event officially starts, and Carol is at the playground with Remy. But I haven't seen Elodie in a while now, which instantly makes my pulse spike.

When she first mentioned coming to yoga night at the winery, all I could think about was getting to see how flexible she was. But now that we're here, I realize I underestimated how uncomfortable I would be with *other* people getting to see her flexibility, especially while she's wearing a teal spandex workout set that leaves nothing to the imagination. Still, I'm looking forward to doing something with her that's become a part of my life in the past few months. I've never had someone to share a hobby with before, and I kind of like it.

Yet another reason I barely recognize myself lately.

Rhonan laughs. "And miss y'all twisting yourselves into pretzels? No way." He hoists his belt up higher on his waist, checking to make sure that his gun is secured. "Even if I am on shift, at least I'm getting paid and subjected to free entertainment just for being here."

Blossom Peak has very little crime, so most days, I wonder what the hell Rhonan does as sheriff. I imagine there's only so many parking tickets he can write. But at least the slow pace of life here allows him to have a bit of life and be there for events like this.

I lean over toward Elliot. "Just wait. There's gonna be some beautiful woman that will make him change his thinking about yoga and before you know it, he'll be on the grass with the rest of us."

"Oh shit. Yeah, I think you're right. Although part of me hopes he stays single forever so I have a buddy to grow old with."

"Swearing off the entire female population now?" Fletcher asks as he rejoins us.

Elliot scratches his jaw, his nails moving roughly through his scruff. "Yeah, I think I'm in the acceptance stage of grief now. That is, I've accepted that a relationship is just not for me and so now I feel more at peace."

The three of us share a look before Fletcher says, "If that's how you feel, buddy, then I hope it works out for you. Does this mean you're not drinking any more either?" He motions to the bottle of water Elliot is holding.

"I'll have you know that I haven't had a drink since we got back from Charlotte, all right?"

"That was three days ago," Rhonan deadpans.

"Still. After breakfast that morning, I just realized I don't like who I am right now." He turns to me. "I want to apologize for what I said to you about Elodie, and the comments I've made to her too. I—" He pushes a hand through his hair. "I think I've been taking out my anger on you because you're happy and with someone now."

"Holy shit." Fletcher holds the back of his hand to Elliot's forehead. "Do you have a fever? Are you feeling okay? Because I'm not sure who this guy is standing in front of us right now."

Elliot bats his hand away. "Oh, shut the fuck up, respectfully. I'm fine, all right? But I might have finally gone to therapy on Monday."

Slapping him on the shoulder, I say, "Well, I appreciate the apology, and I'm proud of you."

Maybe it's time you go to therapy too, Henley?

He shoves me off. "Let's not make a big deal about it, okay?" He scours the courtyard. "Where are the girls, by the way?"

As if a movie montage begins, we all turn to see Laney, Dilynne, and Elodie stride toward us, ponytails swaying and spandex hugging every curve.

My eyes are locked on Elodie, of course, already thinking about what positions I'm going to fold her into later, hoping our yoga session will give me ideas.

"Goddamn," Fletcher mumbles beside me.

"Right?" I echo his sentiment.

"Jesus Christ," Elliot grumbles, twisting away from us and adjusting his dick.

"You okay there, buddy?" I ask him.

"Yeah, I'm fine. I've—I've gotta piss. I'll be back in a minute." He stomps in the direction of the bathrooms, but I'm a bit confused by his reaction.

"Hey, angel," Fletcher says as he greets his fiancée, pulling her into his chest.

"Hey, yourself. You ready for this?"

"As ready as I'm gonna be. After last week's game, I need to be stretched out anyway."

"You know I could help you with that," she murmurs against his lips.

Rhonan clears his throat. "Uh, I'm standing right here."

Laney swats at him. "Then go away if you don't like what you're hearing."

Elodie giggles as she slides up to me. "You ready to be shown up by your nanny?"

"Is that a challenge?"

"Come on, Henley. Everyone knows women are more flexible than men."

I lean down and line my lips up to her ear. "Then maybe I need to show you a few things when we get home later."

Her gray eyes darken. Seems she likes that idea just as much as I do.

Laney rubs her hands together. "All right, let's get this night started." She takes her spot up at the front of the courtyard, puts on her head mic, then starts the session.

Elodie and I keep tabs on each other throughout the workout, laughing when we both struggle to keep our bodies in a certain pose. Rhonan is taking pictures from his post on a small hill, laughing to himself as Fletcher, Elliot, and I take turns flipping him off. Fletcher is right in front of his fiancée, soaking up every minute of being able to watch her, and Elliot is behind Dilynne, grumbling as he falls down.

"Do you want some help?" Dilynne offers, her voice low.

"I don't need your fucking help," he spits back at her.

She puts her hands in the air. "Suit yourself, Grumpzilla."

I glance back to check on Elliot, but his eyes are locked on a part of Dilynne that I'm almost positive I haven't caught him staring at before.

"Great, now let's start to wind this down. Everyone transition into child's pose," Laney says into the mic as the entire lawn full of people moves down to their mats, placing their hands out in front of them as they bend in half, their chests to the ground.

"How are you feeling?" Elodie whispers over to me.

"I have sweat dripping down my ass crack, but that's pretty normal for when I do yoga, so not that bad."

She snorts. "Oh my God, Henley."

"What?"

Shaking her head, she says, "I like this side of you."

"Which side is that?"

"The one where you're not afraid to have fun."

Her words hit me square in the chest. I've never had issues with having fun, but my definition of fun used to be very different—careening down the side of a mountain at lightning speed, jumping out of an airplane and waiting until the last possible second to pull my parachute, or seeing how many phone numbers I could get from women in one night.

Now, it's getting my daughter to laugh, cracking jokes with my nanny, and thinking about where I could take her on a date.

"And that's it. Thank you all again for joining us," Laney says, breaking through my thoughts as the entire crowd claps. "Don't forget to get your sample of wine before you leave, and all bottles are twenty percent off for yoga participants tonight." She makes her way from her spot at the top of the lawn, kissing Fletcher first, then traipsing over to Elodie. "So, how was it?"

"It was great. It's been a while since I've done yoga, but it was just like riding a bike."

Laney rubs Elodie's shoulder. "Glad to hear it. That spot where I was is where we're going to set you up to perform too, by the way."

"Perfect."

"Um, I'm sorry. Did you say…perform?"

Elodie turns back to me, her eyes wide as Laney glances between us, her brows drawn together. "Yeah. Didn't Elodie tell you?"

I cross my arms over my chest. "Do I look like she told me?"

Elodie rubs my arm. "I'm sorry, I forgot to mention it. Laney had a performer cancel, so she asked me if I'd be willing to perform for Concert in the Courtyard next week."

Laney's eyes dart between us as Elodie plants her hands on her hips and says, "Is that a problem?"

I shift my gaze away from her, trying to figure out why the thought of her singing here sets me on edge. "No. Not a problem. Just—caught off guard."

"Uh, I'm gonna leave you two to talk," Laney says, catching up to Fletcher where he's standing off to the right chatting with a few fans.

I turn back to Elodie. "So, you're performing?"

"I am, but what I'm wondering is why you're mad about it?"

"I'm not."

"Could have fooled me."

Sighing, I uncross my arms and run a hand through my sweaty hair. "Look, I just wasn't anticipating that bit of news."

"And I'm just trying to understand why you're making such a big deal out of this."

I pull her closer to me. "I fucking love your voice, you know that."

"Then what's got gorilla man reappearing right now?"

The issue is hearing that you're performing was like being backhanded into remembering why you came here in the first place, and why you're probably leaving in a month and a half.

"Looks like you two had fun," Carol says, interrupting our conversation, Remy happily sitting on her hip. "Even though the temperature is dropping, looks like you were still sweating."

I intercept my daughter from her, kissing her cheek and nuzzling her nose. "Yoga isn't as easy as it looks, Carol."

"Well, maybe I'll join you next time."

"I think this was the last session before the events shut down for the winter," Elodie says. "That's what Laney told me, at least."

Carol nods. "Sounds about right. The beginning of November brings harsh, cold weather. After the last concert, it just gets too cold for the winery to host outdoor events. They have plenty indoor ones though. You'll have to come to the Sip & Smut Night."

"Sip & Smut?" Elodie asks.

"Yes. It's a book club for romance lovers and we drink wine."

I pinch the bridge of my nose. "I did not need to know that you attend that, Carol."

She smacks me on the back. "You act like you don't know about my reading collection." Carol leans closer. "I'll never forget the look on Henley's face when I found him reading one of my books. Later, I realized it was a scene in a billionaire romance where the man had his wife bent over a piano." She fans her face. "Truly a scene that lives rent-free in my head."

"I think I'm gonna throw up," I mutter.

Elodie is shaking with laughter. "Oh my God, that sounds amazing. What's the title of that book?"

"I'll leave you two to chat," I say as I make my way across the lawn, over to where Laney is standing with Fletcher.

"Hey. Everything okay with you and Elodie?" Laney asks while greeting my daughter. "Sorry for spilling the beans. Seems to be my role lately, but I figured she would have told you by now."

"Well, that makes two of us."

"In her defense, she wasn't sure she was even going to do it. I kind of pressured her."

"It's fine. I mean, music is her passion. She should be performing, and she should be excited about it."

I peer down at my daughter, not wanting Laney to see the conflict in my eyes—because I'm crazy about Elodie, and probably crazy for letting myself give in to what I feel for her as well.

The truth is, as much as I'm thrown off by her impending performance, I'm fucking proud of her too. She's not giving up on what she wants for her life, so why should I be angry? If anything, that type of action makes my feelings grow for her even more.

Fuck. I'm falling for my nanny.

I shake my head. "Never in a million years did I think I'd find myself in this situation."

Laney rubs my shoulder. "I felt the same way when Fletcher came back into town, but look how that ended up, Henley. Life has a funny way of putting you on the path you're meant to take, something I'm beginning to trust even more as I get older. Just don't give up hope."

Hope is the last thing I've ever relied on—because the last time I did, my parents never returned and I told myself I'd never again get my hopes up about anyone staying.

Chapter 18

Henley

In Sickness & In Health

"Fuck. I can't believe how long it's been since I've been on these slopes." Pulling my goggles from my face, I turn to see Warren doing the same.

"You're missing out, buddy. You become the boss and all of a sudden you've forgotten how to have fun."

"No, I'm just participating in a new type of fun these days," I reply. "I about lost my shit the other night when Remy rolled over twice back-to-back. And then she tried to crawl."

Warren's blank expression makes me laugh. "Wow. Life sure is different for you now, isn't it?"

I rip off my hat and shove it in the pocket of my snowboarding jacket. "Sure is, but I fucking love it."

"Daddy Henley. Never thought I'd see the day."

I reach down and unbuckle the strap on one of my boots, releasing my foot from the snowboard so I can make my way over to a bench. Warren follows me. "You and me both, but hell, Warren. That little girl is the light of my life."

And so is my nanny.

Staring out at the slope we just ran down, the chill in the air bites my cheeks while the white powder nearly blinds me. It's the first week of November, and the first snow fell. Warren was insistent that I join him for a run, and since I couldn't remember the last time I had, I relented, leaving home earlier than normal to make sure we had ample time. Five passes later, and my heart rate is pumping, that familiar adrenaline that I used to chase returning with a vengeance.

"And what about Elodie? How's that going?" Warren bounces his eyebrows as he glances in my direction.

"That's none of your business."

He shoves at my shoulder. "Aw, come on. Anyone with two eyes can see that you're head over heels for her."

I stare down at my hands, avoiding his gaze. "Yeah, well she's only here until Christmas, so not sure where that leaves us."

The truth is, after yoga last week, I've sort of been living in denial, soaking up every moment that I can with her while ignoring the fact that our time together is dwindling by the day. However, I'm having a hard time containing my alter ego, gorilla man, with her impending performance at Hart Winery this coming weekend.

Part of me just wants to come out and ask her what her plans are, if she's still planning on leaving or if I should plan a date so I can tell her how I feel and attempt to put some demons to rest by planning a future with her. But if I do, she's going to ask me what I want, and I'm not ready to voice it out loud—partly because it involves using words

I've never told anyone but my sister, and the thought of saying them to her, only for her to leave scares the shit out of me.

"I'm sorry, man. That sucks."

"Yeah, well, I knew what I was getting myself into."

Warren lets out a sigh. "At least you found someone. I swear, I'm beginning to think I'll never meet anyone in this town. Maybe I need to expand my reach."

"Are you thinking about leaving?"

He shrugs. "Not sure. You know I love the lodge, and I love you." He bats his eyelashes at me. "But I want more."

I scoff. "Yeah, well, I never did and look where that got me. Trust me, when you least expect it, life will give you a lesson that you need."

"And what lesson is that?"

I open my mouth to answer, but an angry voice cuts me off. "Don't you know how to answer your goddamn phone?"

I turn to find my sister trudging through the snow, her eyes ablaze with fury.

"Dilynne?"

"No, it's Mrs. Claus, you moron!" The sound of the snow crunching under her footsteps gets louder as she closes the distance between us, planting her hands on her hips. "Jesus Christ, Henley. I've been trying to call you for the past hour. I finally got ahold of Jess at the lodge who told me you were snowboarding, but she can't leave the restaurant, so I had to drag my ass all the way out here."

I stand from the bench, my anxiety growing rapidly as I take in the expression on her face. "What's wrong?"

"It's Elodie. She's sick."

"What? How?"

"I don't know. Germs are everywhere." Rolling her eyes, she says, "She tried calling you too, but when you didn't respond, she called me and I called Laney. Laney is at the house with her and Remy..."

I rip the strap on my other boot and abandon my snowboard completely. "Fuck. Is she all right?"

Dilynne begins to walk back to the main lodge as I follow her. "I mean, she's not dying, but she has a fever, chills... Honestly, I'm surprised you didn't notice this morning before you left."

"She and Remy were still sleeping."

My sister shakes her head. "Well, that explains it. Long story short, when she woke up and realized she was not feeling well, and when you didn't answer, she called me." Breathing heavily, she says, "I thought you'd want to know."

Pushing a hand through my hair, I start running at full speed to my truck. "Warren!" I call out over my shoulder.

He raises his hand in the air. "I've got it. Go take care of your girl!"

And as I race back home, I pray she's all right—because if she's not, I'll never forgive myself.

***

"Where is she?" I bark out as I stumble through the front door of my house.

Laney jumps from her spot on the couch, clutching Remy to her chest. "Jesus, Henley."

"Elodie...where..."

"She's resting." Laney peers down at Remy to check that she's okay. For a second, I debate going to my daughter, but Laney makes the decision for me. "Go. I've got the baby."

My footsteps are heavy as I make my way down the hallway to Elodie's room, not bothering to knock. As I open the door, the sight of her curled up in bed almost splits my heart in two.

I wasn't sure anyone but my daughter had the power to do that.

"El?" She doesn't respond, so I move toward the bed, stripping off my jacket as I do and tossing it onto the chair in the corner. When I take a seat on the bed, I find her eyes closed, but her brows pinched together. "Elodie?"

A groan leaves her lips as her eyes flutter open. "Henley?"

"Hey sweetheart." I lift my hand to her face, shocked by how hot she is. "Shit, El. You're burning up."

"I'm sorry," she says groggily.

"You're sorry? What the hell do you have to be sorry for?"

"Remy..."

"She's fine. You did the right thing calling Dilynne. She called Laney and then drove all the way out to the lodge to get me. I'm so sorry I didn't answer, baby." I smooth away her hair from her face, noticing how flushed her cheeks are and it's not from embarrassment for once "I was snowboarding with Warren."

"Did you have fun?"

I huff out a laugh. "Don't worry about me."

"You deserve to have fun. I didn't think I would wake up feeling like this, but..."

"Were you feeling off yesterday?"

"A little."

"Why didn't you say anything?"

"Because I don't get sick."

"Newsflash, you're human, El. Humans get sick."

She lets out another groan. "Don't make me laugh, Henley. Everything hurts. I'm so achy."

"Sounds like the flu." I lay the back of my hand on her forehead this time. "Have you taken anything?"

"Some ibuprofen."

"How long ago?"

"I don't know. Wh—what time is it?"

"Just after ten."

"Then maybe around seven. You left early today."

"Because Warren wanted me to go snowboarding with him on the fresh powder. That's the last time I listen to him," I grumble.

She cracks a smile. "Stupid Warren."

I stroke her cheek again, loving how even when she's sick she can still manage to make me smile. "Yeah, stupid Warren. Can I get you anything?"

She groans louder. "I don't even know. I feel so horrible."

Leaning over, I press a kiss to her forehead. "I'll see what I have and come right back, all right?"

"Henley..."

"Yeah, sweetheart?"

"I don't want you to get sick too."

"I'll be fine. I don't get sick." Winking, I leave her room and find Laney still in the living room in the same spot I left her. "She's in bad shape."

"I know. She kept apologizing for calling Dilynne, but..."

"Look, I know you probably have to get to the salon, but I don't think I have any cold medicine here. Do you mind hanging out for a little while longer while I run to the store?"

"Of course. Yvonne is opening for me and I don't have a client until four, so I'm good here."

Crossing the room, I pull Laney into my arms for a hug, kissing Remy's head as I do.

"Thank you."

"Of course, Henley. We're family. We look out for each other."

When we part, I give her a curt nod then grab my truck keys, heading for the store to get everything possible to help Elodie feel better. The only other time I can recall feeling this helpless was when Remy was sick, but now it's the other girl in my life that needs me.

I just hope I don't screw it up.

***

After buying every cold medicine known to man and a few other necessities, I return home to find Laney has managed to get Remy down for her nap. After thanking her again for her help, I unpack the bags from the store and tidy up the house a bit before checking on Elodie again.

When I enter her room, I find her blowing her nose.

"Hey."

She coughs, holding her hand over her mouth. "Henley, you don't want to catch this. You shouldn't be near me."

"The only place I will be until you're better is by your side." Entering the room, I hand Elodie a glass of water and a few pills. "Now, the internet said that since the flu is viral, there's not much we can do until it passes, but I bought everything they suggested to make you comfortable."

"You—you looked up stuff on the internet?"

"I wanted to make sure I was buying the right things." Her eyes start to well with tears, but I cup her face. "Take your medicine." She does as I say and sets her glass on her nightstand. "Good girl. Now, I'm gonna make you some soup, and then you can try all the flavors of popcorn that I got you if you're still hungry."

"You bought me popcorn?"

"Every flavor they had." I push a hand through my hair and shrug. "I know it's probably not the best thing for you to eat right now, but it was one of the things that I knew would make you happy."

"I can't believe you did that, Henley."

"It's my turn to take care of you, El, like you've been taking care of me since you got here." The emotion in her eyes makes me want to reach out and pull her into me, but I also know that I'm not immune to every sickness, so I control myself and slip right back into caretaker mode.

For the next twenty-four hours, I juggle taking care of my daughter and my nanny, checking on her regularly while alternating medicine to keep her fever down, using the same protocol that she taught me when my own daughter was sick. Warren assured me that he is holding down the fort at the lodge, giving me updates here and there, but I'm grateful that I can rely on him to keep the place running while I'm needed at home.

By the morning of the third day, Elodie emerges from her room with color back in her cheeks. "Hey."

"Hi there." Her cough is still present, but it's not nearly as bad as it was. "I don't know how I'm supposed to sing on Saturday."

"We still have a few days to get you in tip-top shape." I wave Remy's hand toward her as she sits on my hip. "Who is that, baby bear? Can you say, Elodie?"

Remy lets out a squeal that makes us both laugh.

"Close enough." Elodie moves toward Remy, but then second guesses herself. "God, I wanna squeeze her, but I don't want to get her sick."

"Yeah, probably best to wait another day." I move around the kitchen. "I'm gonna make you some hot tea for your throat."

"You know, if you ever consider a second career, I think you'd make a fantastic nurse," Elodie says as she takes a seat on one of the stools at the kitchen counter.

I chuckle. "You think so?"

"Oh, absolutely. Besides, the idea of you wearing scrubs?" She hums appreciatively. "Yeah, I can definitely see it."

"I'll keep that in mind."

She clears her throat, watching me as I move. "Seriously though, Henley. I can't thank you enough for the past few days."

I turn and meet her eyes. "There's no need to thank me, El. I did what you would have done for me."

Her smile is small, but it's there. "Still, I've never had anyone take care of me like that."

"That's a damn shame because that's what you deserve."

And I'd do it a thousand times over, I think, feeling my heart slam against my chest as the reality races through me.

This woman has completely flipped my life upside down in three months, but I can't even be mad about it anymore. Instead, all I want to do is make her tea, ask her questions, and stroke her hair when she's sick.

Suddenly those wedding vows about taking care of each other in sickness and in health are starting to make a lot more fucking sense.

"Speaking of what you deserve," I say, preparing what I want to say next. "Once the concert is over, I'd like to take you on a proper date."

Her eyebrows lift. "What?"

"It dawned on me last week that we haven't done that. Between Remy and the trip to Charlotte...things sort of escalated and we haven't even had our first date. I want to show you how grateful I am for you."

She purses her lips. "You show me every day, Henley."

"Well, this is something I also want to do."

The smile she flashes me this time makes me feel like I'm ten feet tall. "All right. I would love to go on a date with you."

"Good. Now, you focus on getting better, and I'll focus on giving you a night you won't forget."

If only I knew that a few nights from now would be a moment that would be burned into my memory for the rest of my life, and not in a good way.

Chapter 19

Henley

Meeting the Parents & Harsh Truths

"Sorry, Mom. I was sicker than a dog and have other things going on right now." Elodie's voice rings out from the kitchen as I enter the house. It's Friday night and the first day I've been back at work all week. Elodie was finally feeling like herself, so I left feeling confident that she could survive the day with Remy so I could get caught up with my business.

Unfortunately, it sounds like she's getting an earful from her mom right now.

"I just don't understand why you couldn't answer the phone," her mother says. As I round the corner, I see Elodie staring down at her phone propped up on the kitchen counter as she sways side to side with Remy on her hip. Her eyes lift to meet mine, rolling before she mouths "hello" to me.

"I literally didn't get out of bed for three days, Mom."

"Who was taking care of the baby then?"

"That would be me," I say, stepping into the camera's view, waving at the woman on the screen who looks just like an older version of the woman standing next to me. "Nice to meet you, Mrs. Olsen. I'm Henley Clark."

Her eyes widen. "Oh, uh...hello there."

"Elodie had the flu. I can attest to that myself."

"See?" Elodie says. "I wasn't ignoring you."

"Well, still. You could have answered my texts."

"I would have but I don't have an answer for you about Thanksgiving. I just need to get through tomorrow, then I'll be able to think."

"What's tomorrow?"

Elodie darts her eyes toward me and then back to her mom. "I'm, uh...performing at the Hart Winery for their last Concert in the Courtyard."

"Really?" Her mom's voice rises an entire octave.

"Yes."

"Are they paying you?"

"Well, no..."

Her mom lets out a heavy sigh. "Elodie Anne," she starts just as her father comes onto the screen now.

"Hey pumpkin," he says then darts his eyes to me. "You must be the boss."

"Yes, sir. Henley Clark. Nice to meet you."

His response is a grunt as he turns his attention back to his daughter. "I think it's time for you to come home, Elodie."

"I'm twenty-five, Dad."

"Exactly. You should have a career by now, or at least be married and working on a family."

I can see the emotion on Elodie's face that she's trying to keep at bay. "Glad to know that's all you think women are good for."

"You know what I mean. Music is a hobby, pumpkin. That's what your mom and I have been trying to tell you..."

"Have you even seen her perform?" I interject. I can't stand here and listen to them speak to her like she's a child who doesn't know how to make her own decisions.

"Of course we have," her father replies. "Do you know how many talent shows her mom sat through?"

"So you weren't there then?" I counter. "Makes sense." Grinding my teeth together, I widen my stance and cross my arms. "Look, I know that we don't know each other, but I'm not one who ever sought out to impress a girl's parents, so I'm going to be frank." I lean closer to the phone and lower my voice. "Your daughter is talented, like jaw-droppingly amazing and hearing the way you dismiss her aspirations makes me think I prefer absent parents to the lack of support you show her."

"Henley," Elodie gasps beside me, but I continue.

"Maybe if you would stop trying to force your ideas on your daughter of what you think her life should be like, you might realize timing is everything. That's certainly something she's taught me."

"Are you done?" her father clips.

"Not even. I'll have you know that getting to know your daughter over the past three months has made me a better man, and if you think her chasing music is a waste of her time, then I invite you to her performance tomorrow where you can see for yourselves how incredible she is."

"I have to work," her father replies.

"Of course you do." My eyes dart to her mom. "What about you?"

"Well, I, uh..."

Elodie reaches for my arm. "Henley, it's okay."

"No, it's not. It's bullshit that they don't support you."

"I'm used to it."

"We support you, sweetie," her mother interjects.

"Then come to her performance tomorrow," I reply.

"I'll—I'll think about it." Her mother's voice is low, but it's loud enough that Elodie is surprised by her response.

"Really?"

"Yes, but only if you promise to come to Thanksgiving."

"Wow, blackmail at its finest." Elodie rolls her eyes and adjusts Remy on her hip. "Fine. I'll be home for Thanksgiving."

"Susan! Wheel of Fortune is about to start and I need a beer!" Elodie's father's voice booms through the background.

"I've got to go," her mom says.

"Okay. See you tomorrow then?" Elodie asks.

"Uh huh." And then her mom ends the call.

Elodie stares down at the phone, processing the end button before she finally lifts her eyes to mine. "I can't believe you just did that."

"I can't believe you let them talk to you that way. I know damn well you've given me more sass for less."

"Well, they're my parents."

"Doesn't matter. You don't deserve to be spoken to that way," I say, pulling her into me by her hips.

Her reply comes out as a whisper. "Thank you for sticking up for me."

I cup the side of her face. "Thank you for letting me." *And thank you for changing my life.*

We stand there, our eyes bouncing back and forth before she presses up on her toes and kisses me softly. And in the back of my mind, I admit what I already know: she might have changed my life, but if I ask her to stay, I'd be just as bad as her parents for asking her to change what she's always wanted for hers.

***

"Her parents really said that?" Fletcher asks as Rhonan shuffles the deck of cards.

"Yeah. I swear, I've never wanted to cuss out a grown man and woman before, but I came really fucking close."

Elliot scoffs. "Trust me, it's not as satisfying as you'd think."

"Speaking from experience?" Rhonan asks as he begins dealing the cards. It's Friday night, and since Fletcher's team played last night, he came home for the rest of the weekend to be with Laney and see Elodie perform. Which is why we decided to sneak in a blackjack night.

"I may have left a few choice words on Tori's voicemail."

I shake my head. "Yeah, well, seeing as how these people are Elodie's parents, I'm not sure I made the best impression even with the little restraint I exercised."

Elliot takes a chip and slides it toward the center of the table, placing his bet. The rest of us follow suit. "Speaking of parents, I have those papers ready for your daughter's egg donor to sign."

"That's awesome. Thanks, man."

"No problem. Just let me know when you're free to meet with Meghan, and I'll have my paralegal set it up. Unless you want to call her yourself?"

"The sooner the better. Just give me a time and I'll be there."

I shake my head. "No, I'd rather all communication go through your office just in case. Just find a time that works for Meghan, and I'll be there. The sooner I get legal custody, the better."

Elliot nods. "Got it. You need another card?" He flicks his chin in the direction of Fletcher.

"Yeah, hit me." Rhonan flips over a five, which brings Fletcher's total to twenty. "Hell yeah." Elliot chooses to stay with his hand totaling eighteen, and I only have twelve, so I ask for a hit and end up busting with twenty-two when Rhonan flips over a ten.

"Shit."

"Never can be sure with twelve," Rhonan says as he flips over his second card and reveals that his hand totals twenty-one.

"Mother fucker," Fletcher says, grumbling as Rhonan takes the chips from all of us. "Anyway...do you think Elodie's parents will show up tomorrow?" he asks, redirecting the conversation back to my issue.

"I honestly don't know. Her dad said that he had to work, but her mom made it sound like she'd be there."

"What if she doesn't show?" Rhonan asks.

I push a hand through my hair and lift my soda to my lips since I still haven't touched alcohol since the night out with Warren. "I think as long as we're all there, Elodie will be okay. Truth be told, we've given her more support in a few months than her parents have her whole damn life."

"So does this mean she's still planning on leaving before Christmas?" Rhonan asks as he passes the cards to Fletcher to deal next.

"I don't know, and part of me doesn't even want to fucking ask."

Fletcher slaps me on the shoulder. "Dude..."

"I know, but..."

"Do you want her to stay?" he asks.

Yes, my mind says, but my mouth says otherwise. "I—I don't know what I want. All I know is that I have feelings for the woman I hired to be my nanny but has turned into so much more than that, and I don't know what to fucking do about it."

Rhonan clears his throat. "Crazy hearing you admit that, man."

"Does that mean the shit-talking is about to begin?"

Rhonan shakes his head. "No. In fact, I was just going to say that hearing you say that out loud shows how much you've changed in the past three months. I'm—I'm fucking impressed. You took your role as a father seriously from the start, Henley." With a dip of his chin, he continues. "That first night you went home with Remy to now? Look at how far you've come. It's not easy raising a child on your own. Trust me, I know."

"Well, none of my confidence and skills would exist without Elodie."

Fletcher shuffles the cards. "Then ask her to stay."

"And what if she says no?" I counter. "I'll be right back where I've always been—alone."

Elliot throws his hands in the air. "Then who the fuck are we?"

"You know what I mean," I say, twisting to face him, but he cuts me off before I can continue.

"No, I don't. In fact, the three of you are the people I can depend on to be there more than anyone. Did I read that wrong? Is it just me who feels that way?" he says, looking to Rhonan and Fletcher.

"You don't get it," I argue before they can chime in.

"No, *you* don't." Elliot's jaw tightens. "I've been going through the shittiest time of my life, Henley, and I know I've been an asshole. But I also know that you three will be there no matter how ugly it gets."

"You still have your family, though," I reply. "My family is Dilynne."

"What about Carol and Nick?" Fletcher adds. "Pretty sure they've been better parents to you than your own."

"Yeah, out of obligation. And if I ask Elodie to stay, I'm afraid she'll either stay because she feels obligated or leave because I forced her hand. I don't want her to make the decision because I asked her to. I want her to make the best decision for herself."

Rhonan furrows his brow. "Do you honestly think that Carol and Nick have stayed in your life out of obligation? When you wrote that letter to the deputy district attorney, asking for you and Dilynne to stay in their care until you both turned eighteen, you know they did that by choice, right? Because they love you."

"It's not real love," I blurt before I can stop myself.

My three best friends stare back at me, bewildered.

"Holy shit," Fletcher says. "That's what you think?"

"It's what I know," I grate out, pointing a finger to the felt under my hands as I clench my jaw. "And I made peace with it a long time ago."

Rhonan scoffs. "Wow, Henley. Jesus, I never realized you were so fucking clueless."

Fletcher glares at me. "You still haven't said it back to them, huh?"

"Who?" My blood pressure is rising the longer this conversation continues, especially because I can feel my insecurities about Elodie lurking in the background to join the party.

Let's just air all of my fears tonight, shall we?

"Carol and Nick," Fletcher finishes, leaving me silent. Our eyes remain locked until a puff of air bursts from his lips. "Yeah, that's what I thought." He leans toward me with narrowed eyes, and I brace for what he's about to say. Sadly, no preparation could make it sting any less. "You ran the first time Nick said it to you, tried to fucking cheat death so that you could ignore how it made you feel, and you've been running from it ever since."

I pound my fist into the table, chips scattering to the floor. "You don't know what the hell you're talking about! And besides, you're one to fucking talk, Fletch."

He moves his face even closer to mine. "No, I'm the one that has every right to call you on your shit because I did the same fucking thing, Henley. I ran from this town to escape my father, and guess what? It still caught up with me. And if you don't face this lie you've been feeding yourself that you don't deserve to be loved, it doesn't matter if Elodie chooses to stay or not, you're going to fuck it up anyway. Because that's what you'll let yourself believe—that you don't deserve her." He sizes me up, a look of disgust gracing his features. "And right now? I'd have to agree. You haven't earned her, Henley. She deserves a man who is willing to face his past to give her a future."

I stand from the table and slam my glass down on it. "You know what? Fuck this. I'm going home."

"She'll never stay for you if you don't think you're worth staying for!" Fletcher yells after me as I storm out of Elliot's house. I stomp out to my truck and drive home with a grip on the steering wheel so tight it feels like I'm trying to strangle the damn thing.

But deep down, I know Fletcher's right.

I'll never be enough for her if I can't believe I am.

My parents fucked me up far worse than just abandoning me at a young age.

They stripped me of my self-worth and made me doubt that I could ever be enough for anyone.

And Elodie deserves a man who knows his own worth and hers. Turns out I'm not that man, and I don't know if I ever will be.

Chapter 20

Henley

Options & Acceptance

"It looks like the whole town showed up tonight." My sister stands beside me, holding Remy.

"They usually do." I lift my water to my lips.

"Yeah, but I also heard that Carolina was bribing people with donuts at Bites & Bliss, so that might have been a factor."

I direct my gaze in the direction of the bar and see Carolina handing out samples of the blueberry donuts that Elodie loves, bragging about Elodie and her voice, as well as her exceptional taste in baked goods.

It's the night of Elodie's performance at Hart Winery, and as my sister pointed out, the place is packed. Gas heaters are spread throughout the courtyard to ward off the chilly November air, especially after the snow we got earlier this week. But the people of Blossom Peak aren't afraid to put on a jacket and bring a few blankets to support one of their own, and in less than an hour, Elodie will have everyone warming up when they start dancing.

I heard her rehearsing in her room when I got home from Elliot's house last night. She probably doesn't know since I didn't bother her and I was too busy pacing my room after my argument with the boys, but all I could think about is how tonight was going to feel—how watching her perform for the first time would remind me of why she came here in the first place, to make a decision about the role that music still plays in her life.

And I think by her deciding to do this, her choice is clear and I need to accept it—music is still what she wants.

"How are you feeling?" Dilynne asks as Remy blows raspberries in her arms.

"I'm not the one performing."

She rolls her eyes. "No shit, Sherlock. But I can tell by the scowl on your face that you've got something on your mind."

My eyes scour the crowd again, looking for any sign of the one person I know Elodie wants to be here. "Elodie's mom said she might come tonight, so I guess I'm on edge."

"Really? I thought her parents weren't supportive."

"Oh, they're not. I gave them an earful about it, though."

My sister laughs at me. "God, I knew this girl was having an effect on you, but I didn't think it would happen this fast."

"She's leaving still, Dil."

Her brow furrows. "Really? Did she tell you that?"

"She didn't have to. This performance says it all." I hold my hand out toward the stage Laney is currently checking over, talking to the sound guy to make sure everything is working right. "This is the life she wants."

"And what do you want?"

I want her, I think to myself. I want to keep her for myself, but I know I'm not the man who gets to keep a woman like her.

"I want her to be happy," I say instead.

"You and Remy do make her happy," my sister counters.

"Music is her first love, and it always will be."

"First loves don't mean shit," my sister fires back. "Trust me. Sometimes the person we give our heart to first is the one we think breaks it the hardest, but then we experience true heartbreak and realize we didn't know shit about love."

I glance over at her. "Sounds like you're speaking from experience."

"Yeah, well…lessons learned are important too. But Henley, you can't deny that there's something real between you two."

"I'm not."

"So why don't you ask her to stay?"

Remy reaches for me, so I take her from my sister and situate her against my chest. "I knew we were on borrowed time, Dilynne. I've known that from the start."

"Have you considered going back to LA with her?" she suggests, which I can't deny has crossed my mind. But it's not that simple.

"I can't, Dil. I have a business and a daughter now, which means my life is here. And if I ask her to stay, she'd be giving up her dreams for me." Shaking my head, I clear my throat. "The last thing I would want is for her to hold that over my head, to resent me down the line."

"Oh, so this is about your baggage."

"I don't have baggage," I lie, knowing damn well that she's right, and so were my friends last night.

My sister huffs out a laugh. "Oh, so you're also in denial, got it."

"Thanks for the support."

"That's what I'm here for. But, you know what I keep thinking about? The Charming Bull. She sang a country set that night and owned the place." She taps her chin, considering her next words. "Nashville isn't as far as Los Angeles, and honestly, that seems like a better fit for her."

"What are you saying?"

My sister leans closer to me, eyes wide. "I'm saying, things can change, and if you're serious about her, maybe she could consider other options."

Is Dilynne right? Is this something Elodie might be willing to do?

"My point is, you've got to stop hiding behind your fears and actually make shit happen. Otherwise, you're going to be left living with regrets."

"You act like it's so simple to just forget what happened to us, how it felt to be forgotten about over and over again," I say, finally voicing part of my fear to my sister.

Her face softens as she places her hand on my shoulder. "I didn't forget a thing, Henley. I remember parts you probably never wanted me to, but I do. Those memories still exist, I just choose not to dwell on them. And you know who restored faith in the world for me besides you?"

"Who?"

"Carol and Nick." She squeezes my upper arm. "We had an amazing gift of a second chance with them. They loved us like we were their own, and I'll never take that for granted." Sighing, she leans toward Remy and kisses her on the cheek. "I've got to go to the bathroom and check on Laney, but save me a seat, will you?"

"Sure."

As I watch my sister walk away, her last few words hit me hard. Have I taken Carol and Nick for granted? Have I been so blinded by anger that I've been reluctant to accept all of the good in my life?

Gazing down at my daughter, I feel the sting of tears in my eyes.

Holy shit.

Dilynne is right.

I'm the one who gets to choose if I keep fixating on my past instead of fighting for my future, a future with my daughter that I never imagined having. But I do, and now it has to be my main focus.

God, I'm such a fucking moron, but at least I have the ability to change that.

"You look like you're having an epiphany," Fletcher says as he comes up behind me.

I twist to face him head on. "Well, I sort of am."

"Is it a good epiphany?"

"Yeah, but not for my heart rate."

Fletcher reaches up and clasps my shoulder. "Look, I wanted to apologize about last night."

"No. You have nothing to apologize for, man. You were right."

"I was a little harsh."

"I needed to hear it, Fletch. In fact, between you and my sister just now, I think something finally clicked."

"Really?"

My eyes move to the right just in time to see Elodie making her way toward the stage for a sound check. A man hands her a microphone and asks her to say a few words. People instantly start clapping and cheering, even though we still have another half hour before she starts performing.

"Fuck."

I—I think I'm in love with her, my mind finishes for me.

Fletcher slaps me on the back. "Yeah, it slams into you fast, buddy."

I turn to face him. "I have to ask her to stay."

"I know."

"If I don't, I'll—"

"Always regret it." He nods. "I know the feeling well, my friend."

And that's when I decide that it's time to make this woman mine, come hell or high water.

***

"Blossom Peak! How are y'all doing tonight?" Elodie greets the crowd, and their cheers go on for minutes.

I show Remy how to clap her hands, assisting her with the motion until she attempts to do it on her own. "Say, 'Go, Elodie!'" Remy squeals when she sees her nanny walking across the stage.

"Well, I'm so honored to be performing for you all tonight, and I hope you like country music." The crowd cheers in response. "Growing up, my momma always had music playing, so this first song goes out to her. And if you're here, Mom, I just wanna say thank you."

A sharp pang of guilt cuts through the center of my chest as I watch Elodie search the crowd for her mom only to come up empty.

I kept trying to hold out hope that her mother would appear, even standing by the entrance to the winery until the very last second and asking Dilynne to save a seat for me and her if she showed up. Unfortunately, the woman I chastised on the phone the other night is nowhere to be found, at least that I've seen for myself.

Laney and Dilynne are seated to my right, Fletcher next to his fiancée, and George Hart next to him. Rhonan, his nanny Joanne, and daughter Ellis are on my left, followed by Elliot. Carolina is in the row behind us, smiling from ear to ear as Elodie starts to sing the lyrics to "Somebody's Hero" by Jamie O'Neal. Dilynne and I share a look, but I try to just focus on Elodie and not how badly I want to drive to Garnet Valley to tell her parents off for real.

Elodie keeps playing through her set, singing crowd favorites by Tim McGraw, Shania Twain, Reba McEntire, and George Strait, and I can't take my eyes off of her the entire time—her smile, her energy, the way you can tell that she feels the music and lyrics in her soul.

Watching her on that stage is making me fall for her even more.

"Thank you so much," she says before taking a sip of her water. "Now, I love singing, but I love writing songs even more and lately, I've had a little bit of inspiration." Her eyes meet mine. Rhonan shoves me from the side as my grin appears. "So, if you're willing, I'd love to play a few new songs I've written for you." The applause is instant. "Perfect. Well, this first one is inspired by a little girl I've had the pleasure of taking care of for the past three months. She's brought so much joy to my life, especially at a time when I thought I'd lost all of mine. It's called, 'Remember Me.'"

My pulse climbs as I listen to the lyrics Elodie wrote about my daughter, echoing her sentiment that she spoke to me about a few weeks ago—how my little girl has made her see the world differently, and how she worries Remy won't remember her because she's so young.

That sting of tears returns because I don't want Elodie to be some-one that only exists in my memory. I want my daughter to know her too, to be raised by her, to look up to her, and run to her when she needs a woman to talk to.

Sure, she'd have Dilynne and Laney, but this little girl deserves a mom and a dad. She deserves the life I didn't have.

Meghan didn't want her, but I think Elodie just might.

When Elodie finishes, Laney is wiping tears from under her eyes and glances over at me. "Wow," she mouths and all I can do is nod.

"Thank you, everyone," Elodie says before reaching for her guitar and strumming the chords to another song she wrote when she was in college about following your heart. When she's done with that one, I check the time on my watch and note that she's got to be toward the end of her set.

"So unfortunately, our time together is coming to an end, but there's one more song I'd love to play for you. You okay with that?" The crowd cheers and I draw the blanket tighter around Remy to ward off the cold. "Perfect. This one doesn't need an explanation because the lyrics speak for themselves. It's called, 'On Borrowed Time.'"

Goosebumps break out on my skin under the layers of my coat, but not from the cold.

No.

It's from listening to this woman tell me in a song everything I've been feeling since she crashed into my life.

Your eyes say more than your mouth,

Your touch says more than your eyes,

And each time you look at me,

All I can think about is our inevitable goodbye.

But what if this didn't have an end?

What if you decided to let me in?

I know you can be that man,

You just have to want it.

I know that you're scared,

Because I'm scared too.

You have the power to destroy me,

And I can do the same to you.

But we can be scared together,

Life can change on a dime,

Or are these feelings only fleeting?

Because we're on borrowed time?

***

"Fuck, you were incredible." My words are barely audible as I mumble against Elodie's lips, leading her to my bedroom after putting Remy to bed in her crib. That little girl passed out the second we started driving back to my house, and at this moment, I'm extremely grateful for that.

"Thank you."

"Seriously, Elodie. I couldn't take my eyes off you," I say as I lift her sweater and throw it to the other side of the room before dropping my lips to her neck and kissing her sensitive skin.

"I know. I could feel your eyes on me."

"I didn't want to look away." When I lift my eyes and meet hers, those gray orbs hypnotize me. Leaning my forehead against hers, I let out a shaky breath. "Fuck, there's so much I want to say to you."

"We can talk later," she says before bringing her lips back to mine, telling me that she needs our physical connection right now more than anything. "I just want to be with you right now." She palms me through my jeans.

"Damn, baby. I need you too." We make quick work of our clothes and then I'm crawling across the bed, hovering over her while testing her wetness with my fingers.

She swallows roughly. "Henley, I'm on the pill and I—" She pauses before saying, "I really don't want anything between us tonight."

I grow even harder from her request. "Jesus, are you sure, El?"

Her nod is confident as she reaches for my cock and strokes the entire length. "Yes. Please..."

I look down to where we're about to be joined as I drag the head of my cock through her slit. "You're gonna feel every inch of me tonight, sweetheart."

She pushes her arms above her head, reaching for the metal bars on the top of my headboard, her breasts rising as her back bows. "That's exactly what I want."

Without another moment of hesitation, I line myself up to her entrance and push forward, watching her stretch around me, feeling her silky heat envelop my cock in one of the most intense sexual experiences of my life. "Fucccckkkk…"

"Holy shit," she moans, pushing herself up on her elbows to watch the juncture between her legs where we're joined. "It's so good, so different, so…"

I reach down and rub her clit softly with my thumb. "You feel incredible, baby. So fucking wet." I bend my head toward hers and capture her lips, continuing to rub her clit and trying to focus on anything but how exquisite she feels.

I've never been bare with a woman before.

But none of them have been her.

Her legs start to quiver as her orgasm blooms. Her breaths grow shallow and her eyes close tight as I keep up my relentless pace. "Henley, I'm—"

"Fall apart for me, baby." She breaks and tweaks her nipples as she does before I lean down, bat her hand away, and take her nipple into my mouth instead. "Goddamn, you're even wetter now."

"I—I can't catch my breath."

I press our foreheads together. "Stay with me, El. Keep letting me make you feel good."

"You always do."

With each flick of my hips, the woman beneath me writhes and meets my thrusts, egging me on, encouraging me to fuck her harder and deeper, edging us both until I can't hold back any longer.

"Fuck, baby. I can't hold back anymore."

"Come for me then, Henley." She lines her lips up to my ear. "Fill me."

"Ah, shit," I groan as the first spurt of cum leaves my body. I keep pumping through my orgasm and Elodie finds her second one, clenching tightly and fluttering all around me.

By the time we're both done, I've collapsed on top of her. "Jesus."

"Henley..." Her lips meet my ear. "Thank you."

I lift my head to meet her eyes. "No, thank you. Fuck, El. I—"

Her yawn cuts me off. "I'm so tired. Can we talk in the morning?"

Pressing my lips to hers, I pull out of her slowly, watching my cum seep out of her pussy as I lean back. "Yeah, baby. That's fine."

And as we lie in bed together and drift off to sleep, I decide that our date on Tuesday is when I'll lay everything out there. I'll tell her how I feel, that I want her to stay, and that I want to make this work.

But I should have seen the writing on the wall—our time was borrowed.

And one phone call was about to prove it.

Chapter 21

Elodie

Give Me a Reason

"Hello?" Remy reaches for the phone at my ear, so I place her in her playpen and catch the phone before it falls from my shoulder.

Lennon's voice comes through the line at increased volume. "Girl, when were you going to tell me that you're famous?"

"Uh, last time I checked, I wasn't."

"Have you been on social media today?"

"No. I logged out of all of my stuff when I moved to Blossom Peak. Why?" My heart rate picks up. "What's going on?"

It's the Monday after my concert at Hart Winery, and yesterday I was basking in the afterglow. Henley cooked breakfast after Remy let us sleep in, and then we took her to the park and visited with Carol and Nick. Surprisingly though, Henley didn't bring up my performance or the fact that my mom never showed, but neither did I—because voicing my disappointment would make it all the more real that my parents truly don't want me to succeed with music.

Luckily, Henley's mind was exactly where I needed it to be when we got home that night—in the gutter. The man made love to me with nothing between us, and that was the moment I knew that I was head over heels in love with him. It's been in the back of my mind for weeks now, but watching him hover over me that night solidified it.

The reverent look in his eyes, the softness of his touch, the way he couldn't form words and instead used his body to show me what he was feeling—it was exactly what I needed in that moment.

And that's how I know that he's what I need too.

I can't wait for our date tomorrow so I can tell him.

"Your performance at the winery is all over the internet. And girl...that song you wrote about your boss's daughter?" Lennon whistles, bringing me back to our conversation. "Freaking gold."

My stomach drops. "Oh my God."

"And when were you going to tell me that you performed at The Charming Bull?" she continues. "You know that place was our stomping ground back in college."

I can hear my pulse in my ears. "Is it bad?"

"Is what bad?"

"The comments? The posts?" I struggle to find the couch behind me so I can sit down in preparation for her response. The last thing I anticipated this morning was finding out that my absence from social media has actually made an impact, and not just on my mental health.

"Do you think I would have called you if they were?"

My hand covers the center of my chest. "Lennon, just answer me, please."

"You're a sensation, Elodie. Seriously, why haven't you posted on social media in months?"

"I just needed space from that grind, of constantly feeling inadequate. That's why I logged off when I left LA." A chime rings in my ear. I lower my phone to see a number flash across the screen that I don't recognize, but the area code is from Los Angeles. "Uh, Lennon?"

"Yeah?"

"I'm getting a call from someone in LA."

"It's probably spam. You know how you put your phone number down in one survey or application for something, and suddenly you're getting random calls from numbers in Greenland? Like, who the hell lives in Greenland?"

"Good point." I press ignore and then slump back against the couch. "So, is that why you called this morning? To tell me that I'm an internet sensation?"

"Yes, and for you to bring me up to speed on your boss. The last time we spoke was after Charlotte when you told me you two slept together." Lennon sighs. "So now that means you're in love with him, right?"

It's my turn to sigh. "I think I've been in love with him since long before that."

"Elodie..."

Groaning, I cover my face with my hand. "Look, I know, okay? I'm pathetic."

"You are not pathetic. I wouldn't have been able to resist a handsome single dad who wears flannels either. So, what does this mean? Are you still going back to LA?"

My phone rings again with the same number, but I press ignore once more.

"I—I don't know. I guess I'm kind of waiting for a sign, like something to help me make that decision. Henley hasn't brought it up. But did I tell you that he invited my mom to my performance the other night?"

"What? No. Girl, your communication with me has been lackluster, at best."

"I'm sorry, but life has been a little crazy and I've sort of been wrapped up in my boss."

"Hey, I understand. If I could wrap my legs around a man that looked like that, I would ignore my best friend too."

"Yeah, well even him defending me wasn't enough to make my mom show up." Sadness overwhelms me. "I can't even believe that I thought she might."

"Well, you know how your parents feel."

"I know, and hearing Henley put them in their place just made me fall for him even more. He said things to them that I wish I had the courage to say."

"He did what?" I recount the night he spoke to them on the phone. "Oh my God, Elodie. That man is in love with you."

My pulse spikes again. "You think?"

"Uh, yeah. A man doesn't do something like that if there aren't real feelings there."

"I'm so crazy about him and his daughter, Lennon." My gaze drifts over to Remy shaking one of her toys around while squawking. "But..." The same number from earlier is calling again. "Uh, Lennon. That number is calling for the third time now."

"Maybe it's important. I'll let you go."

"Thanks. I'll call you later," I say before answering the call with hesitation. "Hello?"

"Hi there. I'm looking for Elodie Olsen."

"This is she."

"Hi, Elodie. My name is Sandra from Regal Records. How are you today?"

"Uh..." I'm momentarily speechless, but not just because a record label is calling me. No, it's because this is the label that Liam works for, making my skin crawl. "I'm good, thank you."

"Great. Is now a good time to speak with you?"

I glance over at Remy who is perfectly content in her playpen. "Sure."

"Perfect. Well, Elodie Olsen, you have made quite the splash on social media this past weekend, and I think I speak for everyone at our label when I say that you are very talented."

"Uh, thank you." I can't feel my hands as Sandra continues to speak.

Her laugh comes through the phone. "Look, I know these calls can seem sort of formal, so let me break something down for you. I found your demo in Liam's old office."

That information makes my body snap back up. "Wait? *Old* office?"

"Oh yeah. That slimeball got exactly what was coming to him, including several charges for sexual harassment." My mouth falls open. "Anyway, I found your demo and was blown away. Then when I looked you up online, clips from your performance this weekend were everywhere, and I just had to reach out to you. Are you busy this afternoon? I'd love for you to stop by the office so we can chat more."

My eyes land on Remy again. "Uh, well...I'm actually in North Carolina."

"Oh, dear. Yeah, that's not a short commute."

"No, it's not," I say through a laugh.

"Well, when's the soonest you can get here?" I hear clicking in the background. "Time is of the essence here, Elodie. The executives are very interested in you, but they have the attention spans of a gnat. Meeting in person will allow them to fall in love with you even faster."

My mind is spinning as I'm trying to process what she's saying and everything that I'm thinking and feeling right now. "Um, I'd have to ask my boss…"

"Hey, I get it. Tell you what, you call me back later after you've talked to your boss. Ideally, you can catch an early flight tomorrow because I really want to introduce you to the executives here at the label and show you around."

"Uh…is this for real?"

"Elodie, this is a good thing," she says quickly. "You have a future in music, my dear. And I'm going to help make you a star."

***

"Holy shit!" Lennon shouts through the phone when I call her back. When I got off the call with Sandra, I had to sit on the couch for a moment to process what happened. Then Remy got fussy so I fed her, changed her, and put her down for her afternoon nap. But now that the call has sunk in, I knew I had to process this turn of events with my best friend.

"Yeah. Say that about a dozen more times and you'll be where I'm at."

"You have to go, Elodie. This is huge! A once-in-a-lifetime opportunity!"

"I know, Lennon," I say as I pace the living room, glancing at the clock and realizing that Henley won't be home for a few more hours, so I still have time to gather my thoughts and decide what I'm going to say to him. "But I feel bad just springing this on Henley."

"Girl, he's a grown man. He can find someone else to watch his kid while you go to L.A. for a few days and possibly get everything you've ever wanted."

"But what if what I wanted has changed?" It's the one question I am still scared to admit the answer to.

"Are you—what are you saying, Elodie?"

Sighing, I sit down on the couch and stare across the living room. "I—I don't know. This is all happening so fast, and I—" I take in a deep breath. "We're supposed to go on a date tomorrow."

"You can't seriously be considering giving up this opportunity for a man?" Lennon snaps. "Girl, I love you, but this is it. This is your chance. If you don't go and at least hear what they have to say, you're going to regret it for the rest of your life."

"You're right. I know you're right. I just..."

"Figure out how to get out there. If Henley truly cares about you, he'll let you go."

That's exactly what I'm afraid of.

***

"Mmmm." Henley's lips meet the juncture between my neck and shoulders as I stand at the stove, stirring the beef stew I made for dinner. "I missed you today," he whispers in my ear, nibbling at my lobe.

"I missed you too." I can feel my voice already starting to crack, so I clear my throat. "How was work?"

He releases me from his hold and moves to the fridge, reaching for a soda. "Busy. I had a lot to catch up on from last week, but people were talking about your performance all day, and I got roped into several conversations about it."

I turn the stove burner off and twist to face him. "Really?"

"Yeah. You made quite the impression on our little town."

My heart is hammering wildly. Is this the time to bring up my phone call today? "Well, uh..."

Remy fusses in her high chair, pulling Henley's attention to her. "Hey, baby bear." He lifts her into his arms and kisses her cheeks. "I missed you too." His eyes meet mine. "Is it just me, or did she grow in the past week?"

"I was thinking that myself, actually." Walking toward them, I reach out and bring her hand to my lips, kissing the top of it. "She feels heavier and taller. Longer?" I shrug. "Not sure how to describe a baby's height."

Henley laughs. "Well, I'm not short so hopefully she inherited her height from me and not her mom."

"Was Meghan short?"

"Not as short as you," he teases before leaning down and kissing me.

"You'd better watch it."

"Oh really? What are you gonna do about it?"

The timer on the oven goes off before I can reply. "Saved by the bell, Henley Clark."

"That's a good thing for you," he tosses back. God, I love talking with him, seeing this lighter side of him and watching him dote on his baby girl.

It's these moments that have made me question everything lately.

I pour two bowls of stew and bring a basket of biscuits over to the table, settling in to eat as my stomach continues to twist, anticipating the conversation we need to have before the night is over. Remy is in her high chair, eating a few baby snacks and Henley is already reaching for a second biscuit. "So, how was your day? Anything exciting happen?" he asks as he lifts his spoon to his mouth.

I move my food around, sensing my hunger diminishing the longer I contemplate what to say. "Actually, I got a, uh...pretty exciting phone call."

"From who?"

"A record label in L.A."

He drops his spoon into his bowl, splashing beef stew onto the table. His face is stoic, lacking any indication of what's going through his mind. Finally, he clears his throat and asks, "Seriously?"

"Yes." Biting my bottom lip, I take in a deep breath and prepare to say the words I've been rehearsing all afternoon. "It's the label Liam worked for."

That gets a reaction out of him. His jaw ticks and he's instantly shaking his head. "Oh, hell no..."

"It wasn't him," I interject quickly. "It was a woman. Her name is Sandra, and she found my demo tapes in Liam's old office. Apparently, he got fired for sexual harassment."

"Good. The fucker deserved it." Henley tears a piece of his biscuit off and shoves it in his mouth, chewing aggressively. "So, what did she say?"

"She wants me to go to L.A. to meet some executives."

His brows lift. "Oh. Well, that's amazing, El."

"She wants me there as soon as possible."

His brow furrows. "How soon?"

"Tomorrow, if possible."

"Tomorrow."

"I know it's last minute, but..." Henley stands from the table, giving me his back as he pushes a hand through his hair. "I'm sorry for even asking. I just..."

"Why the hell are you apologizing, Elodie?" he snaps, twisting his head over his shoulder to look at me. "This is what you wanted, right?"

"Yes, but..." He grumbles something under his breath, but I can't quite make it out. "Are you angry?"

"I—I don't know what I'm feeling right now. The timing of all of this is—"

I stand from my chair and walk over to him, placing my hand on his shoulder. My touch makes him tense up. "I'm sorry about our date."

His shoulders lift as he shrugs. "It is what it is."

"Henley, please look at me." With a heavy sigh, he slowly turns around, but the pain in his eyes almost slices me in two. "I don't want this to...I'm not sure what to say, I just—"

"I need to call Carol and see if she can watch Remy tomorrow," he says abruptly.

"Henley?"

"What, Elodie?"

"Why are you pulling away from me? We can—"

"This is how we knew this would end, right?" He darts his eyes away from me.

"End?"

He clears his throat. "We always knew this was temporary, El. At least now you're getting everything you wanted."

I place my hand on the center of his chest as he continues to avoid my gaze. "Maybe what I wanted has changed," I whisper.

"No." With both hands, he pushes mine away. "You're going. End of discussion."

The tone of his voice instantly makes me angry. "Last time I checked, you're not the boss of me."

He huffs out a laugh. "That's where you're wrong. I technically am your boss, or...I was."

"What are you saying?"

"I'm saying that maybe this is the sign you've been looking for, and your time as Remy's nanny is coming to an end."

My bottom lip starts to tremble. "Henley..."

The corner of his mouth lifts as he shrugs, studying my face. "You have to go, Elodie."

Shaking my head, I don't give up, even if he doesn't seem to care. "No, I don't. What if that's not what I want anymore?"

"You're kidding, right?"

"No, I'm not." Closing the distance between us again, I put both hands on his chest and peer up at him, begging him when I say, "Give me a reason to stay."

He closes his eyes and sighs. "I can't. You have to go, Elodie. It's your dream." When his eyes open, the pain I see reflected in them makes the first tear of many fall. "This is what you've wanted, and you need to show your parents that you've made it happen. Trust me, as someone who would love nothing more than to rub in my parents' faces what I've made of myself despite them, you owe it to yourself."

"But what about us?"

He covers my hands with his. "My life is here."

"I—" Another tear slides down my cheek. "I can't believe you don't want me to stay."

"It doesn't matter what I want, Elodie. I'll be damned if I'm the person who stands in between you and your dreams, sweetheart." My head falls to his chest as the tears flow freely now. "It's okay." His voice cracks. "Our time has come to an end. But just know that you've changed my life, Elodie Olsen—not just with your words, but also your heart."

We stand there in the kitchen, holding one another as I sob, grieving the future that I thought we had while trying to focus on the future I always wanted.

But no matter how much the idea of going to this meeting in L.A. excites me, I can't help but feel like I'm about to leave a piece of my heart in Blossom Peak, and it's a piece I'll never get back.

Chapter 22

Henley

I Need a Fucking Drink

"Be safe." I press one last kiss to the top of Elodie's head as she stands on my front doorstep. It's five o'clock in the morning, and a cab is waiting at the curb to take her to the airport. I wanted to drive her myself, but Remy is still sleeping and part of me didn't think I could get through dropping her off, not knowing if I'd ever see her again.

I know I'm a fucking coward, but I guess this is what happens to me when I feel like my heart is being ripped in two.

"Kiss me," she commands, lifting up on her toes and pulling my face to hers. Our lips meet and I swear, every time we kiss it feels like it won't ever be enough.

But this kiss is the end. It's goodbye. It's likely the last time I'll ever feel her lips against mine.

I know there are such things as airplanes and long-distance relationships. But last night as I held her in my arms after we made love, a part of me made peace with the fact that Elodie and I just weren't meant to last. Maybe her role in my life was to show me the possibility of what I could have if I just opened myself up and faced the baggage I've been carrying around like a security blanket my entire life.

And maybe I was supposed to help her find joy in music again, to realize her talent and passion and give her the space and opportunity to pursue it.

When we part, the sight of her tears almost makes me drop to my knees and beg her to stay.

But I can't. I refuse to be the reason she doesn't follow this through.

I thought I'd be taking her on a date tonight, telling her how I feel, and asking her to create a life with me. Instead, I'm standing here trying to figure out how to let her go.

"I'll call you," she says, but all I can do is nod in response, not sure if I'll answer. Would it make this harder? To hear her voice, hear her excitement at the prospect of her new life?

Or would a clean break make this easier?

I wish I had the answers.

"Bye, Henley." With one last glance over her shoulder, she makes her way down the sidewalk, handing her bags and guitar case to the cab driver. She took what she needed, and I told her I would ship the rest to her once she got settled.

A few moments later, the cab pulls onto the road, and I watch the taillights disappear.

Fuck. She's really gone.

I head back inside, startled by the quiet of the house, my home that didn't feel like one until Remy and Elodie entered it. Everywhere I turn I see reminders of her—the décor she added over the past few months, the couch where she'd sit and write songs with her guitar in hand, and even the spot in the hallway where I saw her bare ass for the first time.

At least that memory earns a chuckle, even if it hurts.

As I walk down the hall, I debate going into my daughter's room that Elodie helped me decorate but decide against it, not wanting to wake my baby girl before she's ready. Her sleep is the number one factor that decides her mood. Instead, I head to the next room and open the door, finding the bed where Elodie used to sleep empty but freshly made.

Of course she made the damn bed before she left.

But it's not just the perfectly placed blankets that catch my eye—it's the book and envelope sitting in the middle of it.

I rush to pick up the book, opening it to reveal images that steal the air from my lungs.

"Fuck."

Teal and purple papers are decorated in Elodie's beautiful handwriting, "Remy's First Year" etched onto the front page. As I flip through the book, I find pictures that Elodie has taken over the past three months—snapshots of Remy's first bath when I was absolutely terrified that I was going to do something wrong, images of me holding her against my chest on the couch, and in the baby carrier when we went to the movie night at the winery. There are even pictures of her and Remy from their days together at the park or just hanging out at the house, followed by a page that has the lyrics to the song she wrote about my daughter.

As I flip through the last picture and note several more pages that are still blank, my eyes drift to the envelope and I trade the book for that instead. When I pull the paper out and see a handwritten letter from the woman that has claimed the formerly hollow space in my chest, I worry that whatever she's left in this note might just break me.

Henley,

I was saving this as a Christmas gift for you and Remy, but since our time together was cut short, I wanted to make sure that you still received it, even though I had planned to add more.

Capturing memories is something very important to parents, a detail I realized at a young age while helping my mom with her daycare. Children don't stay small for long, and some of those days are long too, so it's easy to take the small moments for granted.

And even though Remy was a surprise for you, I wanted you to have something to look back on, to have documentation of the moments that changed your life.

I also wanted her to have the pictures, and maybe selfishly, a way for me to live on in her memory and the part of her life I got to contribute to.

I can't thank you enough for trusting me to take care of your little girl, to care for her and watch her grow. It is, hands down, one of the best accomplishments of my life so far.

And thank you for letting me in as well, for taking off your gorilla mask long enough to show me the man underneath.

I'm pretty proud of that accomplishment too.

I'll never forget the two of you,

Or the love I felt from you both.

Remy is so lucky to have you as a father. You were made to be a parent, Henley. You're a good man, and I'm grateful that I got to experience your love, even if you could never say the words out loud.

But I need you to know that I feel the same way.

I love you, Henley.

I always will.

Love,

Elodie

By the time I'm done reading her letter, my eyes are full of unshed tears. I toss the paper to the bed, lower my head into my hands, and curse myself for letting that woman walk away, even though I know it was the right thing to do.

And then I let my tears fall.

She's gone. She's really fucking gone.

And now, more than ever, I need a fucking drink.

***

"You know, day drinking is severely underrated," Elliot murmurs around the rim of his glass as we hide out in a booth in the back of Blossom Brews, our local brewhouse and restaurant. I called Warren this morning to take the reins at the lodge so I could sulk. "That's why I was drunk mostly during the day."

"Well, if you felt even half of what I'm feeling right now, I want to apologize for giving you any sort of shit."

Elliot shrugs. "Hey, I'm not denying I was acting like an asshole, but heartbreak fucking sucks, man. I'm only having one drink with you, though. I still need to go back to the office to get a few things done."

"Well, I appreciate you keeping me company." As soon as I gathered myself after reading Elodie's letter, I called Carol to see if she could watch Remy today, and then Elliot was my next call. I knew that out of my friends, he was the one that could relate to what I'm feeling right now the most.

"You know I'm here for you, man. Even if you think me and the boys aren't your family." There's a teasing lilt to his voice, but I still roll my eyes.

"I'm sorry. You know that I appreciate you."

"I do, and I know you'll appreciate me more after tomorrow."

I blow out a breath. "Fuck. I forgot about that."

"Well, here's your formal reminder. Meghan will be at my office at ten in the morning, and she seems to be cooperating. She didn't mention wanting to discuss anything else when I told her what the meeting was for."

"It just still blows my mind that she doesn't want to be in Remy's life."

"Yeah, well...I'm still baffled at how my fiancée was fucking her boss behind my back." He lifts his glass and clinks it against mine. "Cheers to that, right?"

I reach up and rub the center of my chest. "Does it get any better? You know, with time?"

"I mean, there are good and bad days. Like if I see people post photos online from their engagement or weddings, it makes me want to throw my phone at the wall. But then, there are times when I'm working on a divorce case and I hear the way couples talk to each other after being married for years, how they ended up hating the person they thought they wanted to spend the rest of their life with, and I'm glad that I dodged that bullet."

I drain the rest of my beer and signal to our server to pour me another.

"Does Carol know you're planning on getting drunk today?"

"When I dropped off Remy earlier and told her that Elodie was gone, she didn't even ask what I had planned. She just told me to take as much time as I needed. Of course, I feel guilty for not being with my daughter right now, but I just--"

"Don't feel guilty. Your pain is written all over your face, man." Elliot shakes his head. "I know that look. It's been staring back at me in the mirror for the past four months."

"I just can't believe she left," I mutter for the hundredth time just as the waitress comes by with my fresh beer.

"Did you ask her to stay?"

"No. I—I couldn't. I didn't want to be the reason she'd always wonder what if, the person that stood between her and the chance to have a career in music." Shaking my head, I lift my glass to my mouth and drain half of it, smacking my lips as I place it back down. "But the timing of it all is still fucking eating away at me. We were supposed to go on a date tonight. I had it all planned out, and I was gonna tell her how I feel about her…"

"Fuck, I'm sorry."

My phone rings from its spot next to me on the booth. I practically launch upright, like a catapult of hope made me spring back to life. But when I see Fletcher's request for a video call on the screen, that hope evaporates.

Elodie wouldn't be calling me yet anyway. She's probably just landed in L.A. The record label was sending her a driver to pick her up at the airport, and I'm sure she has a hotel to check into before attending meetings on top of meetings.

She's a celebrity now, and I'm just the single dad she worked for on her road to fame.

When I answer the call, I prop the phone up on the table using the bottle of ketchup behind it so both Elliot and I can see our friend on the screen, and straighten my flannel that bunched up around my shoulders. "Hey, Fletch."

His face instantly grows confused. "What the hell is wrong with you? You look like your dog just died."

"We're day drinking," Elliot says, casting his gaze to me. "Elodie left for Los Angeles this morning."

"Fuck, then that explains the text she sent Laney." He reaches up and scratches the side of his head. "That's part of the reason why I was calling. Laney wanted to know what happened. Elodie made it sound like she was leaving for good."

"A record label wants her, man. Her performance at the winery is all over the internet and they wanted her out in L.A. as soon as possible," I grate out before lifting my glass to my lips again, finally starting to feel the effects of the alcohol after four beers.

"Shit." Fletcher lets out a heavy breath. "Well, now what?"

I glare at him. "What do you mean?"

"I mean, how is this going to work with you two?"

"It's not. She's gone. We're done."

Fletcher closes his eyes, clenches his jaw, and pinches the bridge of his nose. "Jesus Christ, Henley. Please don't tell me you just let her go?"

"What was I supposed to do, Fletcher? I'm not going to be the reason she doesn't achieve her dreams."

He smacks the table in front of him. "You're a goddamn idiot. You love her! I saw your face when it fucking hit you the other night."

"Looks like it doesn't matter," I fire back as my voice rises, drawing the attention of people around us.

Elliot scours the room then taps the table in front of me, gathering my attention. "Hey, keep it down, all right?"

"He started it," I quip, pointing to the phone.

"And you ended it by not fighting for her," Fletcher fires back.

"I'm not going to compete with her music, Fletch. Don't you get it? That would be like Laney asking you to give up football."

Fletcher shakes his head. "See? That's where your lack of emotional intelligence is screwing you over."

Elliot rolls his eyes. "Dr. Fletcher Adams, the therapist, has now entered the chat."

"Fuck you, Elliot." Fletcher flips us off through the screen. "But you know I'm right. Laney would never ask me to give up football because she knows what it means to me, but that doesn't mean that I wouldn't if it came down to the choice between the game and her."

My eyes snap back to him. "Seriously?"

"Yeah, man. We've both made sacrifices over the past few months so that we can both keep doing what we love but also love each other." He leans closer to the screen. "Because that's what you do when you *love* somebody, Henley. You compromise and sacrifice and do everything possible to keep them in your life."

My jaw is so tight right now that I think I might crack a fucking tooth. "And what if she doesn't feel the same way? What if she doesn't want both?"

"Did you ask her that?"

"No."

"Then you're fucking assuming, and you know what happens when you assume, right?"

"You make an ass out of you and me," Elliot answers for him, shaking his head. "I had a law professor that said that all the fucking time." He spells the word out phonetically. "Ass-u-me."

I flash him my best deadpan stare. "Thank you for that enlightening explanation."

"Well, it's the fucking truth," Fletcher adds. "You know, there's something my therapist said to me that completely changed how I look at love now."

"Okay..."

"He said we don't fall in love with the other person as much as we fall in love with who that person allows us to be." *Fuck*. "So let me ask you this: Did Elodie allow you to be a version of yourself that you liked, Henley?"

I don't even have to think about my answer. "Yes."

The woman opened up my eyes to so much that I can't even form my thoughts into words.

I know, shocking.

"Then that sounds like a person you should try to hold onto, no matter what obstacles stand in your way."

***

"You nervous?" Elliot straightens the papers in front of him, sitting on my right at the conference table in his family's law office.

"No."

"Then stop shaking the table."

"I'm not."

He reaches down and pushes my leg into the ground, forcing my knee to stop bouncing up and down. "Yes, you are."

A knock at the door interrupts my next reply, and Meghan walks in, looking freshly tanned and smiling from ear to ear. "Ms. Cooke is here," Wendy, the front receptionist announces after Meghan walks past her.

"Thanks, Wendy."

"Of course. Let me know if you need anything." Wendy leaves just as Meghan takes a seat across from me.

"Hi, Henley," she says, far too cheerily for my liking given the nature of this meeting.

"Um, hello." Confusion swirls through my head as I take in the woman sitting across from me, wondering what the hell I ever saw in her that made me pursue her that night.

I can see the features in her face that our daughter inherited—her nose, her lips, and the shape of her eyes, but that's it. There's no warmth radiating from her, no empathy in her voice, and she certainly doesn't seem conflicted about handing over her parental rights to her child.

Elliot clears his throat. "Good morning, Ms. Cooke."

"Please just call me Meghan."

Elliot nods. "Meghan. As my paralegal, Fiona, explained on the phone, we wanted to meet with you today for you to sign over all legal rights to your daughter, Remington Jane Clark."

"Yup."

That's it. One word. No hesitation.

"Okay then." Elliot slides the papers across the table to her. "There are tabs on the lines where I need you to sign." Meghan picks up the pen sitting on her right and scribbles her name quickly, not even bothering to read what she's signing. "Please keep in mind that there is a clause in this contract that you cannot reach out to the child in question before she turns eighteen if you change your mind at any point."

Meghan just shrugs. "Fine by me." She flips to the second and third pages, and once complete, slides them back over to Elliot. "Anything else?"

"That's it?" I bark out. "You seriously aren't even going to bat an eyelash about giving up all rights to your daughter?"

She scoffs. "I told you when I dropped her off with you, Henley, that I didn't want to be a mom." Tossing her hair over her shoulder, she continues. "I'm living my best life. I just got back from a week in Aruba with my new boyfriend, and we're going to Paris next week."

I lean back in my chair. "Holy shit. You don't care at all, do you?"

"She has you now. She won't miss me in her life if she can't remember me, and besides, children just drag you down." She stands from her chair and slings her purse back over her shoulder. "Are we good then?"

Elliot taps the table in front of him as he checks her signatures. "Yup. All good."

"Great. Good luck!" I stare at her back until she opens the door and disappears down the hallway she walked through to get here.

"Wow," Elliot says, tapping the stack of papers back into line. "That was way easier than I expected, but it's probably a good thing."

The only thing I can do right now is blink as I process what just happened.

She didn't even hesitate, didn't even ask me to reconsider.

She just left our daughter without a second thought—just like my parents did to me and Dilynne.

I exhale as the realization hits me. "Fuck."

"You okay?"

I bury my head in my hands as a montage of my childhood slams into me, and then Carol and Nick pop up—the two people who took us in, cared for us like their own, and loved us when they never had to.

I'm such a fucking idiot.

Launching up from my chair, I straighten my jacket. "Do you need anything else from me?"

"No, but where's the fire?" His head swivels on his neck.

My throat grows tight. "I just—I need to go."

"Okay, do what you need to do. I'll make sure I get you a copy of the papers as soon as possible."

Racing out of the office, I manage to catch Meghan just as she's getting in her car. "Meghan!"

"Henley? Did I forget to sign a page, or…"

"Thank you," I blurt out, partly out of breath.

"For?"

"For giving me my daughter, for changing how I view the world, and for helping me see that the best thing you've done for our daughter is leave her life for good."

She actually seems taken aback by those last few words, but it's the truth. My daughter will never know the pain of being left behind—because I'll love her so fiercely there won't be room for doubt.

Just like Nick and Carol did for me and my sister.

She clears her throat. "Is that it?"

"Yeah, that's it. Have a nice life."

Rolling her eyes, she slides into her BMW and peels out of the parking lot, and I watch her leave. But I don't feel even an ounce of remorse, or sadness—not like I did when I watched Elodie drive out of my life yesterday.

Before I can dwell on that though any further, I hop in my truck and cross town to my next stop, ready to take care of something that's been a long time coming.

Chapter 23

Henley

Saying It Out Loud

"Peek-a-boo!" Remy's giggle hits my ears the second I walk into my foster parents' house. Carol is hiding behind a blanket as Remy sits in the corner of the couch, dropping it quickly to surprise her, making her laugh.

The sound almost makes me fucking cry.

Instead, I let out a sigh of contentment then strip off my jacket as I make my way into the living room.

Carol looks up from her spot on the couch. "That didn't take long."

"Well, Meghan clearly knew what she was agreeing to." I take a seat on the loveseat next to the couch and reach out to kiss my daughter's hand. "She's out of our lives for good."

Carol's smile is soft. "How do you feel about it?"

"Honestly? Relieved." I blow out a breath. "Even though I don't think I'll fully understand Meghan's decision, I'm grateful that she made it now instead of hurting my baby bear." As soon as the nickname leaves my lips, that pang of pain radiates in my chest.

"This little girl will never be short on love, Henley." Carol winks at me. "Just like you and Dilynne. You have so many people that care about you two."

The knot in my throat gets larger. "Uh, speaking of that. Where's Nick?"

"He's in the garage. Why?"

"I sort of wanted to talk to you two." Carol's brows draw together. "Give me a second." When I stand, I head straight for the garage to find Nick tinkering around with a motor part on his workbench. If my sister were here, she'd be standing right next to him, swapping vocabulary that I only know bits and pieces of.

But seeing him in his element does something to me—it makes me realize that this man gave me good memories to replace the horrible ones my own father left for me—the ones I'm ready to leave behind completely.

He stepped up for two kids whose childhood was the kind from nightmares.

He supported us in everything we wanted to do, regardless if he understood it or not.

And he filled a spot in our lives—not out of obligation, like I thought—but out of the goodness of his heart, because he was meant to be the father I never had.

"Nick?" I manage to croak out, drawing his attention to me.

His head swivels over his shoulder. "Hey, Henley. How'd everything go today?"

"Good. Easier than I imagined, actually. But, uh..." I reach up and rub the back of my neck. "I wanted to talk to you about something."

He drops the tool from his hand on the bench. "Is everything okay?"

"Yes and no."

"Okay…"

I motion for him to follow me back inside, joining Carol again in the living room, Remy on her lap now. When I take my seat back on the loveseat adjacent to them, I struggle with how to start. "You two deserve to hear something from me after far too long."

"Henley," Carol starts, concern etched in every line of her face, but I hold up my hand to stop her.

"Please, just…let me try to get through this." She nods and glances over at Nick as he takes his hand in hers.

They're a team.

And I fucking want that too.

One thing at a time, Henley.

"Today I watched Remy's mom leave her daughter behind without blinking. She chose to continue her life without her, acting like she never existed, and something hit me as I watched it unfold. My parents did the same thing to me and Dilynne. We were an afterthought, forgotten kids that got tossed around in the foster system until we met you."

"I remember the first time I saw you," Nick chimes in. "You were so angry."

I huff out a laugh. "Turns out I still am, but I'm working on it." He nods, so I continue. "When I wrote that letter for us to stay with you, I did it for Dilynne. I knew she was happy here, but deep down, I realized I did for me too." My eyes start to sting. "You showed me what it was like to be loved for the first time in my life, and even said the words to me, but I didn't want to believe it. I—I didn't want to accept it." Looking at my daughter, I smile. "But I get it now. I get what it feels like to love someone more than you ever imagined you could, to want to protect them from pain and a life without someone to lean on." My eyes cast back to Carol and Nick, who both have tears in their eyes. "You two always let me be me. You never tried to change me, you accepted me for who I was, and I'm not sure where I would have ended up if it weren't for the two of you."

"Henley," Nick says, wiping under his eye. "You and Dilynne put us down a path we didn't expect either, son. You showed us parts of ourselves that never got the love we couldn't give to children of our own, so we gave it to you."

I take in a deep breath and prepare to say what I should have said that night when my sister graduated from high school and I thought that running from my past would make me feel free. My daredevil days were how I tried to forget it. That adrenaline I needed to chase was so I could fucking feel something other than disappointment.

Turns out, it was the love from a woman with a beautiful voice that I needed to thaw the ice walls I've been hiding behind.

"I—I love you both very much, and you deserve to finally hear that." Carol's bottom lip starts to tremble. "I get what that means now, to want to put someone's happiness above your own, to go to the ends of the earth to make their life better." My hands are shaking as I say, "I'm just sorry it took me so long to tell you."

Nick chuckles. "We know you love us, Henley. You never had to say the words because you showed us with your actions and your heart."

Carol chimes in. "I'm so proud of the man you've become, and certainly how much you've grown since becoming a father." She glances down at Remy on her lap, who's smiling across the space at me. "You may not be our son by blood, but you are a part of our family."

"And now Remy has you too." My little girl has a family that Meghan never could have given her, and that makes me feel even more relieved that she's gone.

Carol bounces her on her lap. "We never could have kids of our own," she says, looking over at her husband. "I remember when we were struggling to get pregnant and I saw that quote in the infertility doctor's office. Do you remember what it said?"

Nick nods. "Children don't always come when you plan for them—they arrive when your soul needs them the most."

Carol turns back to me as a tear slips down her cheek. "You and Dilynne came into our lives and transformed us too, just like Remy did to you. And now look? We have two people in our lives that we consider our own, and still ended up with a grandchild. Who would have thought, huh?"

"Best twist of fate, ever." Nick kisses her lips and then turns to me. "Your capacity for love is far greater than you think, Henley. Saying the words is only part of it. And even though I can't deny that hearing them fills something inside of me, what would make me even more content in this moment, is you admitting that Elodie is someone that you want to show that love to, and doing everything you can to fight for her."

His words light the fire under my ass that's been smoldering for the past twenty-four hours. "Actually, there's a favor I need from you two."

Carol throws her hand in the air while rolling her eyes. "Ohhhh...so now that you've told us that you love us, you're just gonna start asking for favors and think we're going to agree to any and everything, huh?"

An amused smile forms on my lips. "Well, yeah."

Nick laughs and grabs Remy from Carol's lap. "If it involves watching this little one so you can go get your girl, then I think the answer is clear."

"I really do love you both," I say, my voice cracking as I soak in the moment right in front of me, the strongest urge to take a picture overwhelming my senses.

And that's when it hits me.

I know just how to show Elodie that she's worth the fight, the memories, and the words I've never told anyone else.

I just hope I'm not too late.

Chapter 24

Elodie

Is it a Murderer?

No, it's...

"You're really sure about this?" Lennon asks me through the phone as I lean against the headboard of my hotel bed. It's been four days of non-stop meetings, parties, and calls. I now have contracts lined up for a publicist, an agent, a record label, and I'm still not done putting everything in my new life into place.

"I'm sure. These past few days have been eye-opening."

"No regrets, right?"

I shake my head, even though I'm all alone. Though it feels like the fibers of my soul have been severed with little hope of being repaired, I'm confident that my decision today will put me on the path to correct that.

"No. I just think the fantasy is so much better than reality in this case," I say, just as there's a knock on my hotel door. I ordered room service about thirty minutes ago, desperate to eat a meal alone so I can act like a trash panda and not worry about being judged.

"But the fantasies include red carpets and award shows," Lennon says as I stand from my bed and make my way toward the door.

"Those can still exist, Lennon..." My words die on my lips as I open the door to find the last person I was expecting. "Oh my God."

"What?"

"Lennon...I have to go."

"Are you okay? Is it a murderer?"

"No. It's Henley." I end the call and drop the phone from my ear, vowing to call her back later while staring up at the tower of a man hovering over me in the doorway.

"Hey, sweetheart."

"I—uh—" Pushing my hair from my face, I manage to form a sentence. "Um, what are you doing here, Henley?"

"Is this a bad time?"

I peer back into my empty hotel room. "Well, as you can see, I'm entertaining about one hundred people."

The corner of his mouth lifts. "Fuck, I missed you, El."

But I don't know what to say to that. The last time I was standing in this position with this man, he was telling me to leave, and now he's here? In Los Angeles? And we haven't spoken all week.

"How did you get up here? How did you know what room I'm in?"

"I have my ways," he says, pushing the door open further and waltzing right into my room like he owns the place. He has a duffle bag slung over his shoulder, and he's wearing dark jeans and a plain black shirt under his unbuttoned flannel.

Damn him and those flannels.

"What are you doing here, Henley?" I ask again as he places his duffle bag on the chair in the corner, stripping off his flannel next and tossing it on top. When he turns to face me, his smile almost steals the breath from my lungs.

He looks lighter, like a dark cloud finally stopped following him around. He seems taller too, his spine straighter and his stance more grounded.

And then he says something that makes me forget how to breathe.

"I love you, Elodie."

I gasp, covering my chest with my hands. "I'm sorry. Did you just say that you...*love me?*"

"Fuck," he breathes out, followed by a low chuckle. "That wasn't what I planned to say to you the minute I got here, but it just...came out."

"I haven't spoken to you since I left and...You—you love me?"

His feet carry him across the room to me, stopping when there's only an inch of space between us. "I do. I think I finally realize what that word means because the second you left my life, I felt like a piece of me went with you. All I could feel was your absence. And when Meghan signed over her rights to Remy, all I could think about is how you would never do that, how you've loved my daughter like she was your own since the day we met." He reaches up to cup my face, pulling me into him by my hip with his other hand. "Can we talk?"

Tears are threatening to spill from my eyes, but I manage a nod. He grabs my hand and leads me to the bed, where we sit facing each other. "What else could you possibly have to say after that speech?"

He laughs, then nuzzles his nose with mine. "Oh, I'm just getting started, El."

El. Sweetheart.

The terms of endearment that have haunted my dreams during our time apart sound like a melody coming from his lips that was only made for me.

"Letting you walk away without fighting for you was the biggest mistake of my life, and trust me, I've made plenty."

"You weren't the only one who didn't fight, Henley. I—I didn't want to leave you, but I did anyway."

"Yes, but I thought I was doing what was best for you when I told you to leave."

I reach up and frame his jaw with my hand. "What's best for me is having you and Remy in my life. You two are my family, my purpose."

"What about music?" he asks, a hint of hesitation in his voice. "You belong on a stage, singing and sharing your songs with the world. Your words—they've changed me in ways I can't even explain. I can't imagine how many more lives you could touch."

I scoot closer to him, which he takes as an invitation to slide my legs over his hips, straddling him now as he leans back so he can still see my eyes. "You see, while you were figuring out a way to push me away, I was figuring out what I could do to show you that I would never stop fighting for you and what we have. You've changed me too, Henley. You and your daughter showed me that some dreams are meant to shift and morph, to form something new and different from what you envisioned, but still equally beautiful." I frame his face with both of my hands. "You are worth the fight, Henley, so I fought for a contract this week that allows me to keep you with me. My life with you is my new dream, so why can't I have both?"

"What do you mean?"

I prepare to tell him what I planned on saying eventually, after this whirlwind of a week was over. "Sandra was fully intent on signing me as a new recording artist with the label, but I realized during my last performance that I don't want the spotlight. I just want to write songs, words that make people feel something. So, instead of being the one singing them, I'm now on the label as a songwriter, which means I can work from anywhere."

"Anywhere?" His lips curve into a smile.

"Yes, even somewhere like Blossom Peak."

"Fuck, Elodie." He brings my face to his, kissing me softly. "Are you sure?"

"Yes, Henley. I want a quiet life, but I still want music to be a part of it. You and Remy helped me figure out what I wanted, even though you thought you knew what that was."

"Watching you walk away fucking killed me, sweetheart. But your absence was what I needed to realize a few things." He kisses my cheek and then my lips. "First, my daughter is the luckiest girl in the world to have so many people in her life that love her, even if her biological mom isn't one of them. Watching Meghan walk away from her made something else click for me—how selfish I'd been to hold a grudge against my parents for leaving me, when I had two of the best foster parents a kid could have asked for."

"Carol and Nick are one of a kind, Henley. I could have told you that."

"Yeah, well? I finally told them that I loved them. How's that for growth?"

I gasp. "Are you joking?"

"I think you should know better than to assume I would joke about saying words like that." Pulling him to me, I kiss him again—deeply and with every fiber of my body. "You made me a better man than I was before you crashed into my life," he breathes out when we part. "I want to go to therapy, to bury these demons of mine once and for all. I feel like I can now, knowing you'll be there cheering me on. I'm yours,

Elodie, in every essence of the word." He brings one of my hands to the center of his chest. "I've never asked someone to stay, but I want you to be the first. Will you stay with me? And Remy? And give me the family I couldn't imagine living without now?"

"I love you so much, Henley Clark," I whisper against his lips.

"Is that a yes?" he whispers back.

"What do you think?"

"I think you need to use your words."

"I just did. How about you use yours?"

"I gave you all of mine, Elodie, even the ones that no one else got to hear."

"Then I'll give you mine for the rest of our lives. How does that sound?"

"It sounds like love."

I rest my forehead on his again. "That's exactly what it is, Henley. The type of love that songs are written about."

***

"Mmmm." The soft flick of a tongue against my clit pulls me from sleep. As my eyes flutter open, I see Henley staring up at me from between my legs. "Henley..."

"I'm here, baby. I had to fucking taste you again the second I woke up. Make sure this was real." His tongue returns to my clit, slowly circling the nub before he slides one finger inside me.

A moan escapes me. "So good."

"Fucking hell. This pussy is perfection," he mutters against me. "Heaven under my tongue."

I bury my hand in his hair as he licks me, exploring every inch of my most sensitive flesh. But I don't want to come under his tongue. I want to come with him buried deep inside me.

Even though we had sex twice last night to make up for our time apart, I can't stand the thought of not feeling this man between my legs again, of holding him in my arms and hearing those words fall from his lips again as he comes.

"*I love you, Elodie.*"

Yeah, I think those are my new favorite words in the world, and they don't even need to be accompanied by music.

"Henley, I need your cock. Now…"

He lifts his head and crawls over me, sliding in with one slow thrust. "You need me buried inside of you again, huh, sweetheart?"

"Yes." My back arches from the bed as his lips capture my nipple and tease the bud, his pace relentless as he thrusts deep and hard, filling me completely.

"This pussy was made for my cock, wasn't it?"

"Yes."

"And *you* were made for *me*, Elodie." My eyes find his again as his tongue darts out to wet his lips and he presses them to my own. "I love you," he murmurs against my mouth. "I love you so fucking much."

"God, I love you too." My fingers run through his hair, tightening on the strands as he picks up his pace. "Fuck, I'm close."

He reaches between us and rubs my clit with his thumb. "I need to watch you come, Elodie. There's nothing I want more than to watch you fall apart." He speeds up his movements, taking me higher and higher until I crash over the peak. As I moan and scream through my release, his groans grow in volume until his voice draws out. "Fuccck-kk…" And then he collapses on top of me.

Once we're spent and cleaned up, we return to the bed under the sheets with nothing between us, skin on skin. "Can we call Remy today?" I ask as I drag my nails through his chest hair. "I miss my baby bear."

"She misses you too."

"How do you know?"

Henley grows quiet for a moment. "The first night you weren't there, she fought going to sleep. I knew she was confused because a part of her routine was gone—*you*. So, I found a clip online of you singing that song you wrote for her and played it for her. She fell asleep almost instantly."

"Oh my God." My eyes sting with tears. "Henley, I—I want to go back to Blossom Peak right now."

His chuckle vibrates against my cheek. "I'm ready when you are, but I imagine you're not finished here yet."

"No," I pout. "I have a few more meetings with the label, and then I have to fly out to Nashville."

"What's in Nashville?"

"Oh, I forgot to tell you last night." I twist to face him, resting my chin on his chest. "My main point of contact will be in Nashville since they want me working with country artists, so even less of a commute. And that way I can still be Remy's nanny."

He drags a finger down my cheek. "I'm so fucking proud of you, Elodie."

"Thank you. I couldn't have done this without you."

"That's not true. And by the way, Carol agreed to help with care for Remy when you have to work, so you can be in our lives, but not as Remy's nanny. You're my girlfriend moving forward."

"But..."

"And one day, you'll be more to my daughter than just my girl-friend, but we can talk about that later."

Emotion clogs my throat, but I swallow it down. "I also didn't get a chance to tell you this last night, but my song for Remy has already been secured for an artist. That's what prompted Sandra to call me. The singer requested it."

"Who is it?"

"I—I can't say yet."

He turns over, placing me flat on the bed beneath him. "But I'm your man. The secret privilege doesn't count with me."

"Is that so?"

"Yup. Official rule. I just made it up."

"Well, I'll have to check the by-laws."

"Better get on that."

Laughing, I stare up at him. "You know, before you, I sang about love but I didn't fully understand it."

"I never understood it until you, El."

"But now that I do, I feel an endless supply of inspiration is coming."

He reaches down and tests the wetness between my legs. "Oh, I can give you plenty of that, baby. In fact, I'd better get to work on that right now."

"Henley!"

"Shut up and let me love you, Elodie."

And so I do as I'm told, letting him love me the best way he knows how.

Chapter 25

Henley

Finally Making Plans

"Now I understand why you picked this for our first date." Elodie is halfway up the wall when she glances down at me and shouts loud enough for me to hear her.

"And why is that?" I can't hide my smirk because the view from down here definitely doesn't suck.

"So you could stare at my ass the entire time."

"Who, me? No way." I lift my phone from my pocket and snap a picture of her scaling the rock wall, wearing that teal spandex outfit from yoga all those weeks ago. Reaching down, I adjust my dick in my shorts, grateful that the room is empty except for the two of us.

When I originally planned this date, I knew that I wanted to do something with Elodie besides just dinner or a movie. I wanted something unique, something interactive and fun for us to do together, and since the adventure park side of Sky's the Limit is shut down for the winter, it gave me the perfect opportunity to give us privacy while having fun together—because if there is one thing this woman has reminded me of, it's that I can still be a parent and have fun.

The past three weeks have been a blur. Between Elodie traveling back and forth to Nashville and booking recording time with artists lined up to work with her, and the peak of snow season hitting Blossom Peak, we haven't had much time just the two of us. But now that she's home for the holidays, I'm going to take full advantage of our days together.

I check the time on my phone and realize it's later than I thought.

"You'd better hurry up so I can still feed you before the night is over."

"And what are you gonna feed me?"

"That's a surprise."

Elodie reaches the top of the wall and rings the bell. "I did it!"

"Yeah, you did, baby. Now get back down here."

She pushes away from the wall and slowly slides down the rope that she is attached to in case she falls. Her feet plant on the ground and then she walks over to me, jumping into my arms. "I really loved that."

I capture her lips with mine. "And I loved watching it."

"Pervert."

"Only for you."

"Okay, what's next?"

"Next, we go home."

"What? I thought we were having dinner?"

"We are. It's my turn to cook for you."

After we make the drive back to my house, I open the front door to reveal the entire living room and kitchen decorated with electric tea light candles and yellow hydrangeas, Elodie's favorite color and flower.

"How on earth did you do this?" Her stunned expression is exactly what I wanted to see.

"Let's just say that I have a sister who is beyond eager to help me keep you around this time."

When Elodie and I returned from Los Angeles a few days after I surprised her last month, my sister nearly beat my ass for not telling her everything that happened. But then I explained my talk with Carol and Nick, how the meeting with Meghan helped me see the light, and when Elodie reunited with her and Laney, Dilynne broke down in tears when she told me how much she loved me—how proud she is of me for finally vowing to move past the pain I've been holding onto.

Never thought hearing that from my own sister would make me break down too, but fuck, we've come a long way from where we were as kids.

So, when I told her my plan for Elodie, she was more than willing to help me with this surprise.

"Wow." She peers up at me. "This is beautiful, Henley."

"I'm glad you like it. Now, I want you to go to my bathroom and relax in the tub while I make our dinner. Everything you need for a bath is in there, then we'll eat and I have something I want to give you."

Elodie tips her head to the side. "A girl could get used to this type of spoiling."

"Not too bad for someone that's never been in a relationship before, huh?"

While Elodie is in the bath, I prepare the steak, potatoes, and asparagus, topping it all off with an Oscar-style sauce that I practiced making three times before tonight just to make sure I got it perfect.

We eat and drink wine from Hart Winery, laughing and reminiscing about the past few weeks and how excited we were when Remy started crawling, but how intense it is now that she doesn't stop moving.

When we're finished, I clear our plates and bring over the gift I've been working on, hoping like hell that she feels what I have to say is enough for her.

"What is this?"

"You know, the concept of giving gifts is quite simple. You rip the wrapping paper off of them to reveal what's inside."

Elodie glares at me, a playful smirk on her lips. "I'm not sure I like happy Henley. His sarcasm is a bit over the top. Where's gorilla man?"

My head falls back as I laugh. "Oh, he's still in here, but you've tamed him a bit, sweetheart."

Elodie tears the paper from the book and gives me a confused look when she sees what's inside. "You—you gave me the scrapbook I made for you?"

"I did."

"Uh..."

"Open it up, baby."

Elodie slowly opens the book up and turns past the first few pages she had already filled with pictures, but stops as she realizes there are words on them now. "Henley, you..."

"I added to it," I finish for her, scooting my chair closer to her so that I can point out the new features. "I've been filling in notes next to the pictures of my thoughts, like how terrified I was during her first bath." Elodie chuckles. "And then, I added some photos of my own." Flipping past the pages that Elodie completed, I arrive at the ones I've worked on after she fell asleep—pictures of Elodie and Remy, or the three of us together, like at Remy's first Thanksgiving that we spent with Elodie's parents.

When Elodie insisted on still traveling to her parents' house for the holiday, I was extremely hesitant, even after Elodie revealed that her mom actually did attend her performance and watched from afar.

She was blown away by her daughter, and when Elodie told her mom and dad about her new music career, they actually all broke down together. Turns out, fear can make you say and do things that hurt the ones you love, and Elodie's parents were so scared that she'd end up disappointed, they just wanted her to find something else more realistic.

Joke's on them though, right?

"I've never even seen some of these. When did you take them?" she asks as she flips through the pages, admiring the details from our time together.

"I've been taking pictures of you since the moment you got here, baby." Her eyes meet mine. "I'm still mad I didn't take one of the night I ran out of the house though, when you were playing your guitar and singing to Remy."

"Why?"

"Because that was the night I realized you completely owned me, and I don't want to ever forget that."

She reaches up and cups my face. "You won't. It's just a memory that lives on in your mind instead of on paper."

"Well, there are a few more memories we still need to put on paper," I say, gesturing to the scrapbook, prompting her to keep flipping the pages.

When she gets to the one I'm nervous about, she freezes. "Henley..."

"I'm not proposing now," I clarify. "But one day, we're going to put our wedding picture on this page."

"The day my mommy and daddy got married," Elodie says, reading the title I wrote at the top of the blank page.

"And I want you to adopt my daughter when that happens so that she's yours—because she is. You are her mother, the one that matters, El."

Tears instantly form in her eyes. "I would be honored."

"I'm in this," I say, reaching for her hands and pulling her closer to me. "That's why I did this. I want you to know that you're it for me. You will be my wife, you will be the person I grow old with, and you will be the mother of our daughter and any future children you want to have with me."

Elodie lunges for me, straddling my lap as we laugh and then press our lips together. I bury my hand in her hair and savor the taste of her tongue against mine, memorizing this moment because now that I have it, I don't want to forget it.

I don't want to forget any second I spend with this woman.

"I love you, Henley," she says when I release her lips.

"I love you too, El. And now we have all the time in the world to do this right."

***

"I'd better not get sick after being here," my sister says as she stands next to me in the cafeteria of Blossom Peak Elementary.

"Why would you get sick?"

"Look at all of these kids," she explains, motioning to the crowded room. "It's like a germ cesspool. I feel like I'm going to need to take a bath in antibiotics when I leave."

Elodie snorts from beside us, readjusting Remy in her arms. "I think you'll be fine. Most of the winter colds are done now."

It's March and Career Day at the elementary school, hence why my sister and I are here instead of at our respective businesses. Turns out, when one of your best friends has a kindergartener and she is told she can invite whoever she wants to speak at career day, she invites literally every adult she knows.

Elliot and Fletcher walk through the doors, Laney holding Fletcher's hand. "Jesus, it's utter chaos in here," Elliot says as a group of kids run right past him, making him stumble.

"That's what I said," Dilynne echoes, but Elliot rolls his eyes.

"Hold on. You two actually agreed on something?" Fletcher asks for clarification. "Did hell just freeze over?"

"I don't know. Ask Satan himself." My sister juts her thumb in Elliot's direction.

"Elliot can't be Satan if I'm Lucifer," Fletcher interjects.

Laney pats his chest. "Maybe it's time to pass on the nickname, babe. Besides, Dilynne has a list of them for Elliot, so it's not like just one is going to stick."

"Uncle Fletcher!" Ellis Hart, Rhonan's daughter and the reason we're all here today, comes running up to Fletcher and jumps into his arms. "You made it!"

"I told you that I would." He bops her on her nose then peers around the room. "Where's your dad?"

"I don't know. I hope he won't be late. Ms. Lewis says we're about to start."

"Wait. Who's Ms. Lewis? I thought Mrs. Allen was your teacher," Dilynne asks.

"She left to have her baby. Johnny said that the baby was gonna rip open her vagina."

Elliot practically snorts. "Looks like Johnny knows a little too much."

Ellis tilts her head to the side. "Can babies do that? Do they rip it open with their hands and crawl out?"

"Uh…" Fletcher looks to the rest of us for guidance. "A little help here, people."

Luckily, Rhonan arrives at that moment, practically panting as he jogs through the doors to the cafeteria, dressed in his deputy uniform. "Daddy!" Ellis shouts, wiggling out of Fletcher's arms before running across the room to him.

"Thank God I got out of answering that question," Fletcher mumbles, pulling Laney back into his arms as she laughs.

"Yeah, we don't need another stripper incident," she says.

Elodie's brows draw together. "Stripper incident?"

Fletcher shakes his head. "Don't ask."

Laughing, I pull Elodie into my arms and kiss the top of her head. "Let's just say that I won't be letting Remy hang around Uncle Fletcher when she starts asking the tough questions."

Rhonan walks toward us, carrying Ellis in his arms. "I didn't think I was gonna make it," he says out of breath before setting his daughter down on the ground.

"You look like you just ran a marathon," Laney says to her older brother.

"Actually, I was chasing after a damn dog."

"I didn't know that was in your job description," Elliot says with a smirk.

"It's not." Rhonan pushes a hand through his unruly hair, trying to tame it. "It's my new neighbor's dog, and he happens to be a bit of an escape artist."

"Wait. You have a new neighbor? Someone is renting that house now?" Laney asks.

"Yeah, and it's…" But he doesn't finish his sentence because a beautiful, tall blonde picks up the microphone at the front of the cafeteria and drowns him out.

"Good morning, everyone," she says, her voice cheery. "If you could all take your seats, please, we will begin Career Day in just a few minutes."

Our group looks toward the rows of chairs in the back as all of the teachers guide the students to sit on the floor in their class groups.

I move toward the back, following my friends, when I realize that Rhonan is still standing in the same spot. Returning to him, I ask, "Dude. You okay?"

"Fuck my life," he grates out, staring at the woman at the front of the room as she smiles at the kids sitting by her feet.

"What's going on?" Fletcher asks as Elliot comes up next to him.

"That's Ms. Lewis!" Ellis shouts, pulling on Rhonan's hand. "That's my new teacher, Daddy."

"She's—she's your substitute?" Rhonan stutters.

"Yes. And she's so nice and pretty. Isn't she pretty, Daddy?"

Rhonan remains frozen as I glance over at Elliot and Fletcher, wondering what the fuck is happening. "Uh, Rhonan?"

"Go take your seat, Ellis," he says before Ellis runs off. Closing his eyes, he blows out a breath and mutters, "This is just my luck."

"Care to fill us in?" I add.

"That's the woman I…" He mutters low enough that only we can hear him, but he doesn't finish his thought.

"Wait. She's the one from The Charming Bull, isn't she?" Elliot interjects. "Didn't she go to the bathroom and never come back?"

"Thank you for that," Rhonan grates out, glaring at Elliot.

"Shit. She ghosted you?" Fletcher asks.

Sighing, Rhonan nods. "Yeah. And apparently she also happens to be my new neighbor."

"Fuck," Fletcher says. "And now…"

"And now? Apparently, she's also Ellis's teacher for the next three months," he finishes, leaving us all stunned, and wondering how the hell the end of the school year is going to pan out for our friend and his daughter given this woman has left a chip on our best friend's shoulder.

THE END

***

Need more of Henley and Elodie and a peek at their future? Get an exclusive bonus epilogue here.

Scan for the
Bonus Epilogue

Also By Harlow James

Somehow You Knew (Gage and Hazel)

***

The Ladies Who Brunch (rom-coms with a ton of spice)
Never Say Never (Charlotte and Damien)
No One Else (Amelia and Ethan)
Now's The Time (Penelope and Maddox)
Not As Planned (Noelle and Grant)
Nice Guys Still Finish (Jeffrey and Ariel)

***

The Newberry Springs (Gibson Brothers) Series
Everything to Lose (Wyatt & Kelsea)
Everything He Couldn't (Walker & Evelyn)
Everything But You (Forrest & Shauna)

***

The California Billionaires Series (rom coms with heart and heat)
My Unexpected Serenity (Wes and Shayla)
My Unexpected Vow (Hayes and Waverly)
My Unexpected Family (Silas and Chloe)

***

The Emerson Falls Series (smalltown romance with a found family friend group)

Tangled (Kane & Olivia)

Enticed (Cooper & Clara)

Captivated (Cash and Piper)

Revived (Luke and Rachel)

Devoted (Brooks and Jess)

***

Lost and Found in Copper Ridge

A holiday romance in which two people book a stay in a cabin for the same amount of time thanks to a serendipitous $5 bill.

Guilty as Charged

An intense opposites attract standalone that will melt your kindle. He's an ex-con construction worker. She's a lawyer looking for passion.

McKenzie's Turn to Fall

A holiday romance where a romance author falls for her neighborhood butcher.

Acknowledgements

It feels AMAZING to finally have this book out in the world, especially after the trouble it caused me.
The first draft of this book was NOT what you just read. LOL But I am beyond thrilled with the final result AND this series. It's fresh, emotional, and steamy. These men are down bad for their girls, and are willing to put in the work to keep them.
With each new series, I pinch myself that I get to write love stories and people read them. It is truly is an honor, and I hope to keep doing this for many years to come.

To my husband: Thank you for believing in me and cheering me on every step of the way. Thank you for traveling with me, investing in my success, and being my person, my best friend, the man that inspires all of my book boyfriends, and my official Book Bitch. I love you.

To my beta readers: Emily, Keely, Carolina, and Kelly: you four are the best voices I have in my corner. Each of you gives me the advice, feedback, and support that I need in your own way. I'm so grateful to have the four of you on my team still after all this time. I love you all and appreciate you more than you'll ever know.

To Kait, my P.A.: Hiring you has been one of the best decisions I've ever made. Your friendship and professional support have helped me so much this year. Thank you for being my newest cheerleader!

To Jess, my social media manager: You have single-handedly made my life better! I have so much more time to focus on writing and other aspects of my business thanks to you. Your time and creativity is appreciated SO much. Thank you from the bottom of my heart for doing what you do for me.

To Kari, my content team leader: I'm SO honored that you agreed to help me with this new aspect of my team! You are such an incredible support and I'm looking forward to how much we can grow this team together.

And to my readers: thank you for supporting me, whether you've been here since the beginning, or you're brand new. I LOVE this hobby turned business of mine. It's an amazing feeling to be able to create art for someone to enjoy and forming a relationship from that. I never take my readers for granted and know that there would be no Harlow James without you.

So thank you for supporting a wife and mom who found a hobby that she loves.
And a future career that I'm working toward with each passing day.

About the author

Harlow James is a wife and mother who fell in love with romance novels, so she decided to write her own.

Her books are the perfect blend of heartwarming, addictive, and steamy romance. If you love stories with a guaranteed Happily Ever After, then Harlow is your new best friend.

When she's not writing, she can be found working her day job, reading every romance novel she can find time for, laughing with her husband and kids, watching re-runs of FRIENDS, and spending time cooking for her family and friends while drinking margaritas.

Connect with Harlow James

Follow me on Amazon

Follow me on Instagram

Follow me on Facebook

Join my Facebook Group: https://www.facebook.com/groups/494 991441142710/

Follow me on Goodreads

Follow me on Book Bub

Subscribe to my Newsletter for Updates on New Releases and Give-

aways

Website